BATMAN ADVENTURES

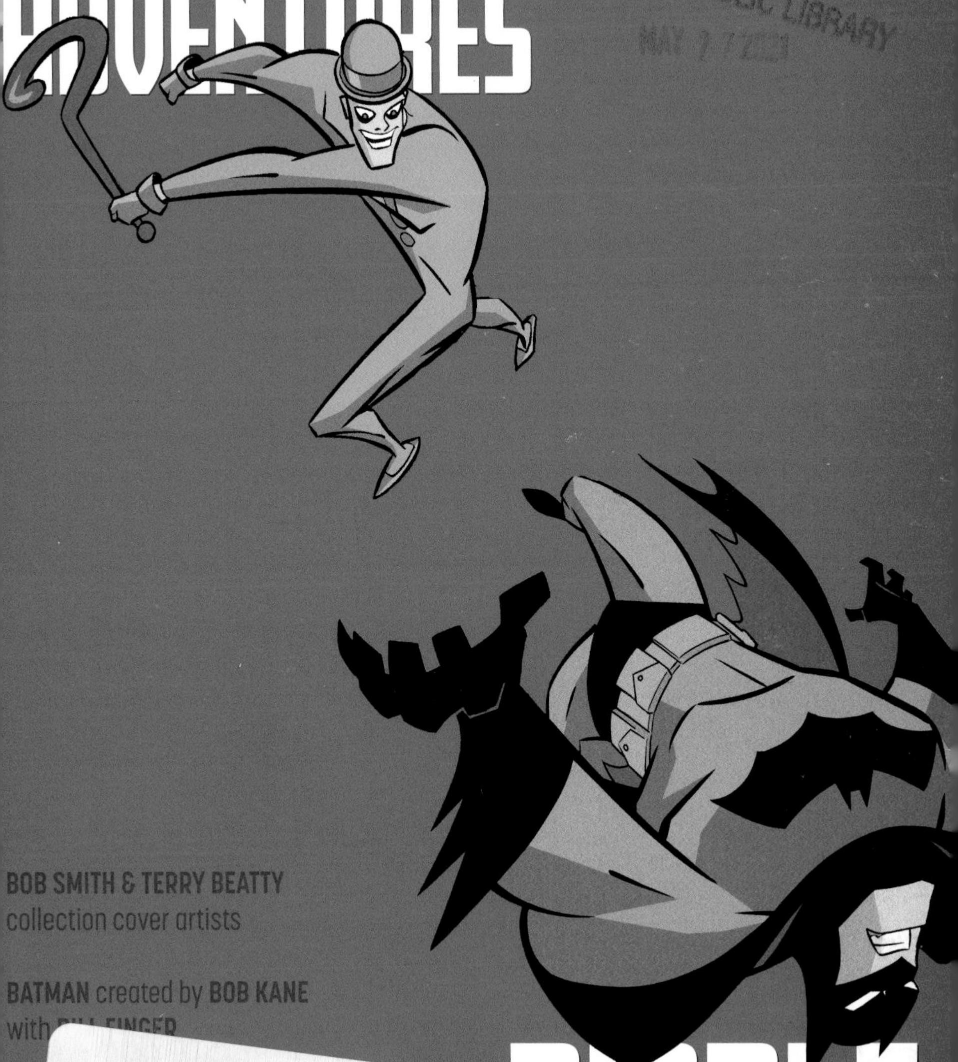

BOB SMITH & TERRY BEATTY
collection cover artists

BATMAN created by **BOB KANE**
with **BILL FINGER**

RIDDLE ME THIS

JOAN HILTY
BOB SCHRECK
DARREN VINCENZO
Editors - Original Series

JOSEPH ILLIDGE
Associate Editor - Original Series

FRANK BERRIOS
HARVEY RICHARDS
Assistant Editors - Original Series

JEB WOODARD
Editor - Collected Edition

STEVE COOK
Design Director - Books

AMIE BROCKWAY-METCALF
Publication Design

KATE DURRÉ
Publication Production

MARIE JAVINS
Editor-in-Chief, DC Comics

DANIEL CHERRY III
Senior VP - General Manager

JIM LEE
Publisher & Chief Creative Officer

DON FALLETTI
VP - Manufacturing Operations & Workflow Management

LAWRENCE GANEM
VP - Talent Services

ALISON GILL
Senior VP - Manufacturing & Operations

NICK J. NAPOLITANO
VP - Manufacturing Administration & Design

NANCY SPEARS
VP - Revenue

MICHELE R. WELLS
VP & Executive Editor, Young Reader

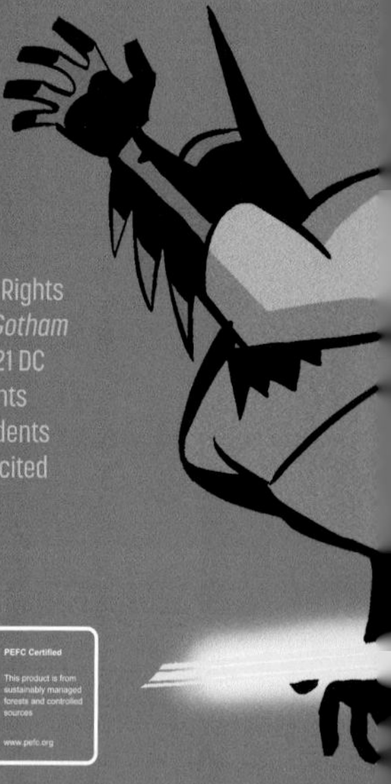

BATMAN ADVENTURES: RIDDLE ME THIS

DC Comics, 2900 West Alameda Ave., Burbank, CA 91505
Printed by LSC Communications, Crawfordsville, IN. 2/26/21. First Printing.
ISBN: 978-1-77950-936-9

Library of Congress Cataloging-in-Publication Data is available.

PEFC Certified

This product is from
sustainably managed
forests and controlled
sources

PEFC/09-31-337   www.pefc.org

CONTENTS

Chapter 1:
The Oldest One in the Book! 5

Chapter 2:
Notes 29

Chapter 3:
Identity Theft 53

Chapter 4:
The Real Deal 77

Chapter 5:
Poker Face 101

Preview:
Dear DC Super-Villains 125

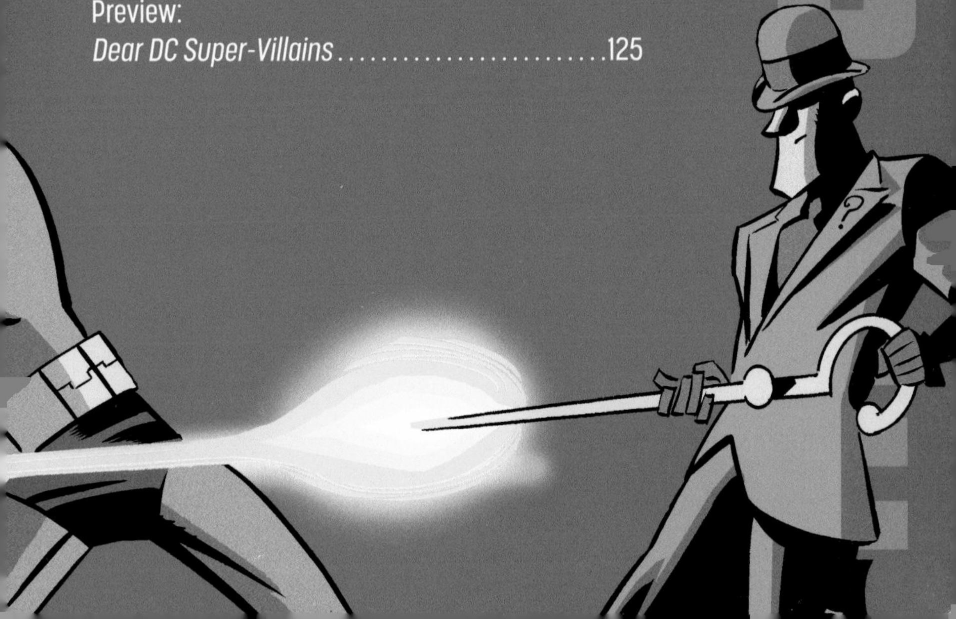

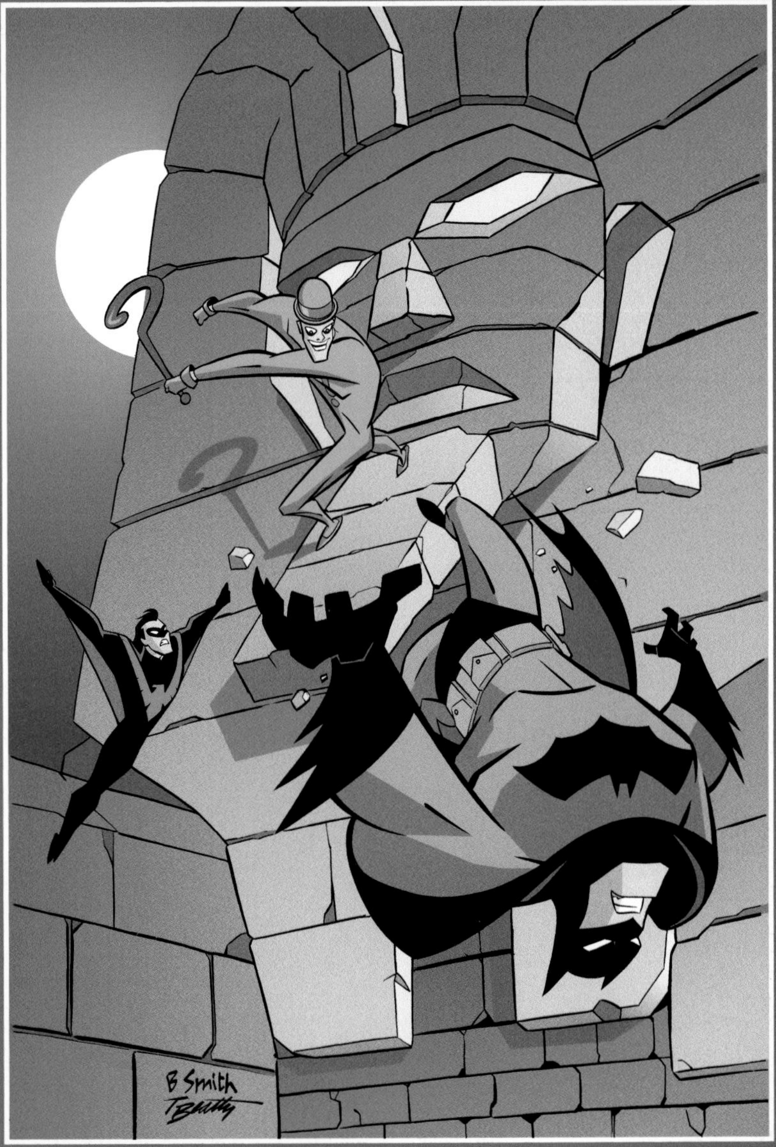
B Smith

CHAPTER 1: THE OLDEST ONE IN THE BOOK!

RIDDLE ME THIS

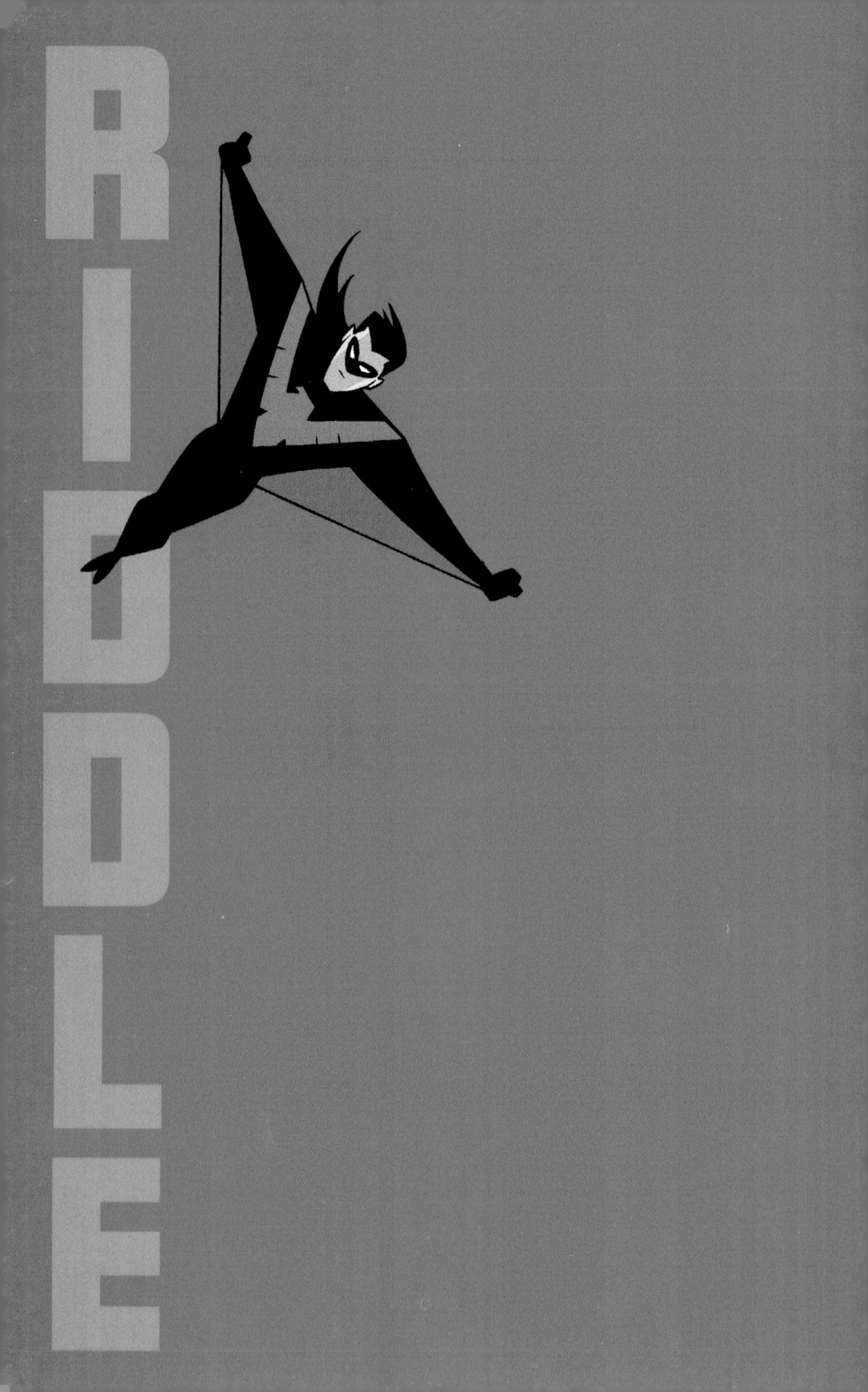

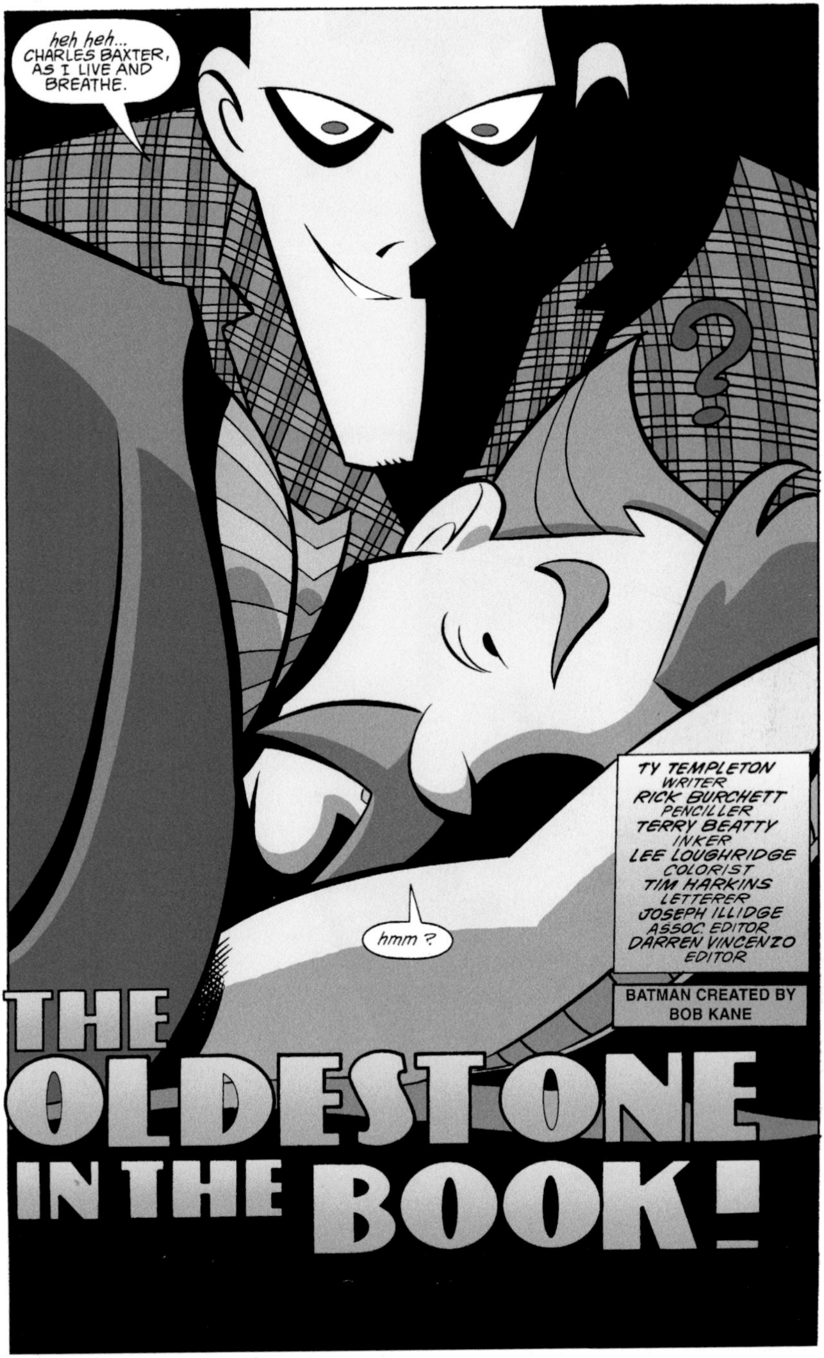
heh heh... CHARLES BAXTER, AS I LIVE AND BREATHE.
hmm ?
TY TEMPLETON WRITER
RICK BURCHETT PENCILLER
TERRY BEATTY INKER
LEE LOUGHRIDGE COLORIST
TIM HARKINS LETTERER
JOSEPH ILLIDGE ASSOC. EDITOR
DARREN VINCENZO EDITOR
BATMAN CREATED BY BOB KANE
THE OLDEST ONE IN THE BOOK!

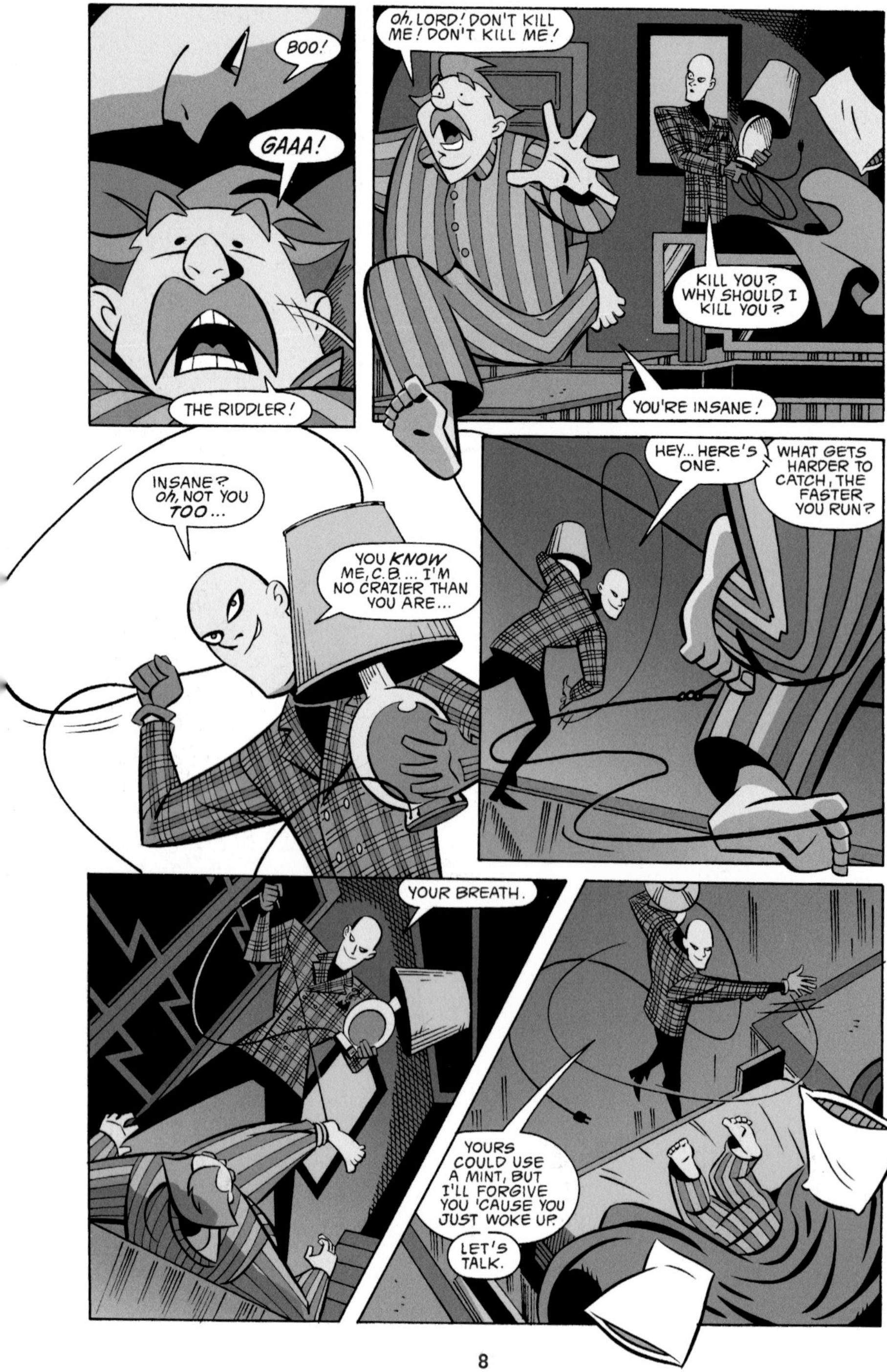
BOO!
GAAA!
THE RIDDLER!
Oh, LORD! DON'T KILL ME! DON'T KILL ME!
KILL YOU? WHY SHOULD I KILL YOU?
YOU'RE INSANE!
INSANE? Oh, NOT YOU TOO...
YOU KNOW ME, C.B. ... I'M NO CRAZIER THAN YOU ARE...
HEY... HERE'S ONE.
WHAT GETS HARDER TO CATCH, THE FASTER YOU RUN?
YOUR BREATH.
YOURS COULD USE A MINT, BUT I'LL FORGIVE YOU 'CAUSE YOU JUST WOKE UP.
LET'S TALK.

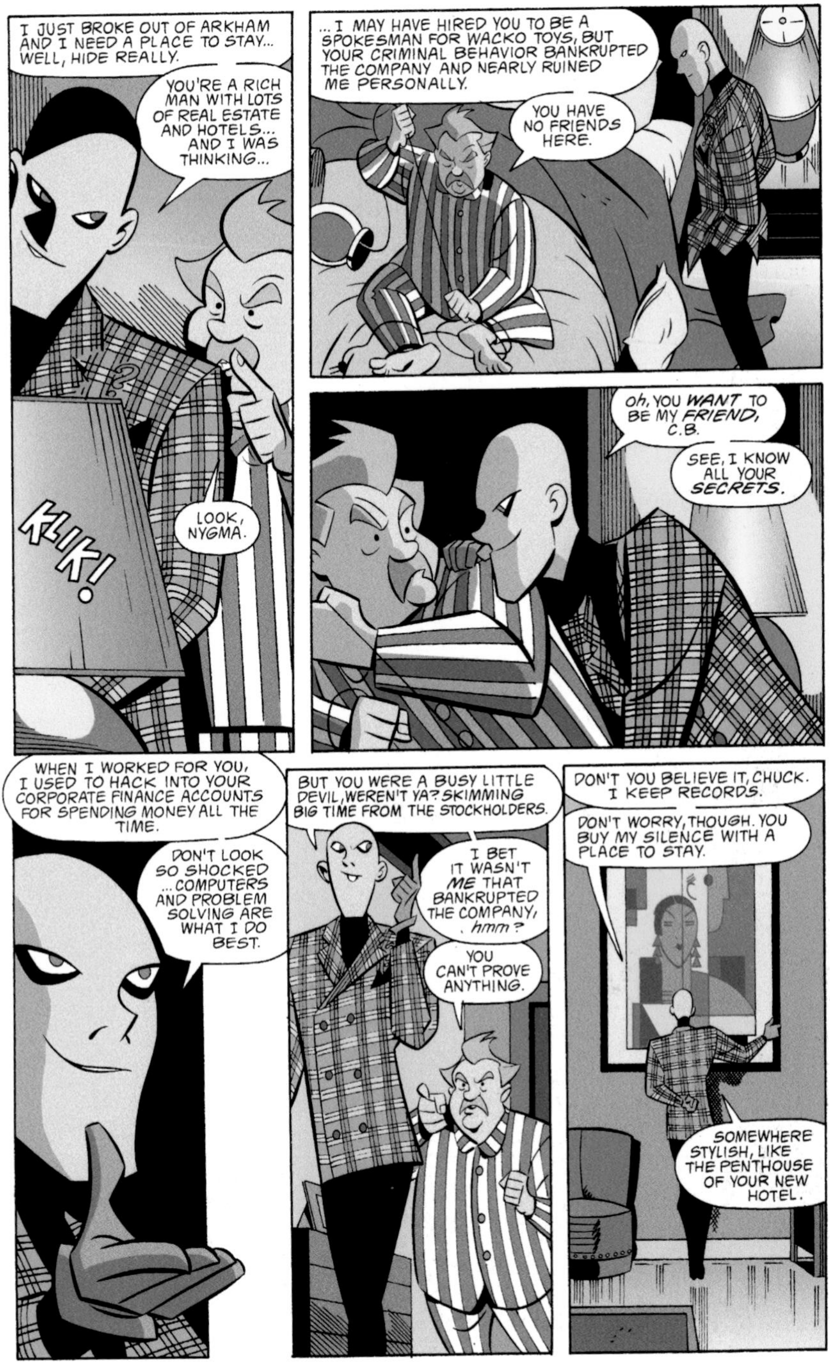
I JUST BROKE OUT OF ARKHAM AND I NEED A PLACE TO STAY... WELL, HIDE REALLY.
YOU'RE A RICH MAN WITH LOTS OF REAL ESTATE AND HOTELS... AND I WAS THINKING...
KLIK!
LOOK, NYGMA.
...I MAY HAVE HIRED YOU TO BE A SPOKESMAN FOR WACKO TOYS, BUT YOUR CRIMINAL BEHAVIOR BANKRUPTED THE COMPANY AND NEARLY RUINED ME PERSONALLY.
YOU HAVE NO FRIENDS HERE.
Oh, YOU WANT TO BE MY FRIEND, C.B.
SEE, I KNOW ALL YOUR SECRETS.
WHEN I WORKED FOR YOU, I USED TO HACK INTO YOUR CORPORATE FINANCE ACCOUNTS FOR SPENDING MONEY ALL THE TIME.
DON'T LOOK SO SHOCKED ...COMPUTERS AND PROBLEM SOLVING ARE WHAT I DO BEST.
BUT YOU WERE A BUSY LITTLE DEVIL, WEREN'T YA? SKIMMING BIG TIME FROM THE STOCKHOLDERS.
I BET IT WASN'T ME THAT BANKRUPTED THE COMPANY, hmm?
YOU CAN'T PROVE ANYTHING.
DON'T YOU BELIEVE IT, CHUCK. I KEEP RECORDS.
DON'T WORRY, THOUGH. YOU BUY MY SILENCE WITH A PLACE TO STAY.
SOMEWHERE STYLISH, LIKE THE PENTHOUSE OF YOUR NEW HOTEL.

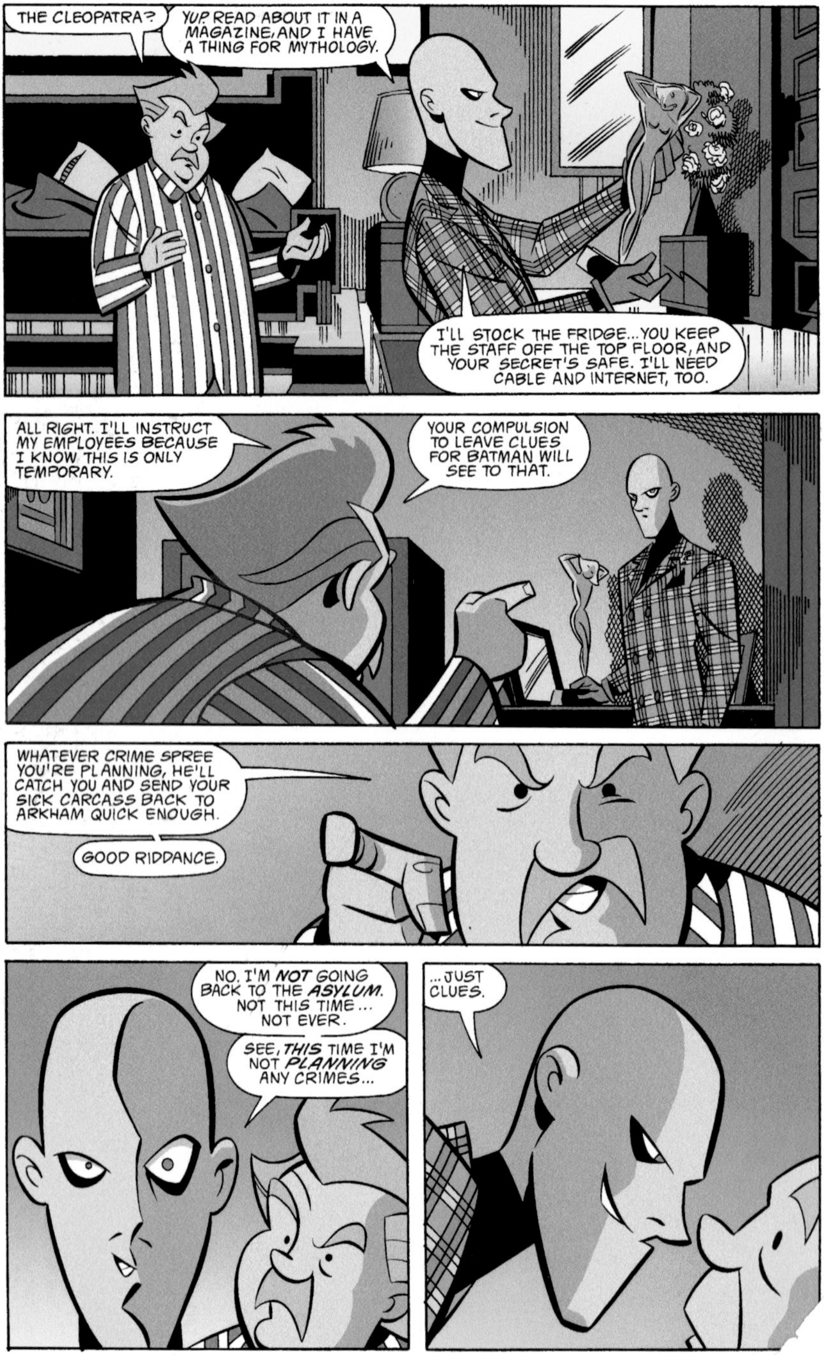
THE CLEOPATRA?
YUP. READ ABOUT IT IN A MAGAZINE, AND I HAVE A THING FOR MYTHOLOGY.
I'LL STOCK THE FRIDGE...YOU KEEP THE STAFF OFF THE TOP FLOOR, AND YOUR SECRET'S SAFE. I'LL NEED CABLE AND INTERNET, TOO.
ALL RIGHT. I'LL INSTRUCT MY EMPLOYEES BECAUSE I KNOW THIS IS ONLY TEMPORARY.
YOUR COMPULSION TO LEAVE CLUES FOR BATMAN WILL SEE TO THAT.
WHATEVER CRIME SPREE YOU'RE PLANNING, HE'LL CATCH YOU AND SEND YOUR SICK CARCASS BACK TO ARKHAM QUICK ENOUGH.
GOOD RIDDANCE.
NO, I'M NOT GOING BACK TO THE ASYLUM. NOT THIS TIME... NOT EVER.
SEE, THIS TIME I'M NOT PLANNING ANY CRIMES...
...JUST CLUES.

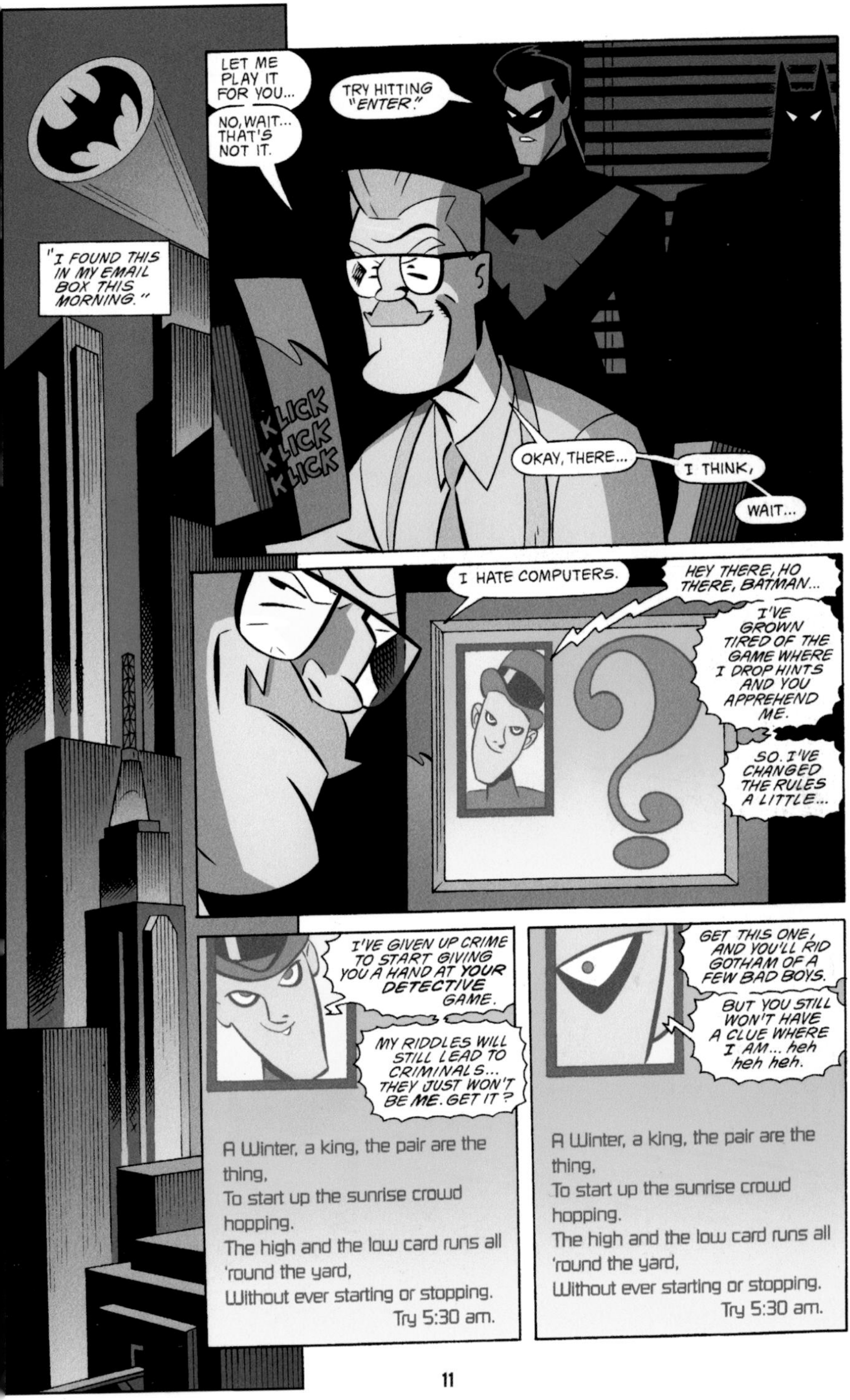
"I FOUND THIS IN MY EMAIL BOX THIS MORNING."
LET ME PLAY IT FOR YOU...
NO, WAIT... THAT'S NOT IT.
TRY HITTING "ENTER."
KLICK KLICK KLICK
OKAY, THERE...
I THINK,
WAIT...
I HATE COMPUTERS.
HEY THERE, HO THERE, BATMAN...
I'VE GROWN TIRED OF THE GAME WHERE I DROP HINTS AND YOU APPREHEND ME.
SO. I'VE CHANGED THE RULES A LITTLE...
I'VE GIVEN UP CRIME TO START GIVING YOU A HAND AT YOUR DETECTIVE GAME.
MY RIDDLES WILL STILL LEAD TO CRIMINALS... THEY JUST WON'T BE ME. GET IT?
A Winter, a king, the pair are the thing,
To start up the sunrise crowd hopping.
The high and the low card runs all 'round the yard,
Without ever starting or stopping.
Try 5:30 am.
GET THIS ONE, AND YOU'LL RID GOTHAM OF A FEW BAD BOYS.
BUT YOU STILL WON'T HAVE A CLUE WHERE I AM... heh heh heh.
A Winter, a king, the pair are the thing,
To start up the sunrise crowd hopping.
The high and the low card runs all 'round the yard,
Without ever starting or stopping.
Try 5:30 am.

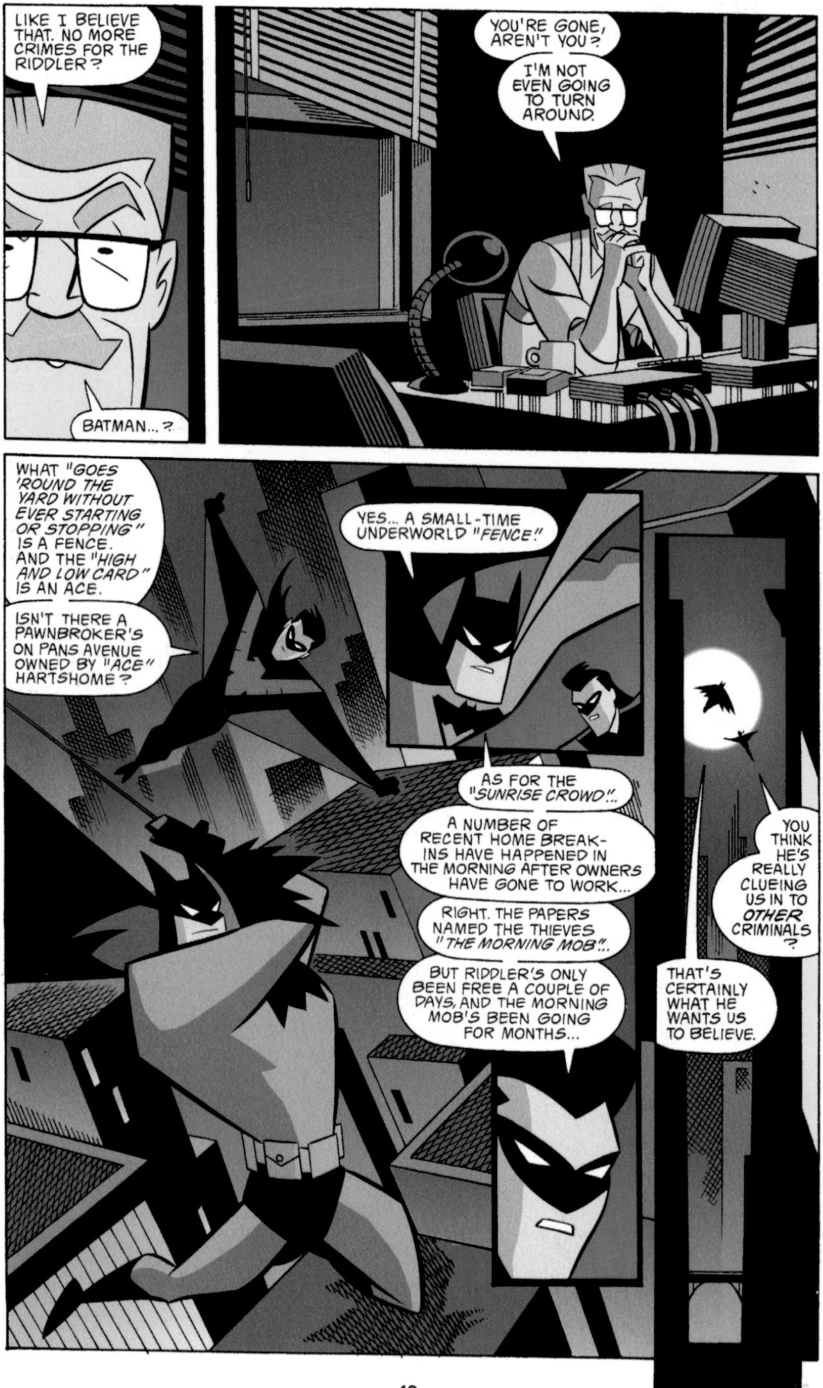
LIKE I BELIEVE THAT. NO MORE CRIMES FOR THE RIDDLER?
BATMAN...?
YOU'RE GONE, AREN'T YOU?
I'M NOT EVEN GOING TO TURN AROUND.
WHAT "GOES 'ROUND THE YARD WITHOUT EVER STARTING OR STOPPING" IS A FENCE. AND THE "HIGH AND LOW CARD" IS AN ACE.
ISN'T THERE A PAWNBROKER'S ON PANS AVENUE OWNED BY "ACE" HARTSHOME?
YES... A SMALL-TIME UNDERWORLD "FENCE."
AS FOR THE "SUNRISE CROWD"...
A NUMBER OF RECENT HOME BREAK-INS HAVE HAPPENED IN THE MORNING AFTER OWNERS HAVE GONE TO WORK...
RIGHT. THE PAPERS NAMED THE THIEVES "THE MORNING MOB"...
BUT RIDDLER'S ONLY BEEN FREE A COUPLE OF DAYS, AND THE MORNING MOB'S BEEN GOING FOR MONTHS...
YOU THINK HE'S REALLY CLUEING US IN TO OTHER CRIMINALS?
THAT'S CERTAINLY WHAT HE WANTS US TO BELIEVE.

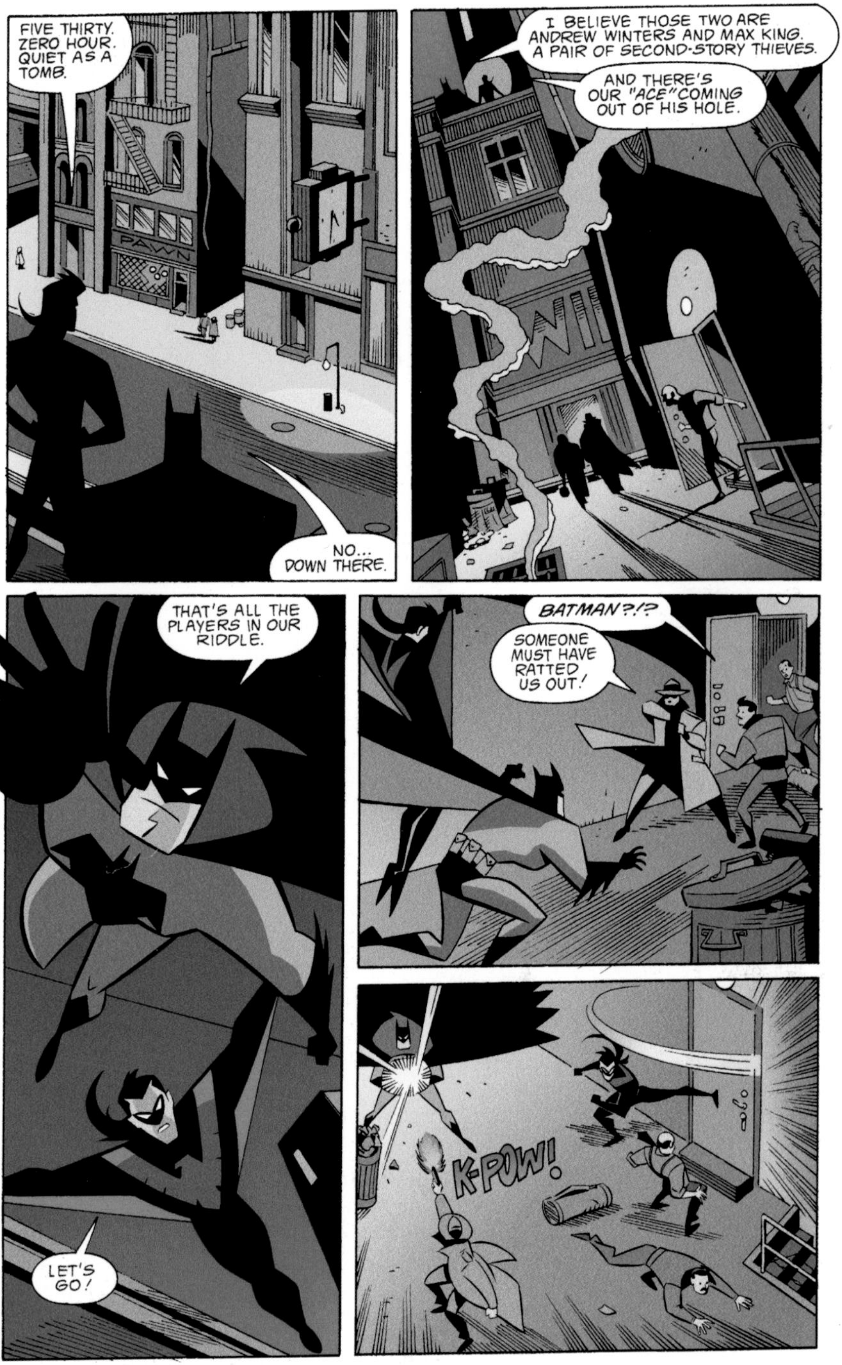
FIVE THIRTY. ZERO HOUR. QUIET AS A TOMB.
PAWN
NO... DOWN THERE.
I BELIEVE THOSE TWO ARE ANDREW WINTERS AND MAX KING. A PAIR OF SECOND-STORY THIEVES.
AND THERE'S OUR "ACE" COMING OUT OF HIS HOLE.
THAT'S ALL THE PLAYERS IN OUR RIDDLE.
LET'S GO!
BATMAN?!?
SOMEONE MUST HAVE RATTED US OUT!
K-POW!

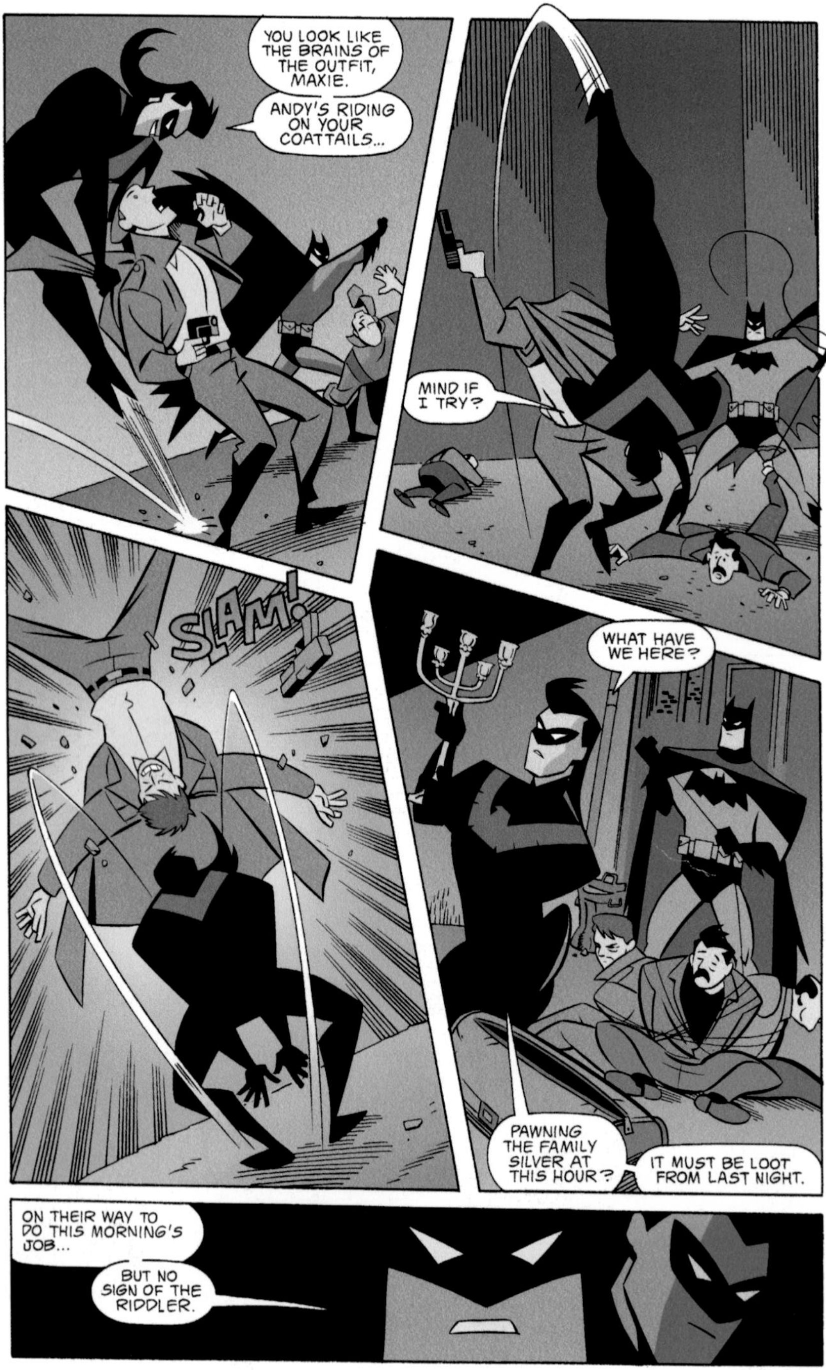

YOU LOOK LIKE THE BRAINS OF THE OUTFIT, MAXIE.
ANDY'S RIDING ON YOUR COATTAILS...
MIND IF I TRY?
SLAM!
WHAT HAVE WE HERE?
PAWNING THE FAMILY SILVER AT THIS HOUR?
IT MUST BE LOOT FROM LAST NIGHT.
ON THEIR WAY TO DO THIS MORNING'S JOB...
BUT NO SIGN OF THE RIDDLER.

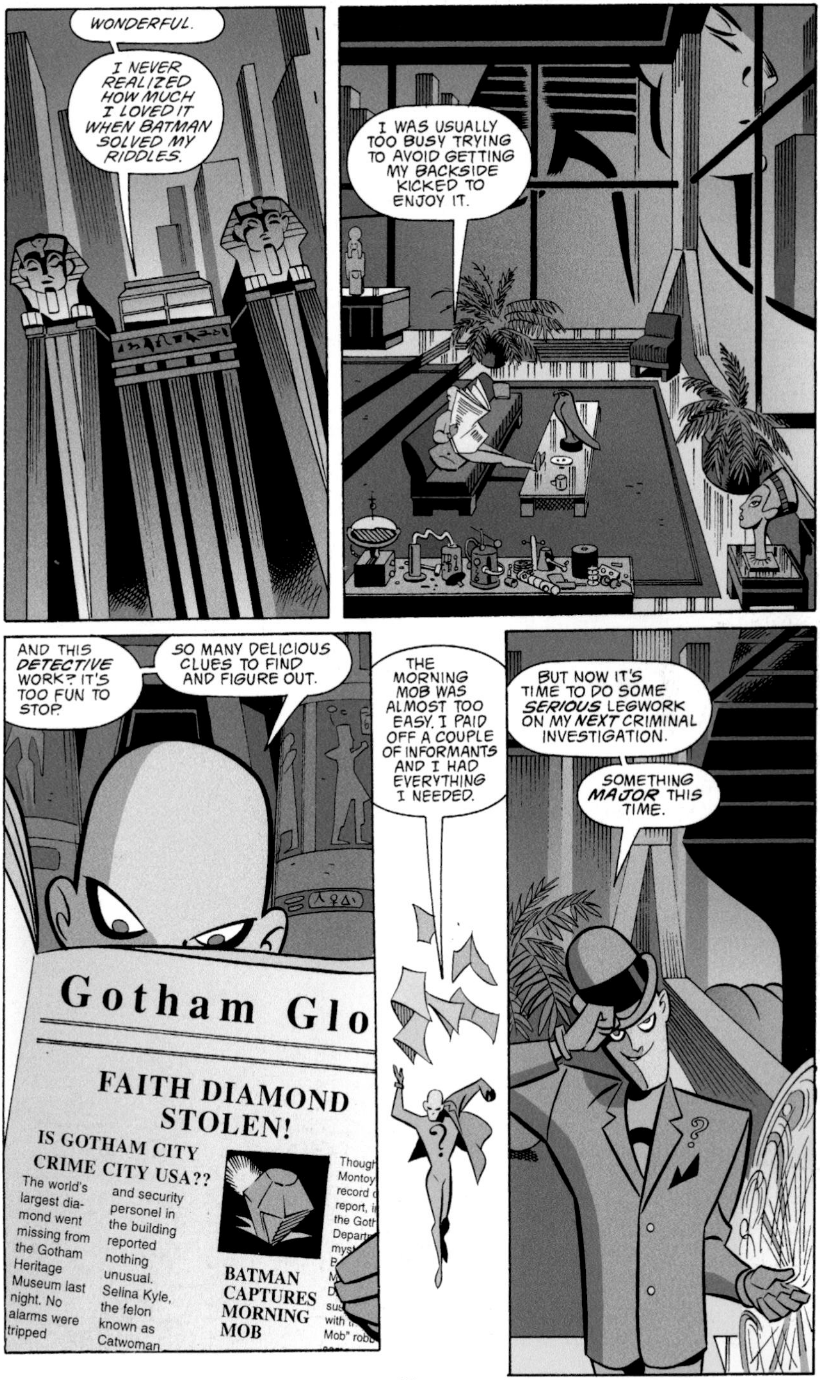
WONDERFUL.
I NEVER REALIZED HOW MUCH I LOVED IT WHEN BATMAN SOLVED MY RIDDLES.
I WAS USUALLY TOO BUSY TRYING TO AVOID GETTING MY BACKSIDE KICKED TO ENJOY IT.
AND THIS DETECTIVE WORK? IT'S TOO FUN TO STOP.
SO MANY DELICIOUS CLUES TO FIND AND FIGURE OUT.
Gotham Glo
FAITH DIAMOND STOLEN!
IS GOTHAM CITY CRIME CITY USA??
The world's largest diamond went missing from the Gotham Heritage Museum last night. No alarms were tripped
and security personel in the building reported nothing unusual. Selina Kyle, the felon known as Catwoman
BATMAN CAPTURES MORNING MOB
THE MORNING MOB WAS ALMOST TOO EASY. I PAID OFF A COUPLE OF INFORMANTS AND I HAD EVERYTHING I NEEDED.
BUT NOW IT'S TIME TO DO SOME SERIOUS LEGWORK ON MY NEXT CRIMINAL INVESTIGATION.
SOMETHING MAJOR THIS TIME.

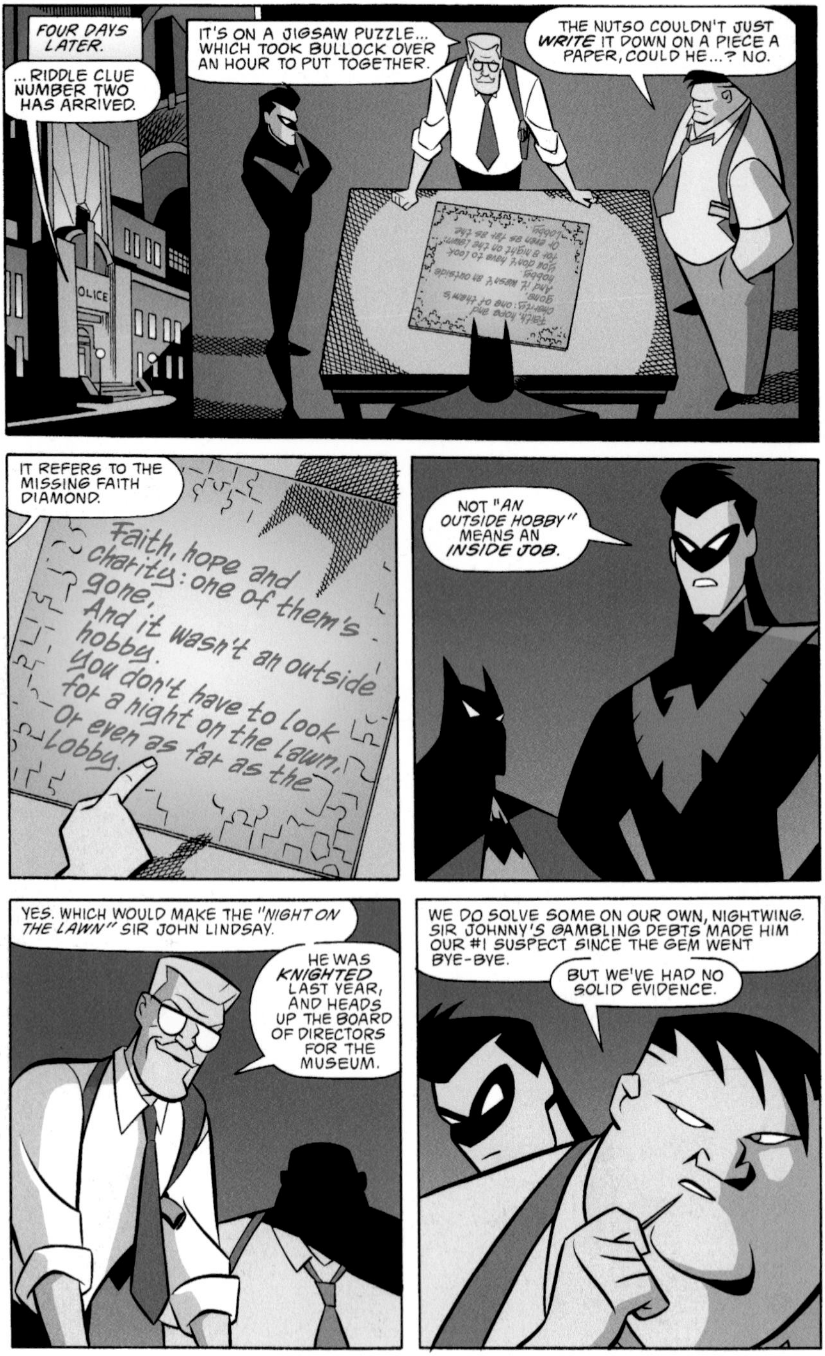
FOUR DAYS LATER.
...RIDDLE CLUE NUMBER TWO HAS ARRIVED.
OLICE
IT'S ON A JIGSAW PUZZLE... WHICH TOOK BULLOCK OVER AN HOUR TO PUT TOGETHER.
THE NUTSO COULDN'T JUST WRITE IT DOWN ON A PIECE A PAPER, COULD HE...? NO.
IT REFERS TO THE MISSING FAITH DIAMOND.
Faith, hope and charity: one of them's gone. And it wasn't an outside hobby. You don't have to look for a night on the lawn, Or even as far as the Lobby.
NOT "AN OUTSIDE HOBBY" MEANS AN INSIDE JOB.
YES. WHICH WOULD MAKE THE "NIGHT ON THE LAWN" SIR JOHN LINDSAY.
HE WAS KNIGHTED LAST YEAR, AND HEADS UP THE BOARD OF DIRECTORS FOR THE MUSEUM.
WE DO SOLVE SOME ON OUR OWN, NIGHTWING. SIR JOHNNY'S GAMBLING DEBTS MADE HIM OUR #1 SUSPECT SINCE THE GEM WENT BYE-BYE.
BUT WE'VE HAD NO SOLID EVIDENCE.

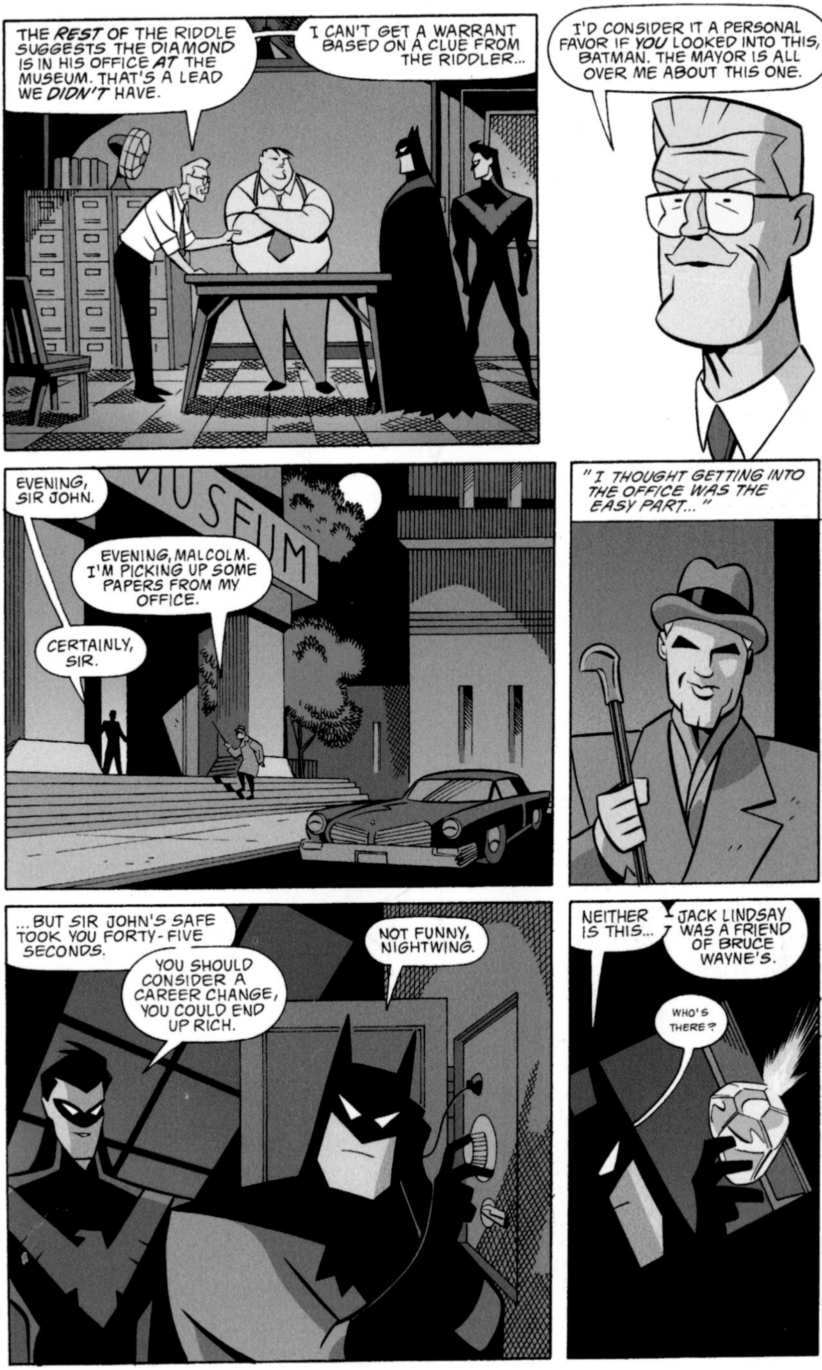
THE REST OF THE RIDDLE SUGGESTS THE DIAMOND IS IN HIS OFFICE AT THE MUSEUM. THAT'S A LEAD WE DIDN'T HAVE.
I CAN'T GET A WARRANT BASED ON A CLUE FROM THE RIDDLER...
I'D CONSIDER IT A PERSONAL FAVOR IF YOU LOOKED INTO THIS, BATMAN. THE MAYOR IS ALL OVER ME ABOUT THIS ONE.
MUSEUM
EVENING, SIR JOHN.
EVENING, MALCOLM. I'M PICKING UP SOME PAPERS FROM MY OFFICE.
CERTAINLY, SIR.
"I THOUGHT GETTING INTO THE OFFICE WAS THE EASY PART..."
...BUT SIR JOHN'S SAFE TOOK YOU FORTY-FIVE SECONDS.
YOU SHOULD CONSIDER A CAREER CHANGE, YOU COULD END UP RICH.
NOT FUNNY, NIGHTWING.
NEITHER IS THIS...
JACK LINDSAY WAS A FRIEND OF BRUCE WAYNE'S.
WHO'S THERE?

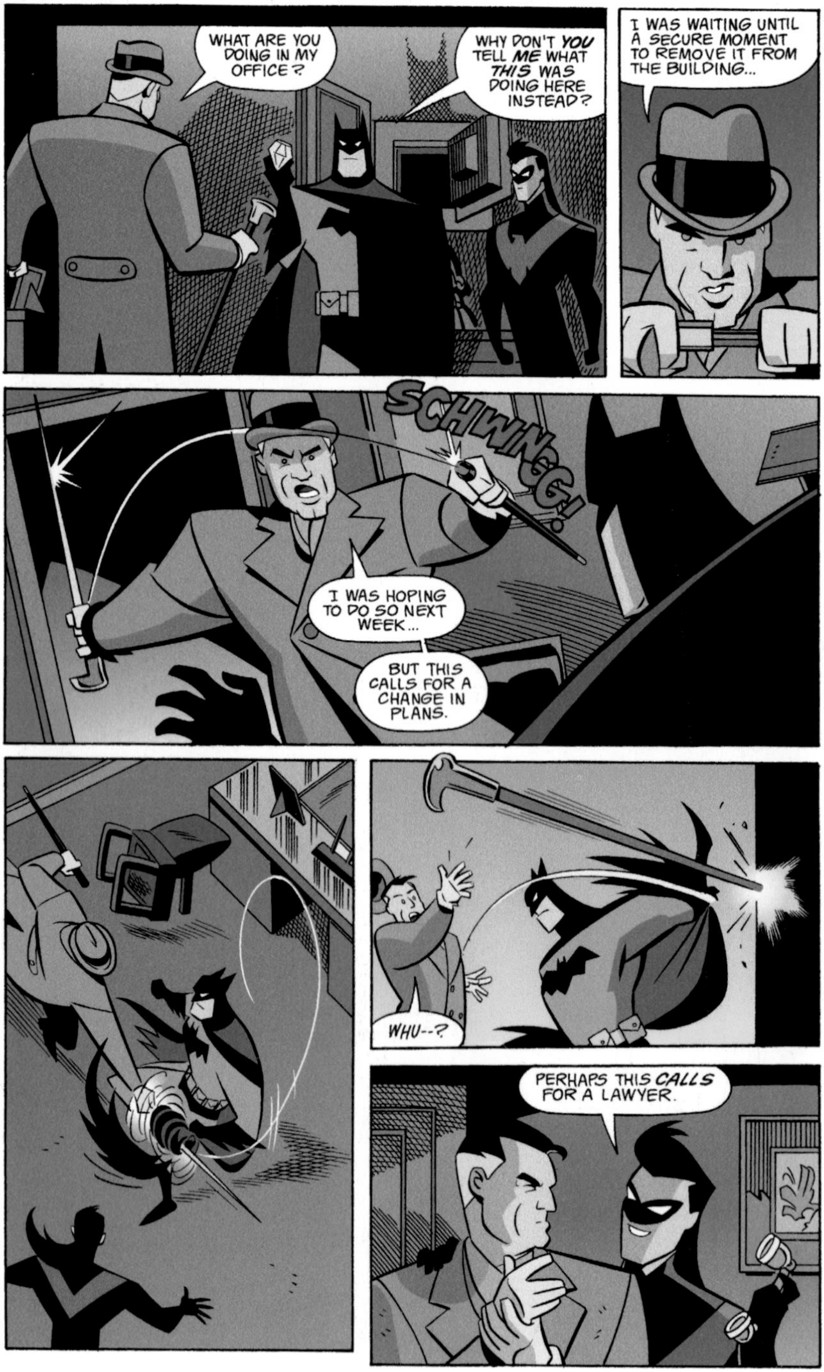
WHAT ARE YOU DOING IN MY OFFICE?
WHY DON'T *YOU* TELL *ME* WHAT *THIS* WAS DOING HERE INSTEAD?
I WAS WAITING UNTIL A SECURE MOMENT TO REMOVE IT FROM THE BUILDING...
SCHWINGG!
I WAS HOPING TO DO SO NEXT WEEK...
BUT THIS CALLS FOR A CHANGE IN PLANS.
WHU--?
PERHAPS THIS *CALLS* FOR A LAWYER.

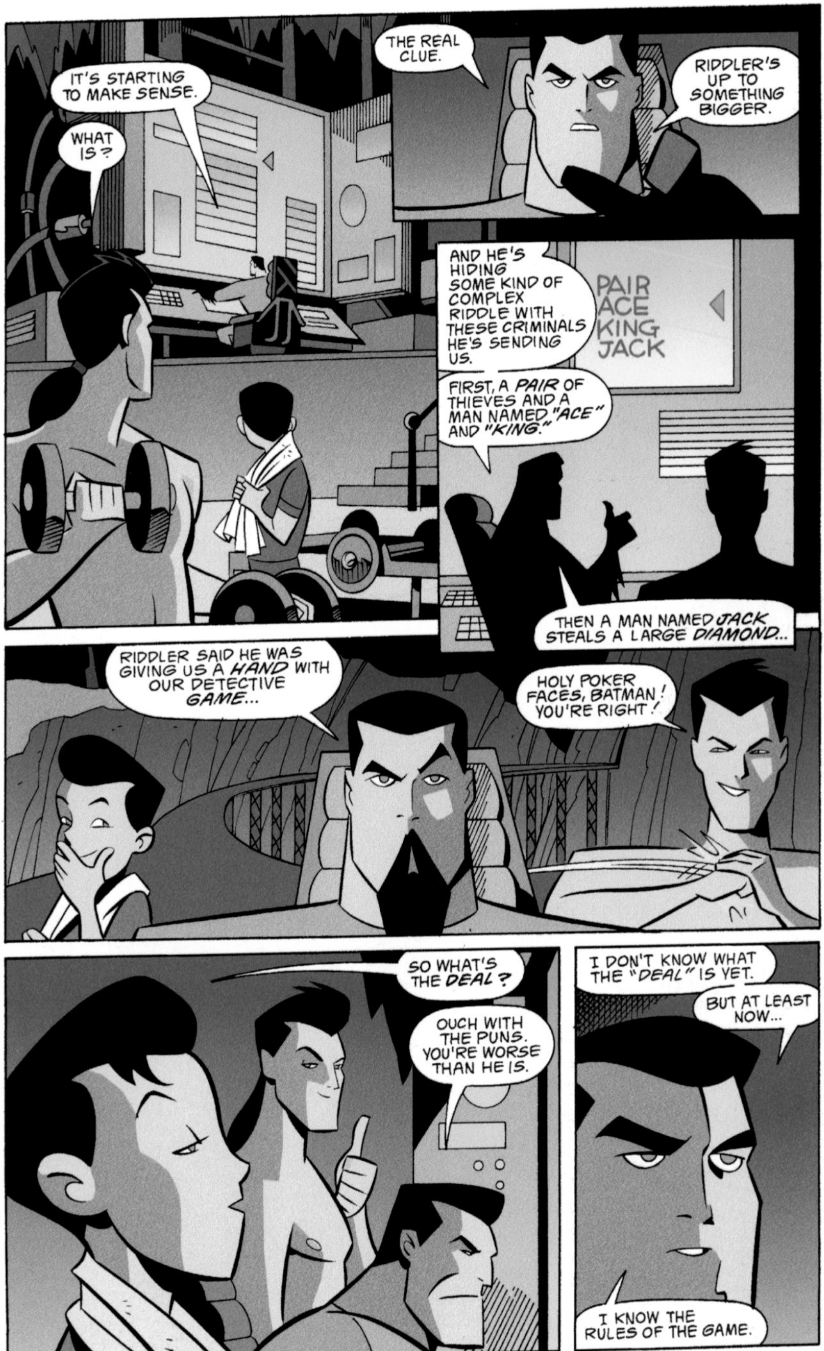
IT'S STARTING TO MAKE SENSE.
WHAT IS?
THE REAL CLUE.
RIDDLER'S UP TO SOMETHING BIGGER.
AND HE'S HIDING SOME KIND OF COMPLEX RIDDLE WITH THESE CRIMINALS HE'S SENDING US.
PAIR
ACE
KING
JACK
FIRST, A *PAIR* OF THIEVES AND A MAN NAMED *"ACE"* AND *"KING."*
THEN A MAN NAMED *JACK* STEALS A LARGE *DIAMOND*...
RIDDLER SAID HE WAS GIVING US A *HAND* WITH OUR DETECTIVE *GAME*...
HOLY POKER FACES, BATMAN! YOU'RE RIGHT!
SO WHAT'S THE *DEAL*?
OUCH WITH THE PUNS. YOU'RE WORSE THAN HE IS.
I DON'T KNOW WHAT THE *"DEAL"* IS YET.
BUT AT LEAST NOW...
I KNOW THE RULES OF THE GAME.

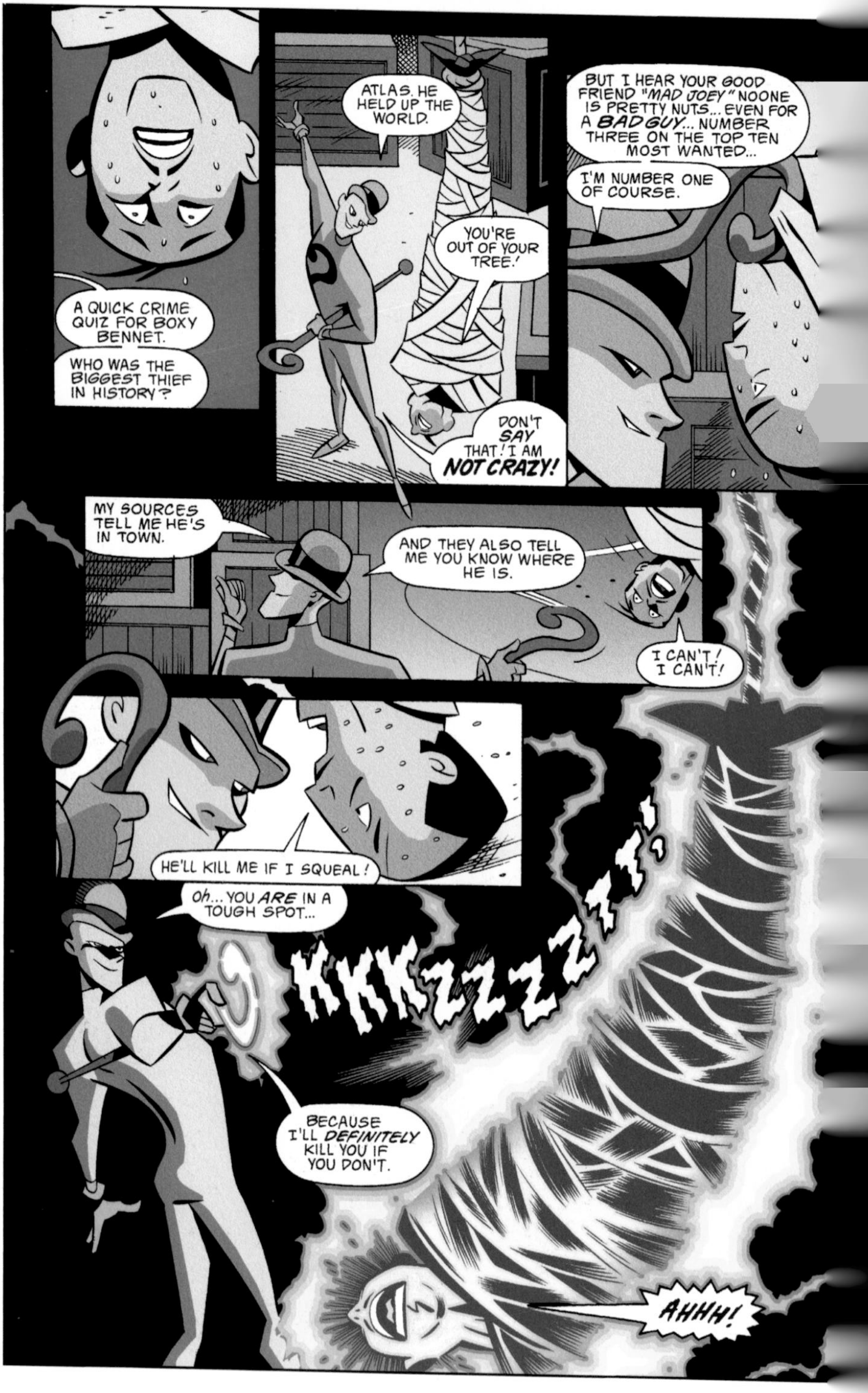

A QUICK CRIME QUIZ FOR BOXY BENNET.
WHO WAS THE BIGGEST THIEF IN HISTORY?
ATLAS. HE HELD UP THE WORLD.
YOU'RE OUT OF YOUR TREE!
DON'T SAY THAT! I AM NOT CRAZY!
BUT I HEAR YOUR GOOD FRIEND "MAD JOEY" NOONE IS PRETTY NUTS... EVEN FOR A BAD GUY... NUMBER THREE ON THE TOP TEN MOST WANTED...
I'M NUMBER ONE OF COURSE.
MY SOURCES TELL ME HE'S IN TOWN.
AND THEY ALSO TELL ME YOU KNOW WHERE HE IS.
I CAN'T! I CAN'T!
HE'LL KILL ME IF I SQUEAL!
Oh... YOU ARE IN A TOUGH SPOT...
KKKZZZZZTTT!
BECAUSE I'LL DEFINITELY KILL YOU IF YOU DON'T.
AHHH!

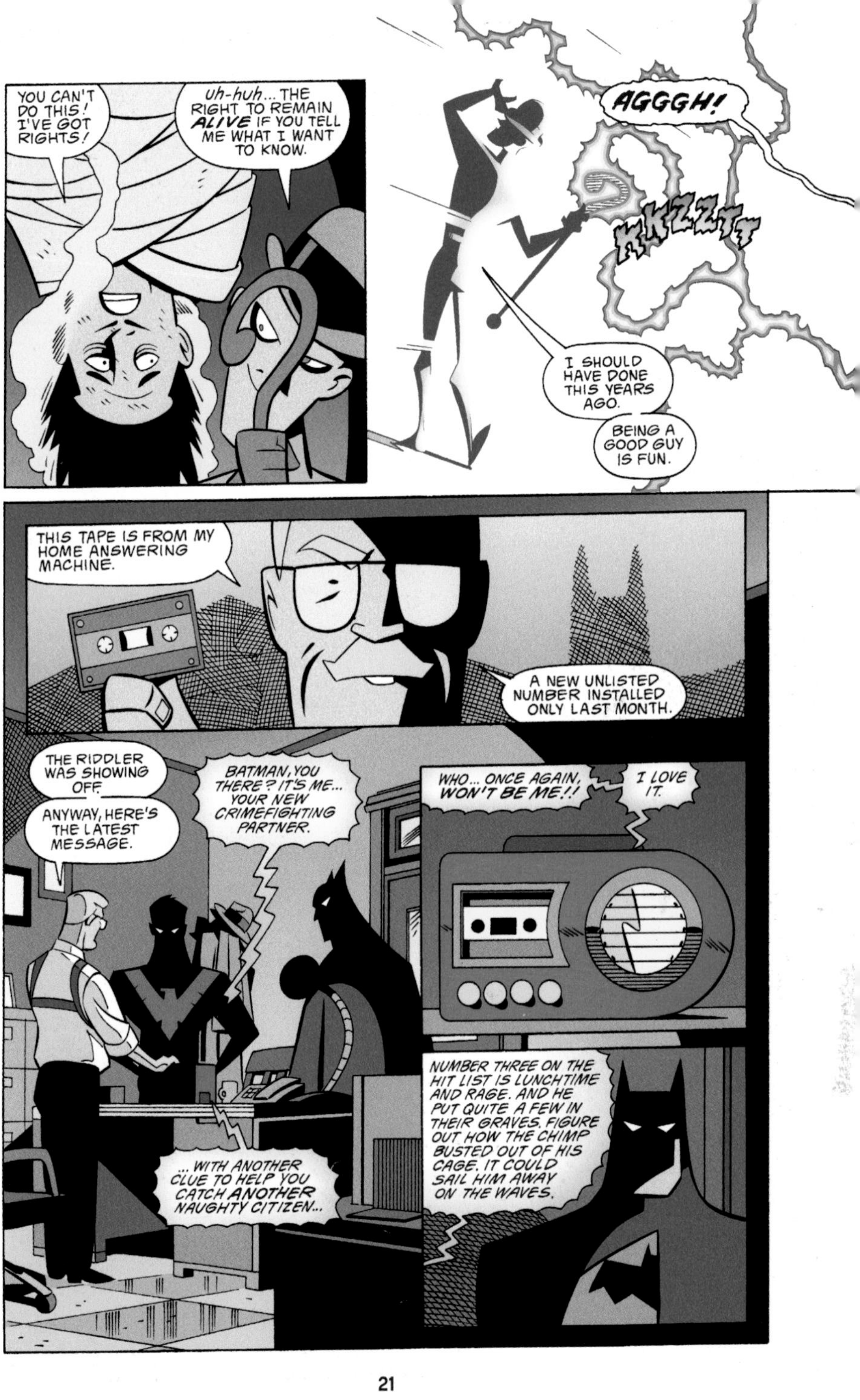

YOU CAN'T DO THIS! I'VE GOT RIGHTS!
uh-huh... THE RIGHT TO REMAIN ALIVE IF YOU TELL ME WHAT I WANT TO KNOW.
AGGGH!
KKZZZTT
I SHOULD HAVE DONE THIS YEARS AGO.
BEING A GOOD GUY IS FUN.
THIS TAPE IS FROM MY HOME ANSWERING MACHINE.
A NEW UNLISTED NUMBER INSTALLED ONLY LAST MONTH.
THE RIDDLER WAS SHOWING OFF.
ANYWAY, HERE'S THE LATEST MESSAGE.
BATMAN, YOU THERE? IT'S ME... YOUR NEW CRIMEFIGHTING PARTNER.
...WITH ANOTHER CLUE TO HELP YOU CATCH ANOTHER NAUGHTY CITIZEN...
WHO... ONCE AGAIN, WON'T BE ME!!
I LOVE IT.
NUMBER THREE ON THE HIT LIST IS LUNCHTIME AND RAGE. AND HE PUT QUITE A FEW IN THEIR GRAVES. FIGURE OUT HOW THE CHIMP BUSTED OUT OF HIS CAGE. IT COULD SAIL HIM AWAY ON THE WAVES.

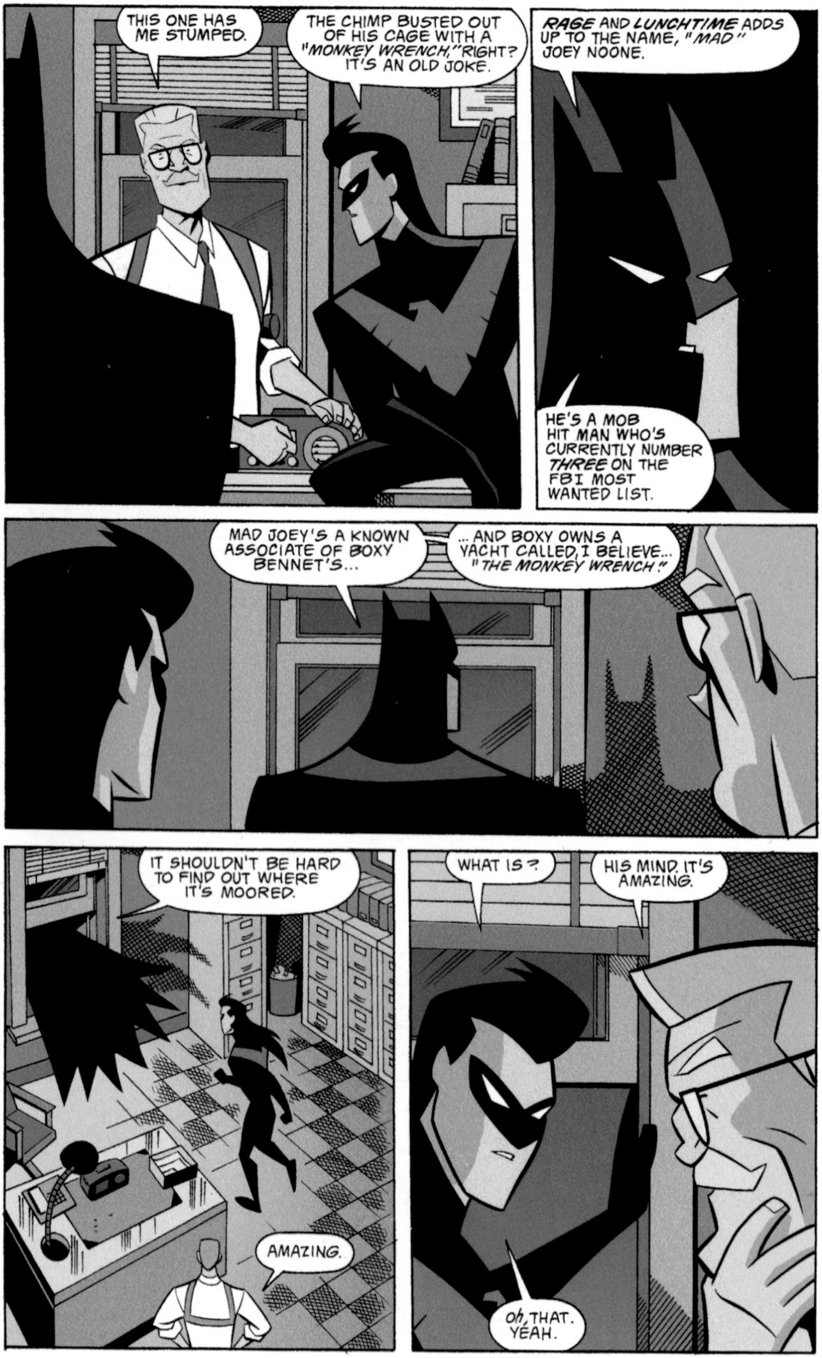
THIS ONE HAS ME STUMPED.
THE CHIMP BUSTED OUT OF HIS CAGE WITH A "MONKEY WRENCH," RIGHT? IT'S AN OLD JOKE.
RAGE AND LUNCHTIME ADDS UP TO THE NAME, "MAD" JOEY NOONE.
HE'S A MOB HIT MAN WHO'S CURRENTLY NUMBER THREE ON THE FBI MOST WANTED LIST.
MAD JOEY'S A KNOWN ASSOCIATE OF BOXY BENNET'S...
... AND BOXY OWNS A YACHT CALLED, I BELIEVE... "THE MONKEY WRENCH."
IT SHOULDN'T BE HARD TO FIND OUT WHERE IT'S MOORED.
AMAZING.
WHAT IS?
HIS MIND. IT'S AMAZING.
Oh, THAT. YEAH.

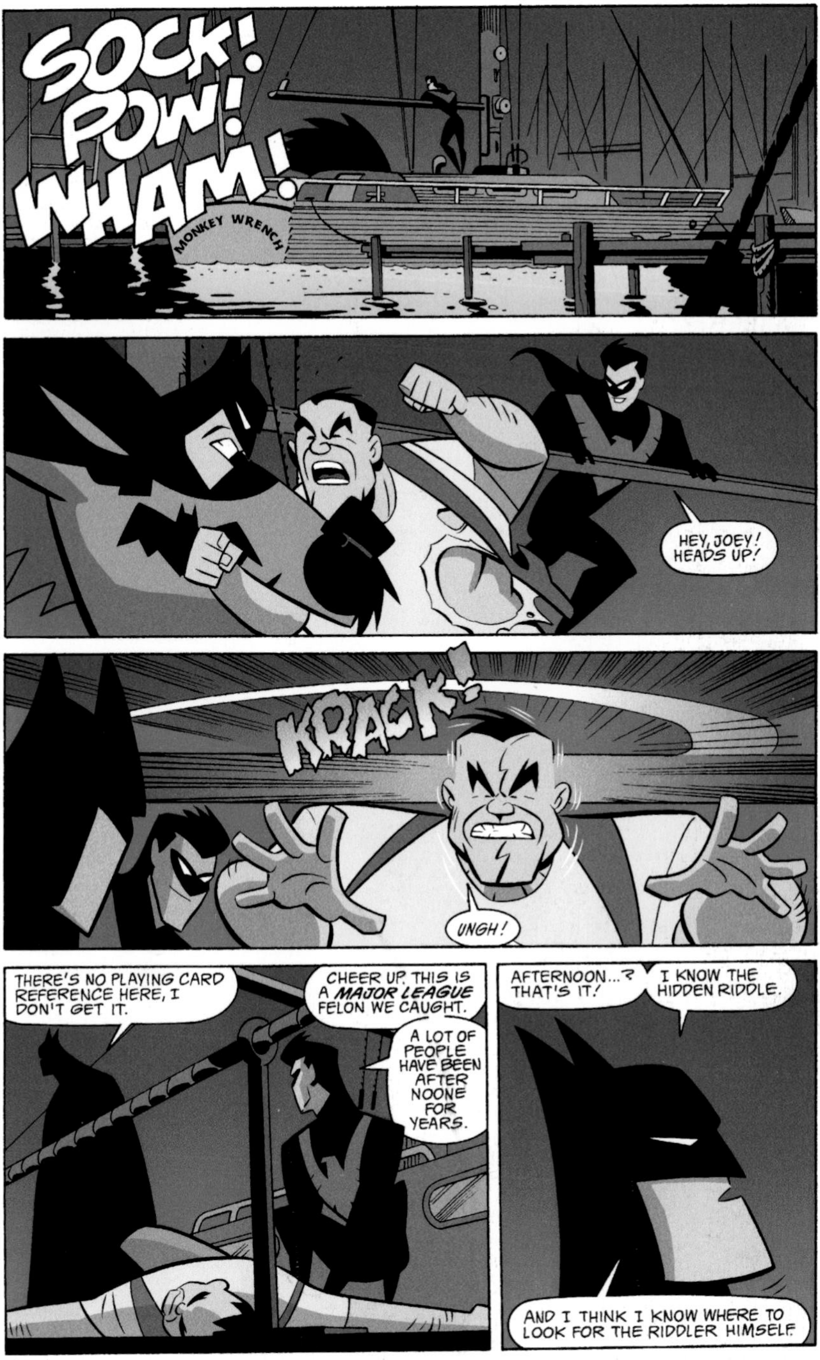
SOCK! POW! WHAM!
MONKEY WRENCH
HEY, JOEY! HEADS UP!
KRACK!
UNGH!
THERE'S NO PLAYING CARD REFERENCE HERE, I DON'T GET IT.
CHEER UP. THIS IS A MAJOR LEAGUE FELON WE CAUGHT.
A LOT OF PEOPLE HAVE BEEN AFTER NOONE FOR YEARS.
AFTERNOON...? THAT'S IT!
I KNOW THE HIDDEN RIDDLE.
AND I THINK I KNOW WHERE TO LOOK FOR THE RIDDLER HIMSELF.

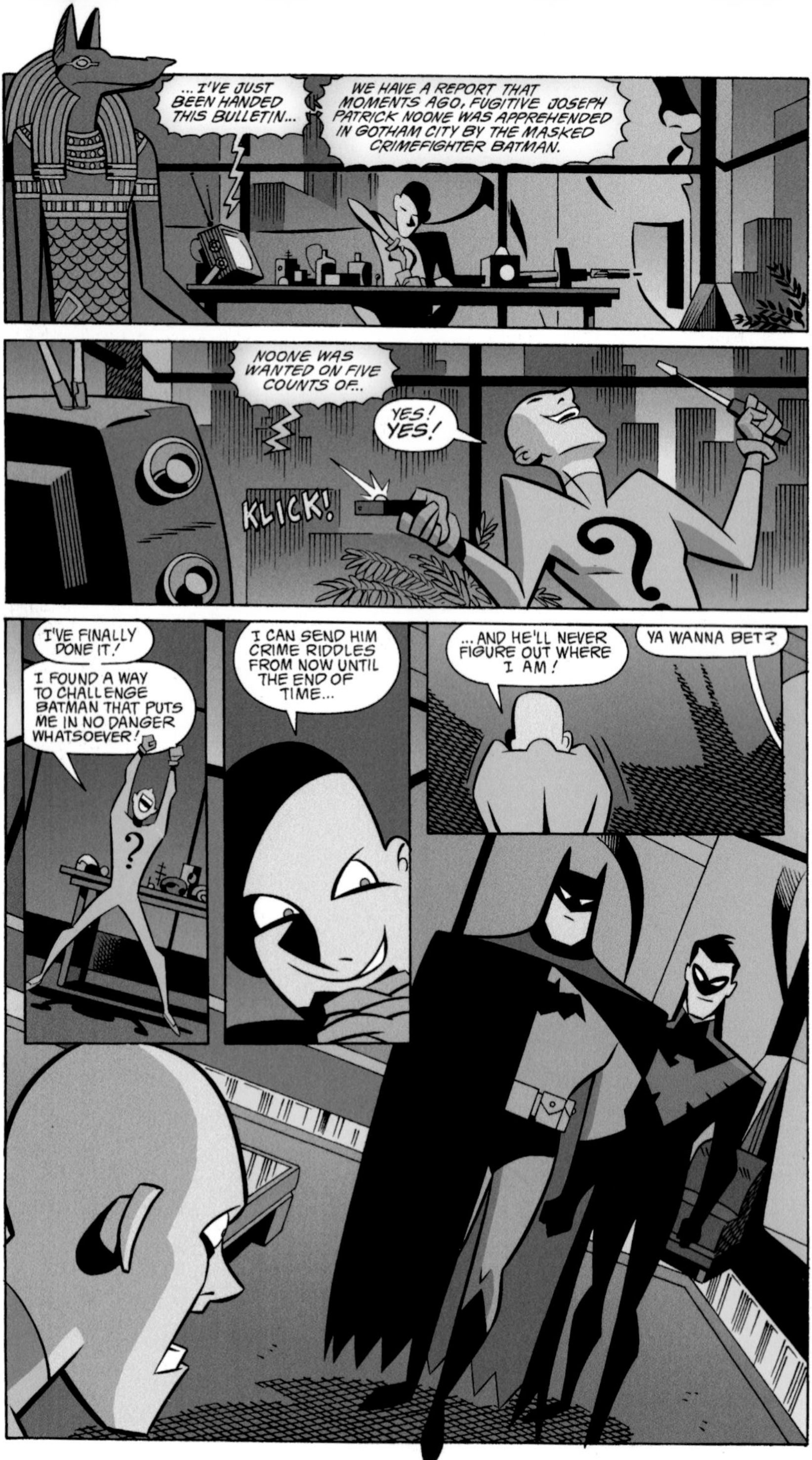

...I'VE JUST BEEN HANDED THIS BULLETIN...
WE HAVE A REPORT THAT MOMENTS AGO, FUGITIVE JOSEPH PATRICK NOONE WAS APPREHENDED IN GOTHAM CITY BY THE MASKED CRIMEFIGHTER BATMAN.
NOONE WAS WANTED ON FIVE COUNTS OF...
YES! YES!
KLICK!
I'VE FINALLY DONE IT!
I FOUND A WAY TO CHALLENGE BATMAN THAT PUTS ME IN NO DANGER WHATSOEVER!
I CAN SEND HIM CRIME RIDDLES FROM NOW UNTIL THE END OF TIME...
...AND HE'LL NEVER FIGURE OUT WHERE I AM!
YA WANNA BET?

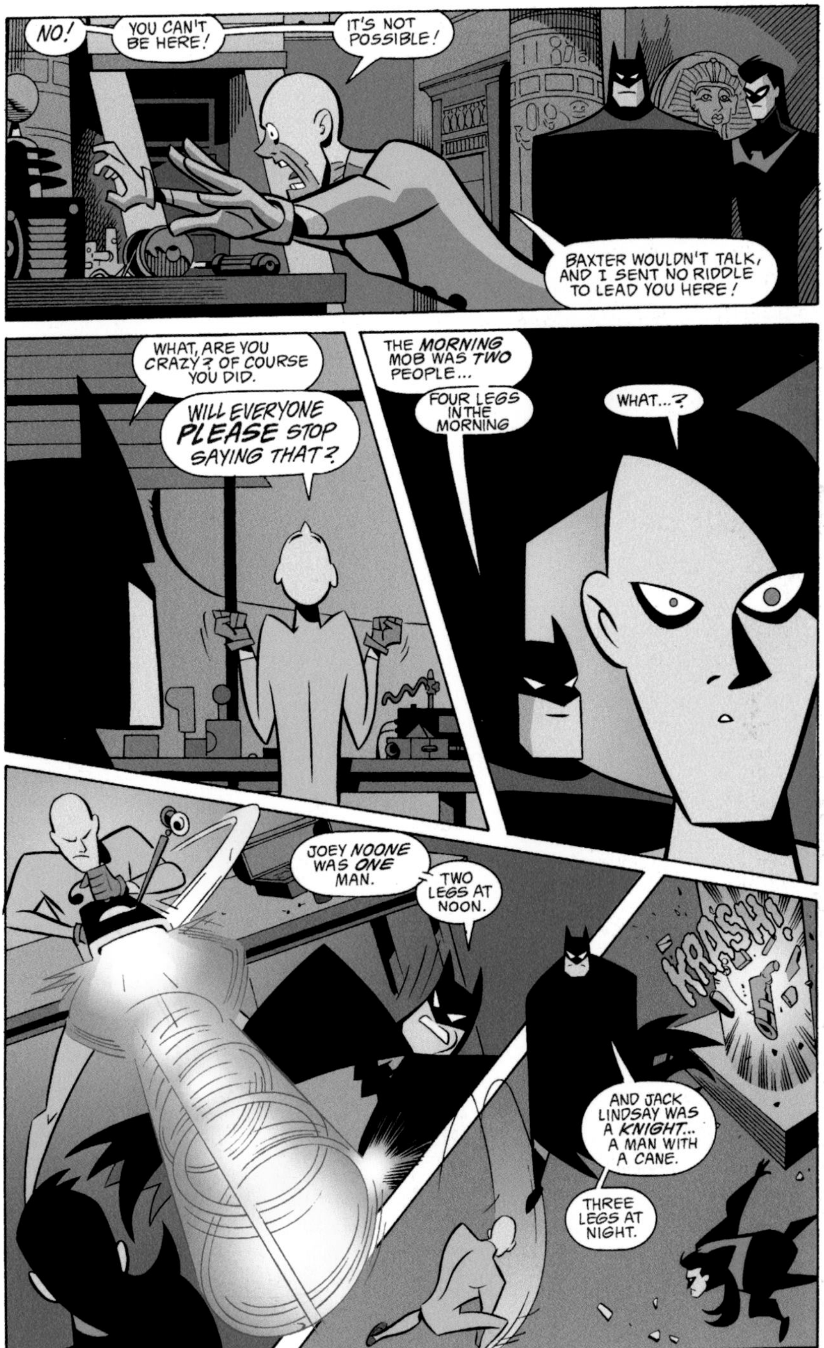
NO!
YOU CAN'T BE HERE!
IT'S NOT POSSIBLE!
BAXTER WOULDN'T TALK, AND I SENT NO RIDDLE TO LEAD YOU HERE!
WHAT, ARE YOU CRAZY? OF COURSE YOU DID.
WILL EVERYONE PLEASE STOP SAYING THAT?
THE MORNING MOB WAS TWO PEOPLE...
FOUR LEGS IN THE MORNING
WHAT...?
JOEY NOONE WAS ONE MAN.
TWO LEGS AT NOON.
KRASH!
AND JACK LINDSAY WAS A KNIGHT... A MAN WITH A CANE.
THREE LEGS AT NIGHT.

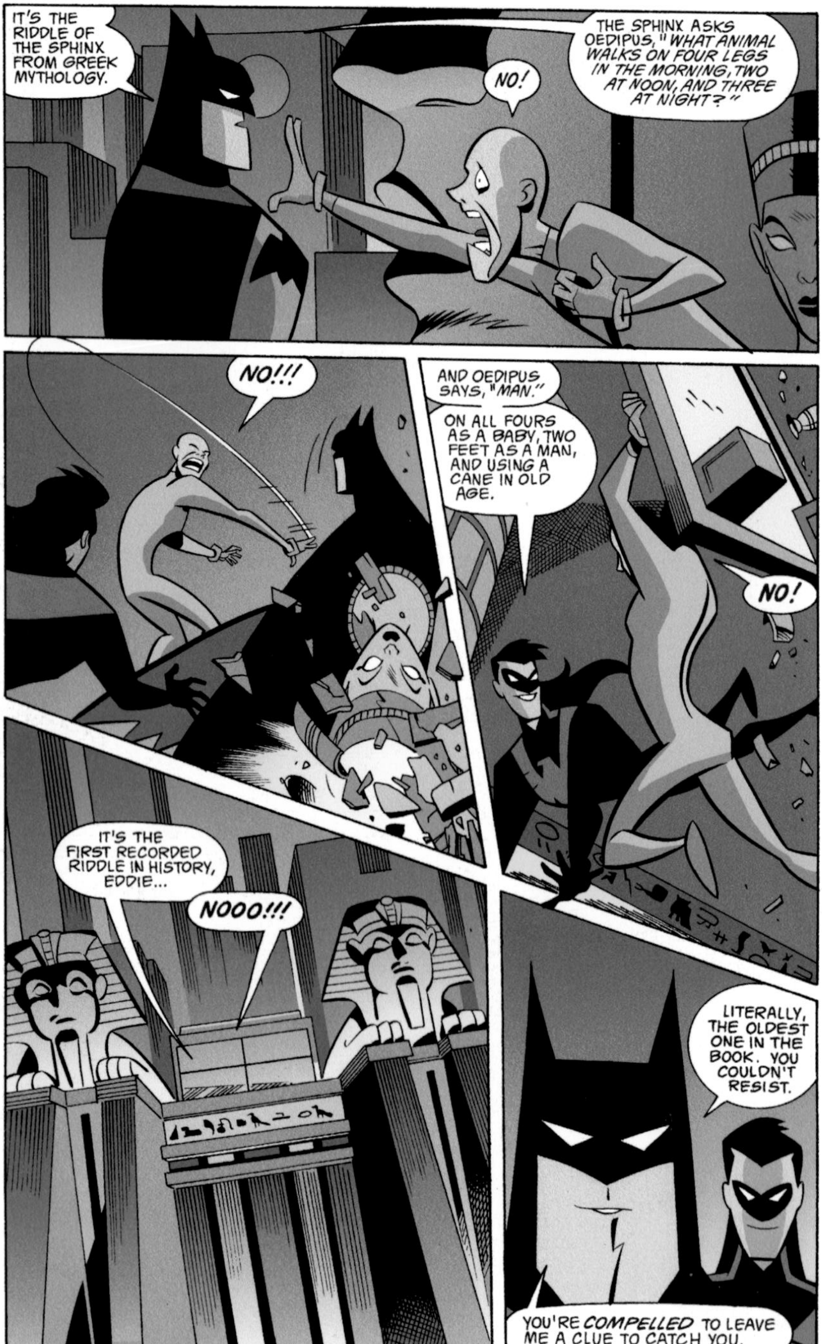
IT'S THE RIDDLE OF THE SPHINX FROM GREEK MYTHOLOGY.
NO!
THE SPHINX ASKS OEDIPUS, "WHAT ANIMAL WALKS ON FOUR LEGS IN THE MORNING, TWO AT NOON, AND THREE AT NIGHT?"
NO!!!
AND OEDIPUS SAYS, "MAN."
ON ALL FOURS AS A BABY, TWO FEET AS A MAN, AND USING A CANE IN OLD AGE.
NO!
IT'S THE FIRST RECORDED RIDDLE IN HISTORY, EDDIE...
NOOO!!!
LITERALLY, THE OLDEST ONE IN THE BOOK. YOU COULDN'T RESIST.
YOU'RE COMPELLED TO LEAVE ME A CLUE TO CATCH YOU.

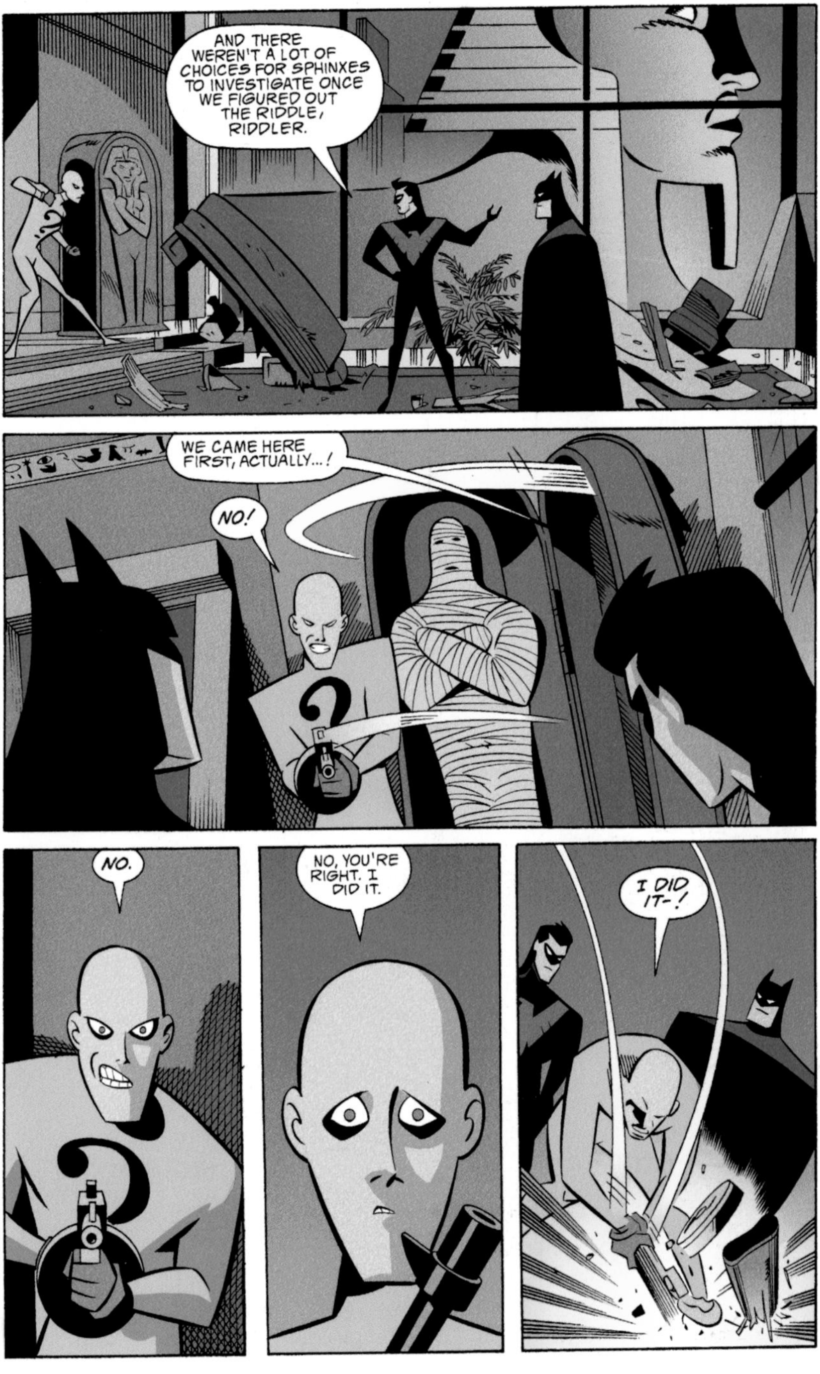
AND THERE WEREN'T A LOT OF CHOICES FOR SPHINXES TO INVESTIGATE ONCE WE FIGURED OUT THE RIDDLE, RIDDLER.
WE CAME HERE FIRST, ACTUALLY...!
NO!
NO.
NO, YOU'RE RIGHT. I DID IT.
I DID IT-!

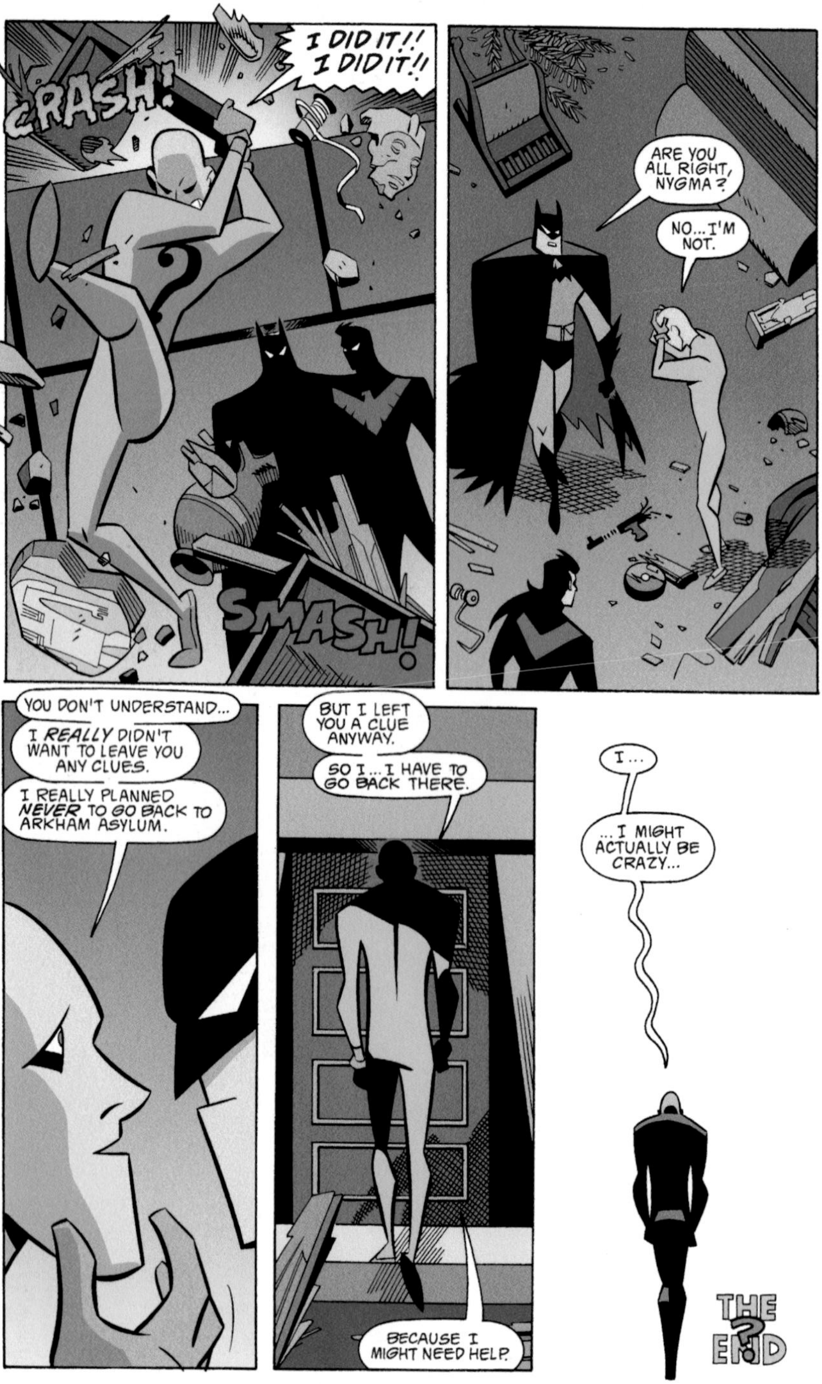
CRASH!
I DID IT!! I DID IT!!
SMASH!
ARE YOU ALL RIGHT, NYGMA?
NO...I'M NOT.
YOU DON'T UNDERSTAND...
I REALLY DIDN'T WANT TO LEAVE YOU ANY CLUES.
I REALLY PLANNED NEVER TO GO BACK TO ARKHAM ASYLUM.
BUT I LEFT YOU A CLUE ANYWAY.
SO I...I HAVE TO GO BACK THERE.
BECAUSE I MIGHT NEED HELP.
I...
...I MIGHT ACTUALLY BE CRAZY...
THE END

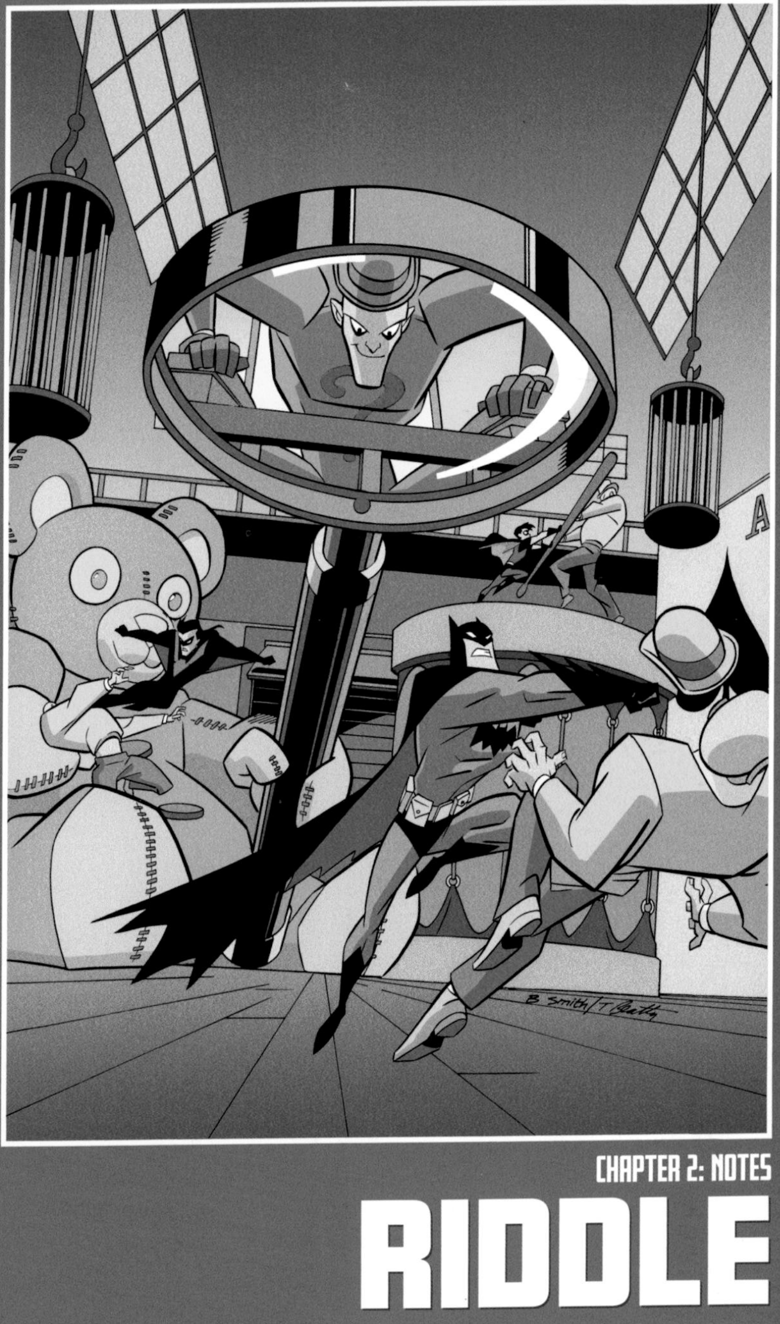

CHAPTER 2: NOTES

RIDDLE ME THIS

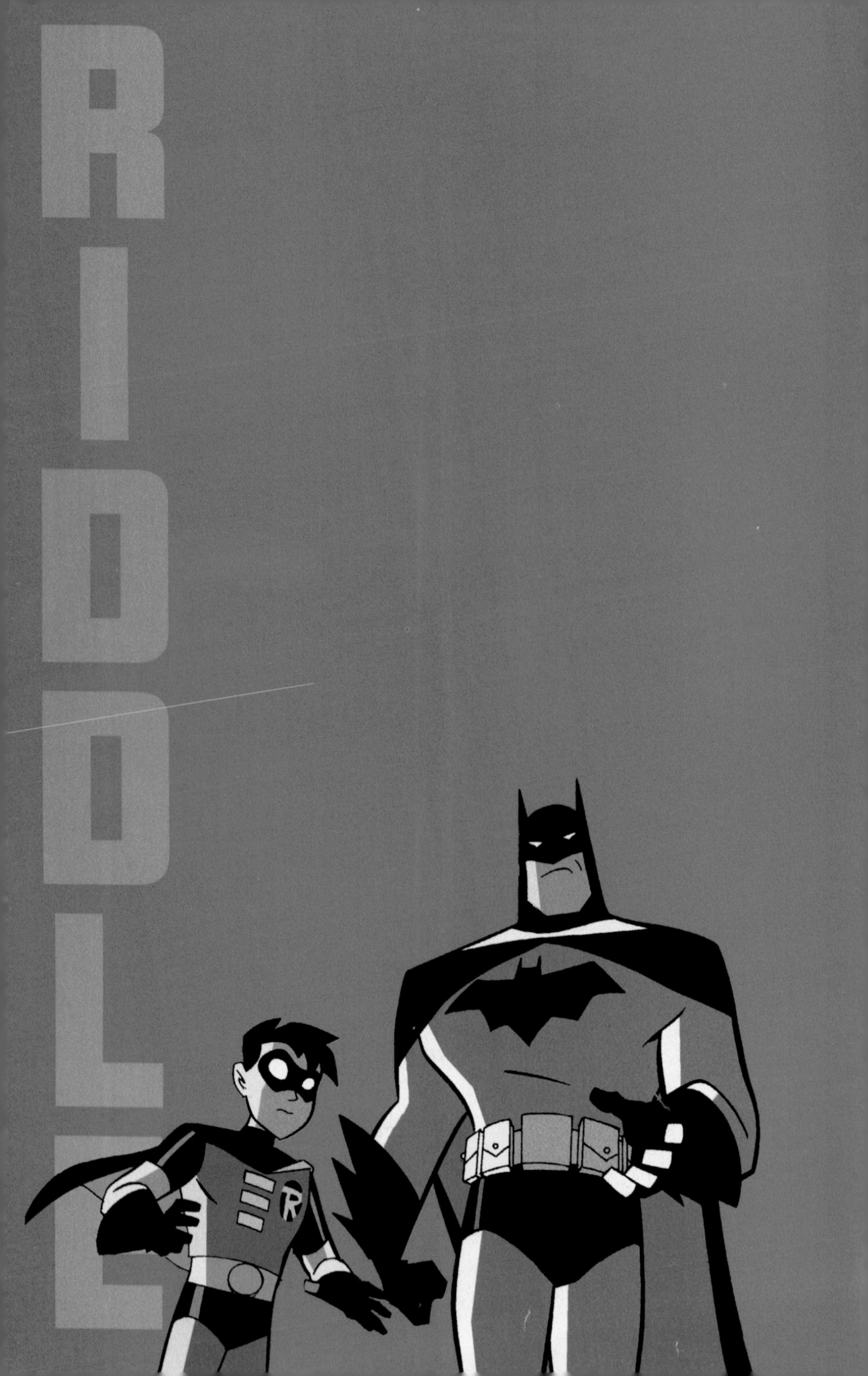
RIDDL

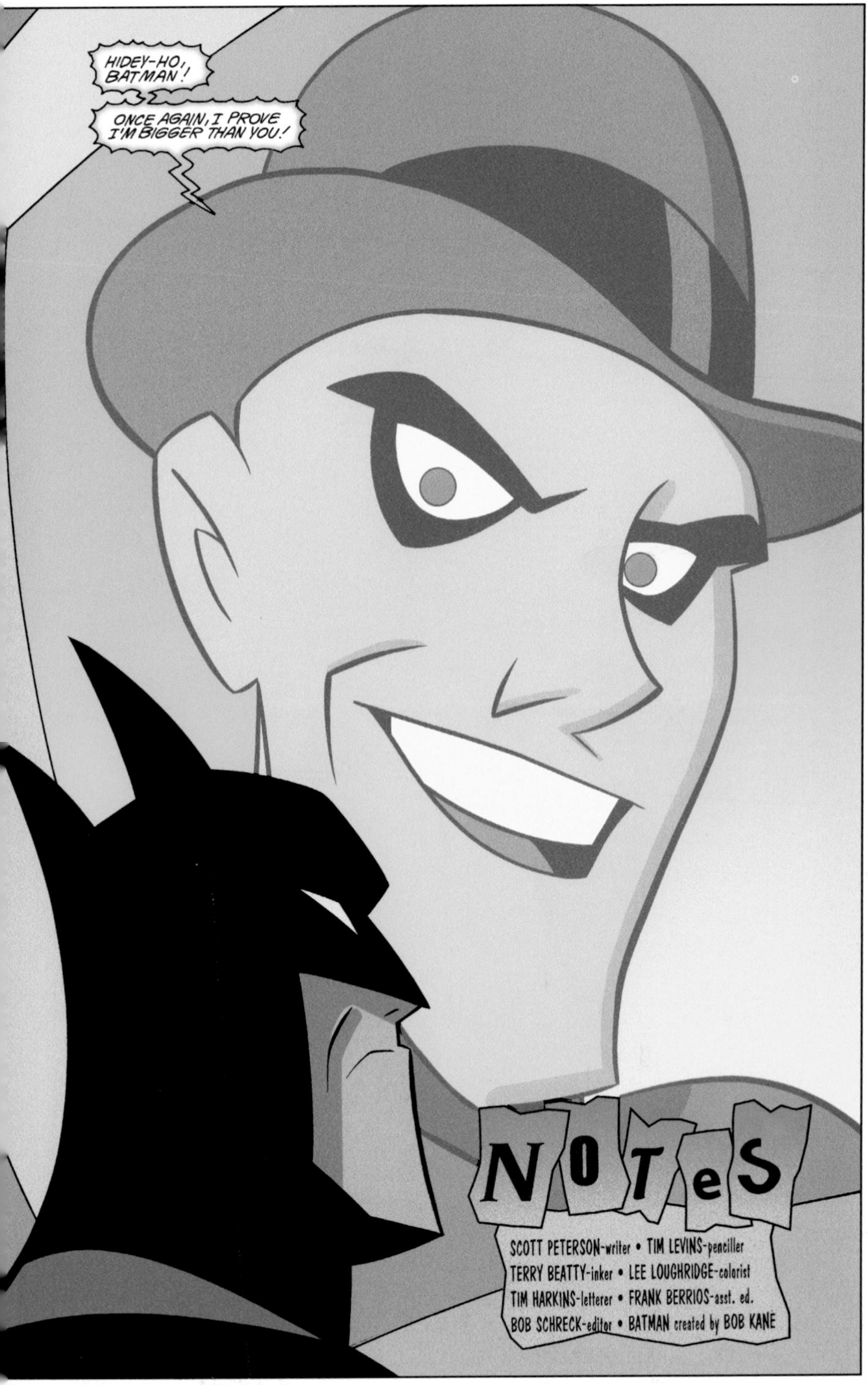
HIDEY-HO, BATMAN!
ONCE AGAIN, I PROVE I'M BIGGER THAN YOU!
NOTES
SCOTT PETERSON-writer • TIM LEVINS-penciller
TERRY BEATTY-inker • LEE LOUGHRIDGE-colorist
TIM HARKINS-letterer • FRANK BERRIOS-asst. ed.
BOB SCHRECK-editor • BATMAN created by BOB KANE

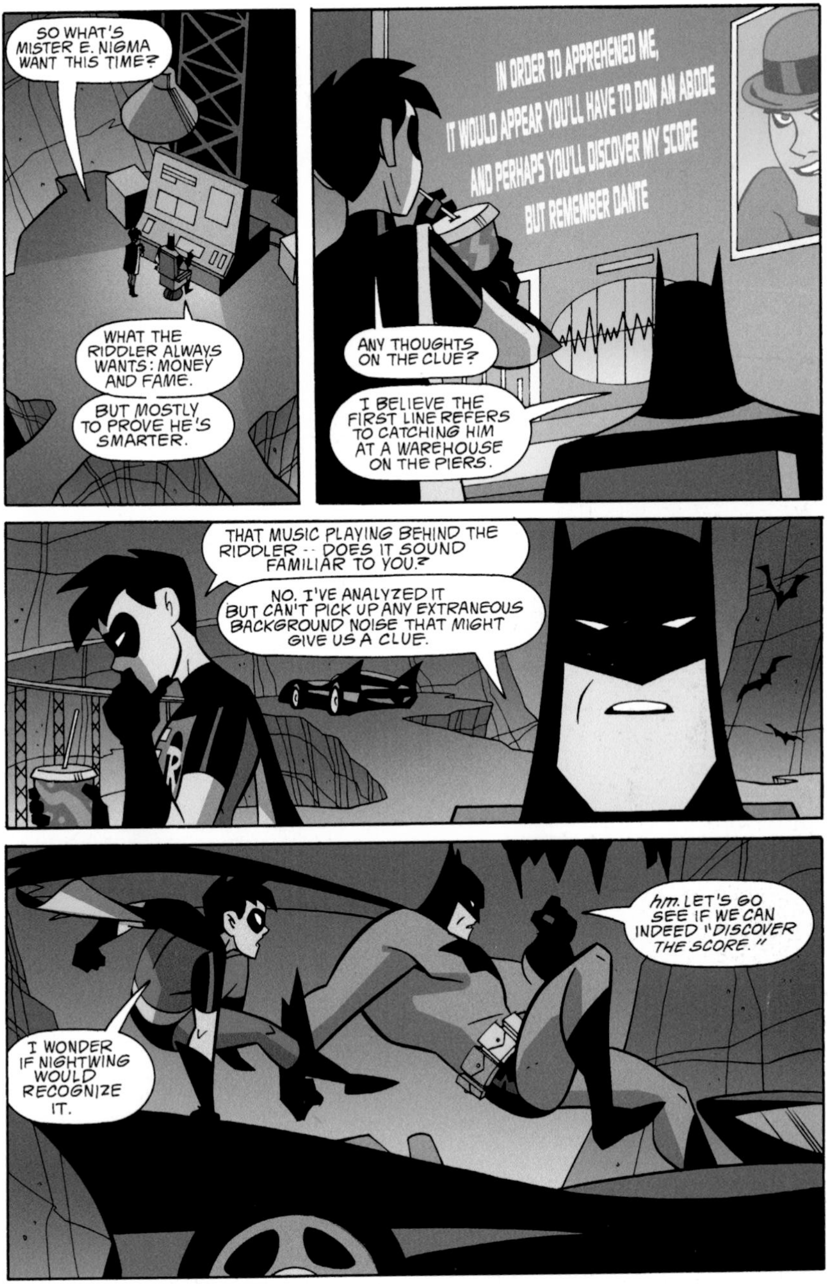
SO WHAT'S MISTER E. NIGMA WANT THIS TIME?
WHAT THE RIDDLER ALWAYS WANTS: MONEY AND FAME.
BUT MOSTLY TO PROVE HE'S SMARTER.
IN ORDER TO APPREHENED ME,
IT WOULD APPEAR YOU'LL HAVE TO DON AN ABODE
AND PERHAPS YOU'LL DISCOVER MY SCORE
BUT REMEMBER DANTE
ANY THOUGHTS ON THE CLUE?
I BELIEVE THE FIRST LINE REFERS TO CATCHING HIM AT A WAREHOUSE ON THE PIERS.
THAT MUSIC PLAYING BEHIND THE RIDDLER -- DOES IT SOUND FAMILIAR TO YOU?
NO. I'VE ANALYZED IT BUT CAN'T PICK UP ANY EXTRANEOUS BACKGROUND NOISE THAT MIGHT GIVE US A CLUE.
hm. LET'S GO SEE IF WE CAN INDEED "DISCOVER THE SCORE."
I WONDER IF NIGHTWING WOULD RECOGNIZE IT.

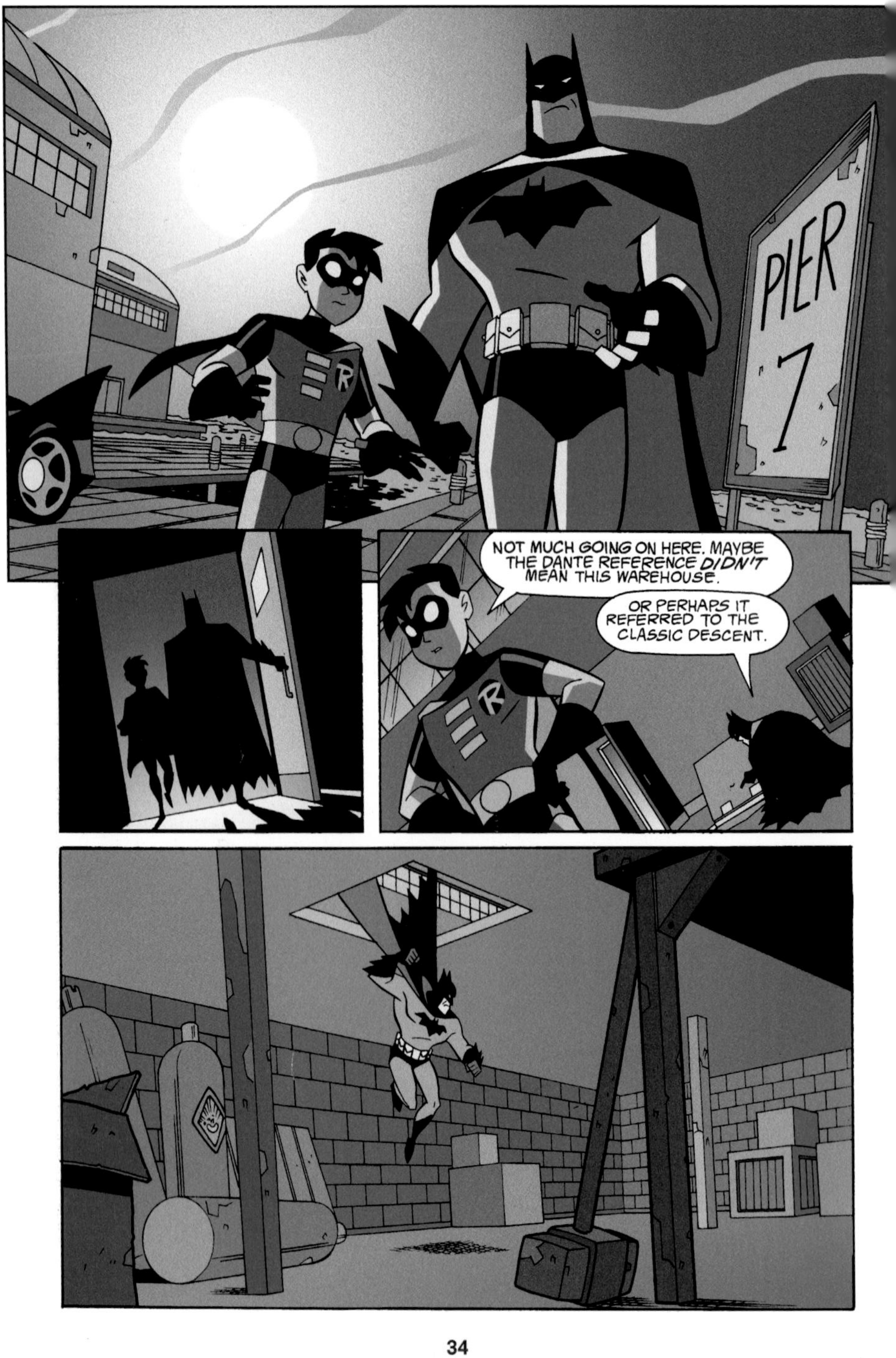
PIER 7
NOT MUCH GOING ON HERE. MAYBE THE DANTE REFERENCE *DIDN'T* MEAN THIS WAREHOUSE.
OR PERHAPS IT REFERRED TO THE CLASSIC DESCENT.

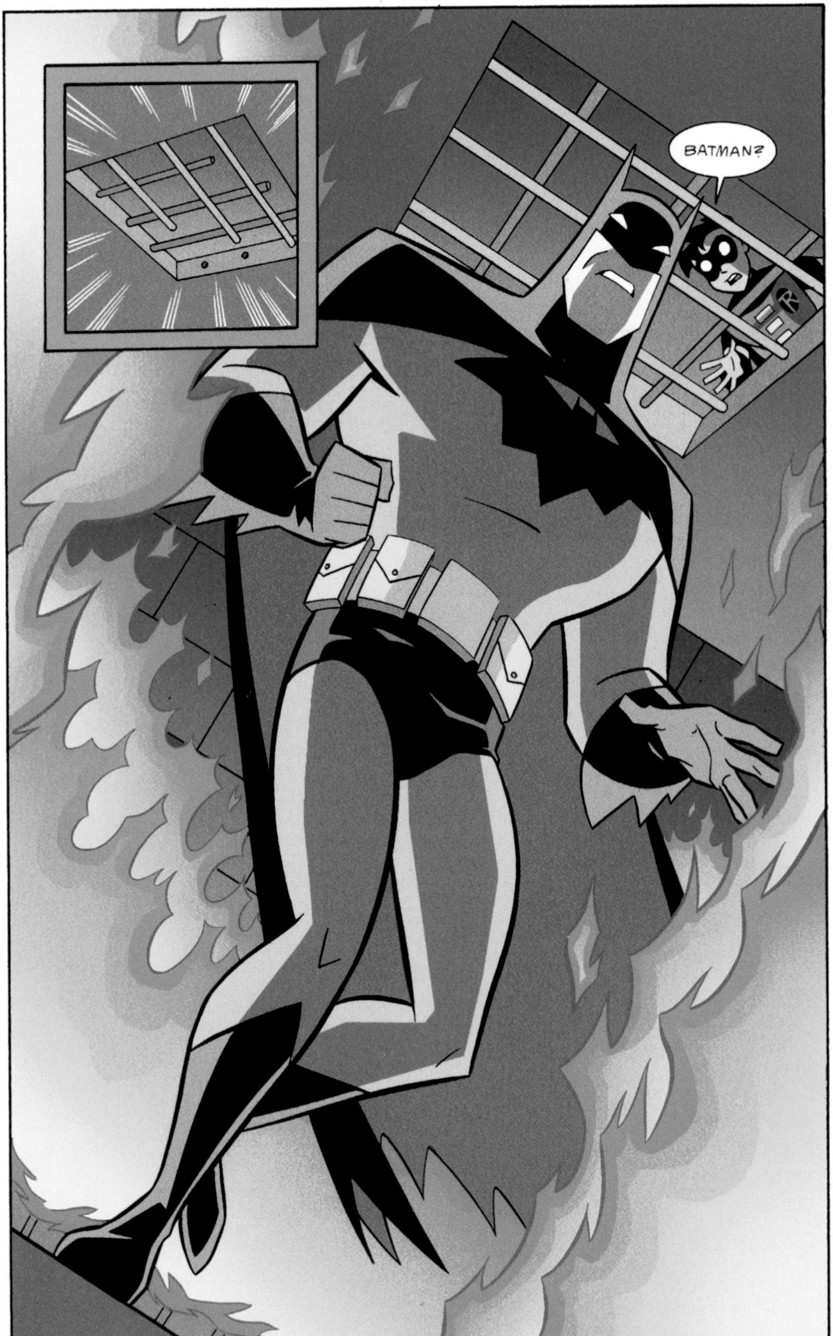
BATMAN?

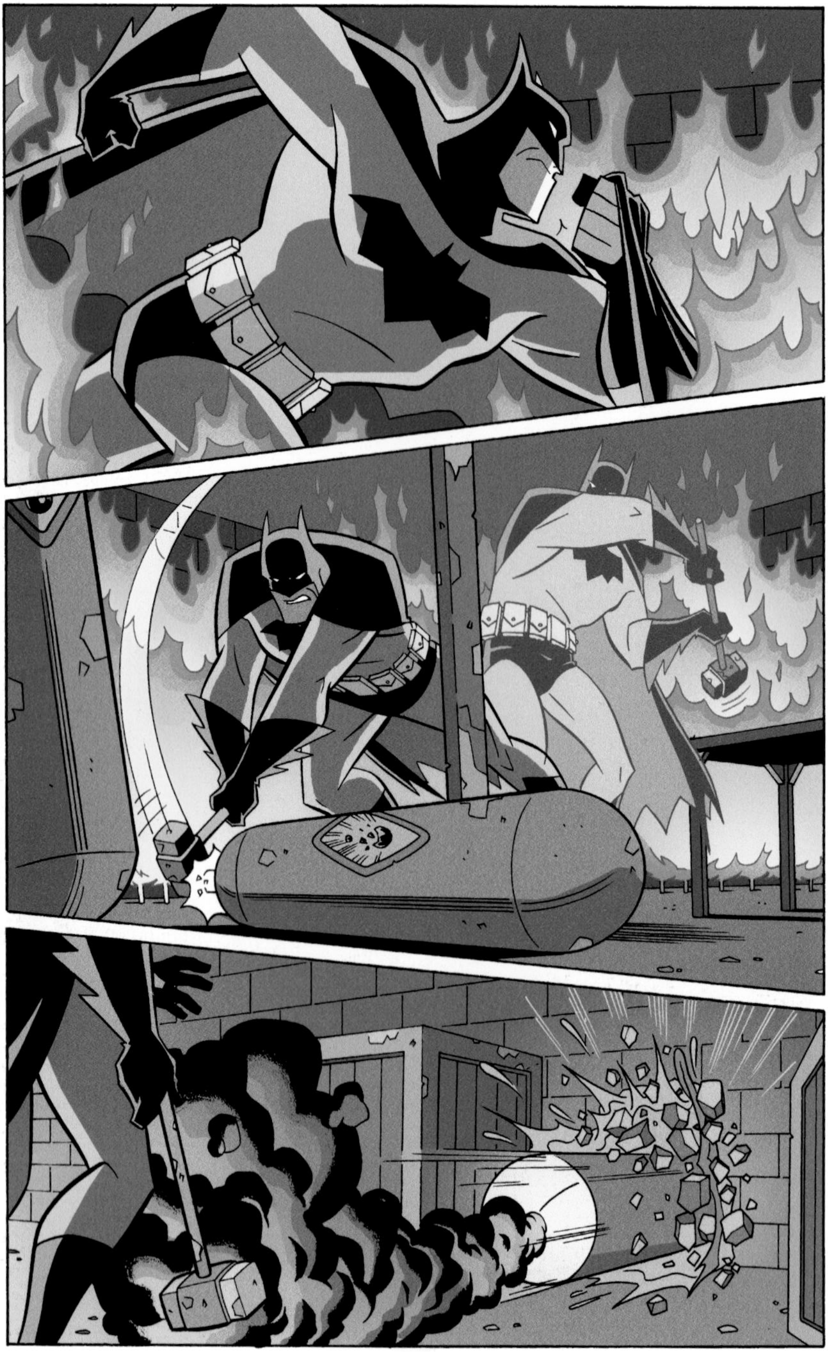

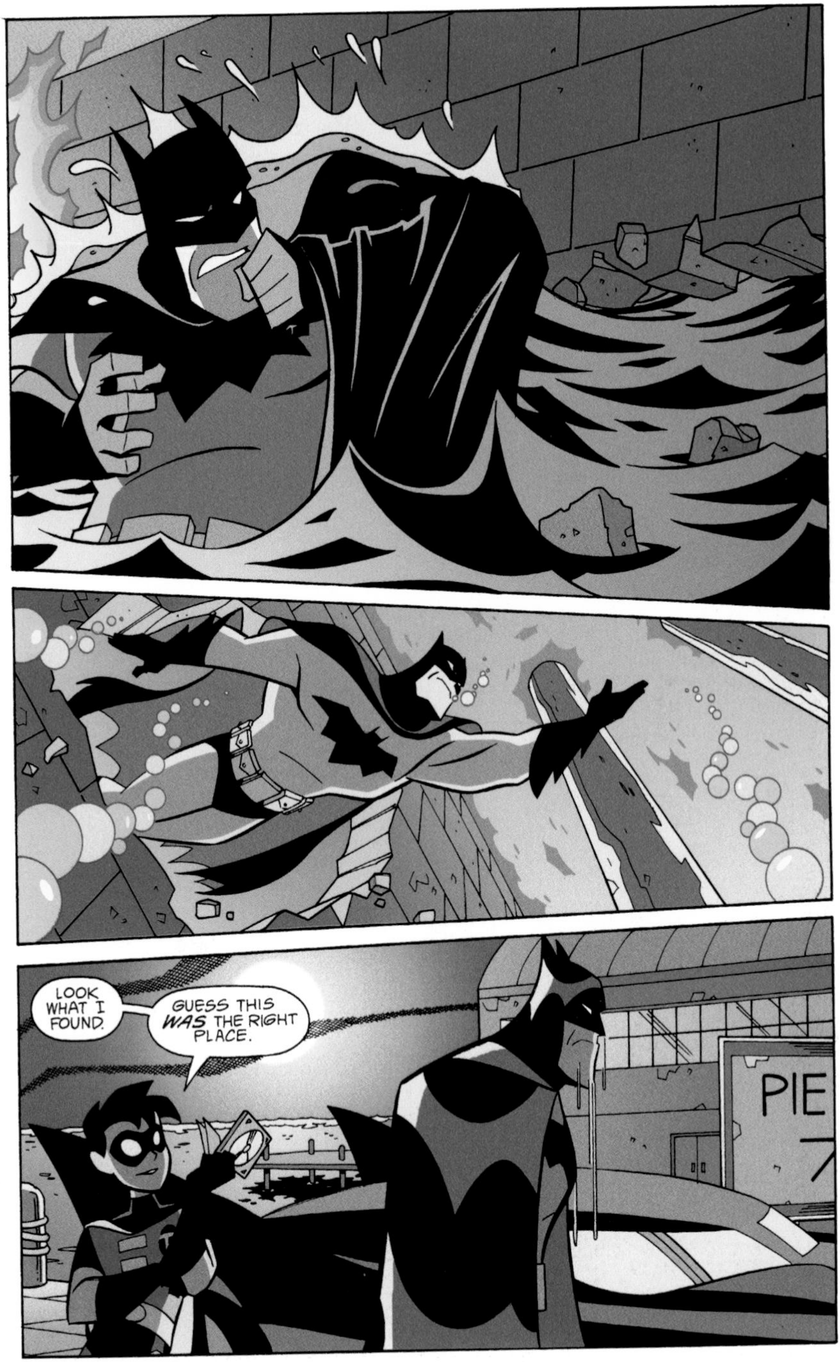
LOOK WHAT I FOUND.
GUESS THIS WAS THE RIGHT PLACE.
PIE

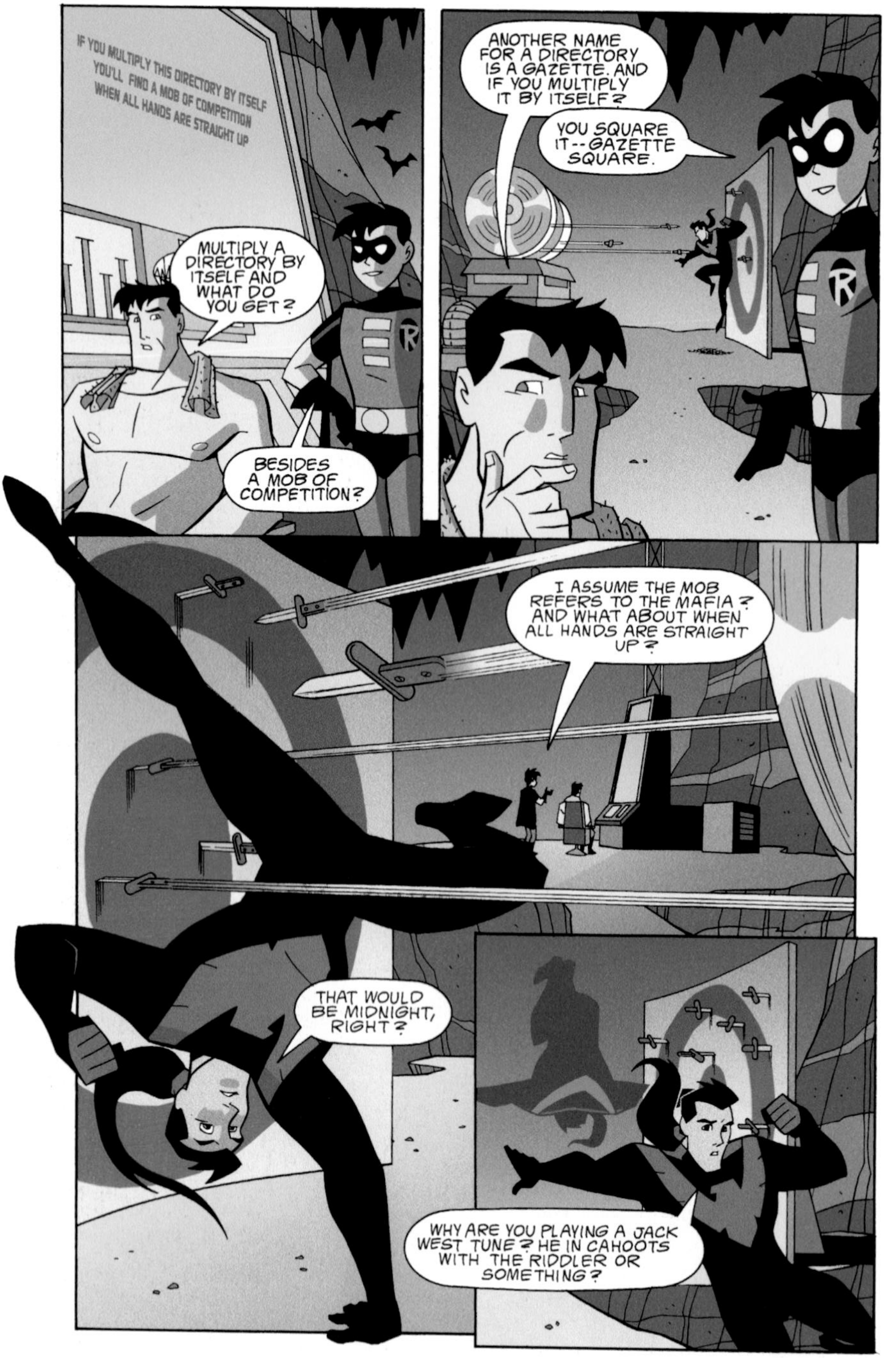
IF YOU MULTIPLY THIS DIRECTORY BY ITSELF
YOU'LL FIND A MOB OF COMPETITION
WHEN ALL HANDS ARE STRAIGHT UP
MULTIPLY A DIRECTORY BY ITSELF AND WHAT DO YOU GET?
BESIDES A MOB OF COMPETITION?
ANOTHER NAME FOR A DIRECTORY IS A GAZETTE. AND IF YOU MULTIPLY IT BY ITSELF?
YOU SQUARE IT--GAZETTE SQUARE.
I ASSUME THE MOB REFERS TO THE MAFIA? AND WHAT ABOUT WHEN ALL HANDS ARE STRAIGHT UP?
THAT WOULD BE MIDNIGHT, RIGHT?
WHY ARE YOU PLAYING A JACK WEST TUNE? HE IN CAHOOTS WITH THE RIDDLER OR SOMETHING?

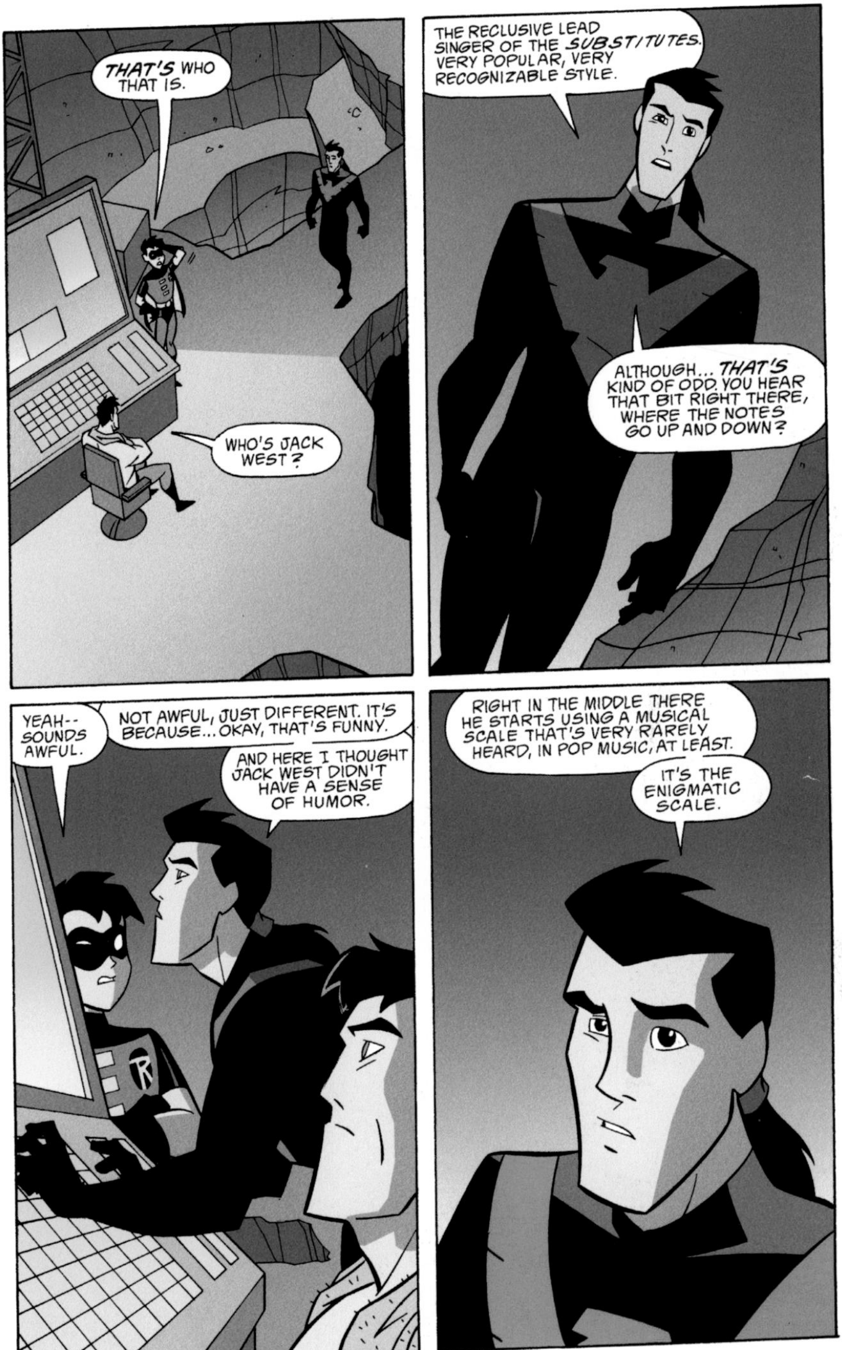
THAT'S WHO THAT IS.
WHO'S JACK WEST?
THE RECLUSIVE LEAD SINGER OF THE SUBSTITUTES. VERY POPULAR, VERY RECOGNIZABLE STYLE.
ALTHOUGH... THAT'S KIND OF ODD. YOU HEAR THAT BIT RIGHT THERE, WHERE THE NOTES GO UP AND DOWN?
YEAH-- SOUNDS AWFUL.
NOT AWFUL, JUST DIFFERENT. IT'S BECAUSE... OKAY, THAT'S FUNNY.
AND HERE I THOUGHT JACK WEST DIDN'T HAVE A SENSE OF HUMOR.
RIGHT IN THE MIDDLE THERE HE STARTS USING A MUSICAL SCALE THAT'S VERY RARELY HEARD, IN POP MUSIC, AT LEAST.
IT'S THE ENIGMATIC SCALE.

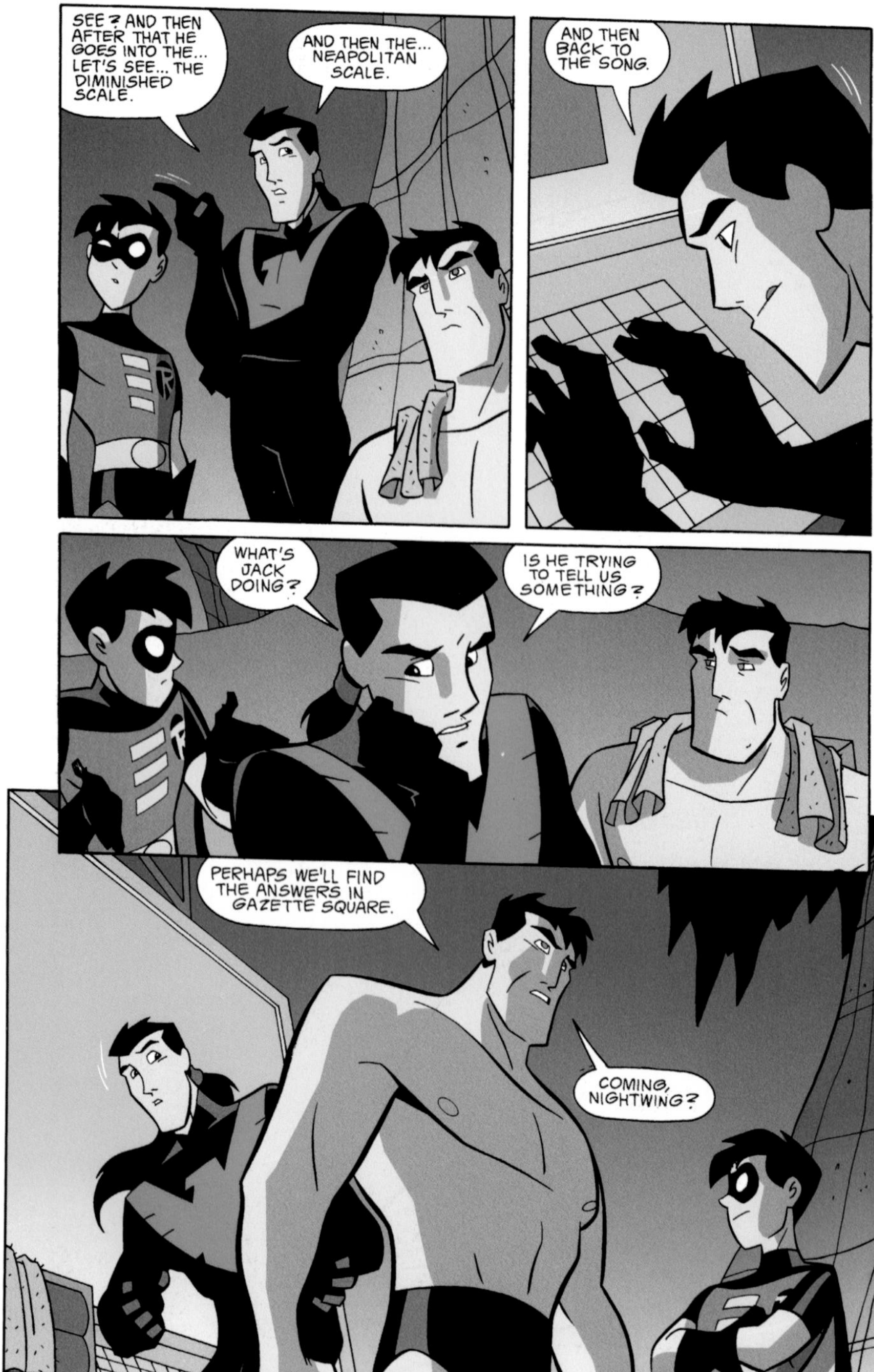

SEE? AND THEN AFTER THAT HE GOES INTO THE... LET'S SEE... THE DIMINISHED SCALE.
AND THEN THE... NEAPOLITAN SCALE.
AND THEN BACK TO THE SONG.
WHAT'S JACK DOING?
IS HE TRYING TO TELL US SOMETHING?
PERHAPS WE'LL FIND THE ANSWERS IN GAZETTE SQUARE.
COMING, NIGHTWING?

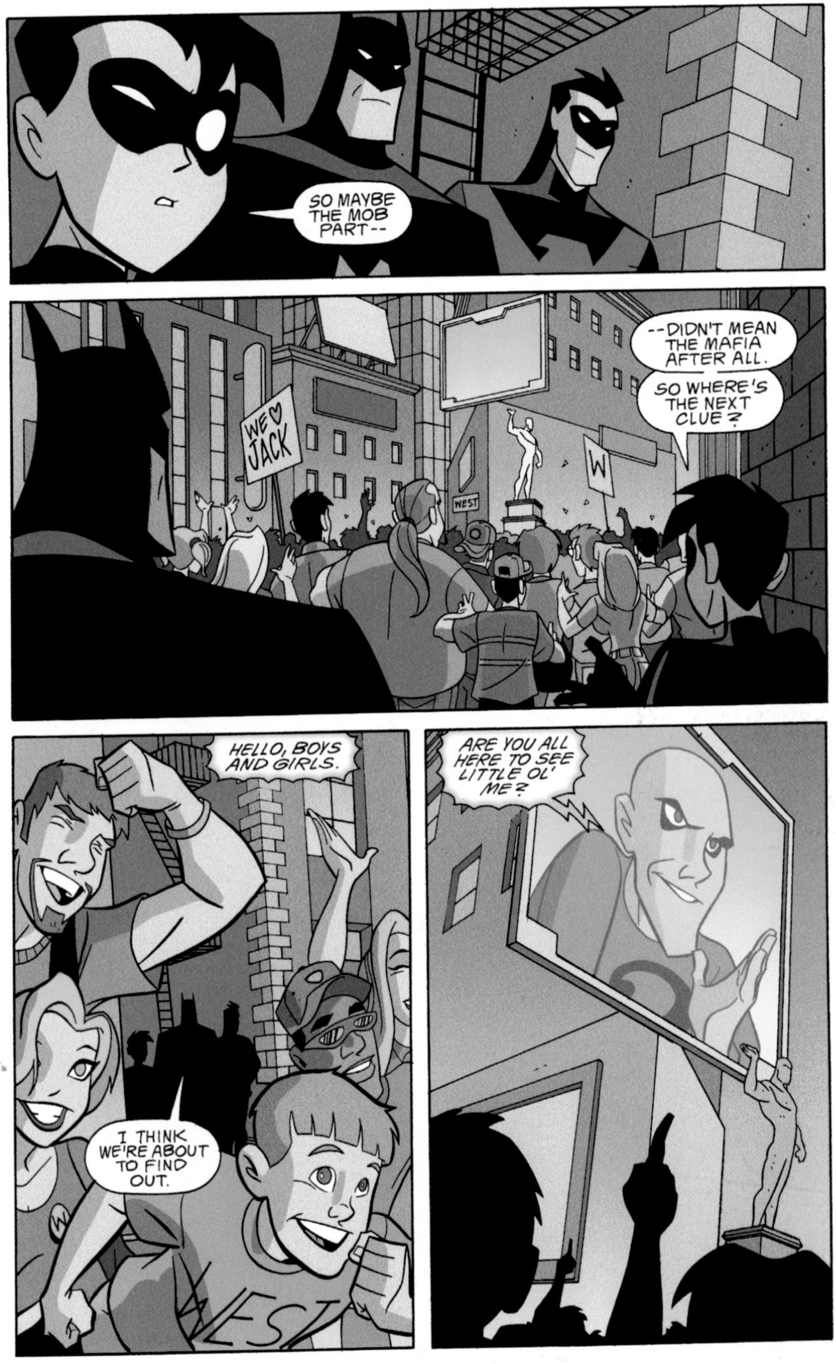
SO MAYBE THE MOB PART--
--DIDN'T MEAN THE MAFIA AFTER ALL.
SO WHERE'S THE NEXT CLUE?
WE ♥ JACK
W
WEST
HELLO, BOYS AND GIRLS.
I THINK WE'RE ABOUT TO FIND OUT.
ARE YOU ALL HERE TO SEE LITTLE OL' ME?

NO, YOU WERE HOPING TO SEE JACK WEST, WEREN'T YOU?

WEST RULES

I'M AFRAID JACK'S ALL TIED UP AT THE MOMENT. BUT HE DID SEND A LITTLE PRESENT FOR ONE OF YOU.

A BRAND-NEW SONG! AND THE DISC IS ON THAT STATUE RIGHT... OVER THERE.

WHO'LL BE THE LUCKY CONTEST WINNER?

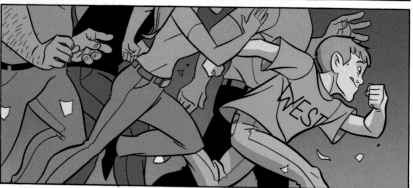

GOT ANY IDEAS *NOW*?

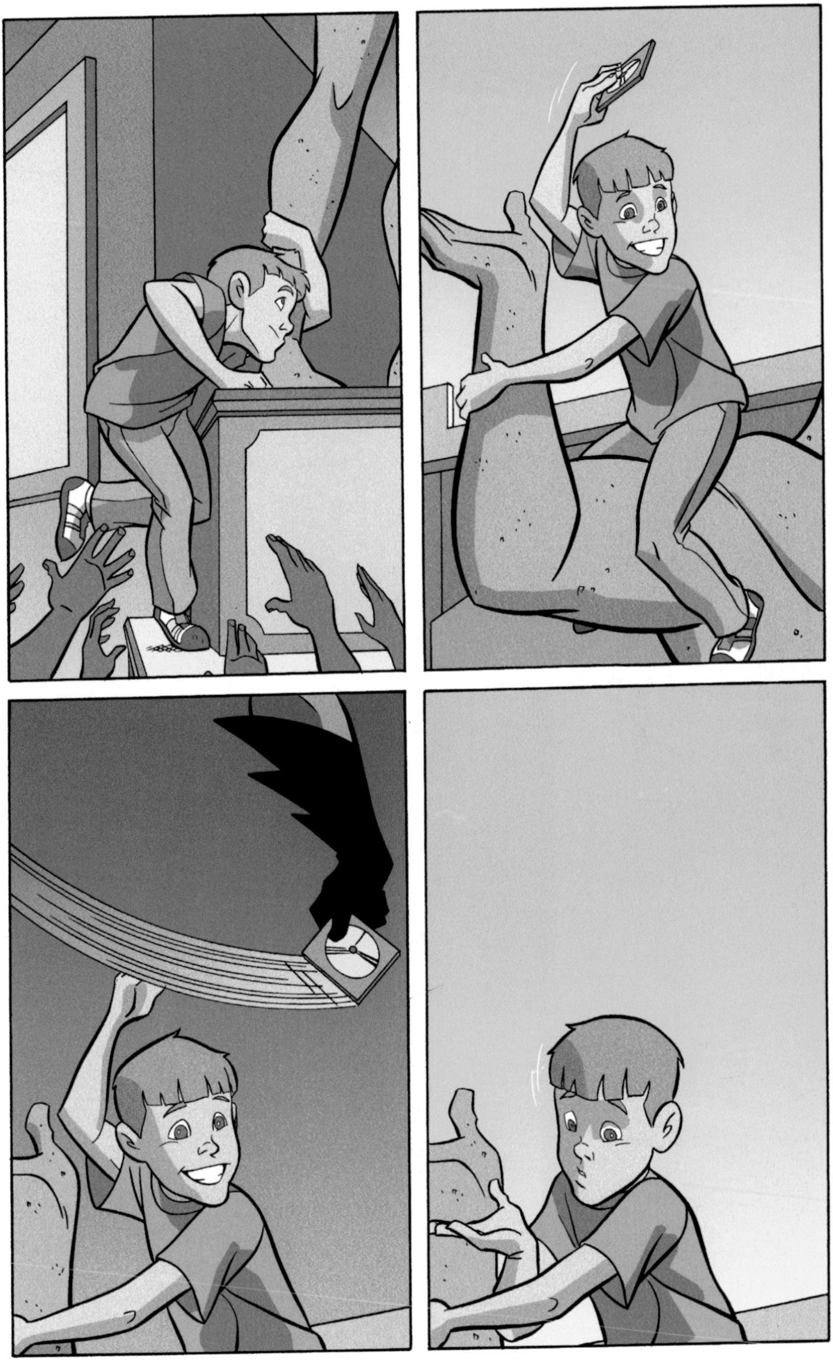

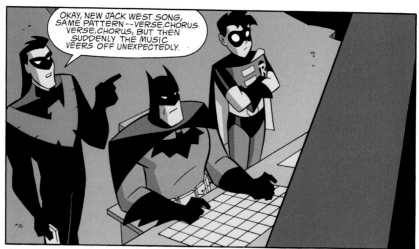

OKAY, NEW JACK WEST SONG, SAME PATTERN--VERSE, CHORUS VERSE, CHORUS, BUT THEN SUDDENLY THE MUSIC VEERS OFF UNEXPECTEDLY.

THE ENIGMATIC SCALE AGAIN, AND THEN A QUOTE THAT SEEMS FAMILIAR AND THEN...

I DON'T KNOW... SOMETHING COMPLETELY ATONAL.

IT'S NOT A SCALE... NOT A MODE... MAYBE THE NOTES SPELL SOMETHING OUT?

01: 07: 45

NOPE, JUST GIBBERISH.

44

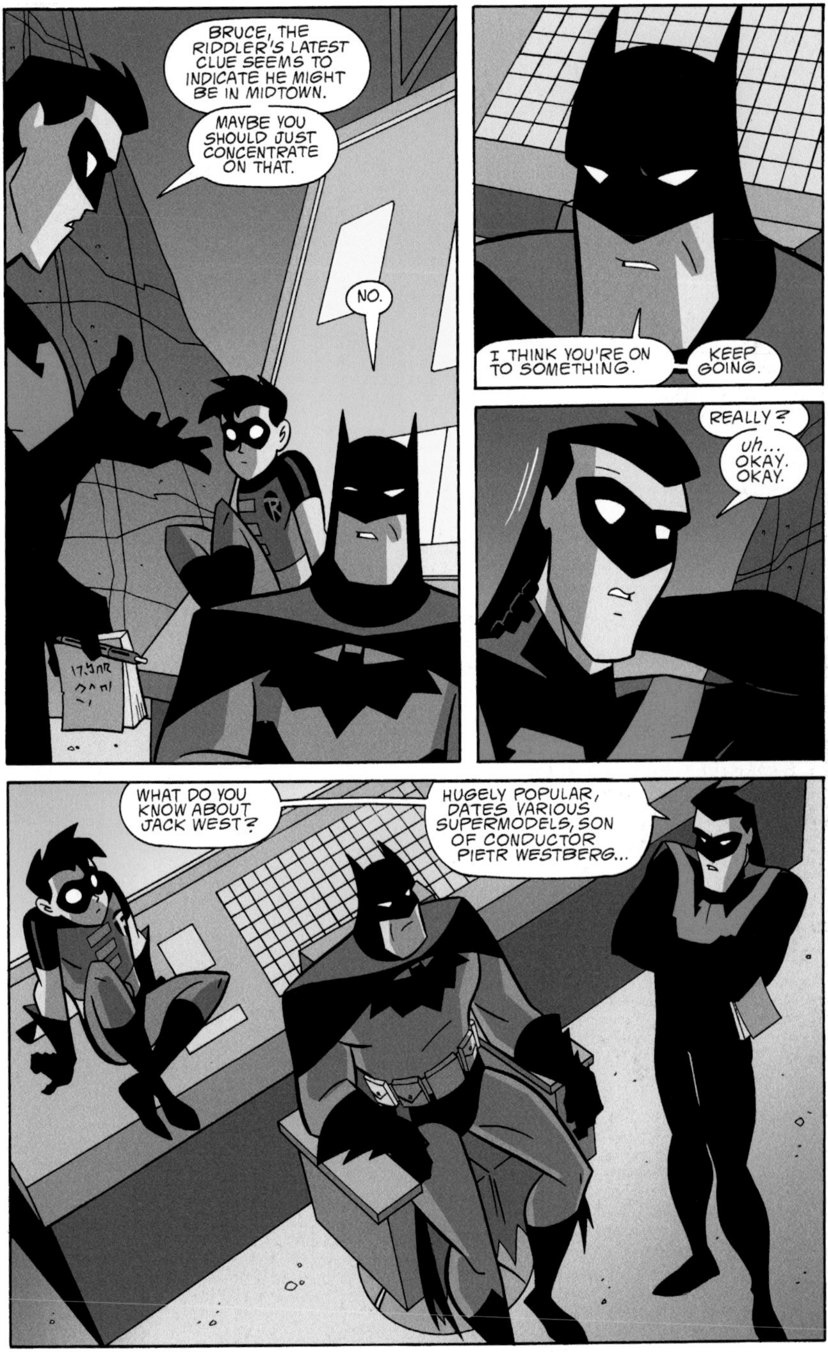

BRUCE, THE RIDDLER'S LATEST CLUE SEEMS TO INDICATE HE MIGHT BE IN MIDTOWN.
MAYBE YOU SHOULD JUST CONCENTRATE ON THAT.
NO.
I THINK YOU'RE ON TO SOMETHING.
KEEP GOING.
REALLY?
uh... OKAY. OKAY.
WHAT DO YOU KNOW ABOUT JACK WEST?
HUGELY POPULAR, DATES VARIOUS SUPERMODELS, SON OF CONDUCTOR PIETR WESTBERG...

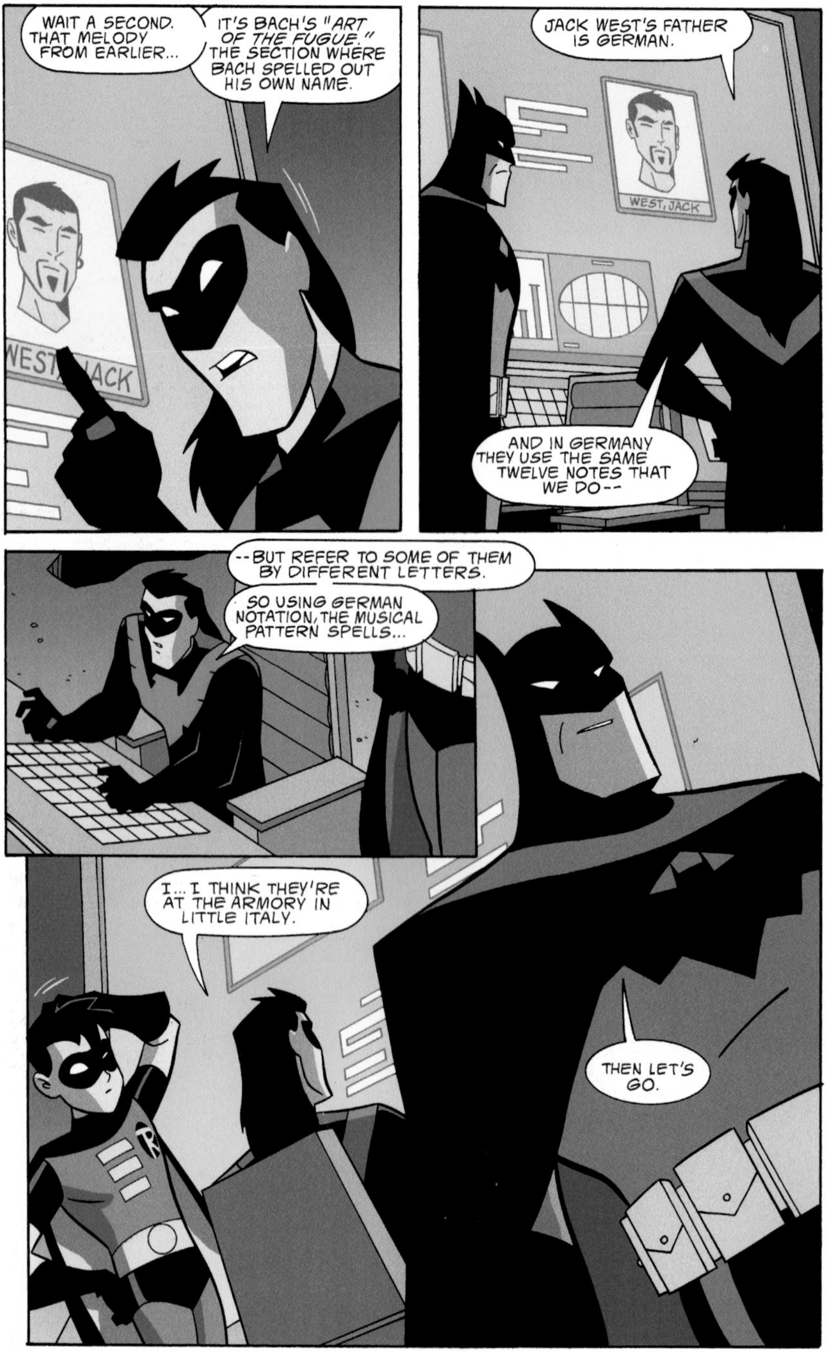
WAIT A SECOND. THAT MELODY FROM EARLIER...
IT'S BACH'S "ART OF THE FUGUE." THE SECTION WHERE BACH SPELLED OUT HIS OWN NAME.
WEST, JACK
JACK WEST'S FATHER IS GERMAN.
WEST, JACK
AND IN GERMANY THEY USE THE SAME TWELVE NOTES THAT WE DO--
--BUT REFER TO SOME OF THEM BY DIFFERENT LETTERS.
SO USING GERMAN NOTATION, THE MUSICAL PATTERN SPELLS...
I... I THINK THEY'RE AT THE ARMORY IN LITTLE ITALY.
THEN LET'S GO.

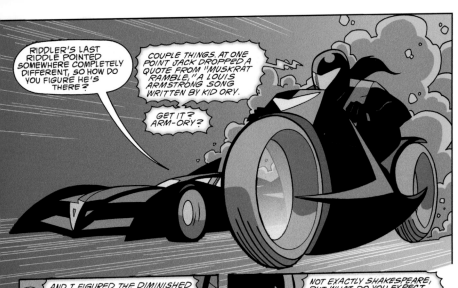

RIDDLER'S LAST RIDDLE POINTED SOMEWHERE COMPLETELY DIFFERENT, SO HOW DO YOU FIGURE HE'S THERE?

COUPLE THINGS. AT ONE POINT JACK DROPPED A QUOTE FROM "MUSKRAT RAMBLE," A LOUIS ARMSTRONG SONG WRITTEN BY KID ORY.

GET IT? ARM-ORY?

AND I FIGURED THE DIMINISHED SCALE PLUS THE NEAPOLITAN SCALE EQUALS LITTLE ITALY.

AND ALL THOSE DISSONANT NOTES? USING GERMAN NOTATION, IT SPELLS "HE CAGED FACE DEAD BEACH."

NOT EXACTLY SHAKESPEARE, BUT WHAT DO YOU EXPECT WITH ONLY EIGHT LETTERS?

AND THE ARMORY DOES OVERLOOK THE HARBOR, WHICH NO ONE WOULD SWIM IN ANYMORE.

I GUESS YOU FIGURED ALL THIS OUT ALREADY, huh?

NO.

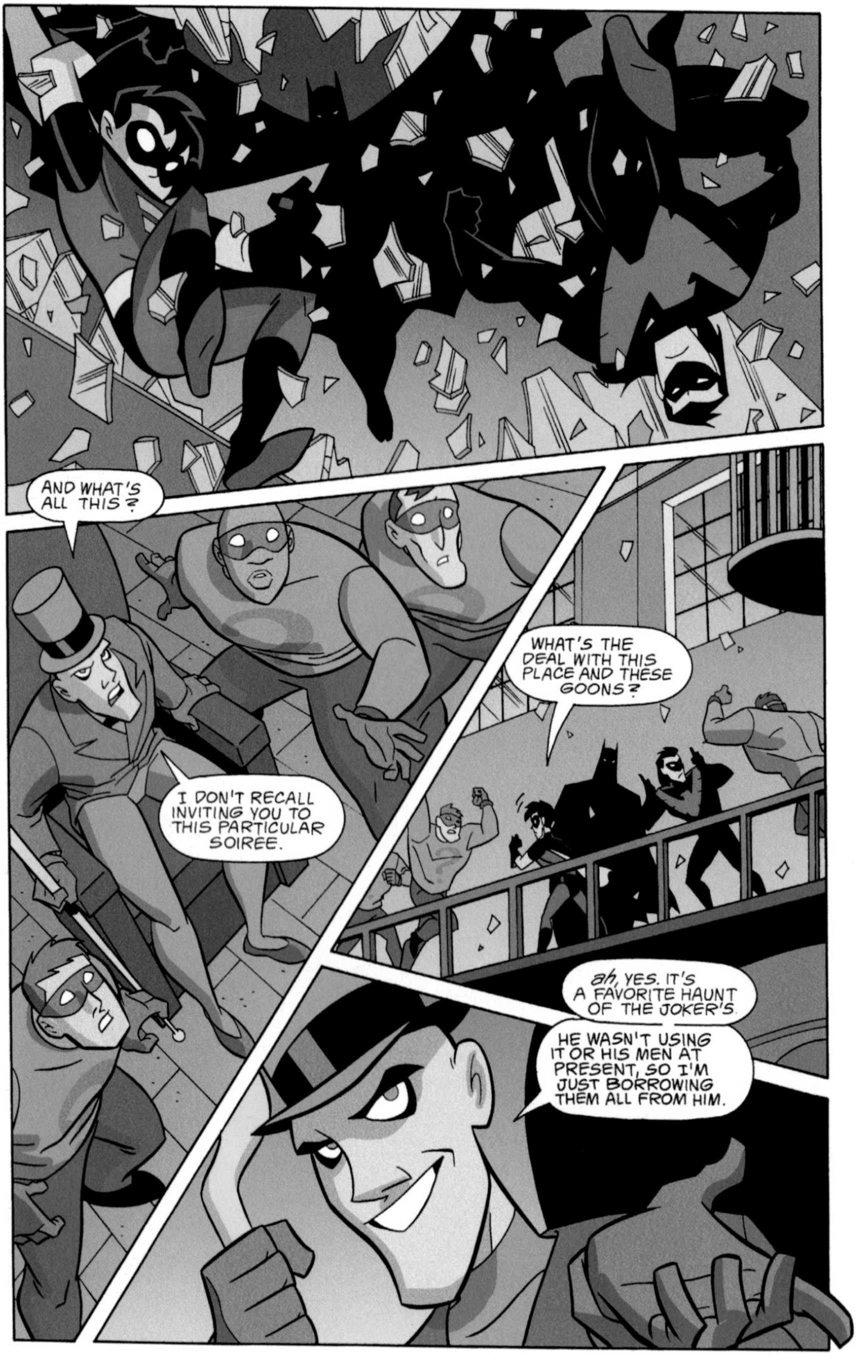
AND WHAT'S ALL THIS?
I DON'T RECALL INVITING YOU TO THIS PARTICULAR SOIREE.
WHAT'S THE DEAL WITH THIS PLACE AND THESE GOONS?
ah, YES. IT'S A FAVORITE HAUNT OF THE JOKER'S.
HE WASN'T USING IT OR HIS MEN AT PRESENT, SO I'M JUST BORROWING THEM ALL FROM HIM.

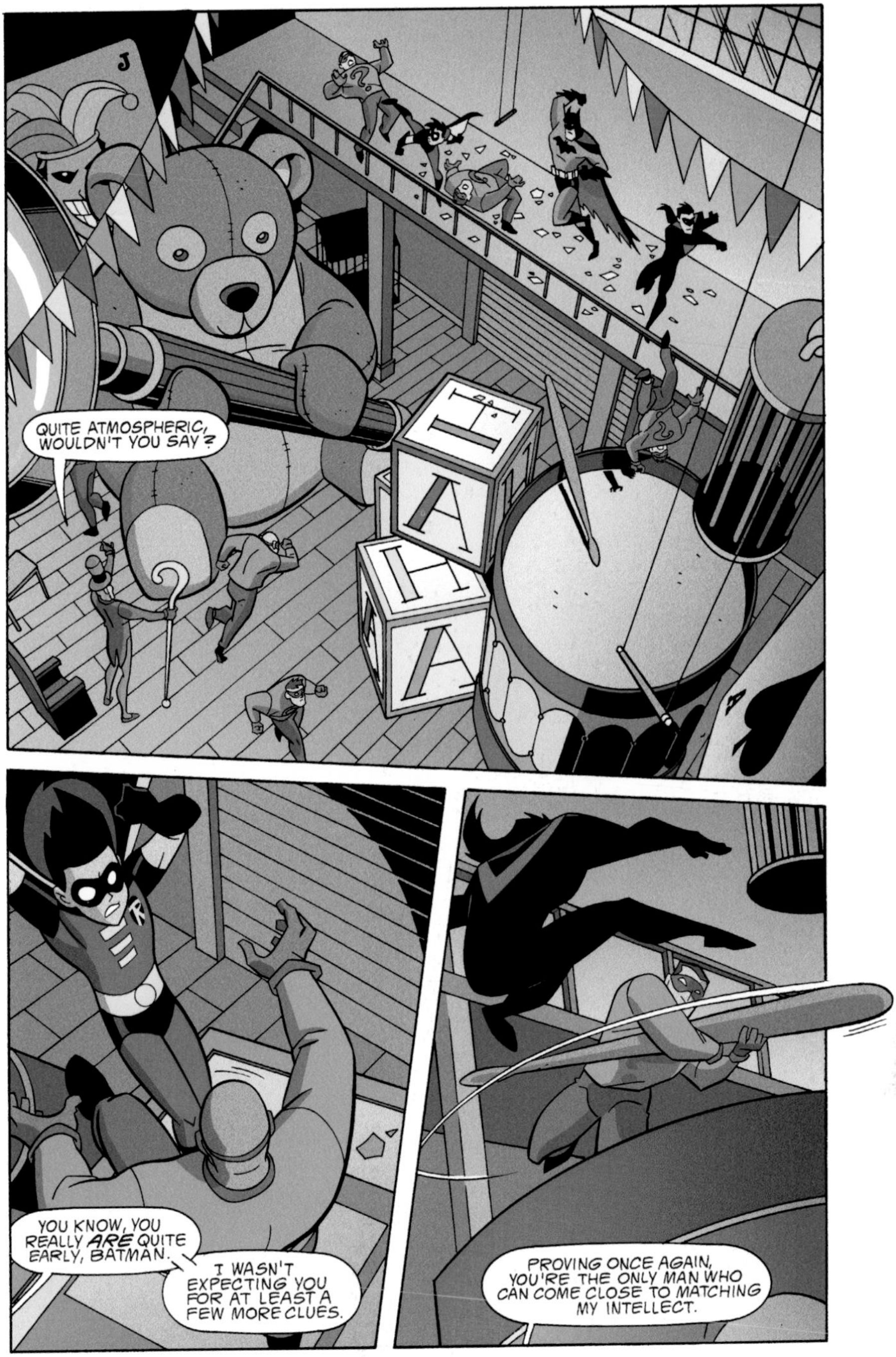
QUITE ATMOSPHERIC, WOULDN'T YOU SAY?
YOU KNOW, YOU REALLY ARE QUITE EARLY, BATMAN.
I WASN'T EXPECTING YOU FOR AT LEAST A FEW MORE CLUES.
PROVING ONCE AGAIN, YOU'RE THE ONLY MAN WHO CAN COME CLOSE TO MATCHING MY INTELLECT.

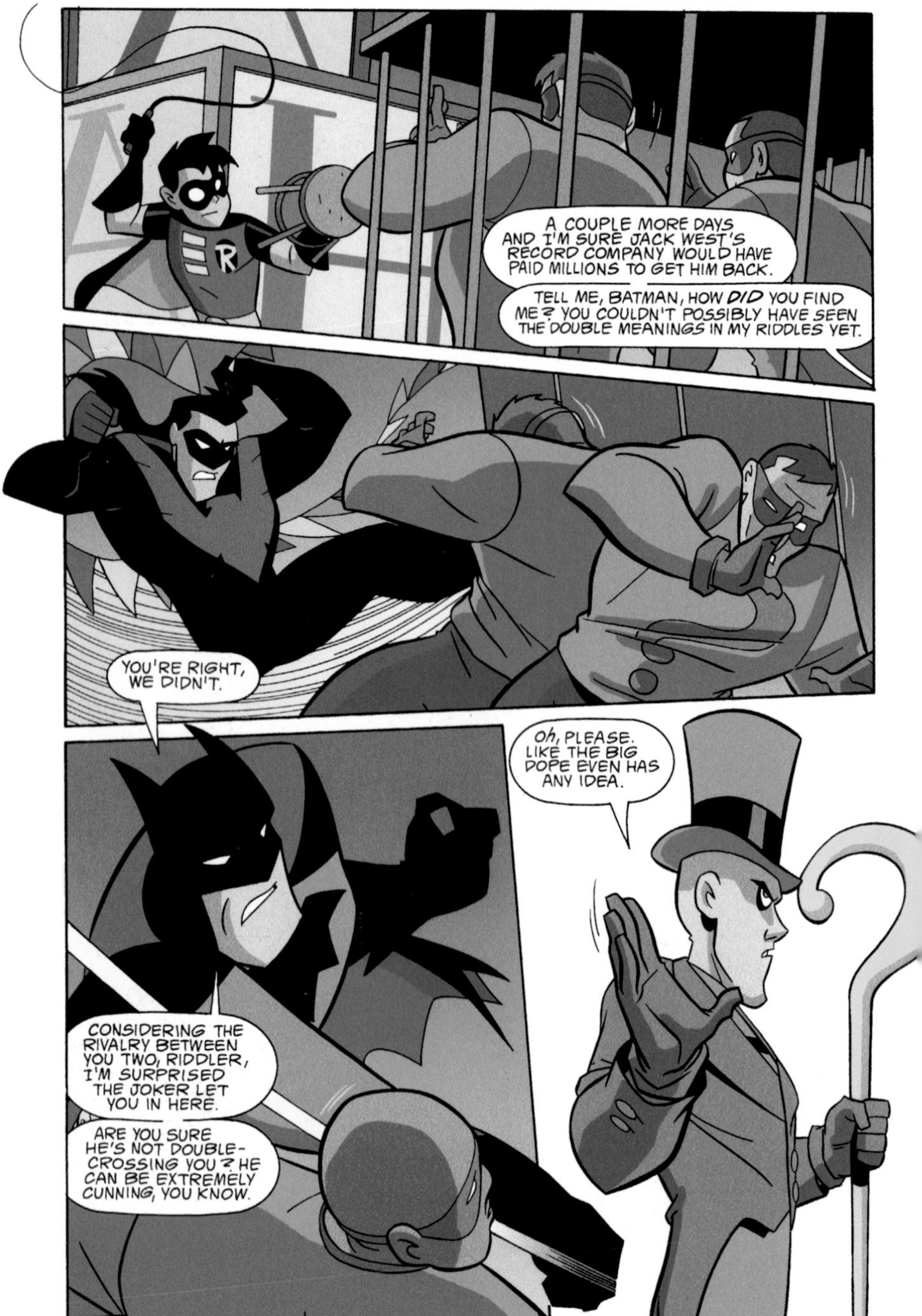
A COUPLE MORE DAYS AND I'M SURE JACK WEST'S RECORD COMPANY WOULD HAVE PAID MILLIONS TO GET HIM BACK.
TELL ME, BATMAN, HOW DID YOU FIND ME? YOU COULDN'T POSSIBLY HAVE SEEN THE DOUBLE MEANINGS IN MY RIDDLES YET.
YOU'RE RIGHT, WE DIDN'T.
Oh, PLEASE. LIKE THE BIG DOPE EVEN HAS ANY IDEA.
CONSIDERING THE RIVALRY BETWEEN YOU TWO, RIDDLER, I'M SURPRISED THE JOKER LET YOU IN HERE.
ARE YOU SURE HE'S NOT DOUBLE-CROSSING YOU? HE CAN BE EXTREMELY CUNNING, YOU KNOW.

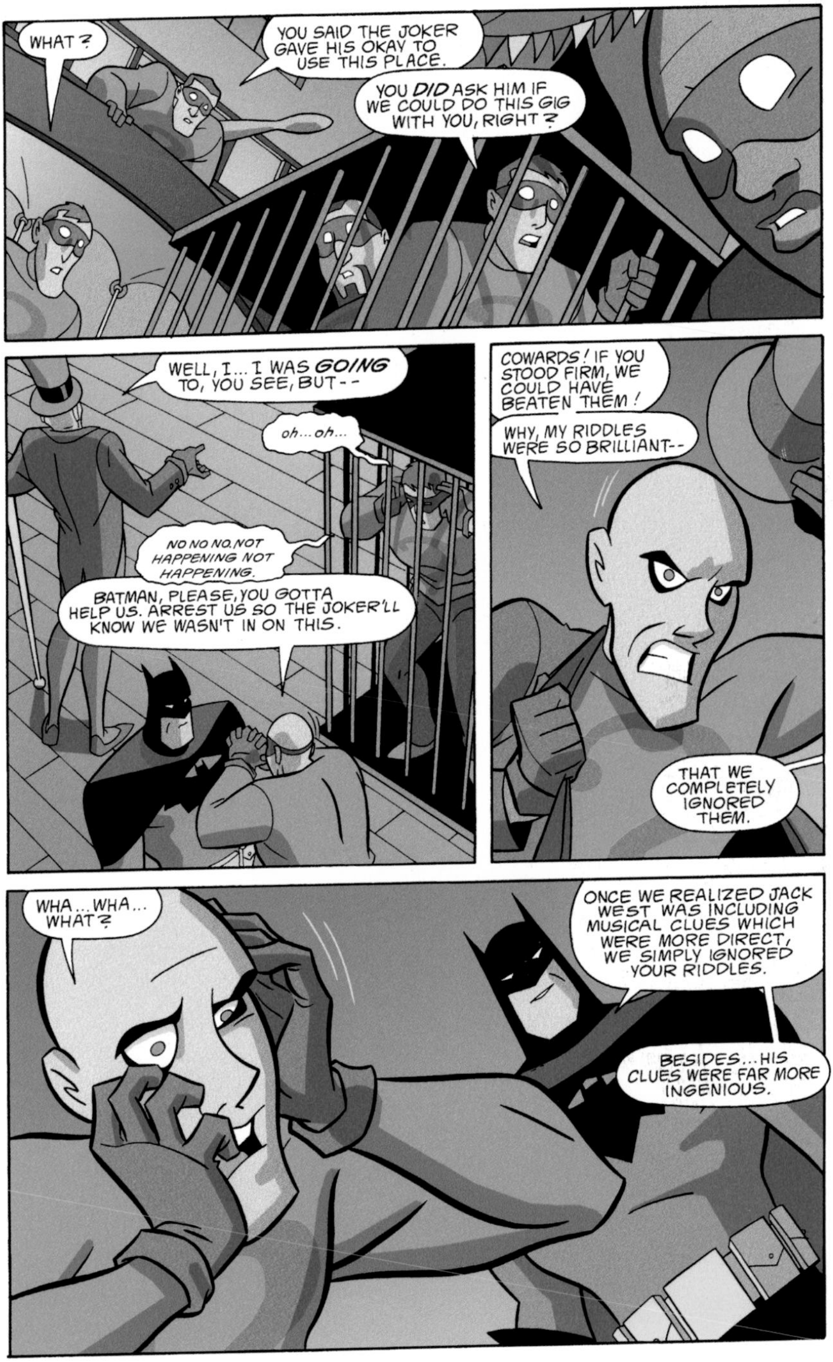
WHAT?
YOU SAID THE JOKER GAVE HIS OKAY TO USE THIS PLACE.
YOU *DID* ASK HIM IF WE COULD DO THIS GIG WITH YOU, RIGHT?
WELL, I... I WAS *GOING* TO, YOU SEE, BUT--
oh... oh...
NO NO NO, NOT HAPPENING NOT HAPPENING.
BATMAN, PLEASE, YOU GOTTA HELP US. ARREST US SO THE JOKER'LL KNOW WE WASN'T IN ON THIS.
COWARDS! IF YOU STOOD FIRM, WE COULD HAVE BEATEN THEM!
WHY, MY RIDDLES WERE SO BRILLIANT--
THAT WE COMPLETELY IGNORED THEM.
WHA... WHA... WHAT?
ONCE WE REALIZED JACK WEST WAS INCLUDING MUSICAL CLUES WHICH WERE MORE DIRECT, WE SIMPLY IGNORED YOUR RIDDLES.
BESIDES... HIS CLUES WERE FAR MORE INGENIOUS.

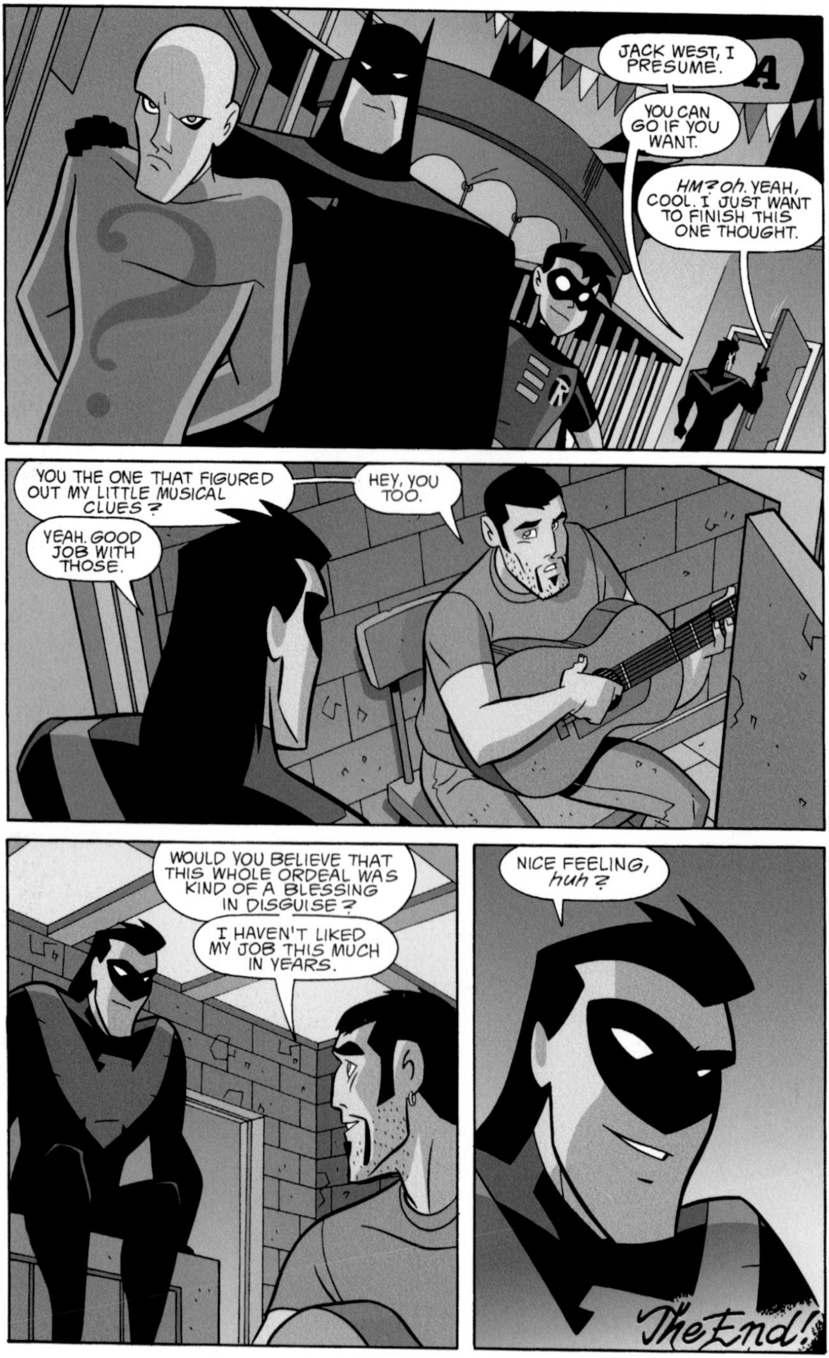
JACK WEST, I PRESUME.
YOU CAN GO IF YOU WANT.
HM? Oh. YEAH, COOL. I JUST WANT TO FINISH THIS ONE THOUGHT.
YOU THE ONE THAT FIGURED OUT MY LITTLE MUSICAL CLUES?
YEAH. GOOD JOB WITH THOSE.
HEY, YOU TOO.
WOULD YOU BELIEVE THAT THIS WHOLE ORDEAL WAS KIND OF A BLESSING IN DISGUISE?
I HAVEN'T LIKED MY JOB THIS MUCH IN YEARS.
NICE FEELING, huh?
The End!

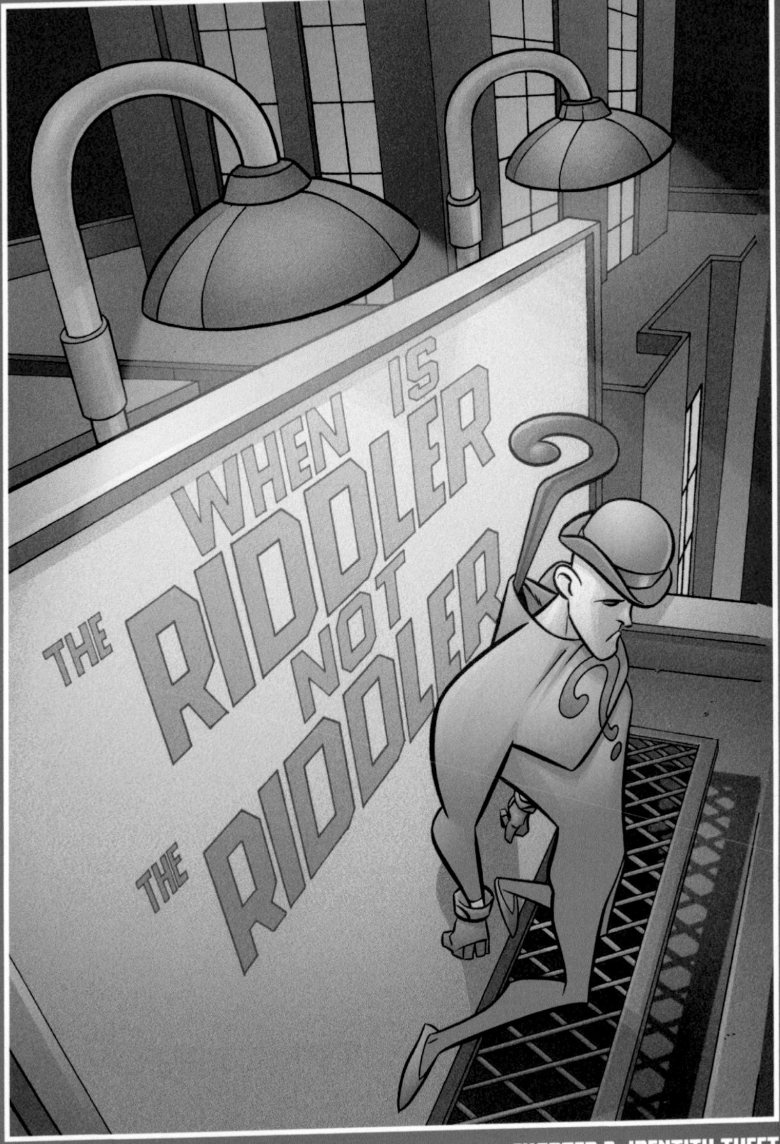
WHEN IS THE RIDDLER NOT THE RIDDLER

CHAPTER 3: IDENTITY THEFT

RIDDLE ME THIS

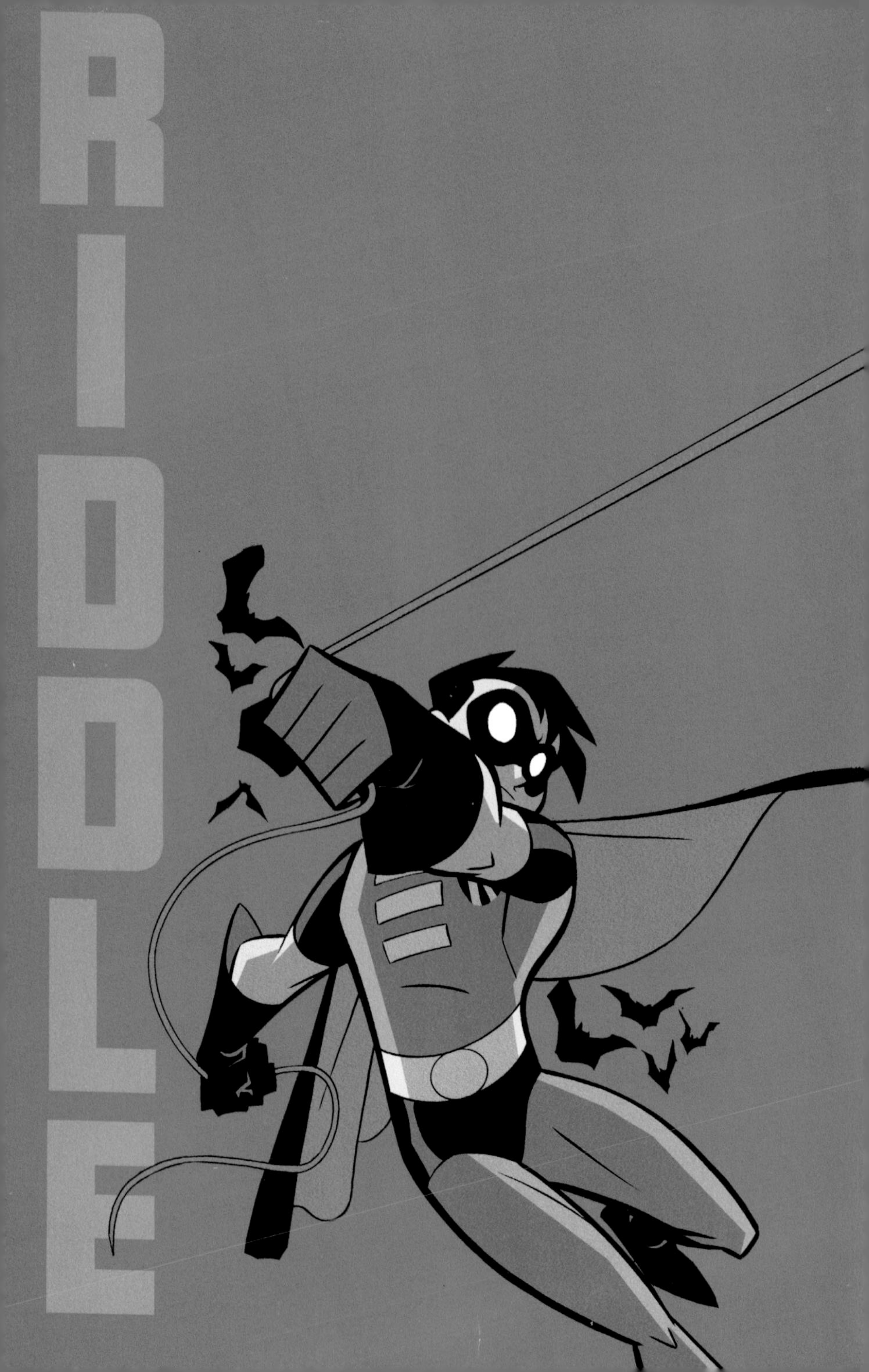
RIDDLE

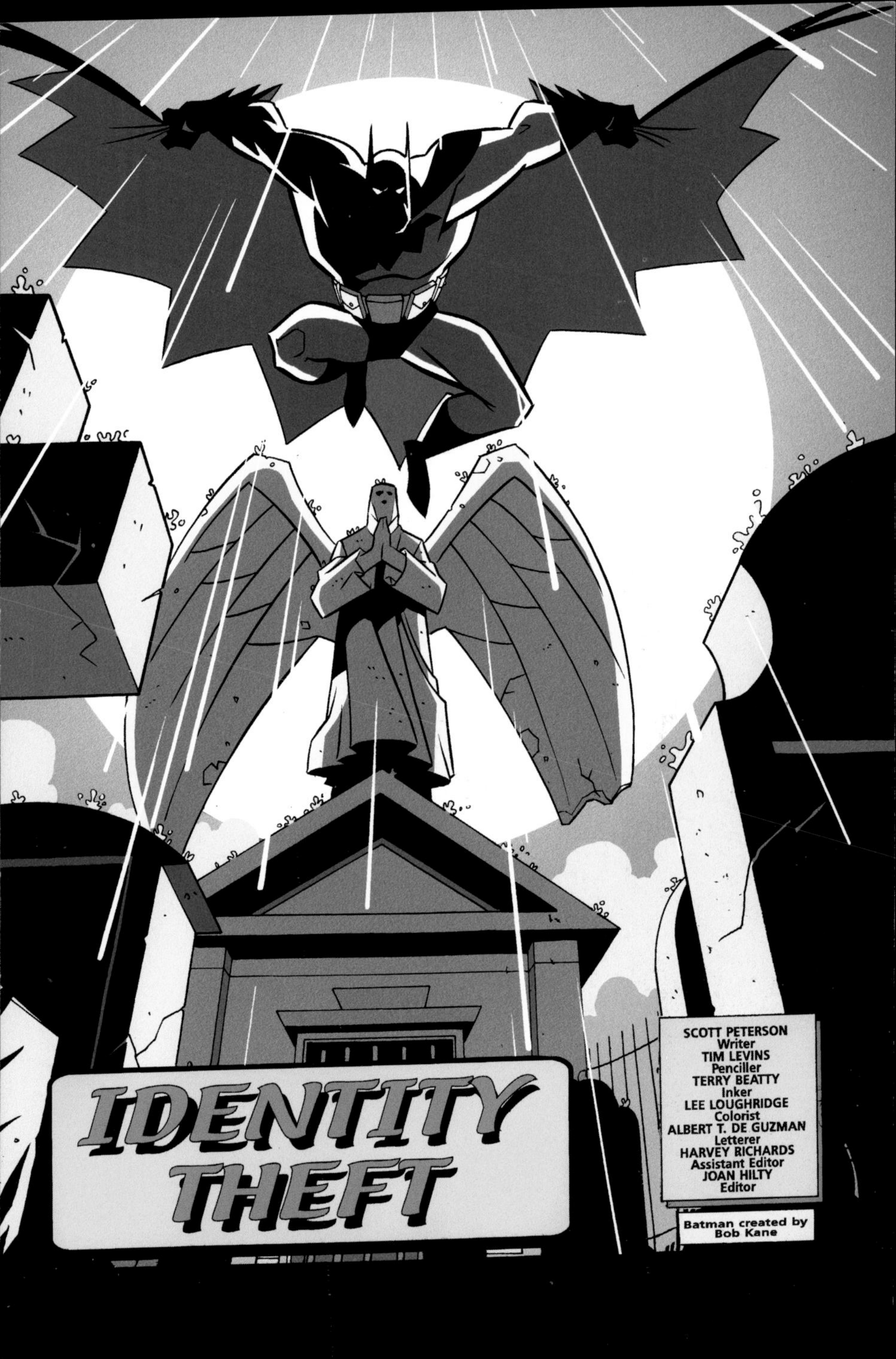
IDENTITY THEFT
SCOTT PETERSON Writer
TIM LEVINS Penciller
TERRY BEATTY Inker
LEE LOUGHRIDGE Colorist
ALBERT T. DE GUZMAN Letterer
HARVEY RICHARDS Assistant Editor
JOAN HILTY Editor
Batman created by Bob Kane

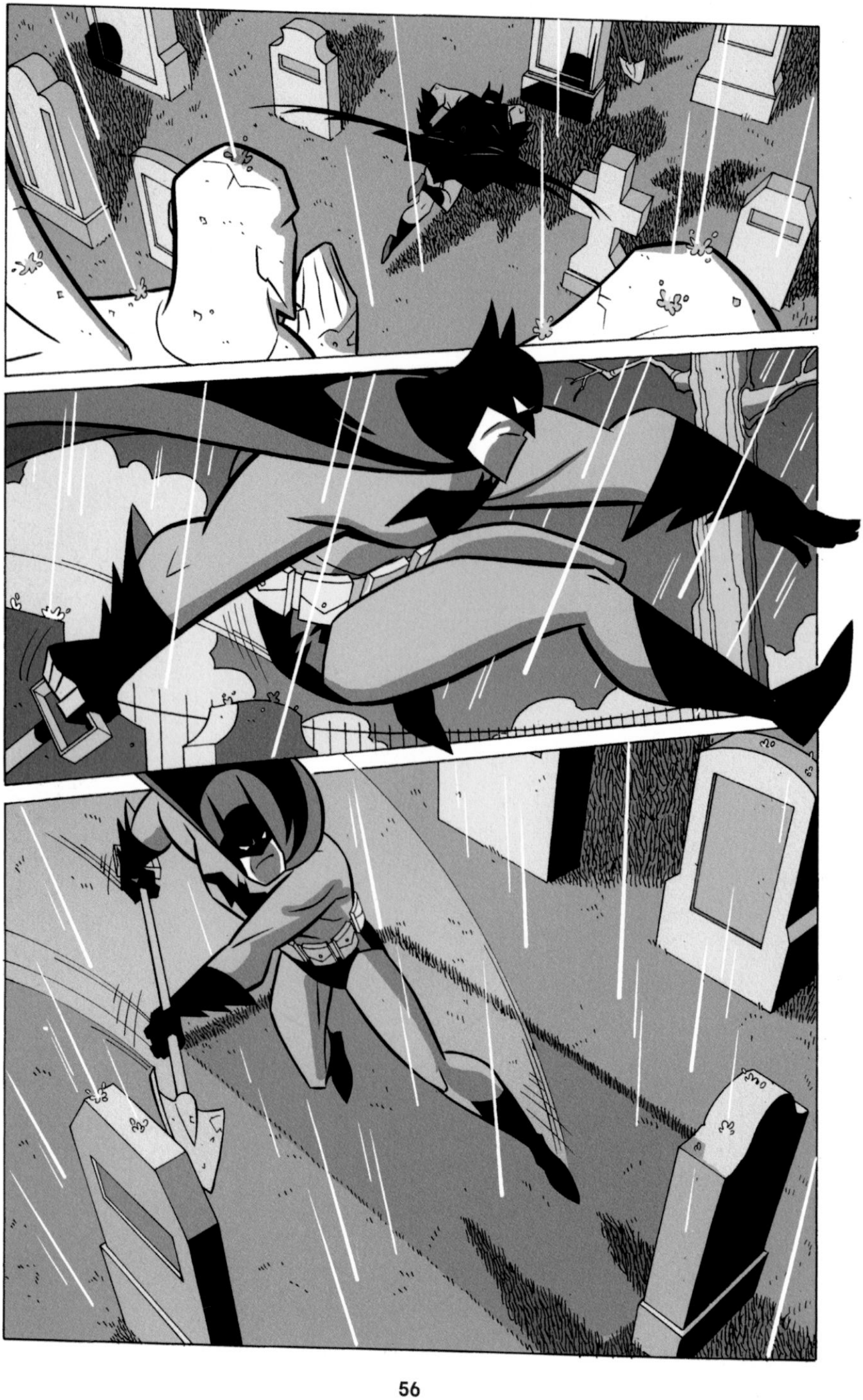

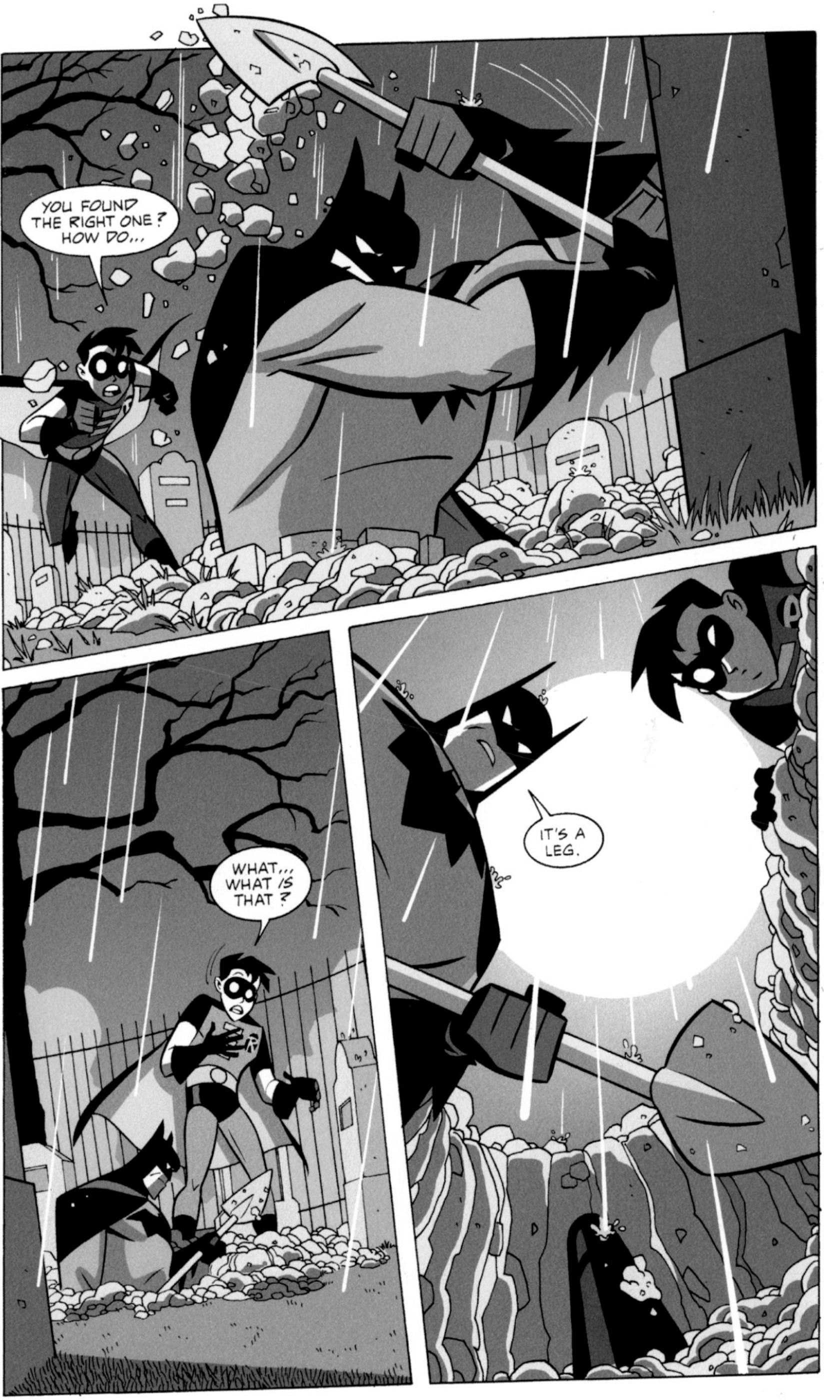
YOU FOUND THE RIGHT ONE? HOW DO...
WHAT... WHAT IS THAT?
IT'S A LEG.

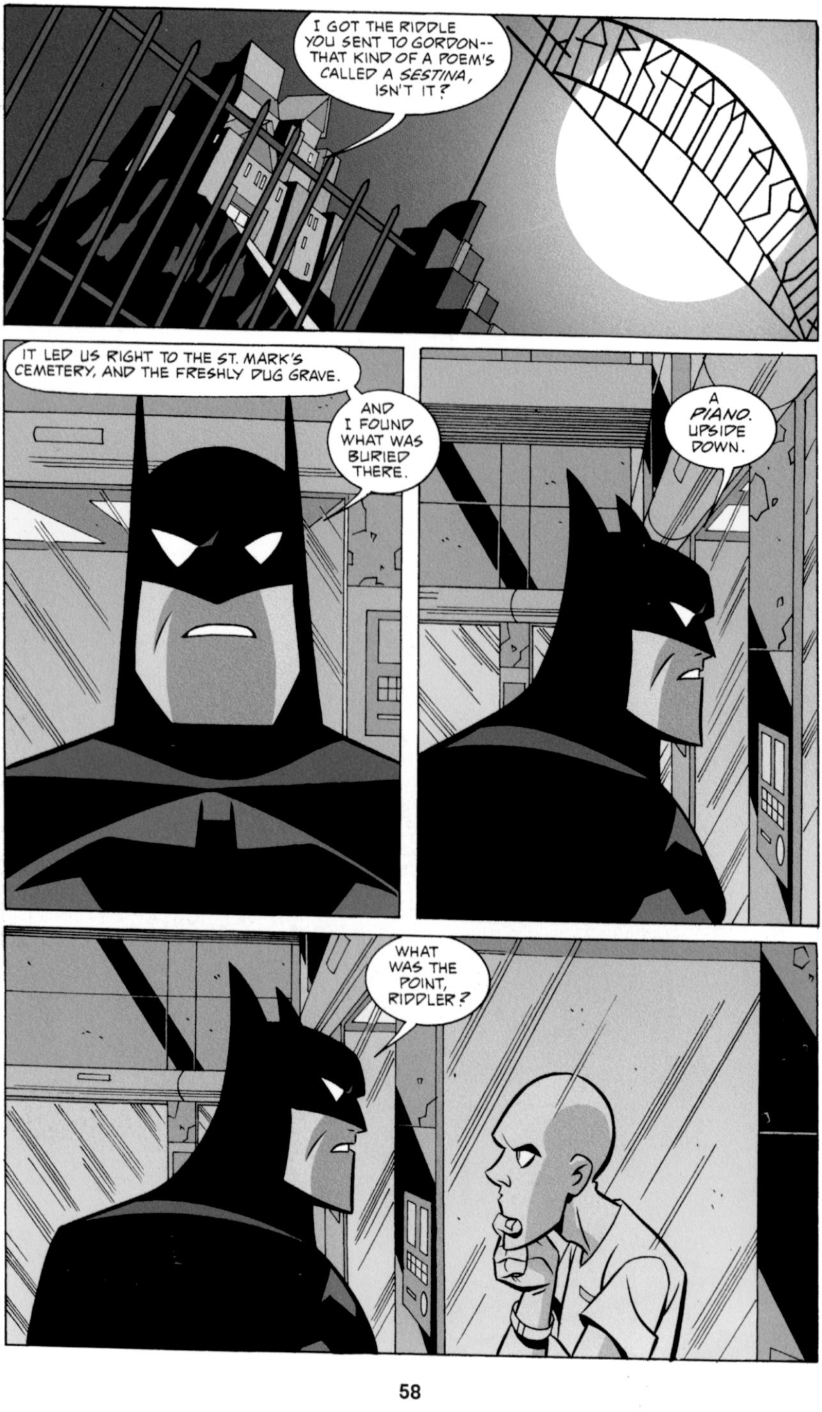
I GOT THE RIDDLE YOU SENT TO GORDON-- THAT KIND OF A POEM'S CALLED A *SESTINA*, ISN'T IT?
IT LED US RIGHT TO THE ST. MARK'S CEMETERY, AND THE FRESHLY DUG GRAVE.
AND I FOUND WHAT WAS BURIED THERE.
A *PIANO*. UPSIDE DOWN.
WHAT WAS THE POINT, RIDDLER?

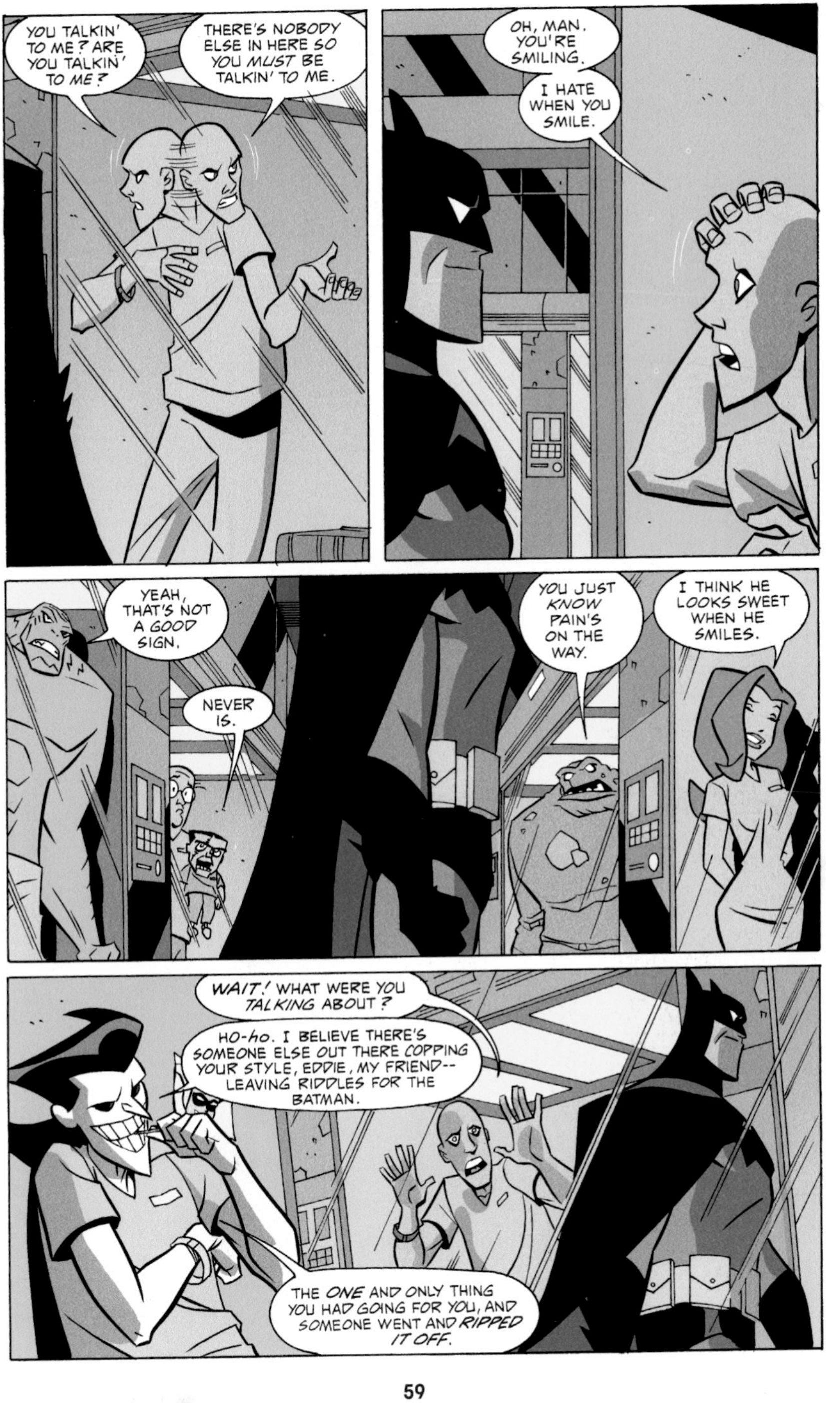
YOU TALKIN' TO ME? ARE YOU TALKIN' TO ME?
THERE'S NOBODY ELSE IN HERE SO YOU MUST BE TALKIN' TO ME.
OH, MAN. YOU'RE SMILING.
I HATE WHEN YOU SMILE.
YEAH, THAT'S NOT A GOOD SIGN.
NEVER IS.
YOU JUST KNOW PAIN'S ON THE WAY.
I THINK HE LOOKS SWEET WHEN HE SMILES.
WAIT! WHAT WERE YOU TALKING ABOUT?
HO-ho. I BELIEVE THERE'S SOMEONE ELSE OUT THERE COPPING YOUR STYLE, EDDIE, MY FRIEND-- LEAVING RIDDLES FOR THE BATMAN.
THE ONE AND ONLY THING YOU HAD GOING FOR YOU, AND SOMEONE WENT AND RIPPED IT OFF.

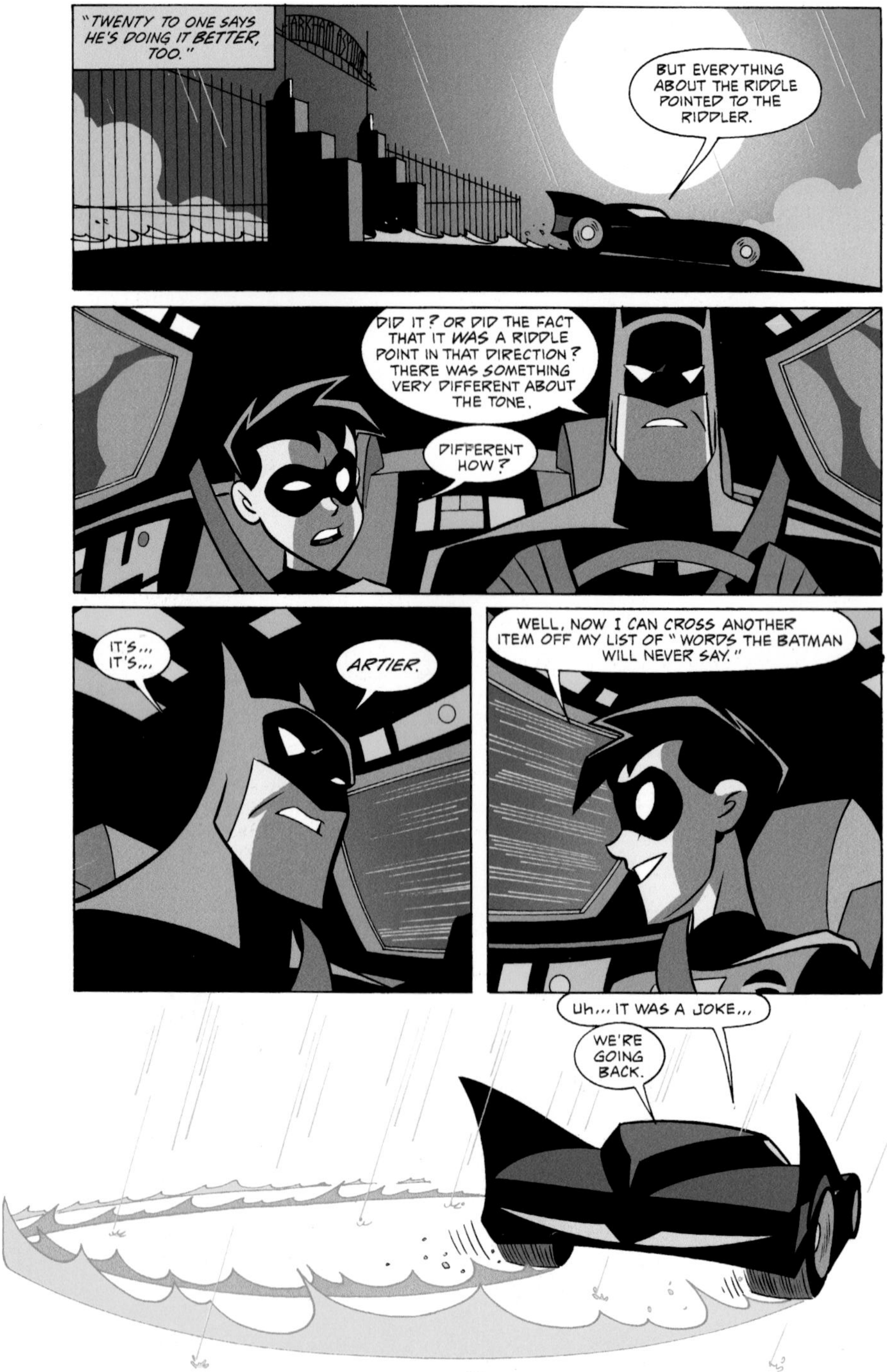
"TWENTY TO ONE SAYS HE'S DOING IT BETTER, TOO."
BUT EVERYTHING ABOUT THE RIDDLE POINTED TO THE RIDDLER.
DID IT? OR DID THE FACT THAT IT WAS A RIDDLE POINT IN THAT DIRECTION? THERE WAS SOMETHING VERY DIFFERENT ABOUT THE TONE.
DIFFERENT HOW?
IT'S... IT'S...
ARTIER.
WELL, NOW I CAN CROSS ANOTHER ITEM OFF MY LIST OF "WORDS THE BATMAN WILL NEVER SAY."
Uh... IT WAS A JOKE...
WE'RE GOING BACK.

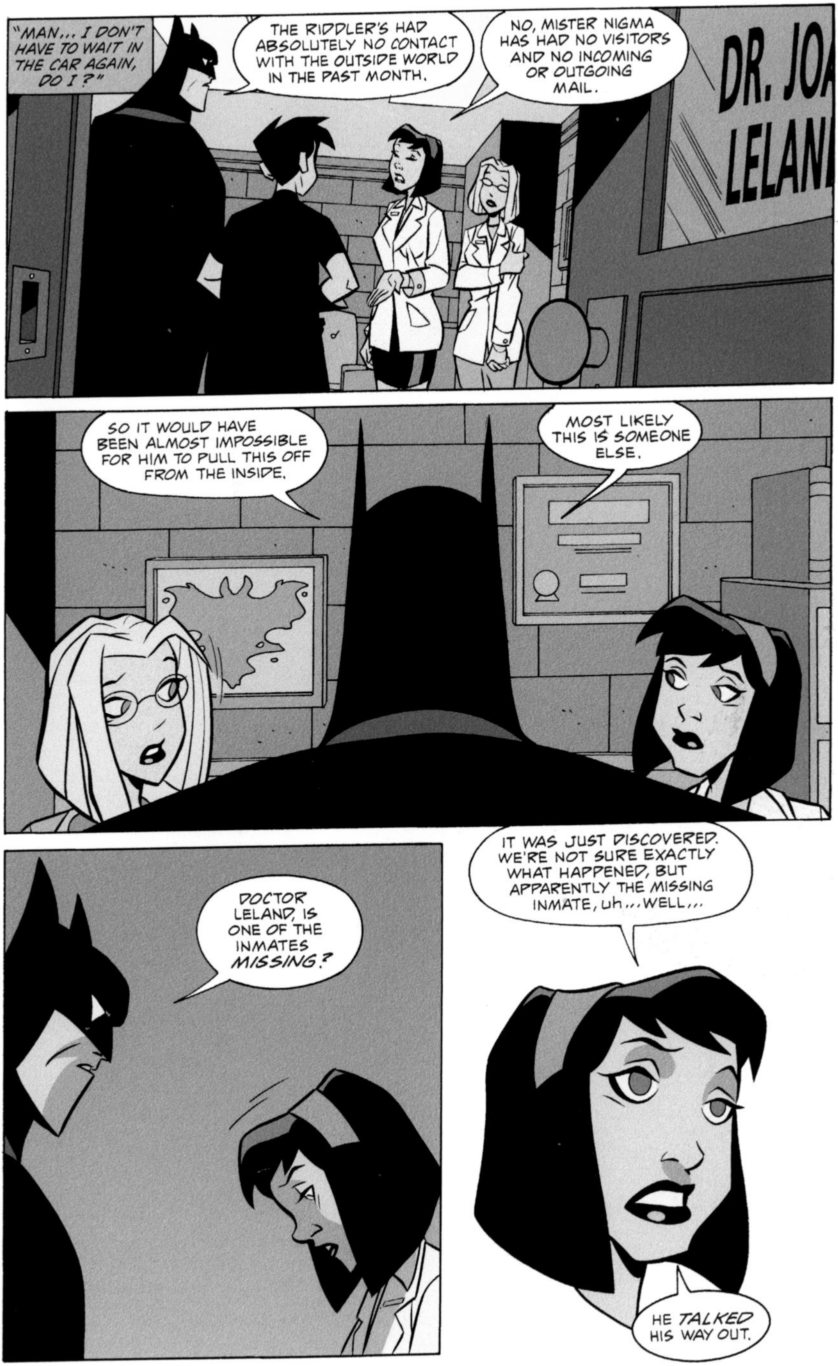
"MAN... I DON'T HAVE TO WAIT IN THE CAR AGAIN, DO I?"
THE RIDDLER'S HAD ABSOLUTELY NO CONTACT WITH THE OUTSIDE WORLD IN THE PAST MONTH.
NO, MISTER NIGMA HAS HAD NO VISITORS AND NO INCOMING OR OUTGOING MAIL.
DR. JOA
LELAN
SO IT WOULD HAVE BEEN ALMOST IMPOSSIBLE FOR HIM TO PULL THIS OFF FROM THE INSIDE.
MOST LIKELY THIS IS SOMEONE ELSE.
DOCTOR LELAND, IS ONE OF THE INMATES *MISSING*?
IT WAS JUST DISCOVERED. WE'RE NOT SURE EXACTLY WHAT HAPPENED, BUT APPARENTLY THE MISSING INMATE, uh... WELL...
HE *TALKED* HIS WAY OUT.

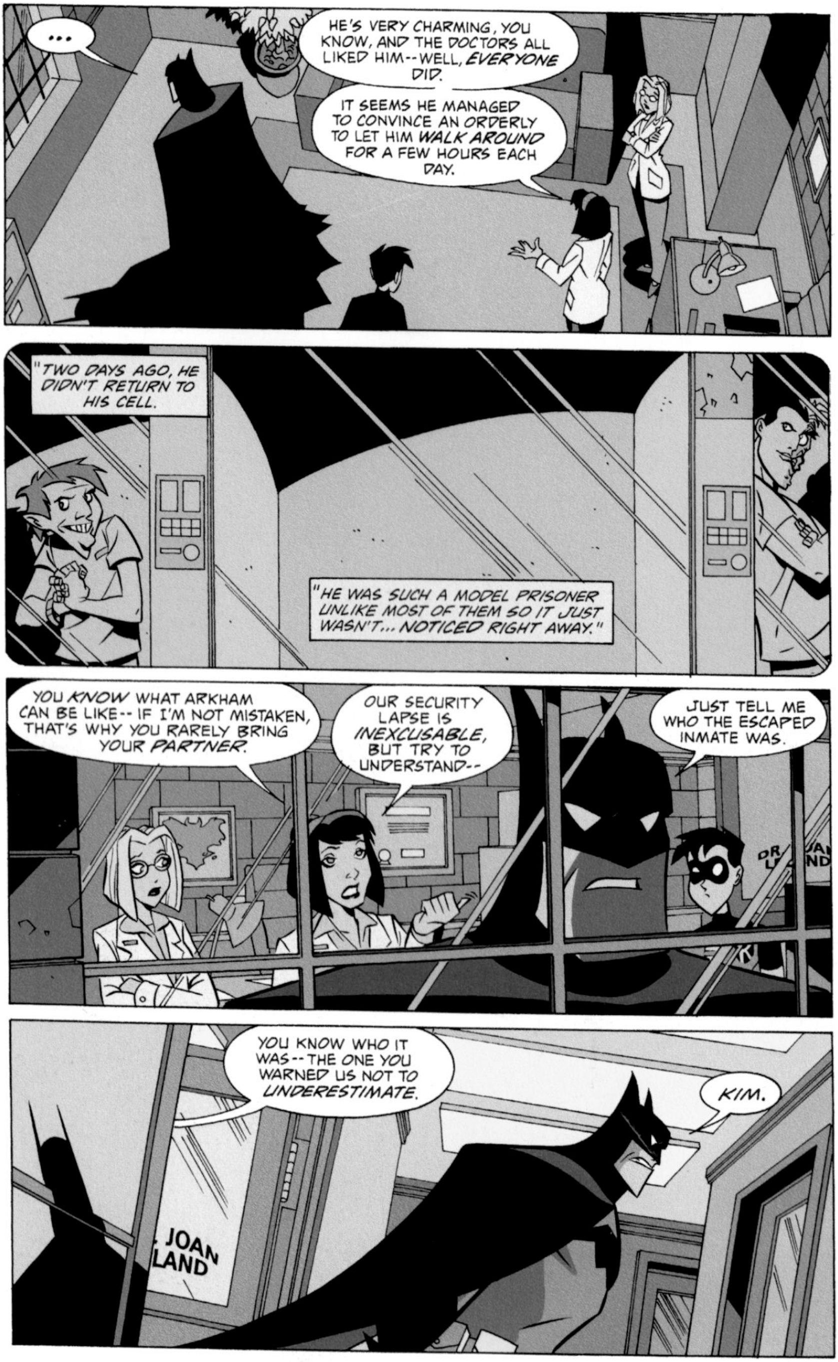
...
HE'S VERY CHARMING, YOU KNOW, AND THE DOCTORS ALL LIKED HIM--WELL, EVERYONE DID.
IT SEEMS HE MANAGED TO CONVINCE AN ORDERLY TO LET HIM WALK AROUND FOR A FEW HOURS EACH DAY.
"TWO DAYS AGO, HE DIDN'T RETURN TO HIS CELL.
"HE WAS SUCH A MODEL PRISONER UNLIKE MOST OF THEM SO IT JUST WASN'T... NOTICED RIGHT AWAY."
YOU KNOW WHAT ARKHAM CAN BE LIKE-- IF I'M NOT MISTAKEN, THAT'S WHY YOU RARELY BRING YOUR PARTNER.
OUR SECURITY LAPSE IS INEXCUSABLE, BUT TRY TO UNDERSTAND--
JUST TELL ME WHO THE ESCAPED INMATE WAS.
YOU KNOW WHO IT WAS-- THE ONE YOU WARNED US NOT TO UNDERESTIMATE.
KIM.
JOAN
LAND

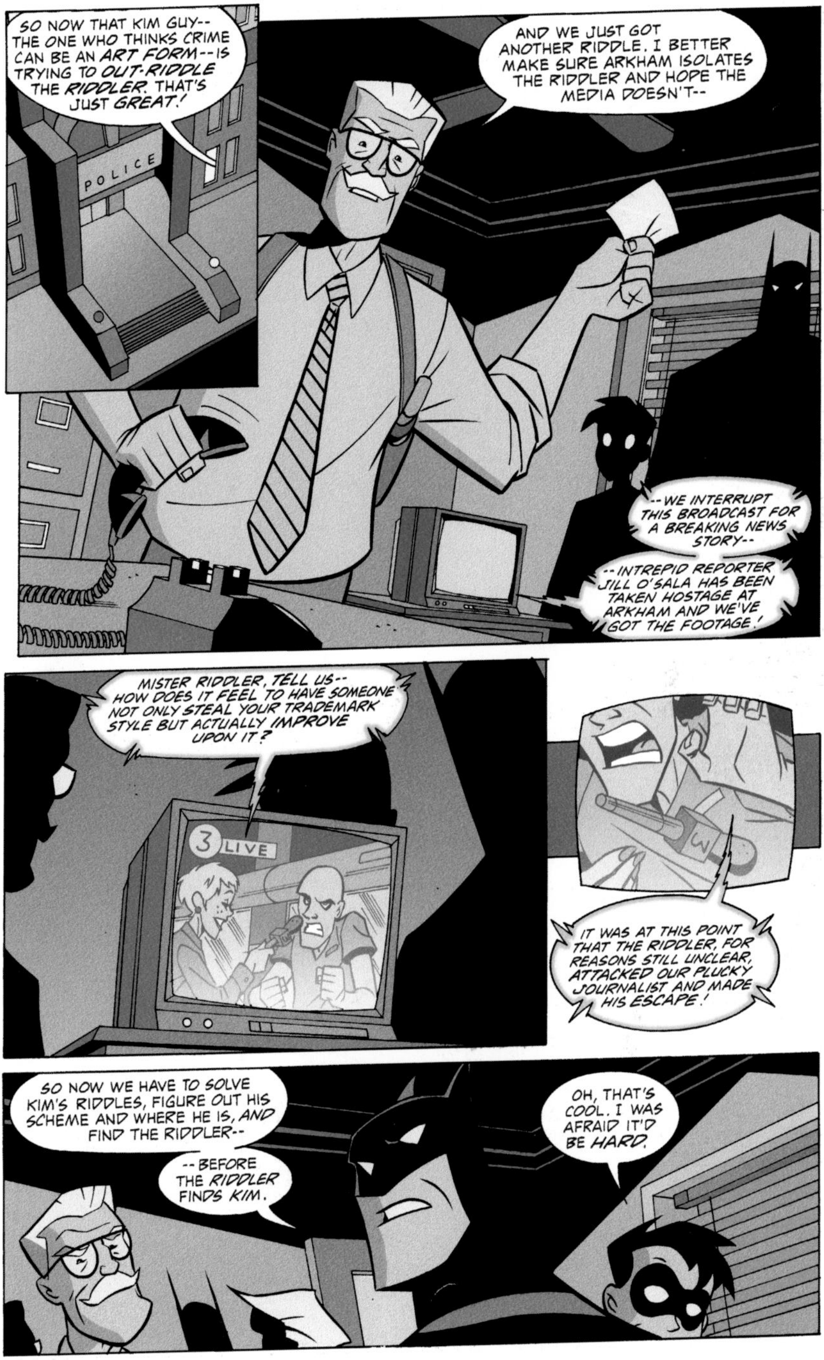
SO NOW THAT KIM GUY-- THE ONE WHO THINKS CRIME CAN BE AN ART FORM--IS TRYING TO OUT-RIDDLE THE RIDDLER. THAT'S JUST GREAT!
POLICE
AND WE JUST GOT ANOTHER RIDDLE. I BETTER MAKE SURE ARKHAM ISOLATES THE RIDDLER AND HOPE THE MEDIA DOESN'T--
--WE INTERRUPT THIS BROADCAST FOR A BREAKING NEWS STORY--
--INTREPID REPORTER JILL O'SALA HAS BEEN TAKEN HOSTAGE AT ARKHAM AND WE'VE GOT THE FOOTAGE!
MISTER RIDDLER, TELL US-- HOW DOES IT FEEL TO HAVE SOMEONE NOT ONLY STEAL YOUR TRADEMARK STYLE BUT ACTUALLY IMPROVE UPON IT?
3 LIVE
IT WAS AT THIS POINT THAT THE RIDDLER, FOR REASONS STILL UNCLEAR, ATTACKED OUR PLUCKY JOURNALIST AND MADE HIS ESCAPE!
SO NOW WE HAVE TO SOLVE KIM'S RIDDLES, FIGURE OUT HIS SCHEME AND WHERE HE IS, AND FIND THE RIDDLER--
--BEFORE THE RIDDLER FINDS KIM.
OH, THAT'S COOL. I WAS AFRAID IT'D BE HARD.

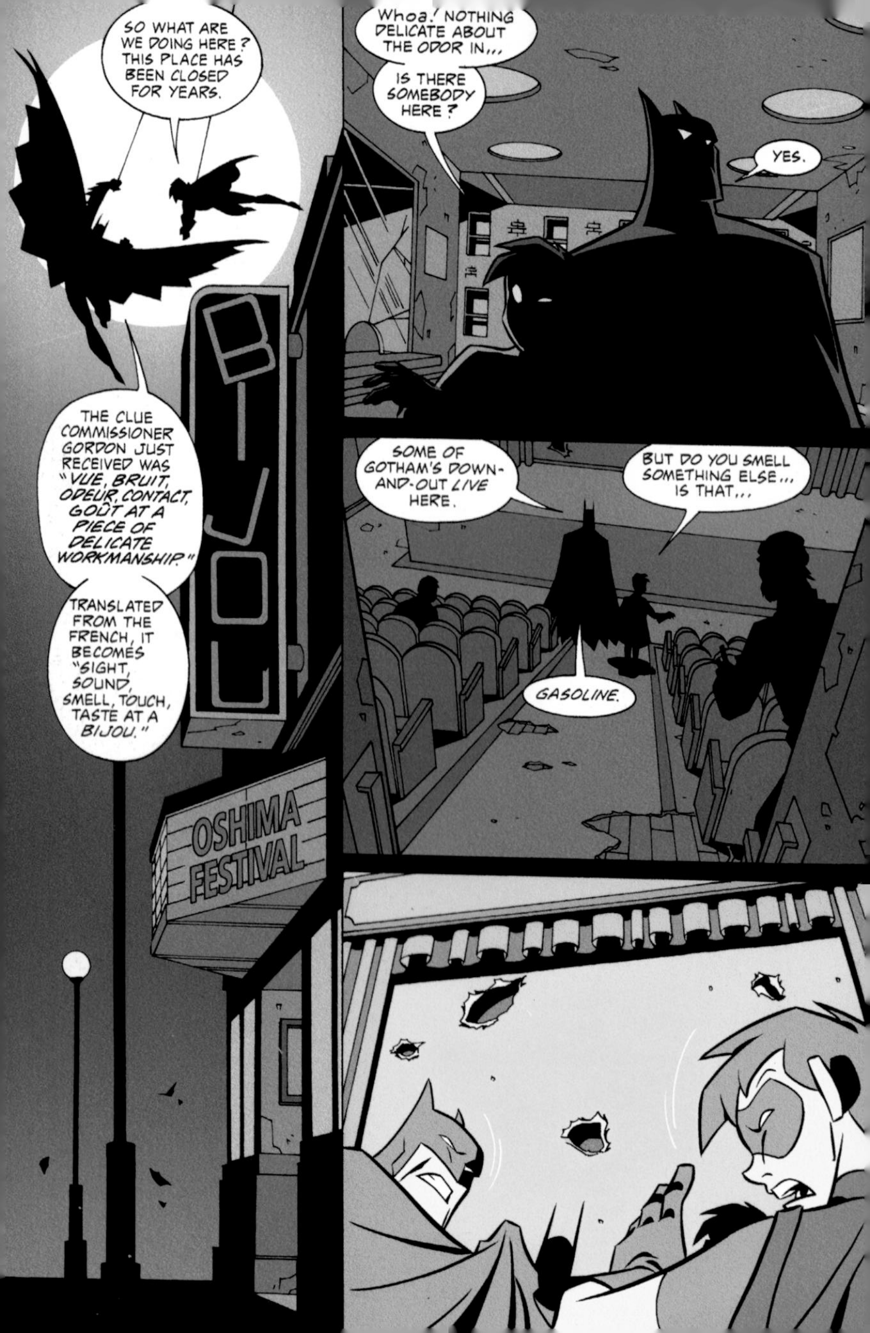
SO WHAT ARE WE DOING HERE? THIS PLACE HAS BEEN CLOSED FOR YEARS.
THE CLUE COMMISSIONER GORDON JUST RECEIVED WAS "VUE, BRUIT, ODEUR, CONTACT, GOÛT AT A PIECE OF DELICATE WORKMANSHIP."
TRANSLATED FROM THE FRENCH, IT BECOMES "SIGHT, SOUND, SMELL, TOUCH, TASTE AT A BIJOU."
BIJOU
OSHIMA FESTIVAL
Whoa! NOTHING DELICATE ABOUT THE ODOR IN...
IS THERE SOMEBODY HERE?
YES.
SOME OF GOTHAM'S DOWN-AND-OUT LIVE HERE.
BUT DO YOU SMELL SOMETHING ELSE... IS THAT...
GASOLINE.

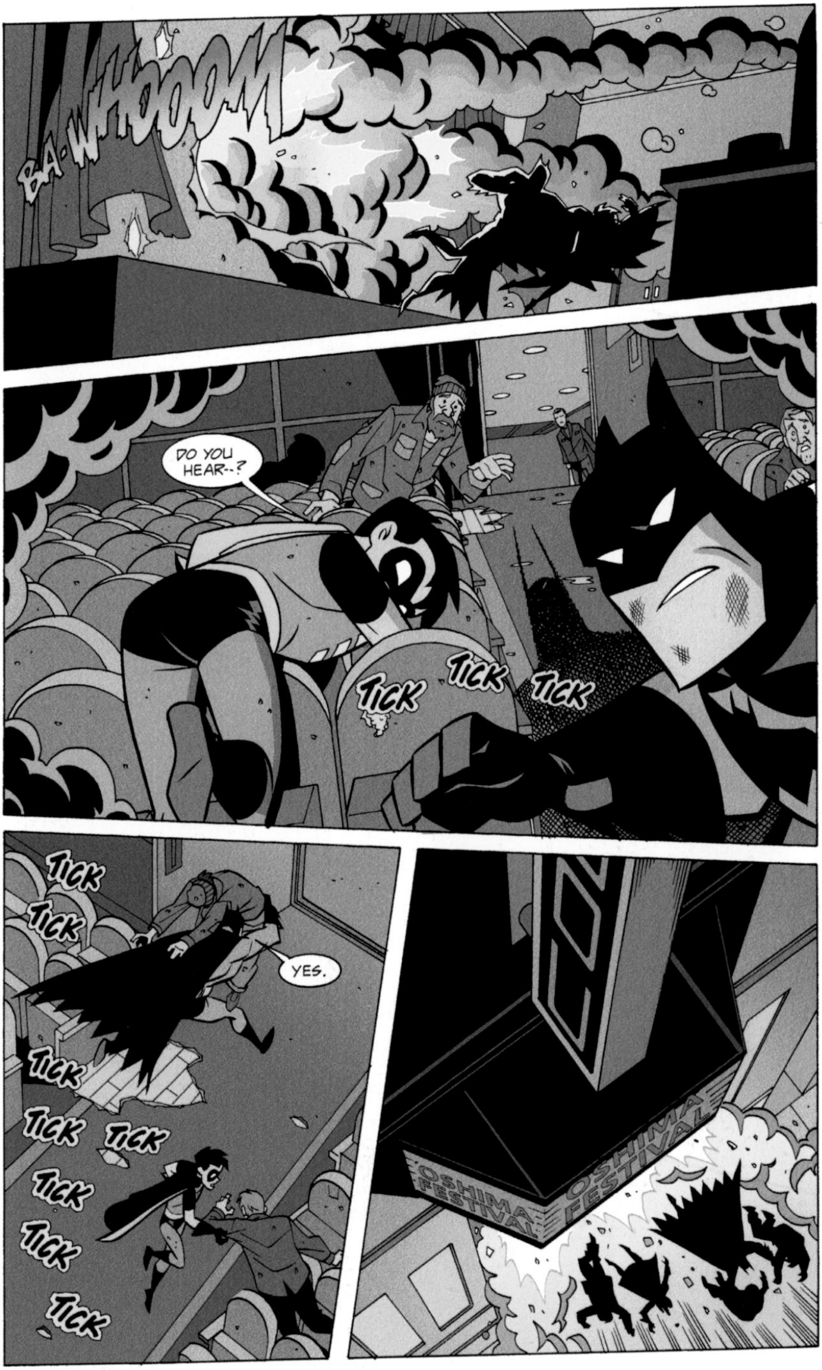
BA-WHOOOM
DO YOU HEAR--?
TICK TICK TICK
TICK
TICK
YES.
TICK
TICK TICK
TICK
TICK
TICK
OSHIMA FESTIVAL
OSHIMA FESTIVAL

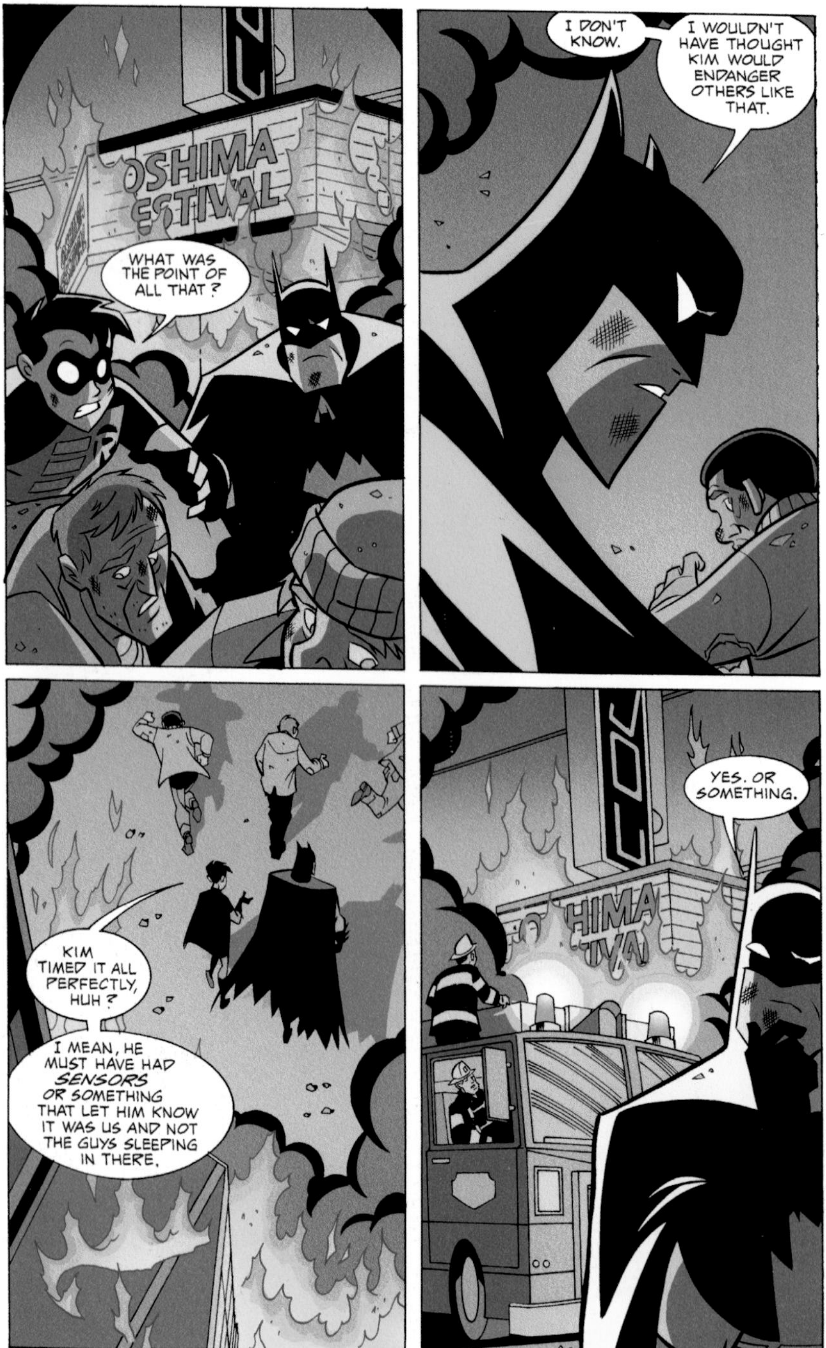
OSHIMA
ESTIVAL
WHAT WAS THE POINT OF ALL THAT?
I DON'T KNOW.
I WOULDN'T HAVE THOUGHT KIM WOULD ENDANGER OTHERS LIKE THAT.
KIM TIMED IT ALL PERFECTLY, HUH?
I MEAN, HE MUST HAVE HAD *SENSORS* OR SOMETHING THAT LET HIM KNOW IT WAS US AND NOT THE GUYS SLEEPING IN THERE.
YES. OR SOMETHING.
HIMA

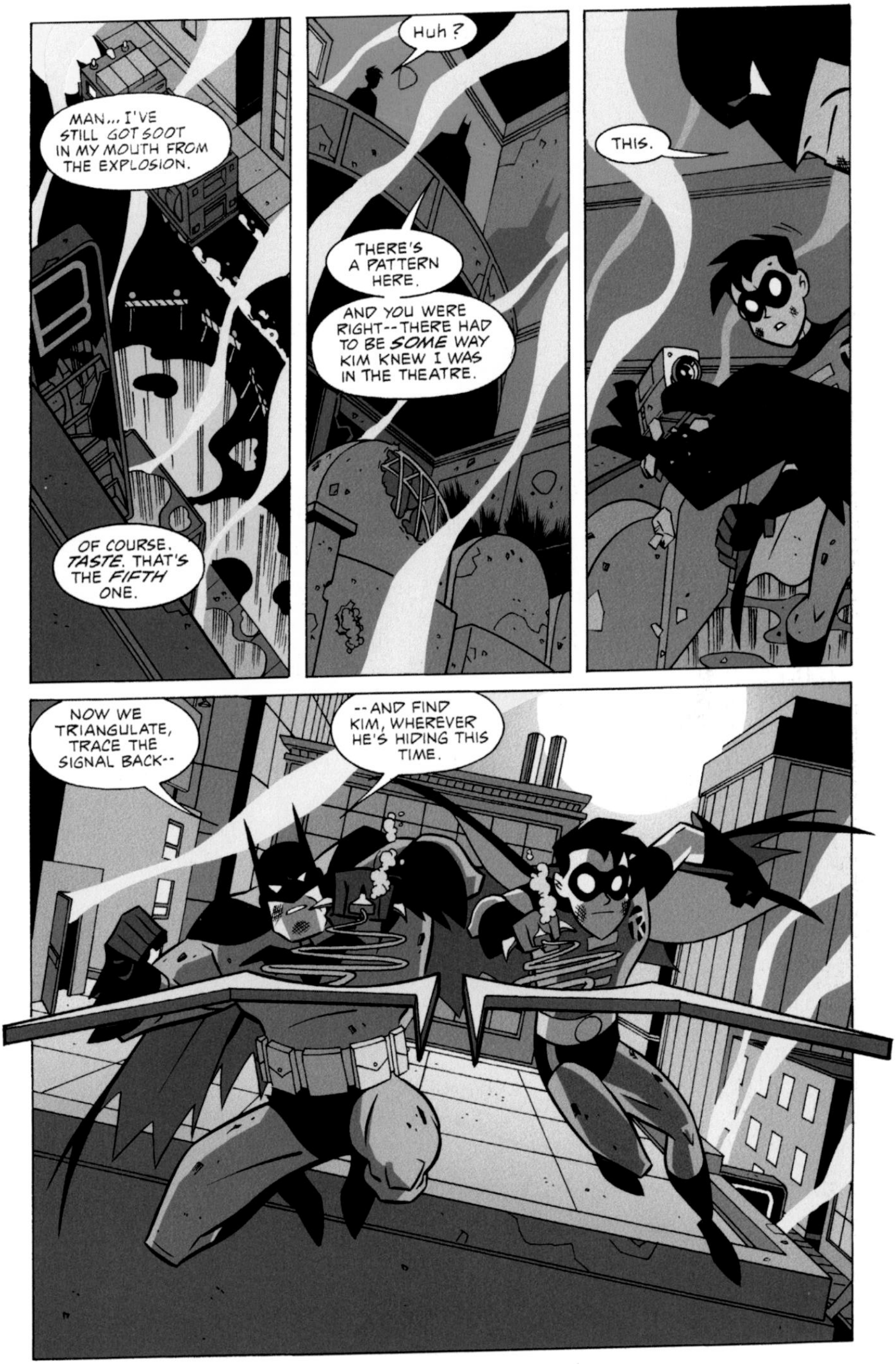
MAN... I'VE STILL GOT SOOT IN MY MOUTH FROM THE EXPLOSION.
OF COURSE. TASTE. THAT'S THE FIFTH ONE.
Huh?
THERE'S A PATTERN HERE.
AND YOU WERE RIGHT--THERE HAD TO BE SOME WAY KIM KNEW I WAS IN THE THEATRE.
THIS.
NOW WE TRIANGULATE, TRACE THE SIGNAL BACK--
--AND FIND KIM, WHEREVER HE'S HIDING THIS TIME.

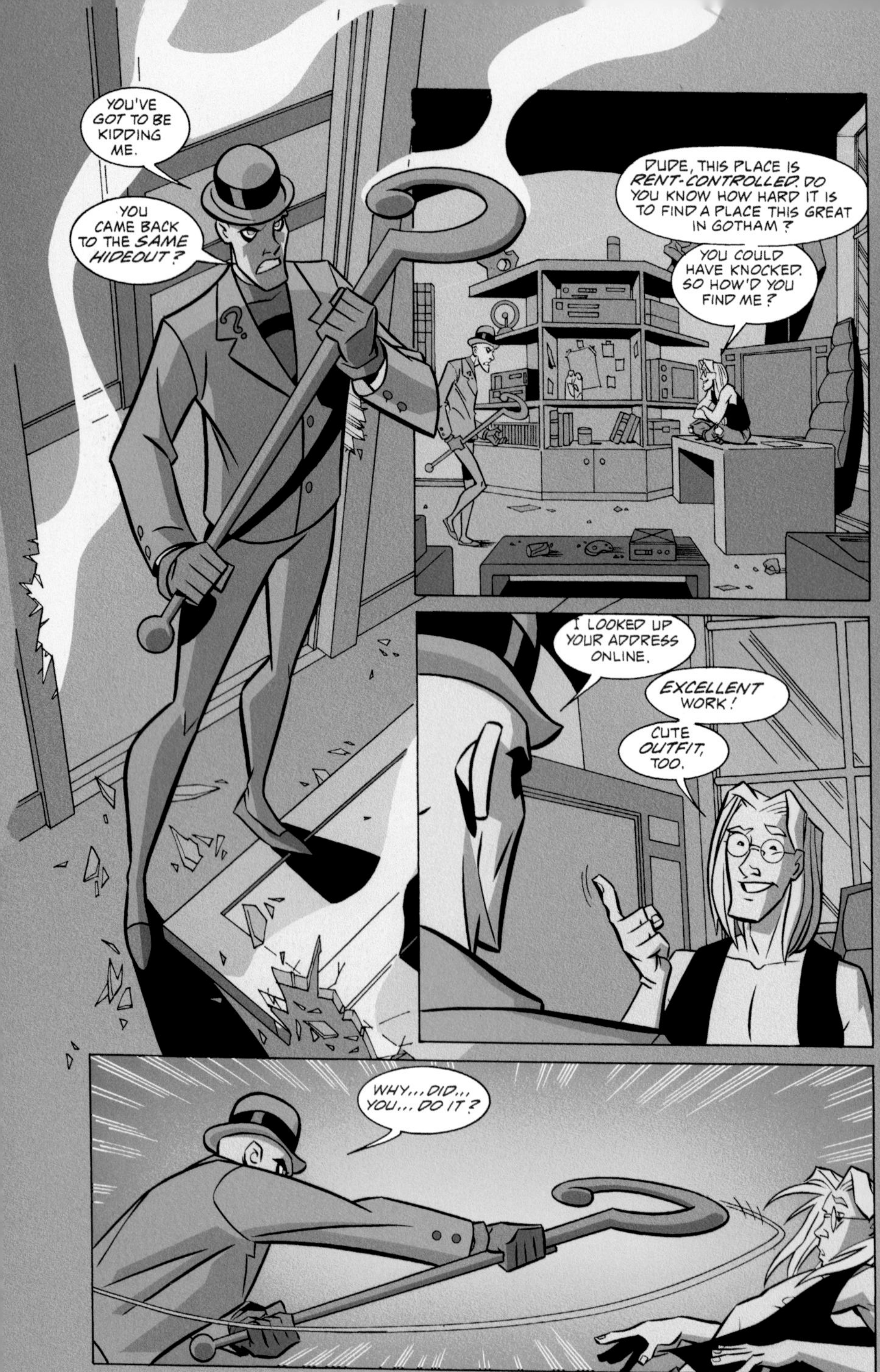
YOU'VE GOT TO BE KIDDING ME.
YOU CAME BACK TO THE SAME HIDEOUT?
DUDE, THIS PLACE IS RENT-CONTROLLED. DO YOU KNOW HOW HARD IT IS TO FIND A PLACE THIS GREAT IN GOTHAM?
YOU COULD HAVE KNOCKED. SO HOW'D YOU FIND ME?
I LOOKED UP YOUR ADDRESS ONLINE.
EXCELLENT WORK!
CUTE OUTFIT, TOO.
WHY... DID... YOU... DO IT?

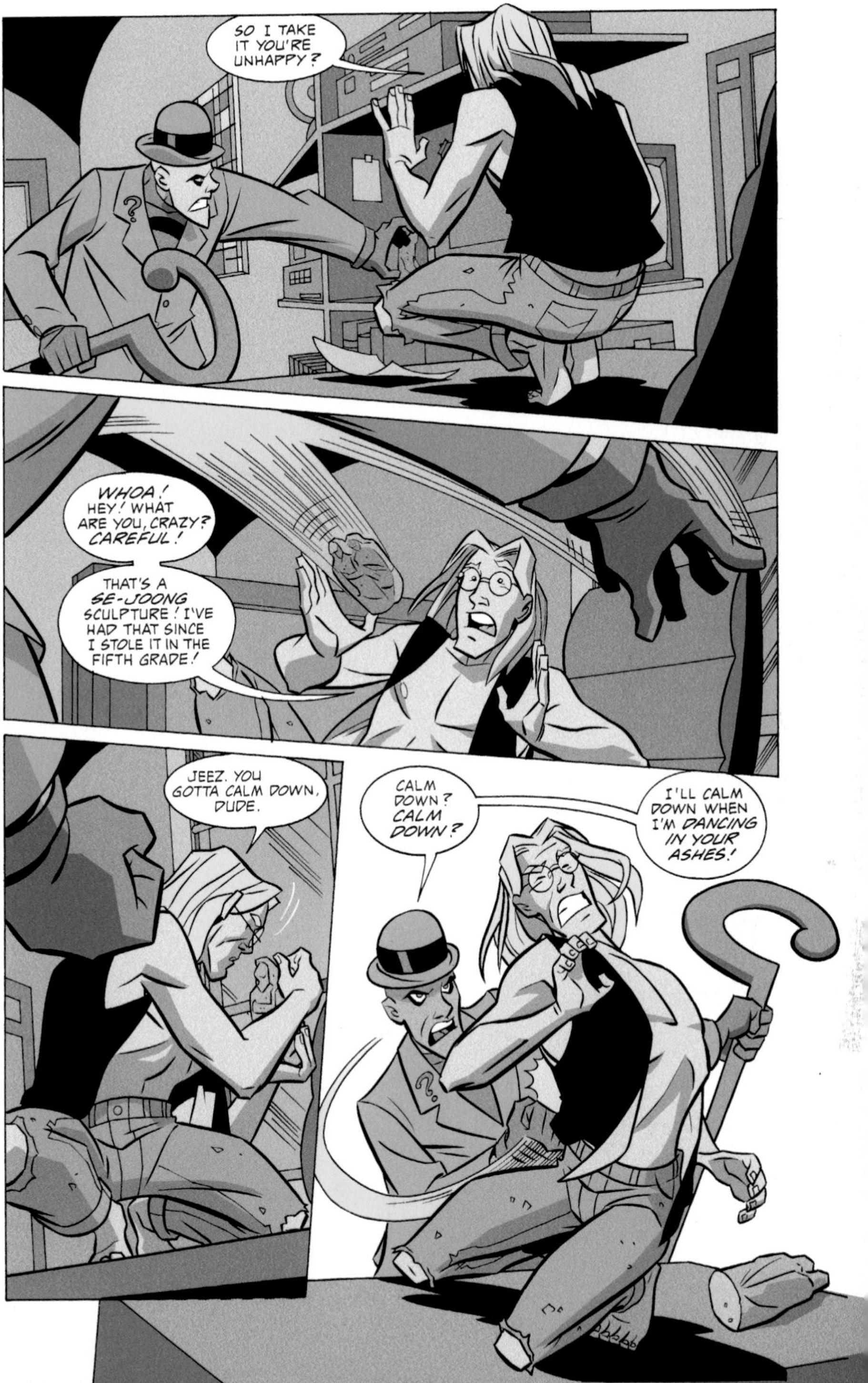
SO I TAKE IT YOU'RE UNHAPPY?
WHOA! HEY! WHAT ARE YOU, CRAZY? CAREFUL!
THAT'S A SE-JOONG SCULPTURE! I'VE HAD THAT SINCE I STOLE IT IN THE FIFTH GRADE!
JEEZ. YOU GOTTA CALM DOWN, DUDE.
CALM DOWN? CALM DOWN?
I'LL CALM DOWN WHEN I'M DANCING IN YOUR ASHES!

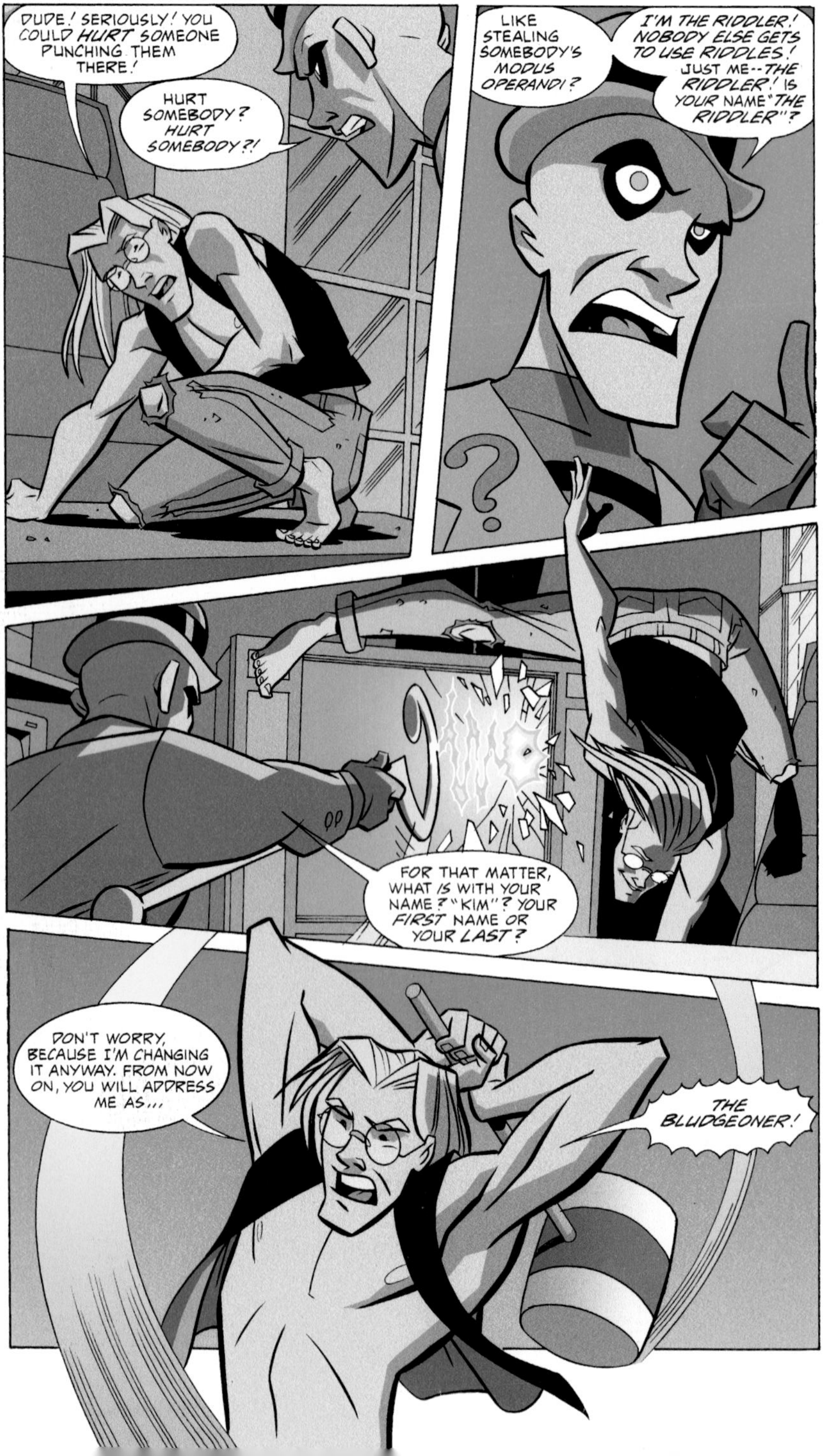
DUDE! SERIOUSLY! YOU COULD HURT SOMEONE PUNCHING THEM THERE!
HURT SOMEBODY? HURT SOMEBODY?!
LIKE STEALING SOMEBODY'S MODUS OPERANDI?
I'M THE RIDDLER! NOBODY ELSE GETS TO USE RIDDLES! JUST ME--THE RIDDLER! IS YOUR NAME "THE RIDDLER"?
FOR THAT MATTER, WHAT IS WITH YOUR NAME? "KIM"? YOUR FIRST NAME OR YOUR LAST?
DON'T WORRY, BECAUSE I'M CHANGING IT ANYWAY. FROM NOW ON, YOU WILL ADDRESS ME AS...
THE BLUDGEONER!

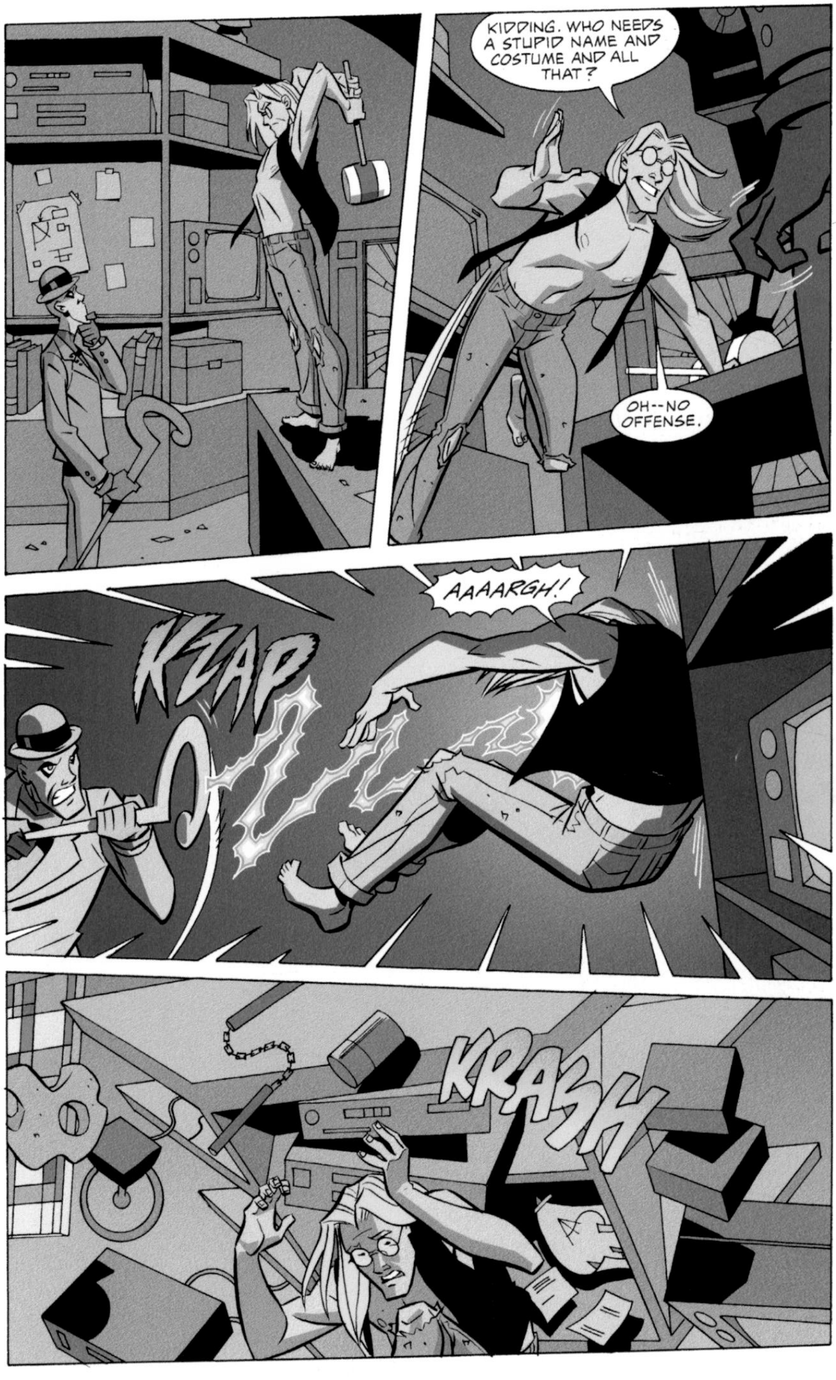

KIDDING. WHO NEEDS A STUPID NAME AND COSTUME AND ALL THAT?
OH--NO OFFENSE.
AAAARGH!
KZAP
KRASH

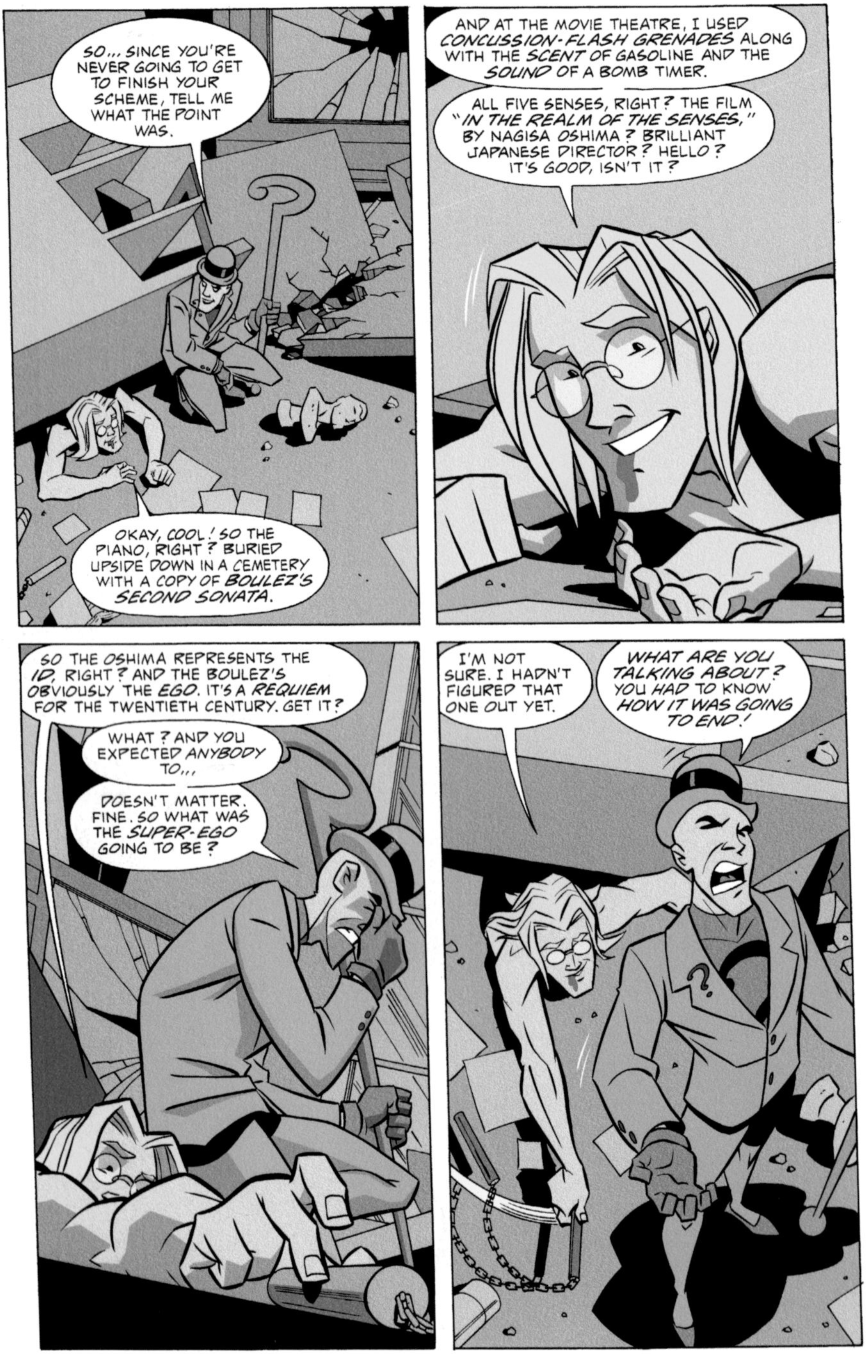
SO... SINCE YOU'RE NEVER GOING TO GET TO FINISH YOUR SCHEME, TELL ME WHAT THE POINT WAS.
OKAY, COOL! SO THE PIANO, RIGHT? BURIED UPSIDE DOWN IN A CEMETERY WITH A COPY OF BOULEZ'S SECOND SONATA.
AND AT THE MOVIE THEATRE, I USED CONCUSSION-FLASH GRENADES ALONG WITH THE SCENT OF GASOLINE AND THE SOUND OF A BOMB TIMER.
ALL FIVE SENSES, RIGHT? THE FILM "IN THE REALM OF THE SENSES," BY NAGISA OSHIMA? BRILLIANT JAPANESE DIRECTOR? HELLO? IT'S GOOD, ISN'T IT?
SO THE OSHIMA REPRESENTS THE ID, RIGHT? AND THE BOULEZ'S OBVIOUSLY THE EGO. IT'S A REQUIEM FOR THE TWENTIETH CENTURY. GET IT?
WHAT? AND YOU EXPECTED ANYBODY TO...
DOESN'T MATTER. FINE. SO WHAT WAS THE SUPER-EGO GOING TO BE?
I'M NOT SURE. I HADN'T FIGURED THAT ONE OUT YET.
WHAT ARE YOU TALKING ABOUT? YOU HAD TO KNOW HOW IT WAS GOING TO END!

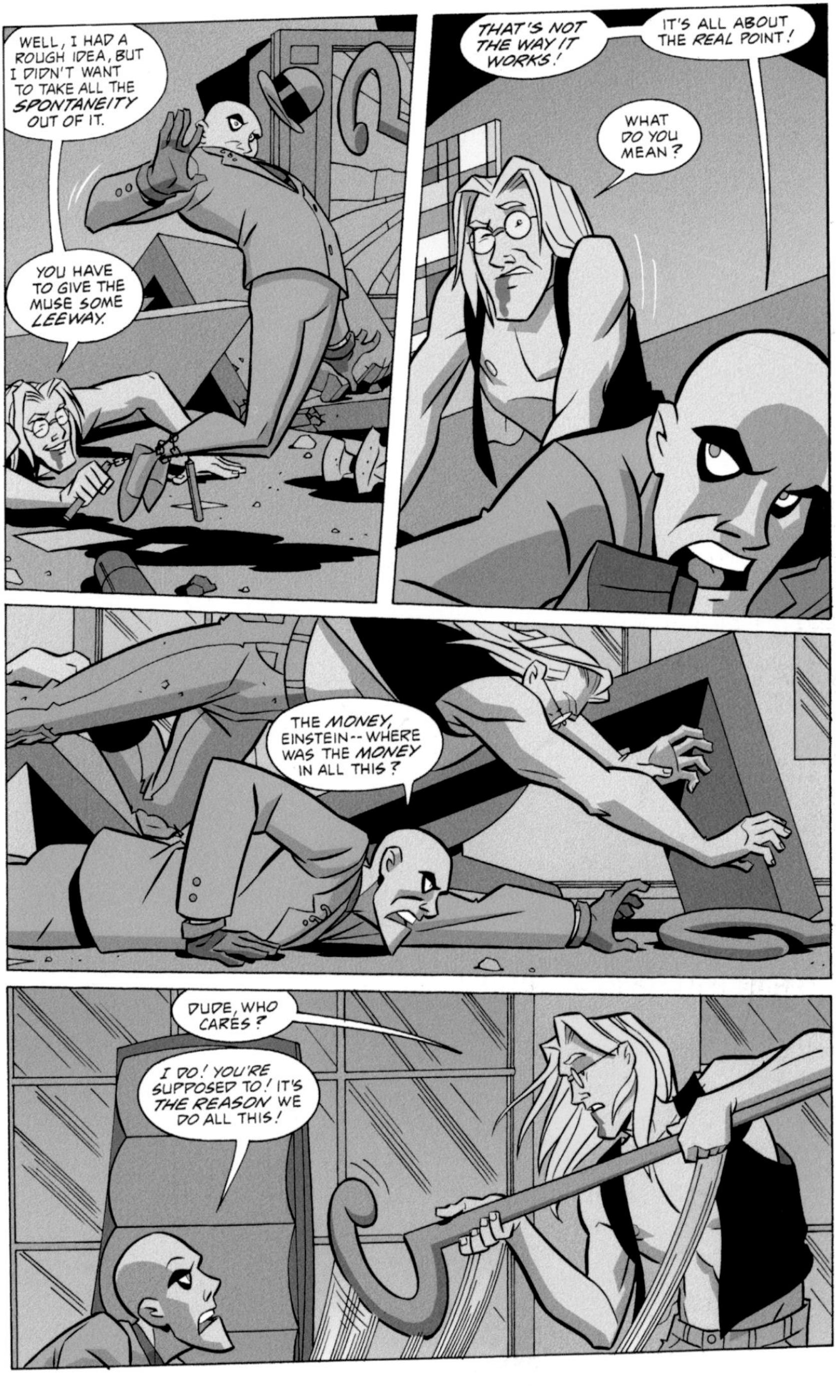

WELL, I HAD A ROUGH IDEA, BUT I DIDN'T WANT TO TAKE ALL THE *SPONTANEITY* OUT OF IT.
YOU HAVE TO GIVE THE MUSE SOME *LEEWAY.*
THAT'S NOT THE WAY IT WORKS!
IT'S ALL ABOUT THE *REAL* POINT!
WHAT DO YOU MEAN?
THE *MONEY,* EINSTEIN-- WHERE WAS THE *MONEY* IN ALL THIS?
DUDE, WHO CARES?
I DO! YOU'RE SUPPOSED TO! IT'S *THE REASON* WE DO ALL THIS!

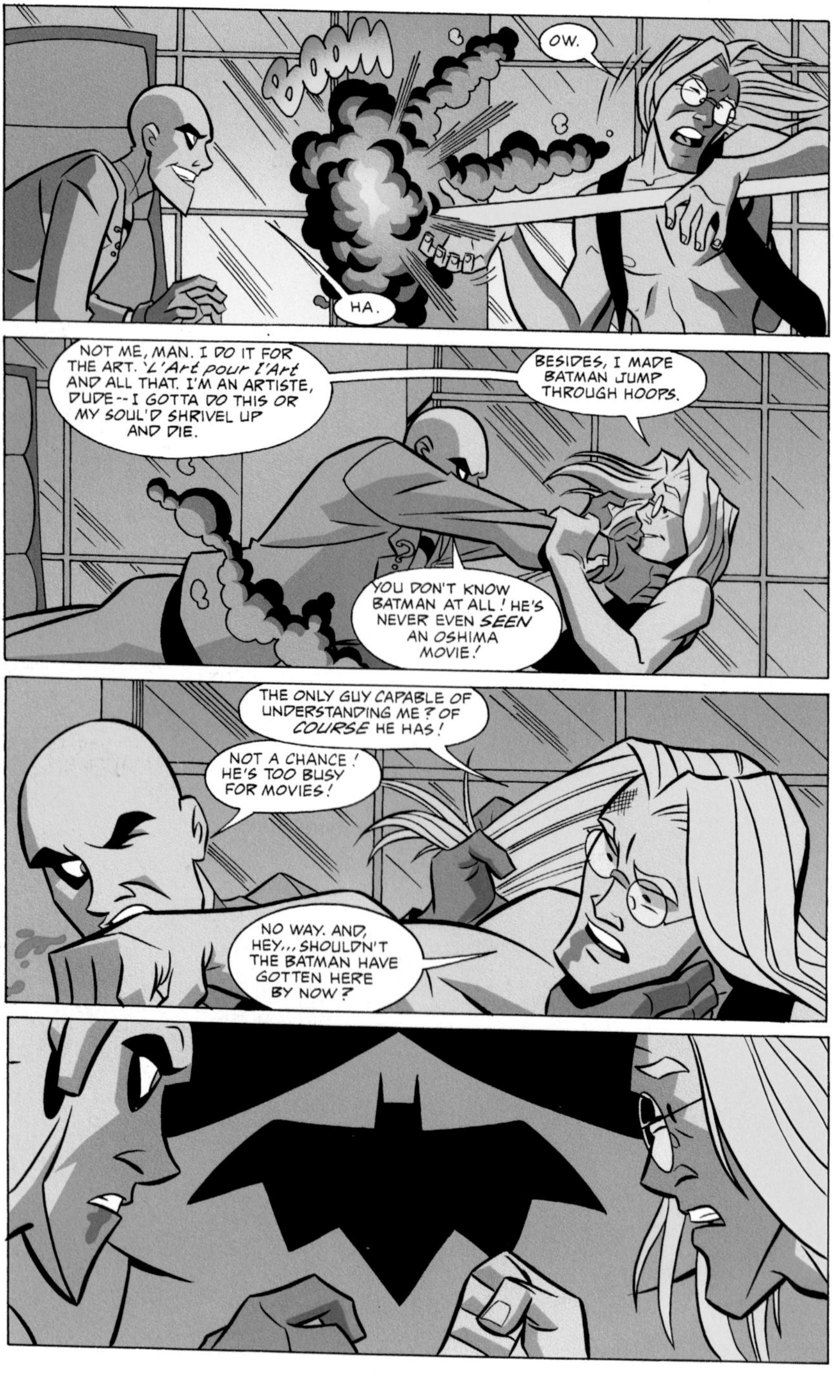
BOOM
OW.
HA.
NOT ME, MAN. I DO IT FOR THE ART. 'L'Art pour l'Art AND ALL THAT. I'M AN ARTISTE, DUDE--I GOTTA DO THIS OR MY SOUL'D SHRIVEL UP AND DIE.
BESIDES, I MADE BATMAN JUMP THROUGH HOOPS.
YOU DON'T KNOW BATMAN AT ALL! HE'S NEVER EVEN SEEN AN OSHIMA MOVIE!
THE ONLY GUY CAPABLE OF UNDERSTANDING ME? OF COURSE HE HAS!
NOT A CHANCE! HE'S TOO BUSY FOR MOVIES!
NO WAY. AND, HEY... SHOULDN'T THE BATMAN HAVE GOTTEN HERE BY NOW?

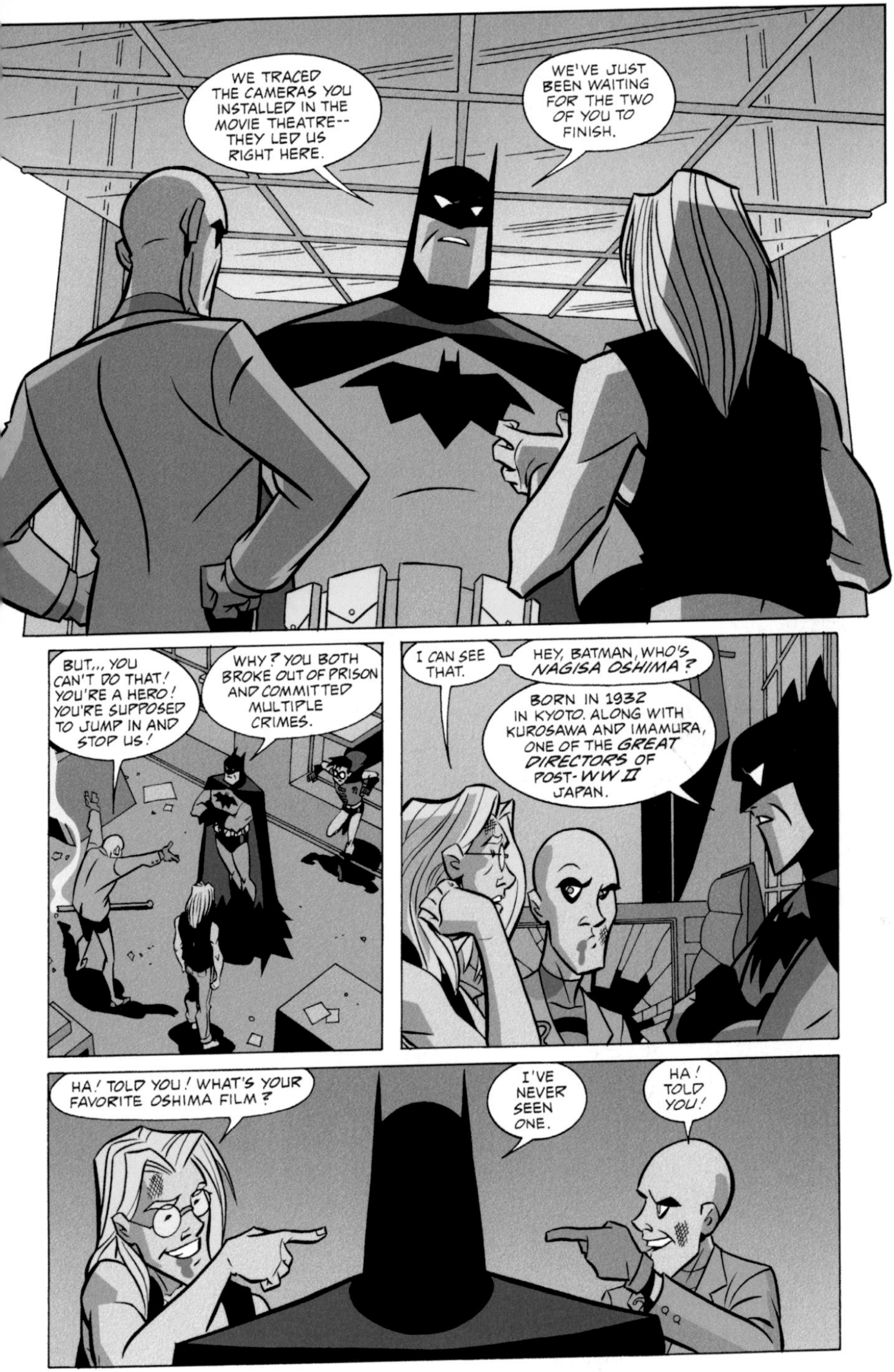
WE TRACED THE CAMERAS YOU INSTALLED IN THE MOVIE THEATRE-- THEY LED US RIGHT HERE.
WE'VE JUST BEEN WAITING FOR THE TWO OF YOU TO FINISH.
BUT... YOU CAN'T DO THAT! YOU'RE A HERO! YOU'RE SUPPOSED TO JUMP IN AND STOP US!
WHY? YOU BOTH BROKE OUT OF PRISON AND COMMITTED MULTIPLE CRIMES.
I CAN SEE THAT.
HEY, BATMAN, WHO'S NAGISA OSHIMA?
BORN IN 1932 IN KYOTO. ALONG WITH KUROSAWA AND IMAMURA, ONE OF THE GREAT DIRECTORS OF POST-WW II JAPAN.
HA! TOLD YOU! WHAT'S YOUR FAVORITE OSHIMA FILM?
I'VE NEVER SEEN ONE.
HA! TOLD YOU!

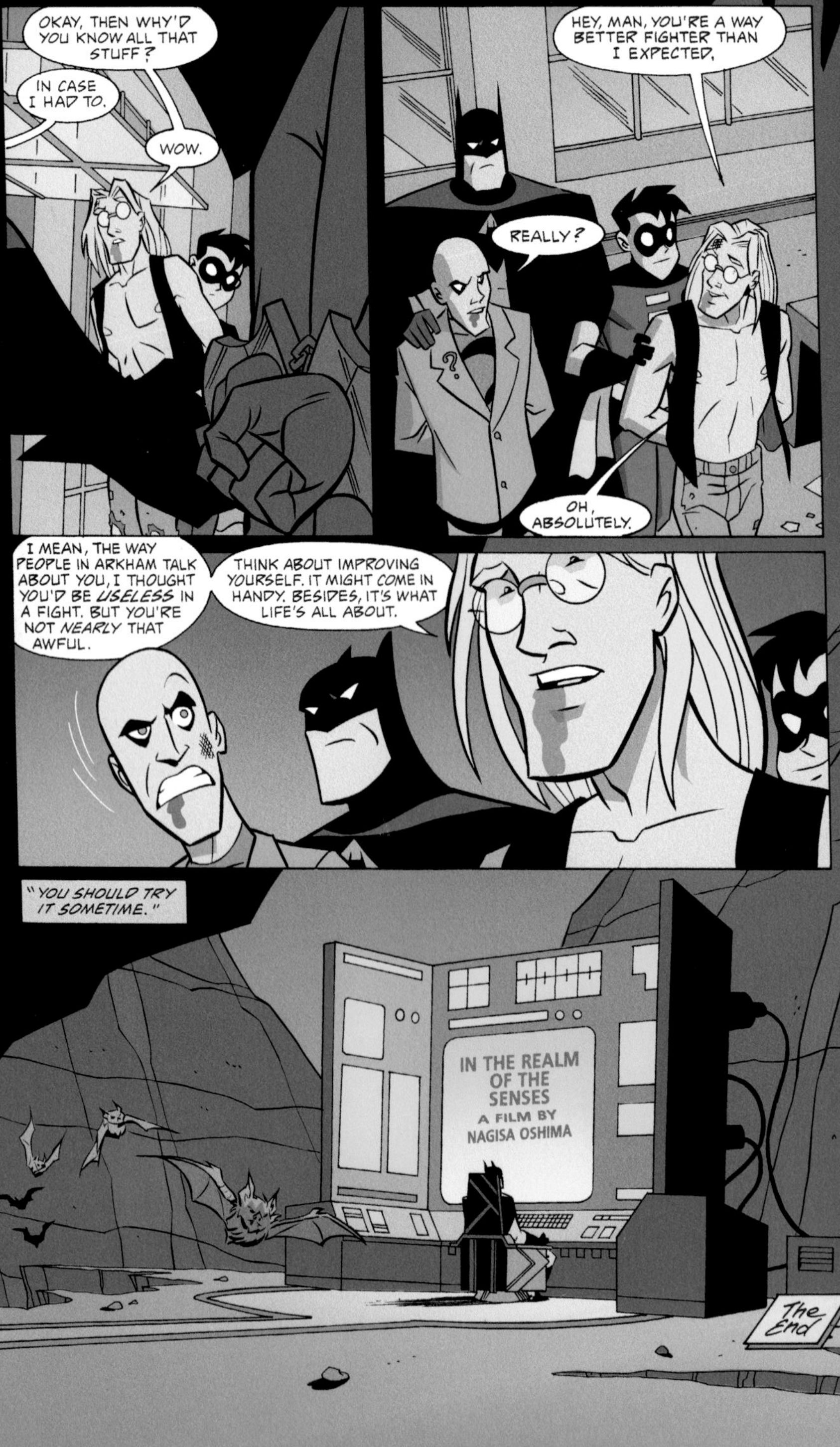
OKAY, THEN WHY'D YOU KNOW ALL THAT STUFF?
IN CASE I HAD TO.
WOW.
HEY, MAN, YOU'RE A WAY BETTER FIGHTER THAN I EXPECTED.
REALLY?
OH, ABSOLUTELY.
I MEAN, THE WAY PEOPLE IN ARKHAM TALK ABOUT YOU, I THOUGHT YOU'D BE USELESS IN A FIGHT. BUT YOU'RE NOT NEARLY THAT AWFUL.
THINK ABOUT IMPROVING YOURSELF. IT MIGHT COME IN HANDY. BESIDES, IT'S WHAT LIFE'S ALL ABOUT.
"YOU SHOULD TRY IT SOMETIME."
IN THE REALM OF THE SENSES
A FILM BY
NAGISA OSHIMA
The End

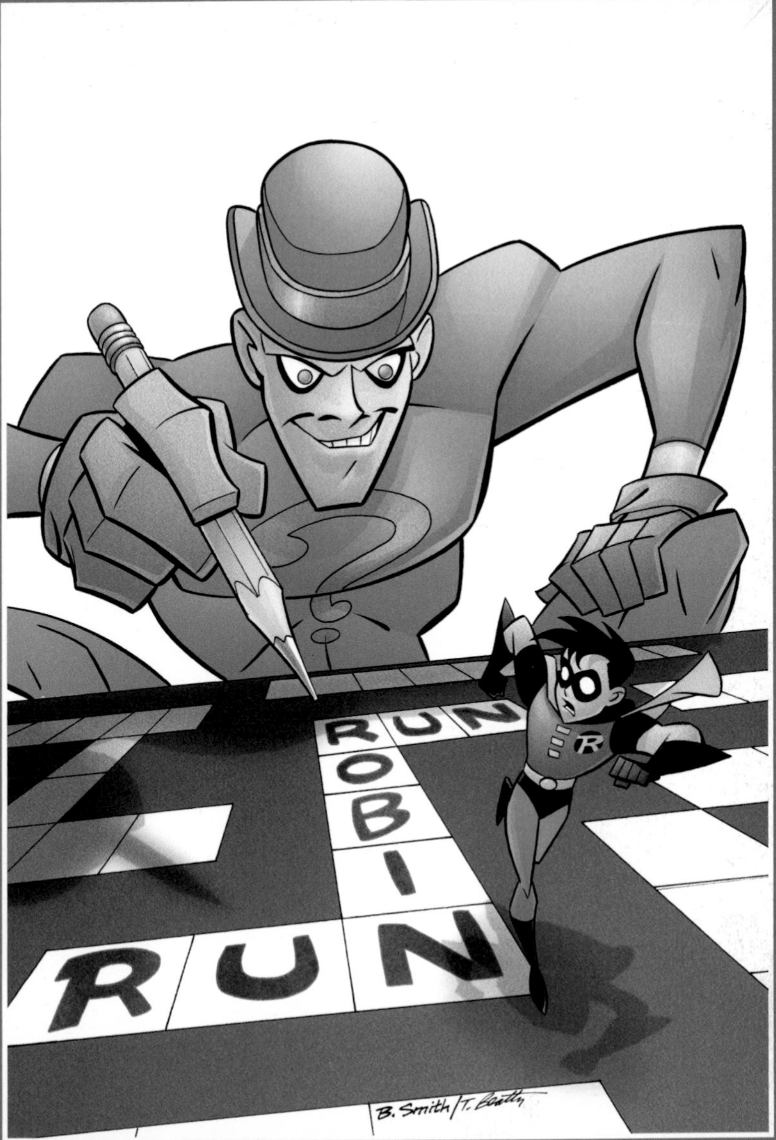
RUN
ROBIN
RUN
B. Smith/T. Beatty

CHAPTER 4: THE REAL DEAL

RIDDLE ME THIS

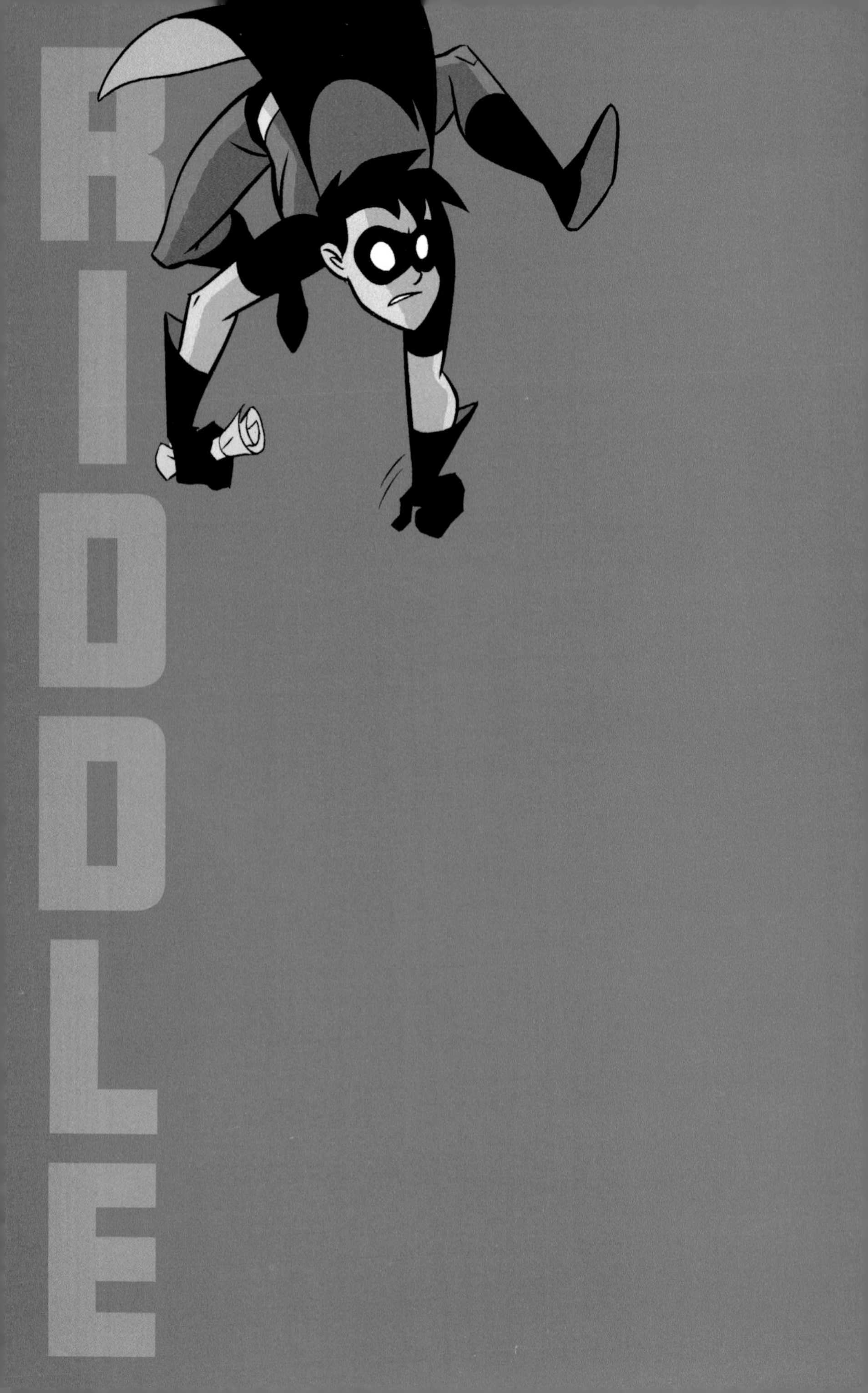
RIDDLE

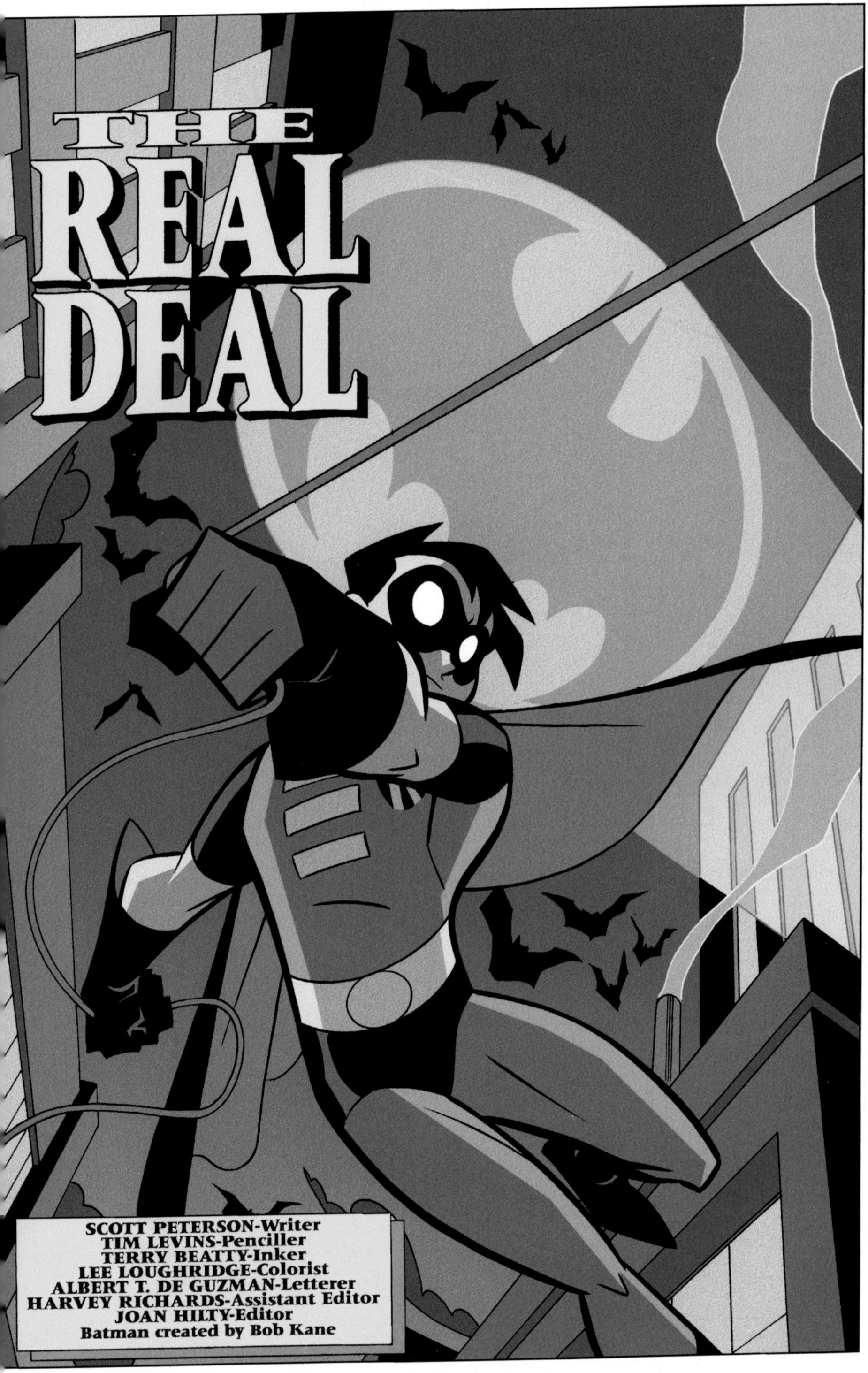
THE REAL DEAL
SCOTT PETERSON-Writer
TIM LEVINS-Penciller
TERRY BEATTY-Inker
LEE LOUGHRIDGE-Colorist
ALBERT T. DE GUZMAN-Letterer
HARVEY RICHARDS-Assistant Editor
JOAN HILTY-Editor
Batman created by Bob Kane

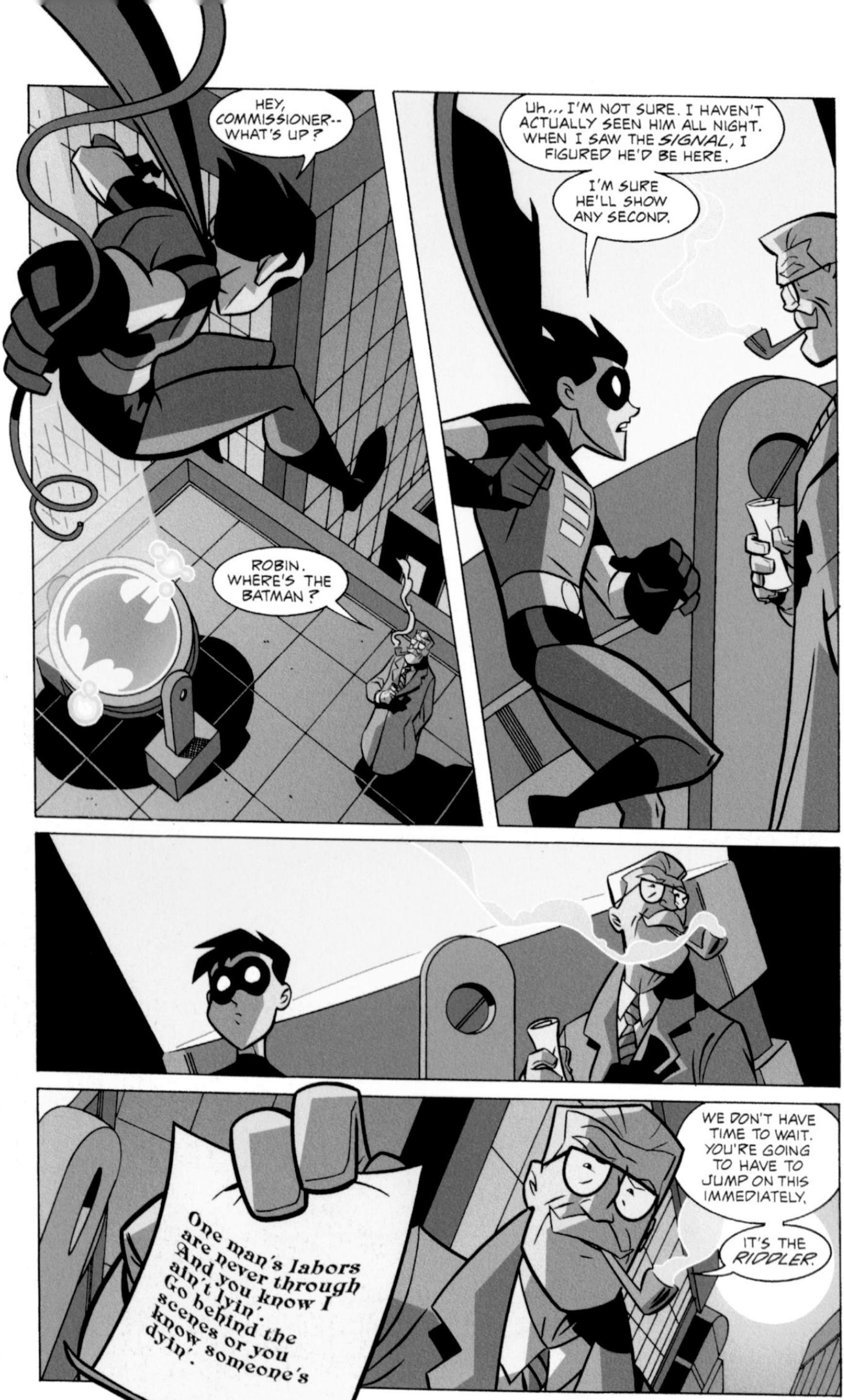

HEY, COMMISSIONER-- WHAT'S UP?
ROBIN. WHERE'S THE BATMAN?
Uh... I'M NOT SURE. I HAVEN'T ACTUALLY SEEN HIM ALL NIGHT. WHEN I SAW THE *SIGNAL*, I FIGURED HE'D BE HERE.
I'M SURE HE'LL SHOW ANY SECOND.
One man's labors are never through And you know I ain't lyin'. Go behind the scenes or you know someone's dyin'.
WE DON'T HAVE TIME TO WAIT. YOU'RE GOING TO HAVE TO JUMP ON THIS IMMEDIATELY.
IT'S THE *RIDDLER*.

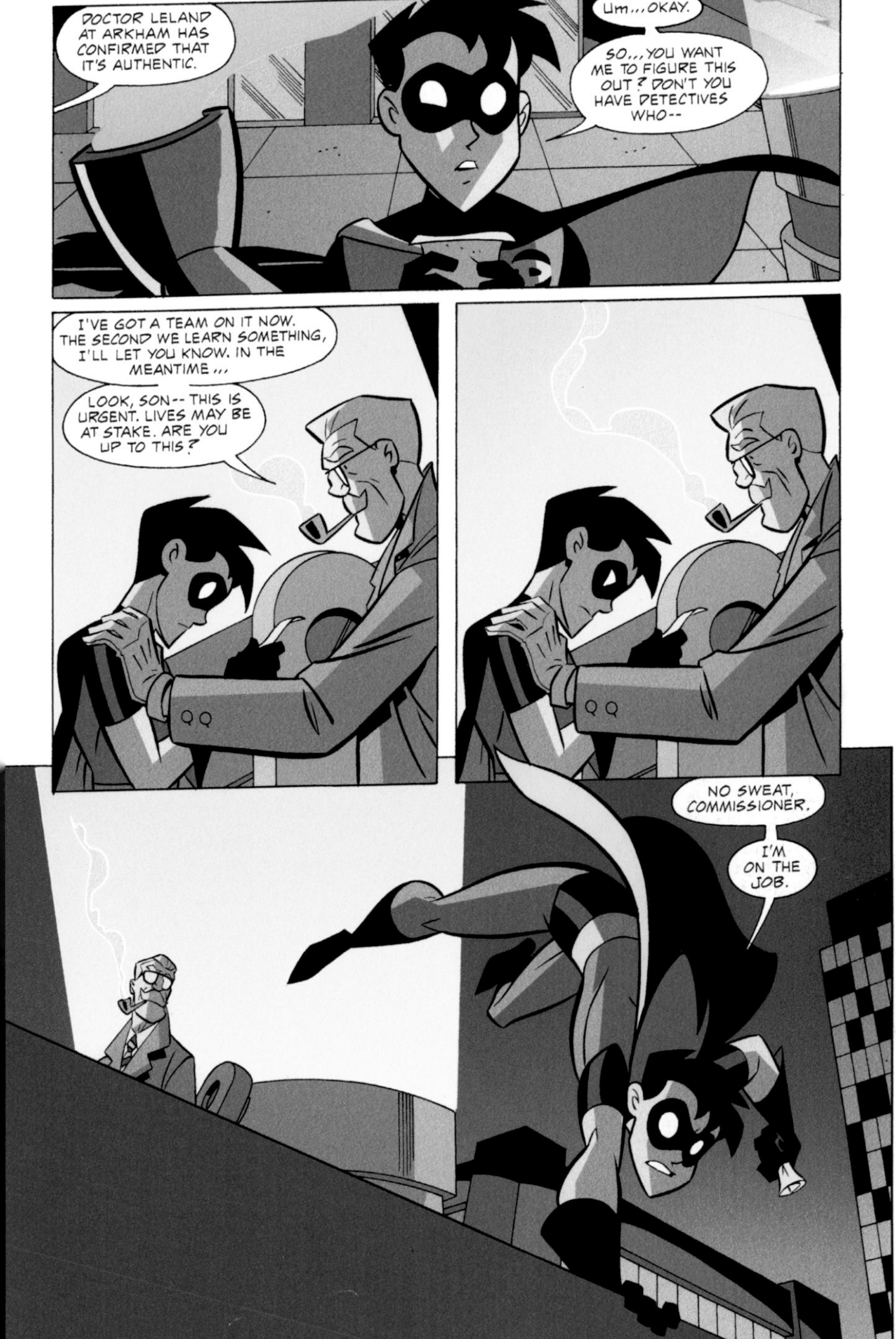
DOCTOR LELAND AT ARKHAM HAS CONFIRMED THAT IT'S AUTHENTIC.
UM... OKAY.
SO... YOU WANT ME TO FIGURE THIS OUT? DON'T YOU HAVE DETECTIVES WHO--
I'VE GOT A TEAM ON IT NOW. THE SECOND WE LEARN SOMETHING, I'LL LET YOU KNOW. IN THE MEANTIME...
LOOK, SON-- THIS IS URGENT. LIVES MAY BE AT STAKE. ARE YOU UP TO THIS?
NO SWEAT, COMMISSIONER.
I'M ON THE JOB.

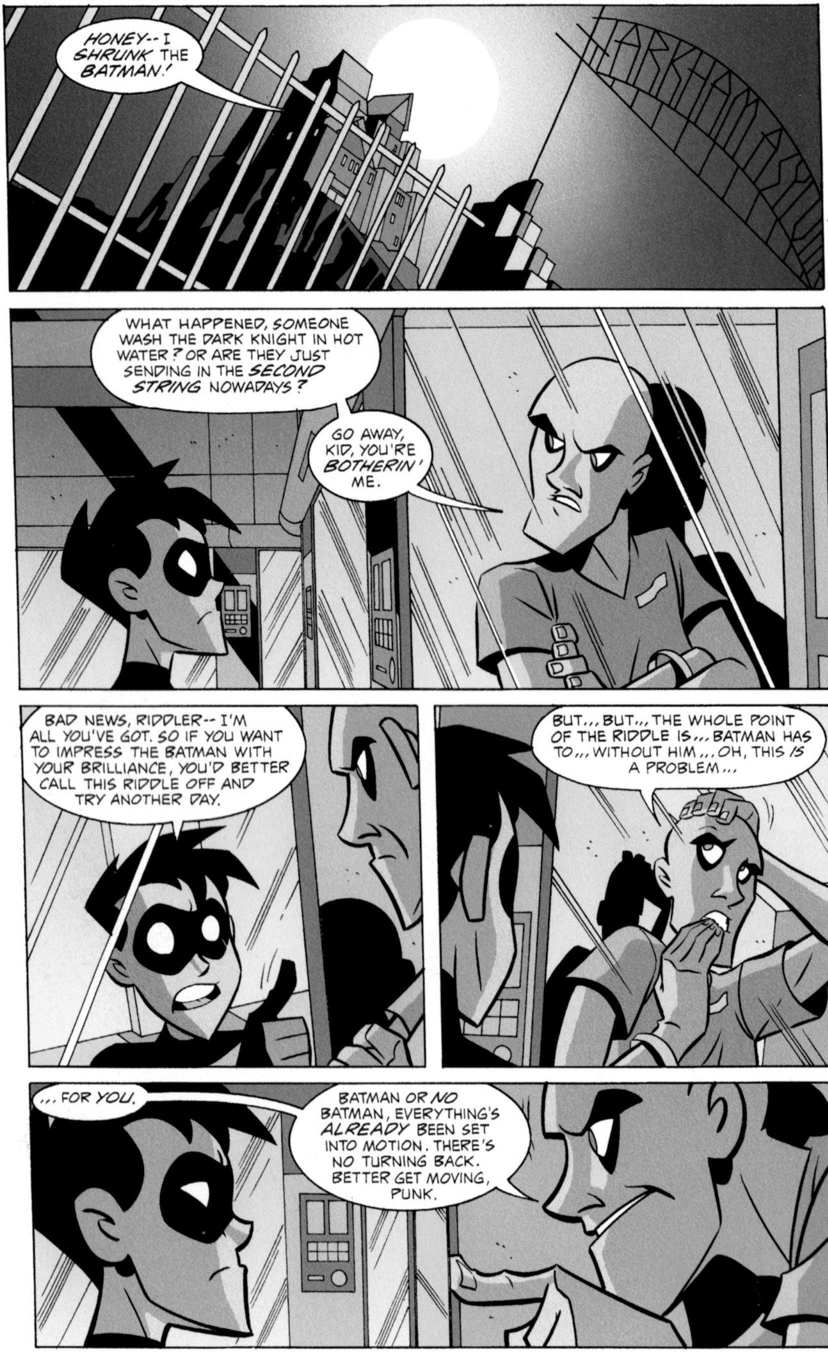
HONEY-- I SHRUNK THE BATMAN!
ARKHAM ASYLUM
WHAT HAPPENED, SOMEONE WASH THE DARK KNIGHT IN HOT WATER? OR ARE THEY JUST SENDING IN THE SECOND STRING NOWADAYS?
GO AWAY, KID, YOU'RE BOTHERIN' ME.
BAD NEWS, RIDDLER-- I'M ALL YOU'VE GOT. SO IF YOU WANT TO IMPRESS THE BATMAN WITH YOUR BRILLIANCE, YOU'D BETTER CALL THIS RIDDLE OFF AND TRY ANOTHER DAY.
BUT... BUT... THE WHOLE POINT OF THE RIDDLE IS... BATMAN HAS TO... WITHOUT HIM... OH, THIS IS A PROBLEM...
...FOR YOU.
BATMAN OR NO BATMAN, EVERYTHING'S ALREADY BEEN SET INTO MOTION. THERE'S NO TURNING BACK. BETTER GET MOVING, PUNK.

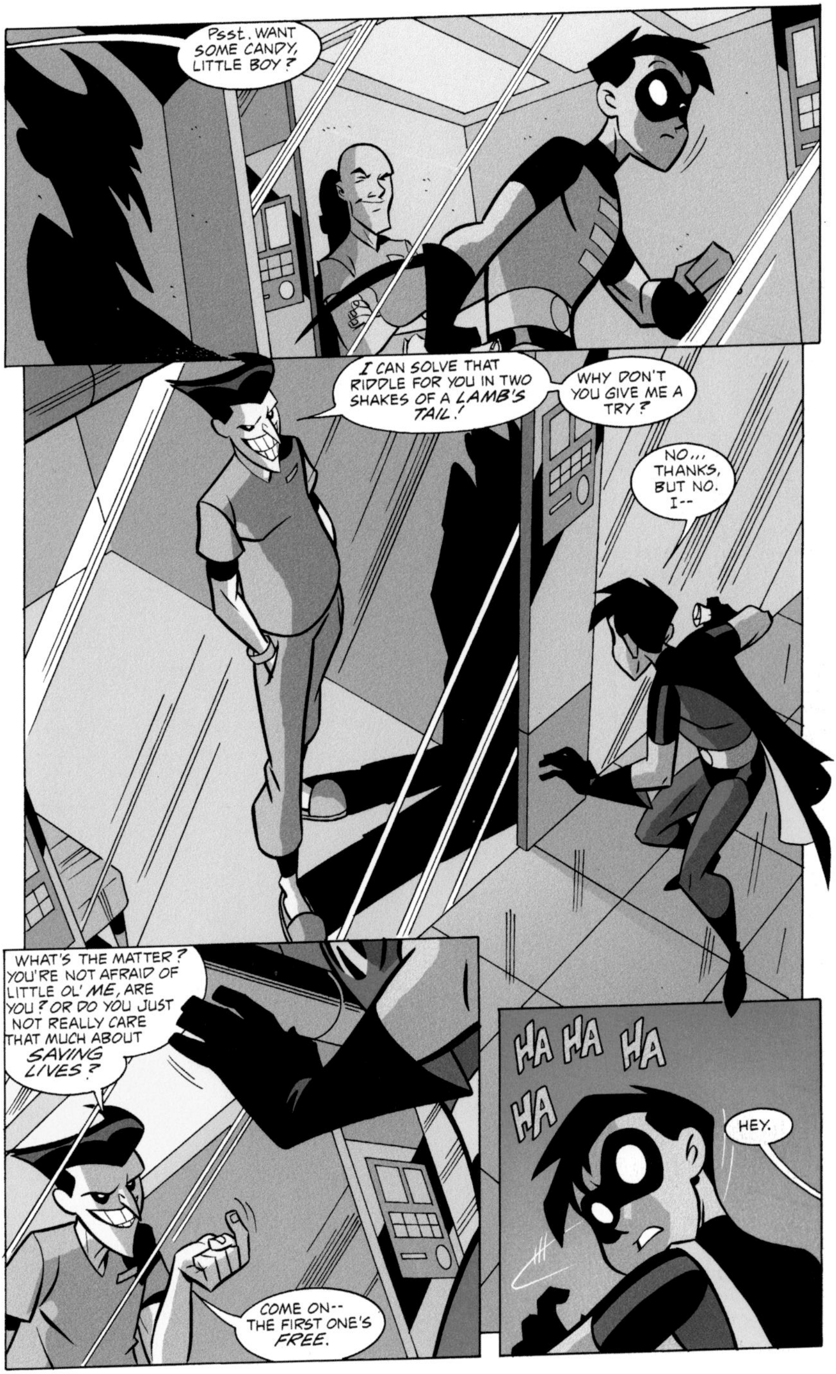
Psst. WANT SOME CANDY, LITTLE BOY?
I CAN SOLVE THAT RIDDLE FOR YOU IN TWO SHAKES OF A LAMB'S TAIL!
WHY DON'T YOU GIVE ME A TRY?
NO... THANKS, BUT NO. I--
WHAT'S THE MATTER? YOU'RE NOT AFRAID OF LITTLE OL' ME, ARE YOU? OR DO YOU JUST NOT REALLY CARE THAT MUCH ABOUT SAVING LIVES?
COME ON-- THE FIRST ONE'S FREE.
HA HA HA HA
HEY.

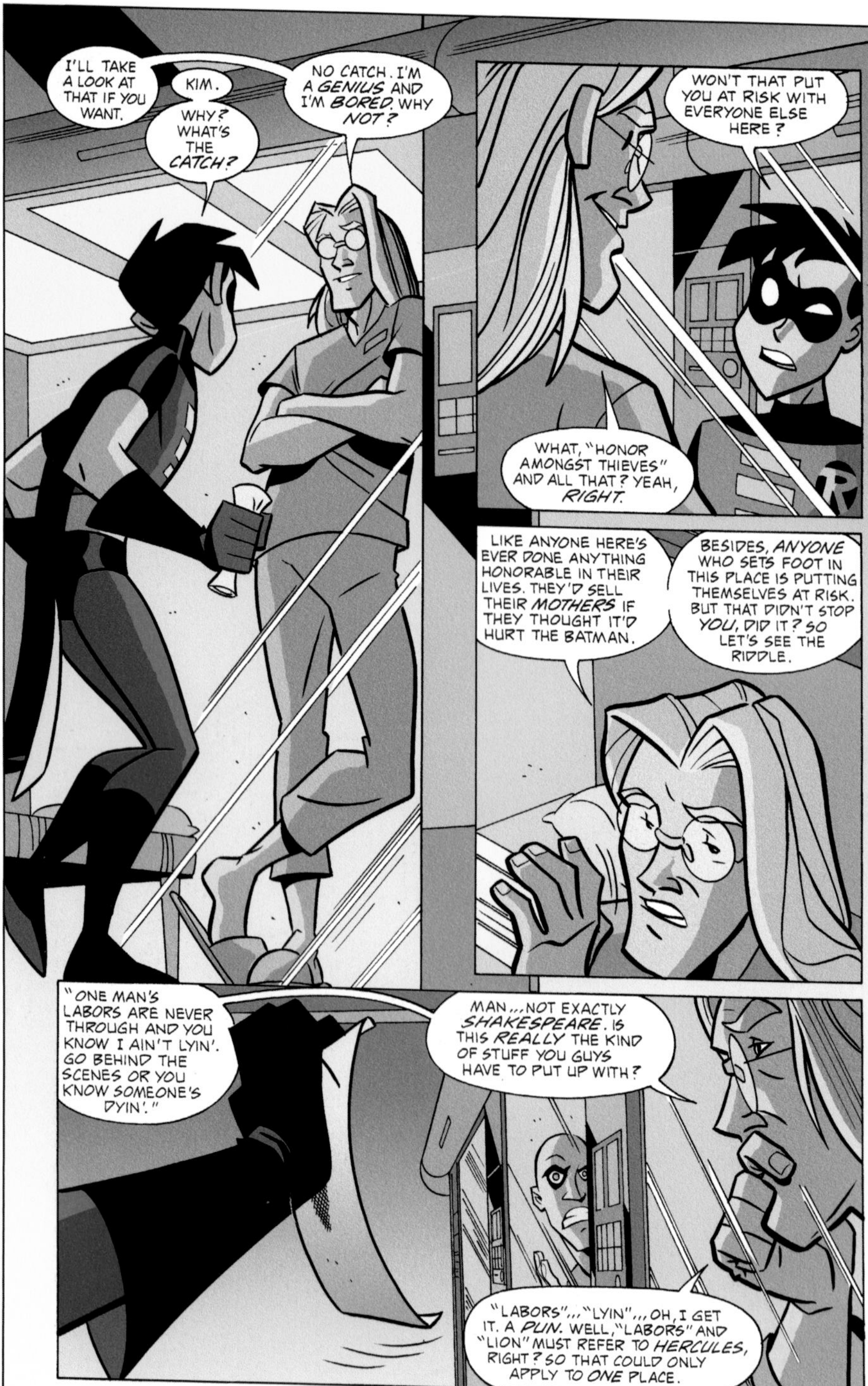
I'LL TAKE A LOOK AT THAT IF YOU WANT.
KIM.
WHY? WHAT'S THE CATCH?
NO CATCH. I'M A GENIUS AND I'M BORED. WHY NOT?
WON'T THAT PUT YOU AT RISK WITH EVERYONE ELSE HERE?
WHAT, "HONOR AMONGST THIEVES" AND ALL THAT? YEAH, RIGHT.
LIKE ANYONE HERE'S EVER DONE ANYTHING HONORABLE IN THEIR LIVES. THEY'D SELL THEIR MOTHERS IF THEY THOUGHT IT'D HURT THE BATMAN.
BESIDES, ANYONE WHO SETS FOOT IN THIS PLACE IS PUTTING THEMSELVES AT RISK. BUT THAT DIDN'T STOP YOU, DID IT? SO LET'S SEE THE RIDDLE.
"ONE MAN'S LABORS ARE NEVER THROUGH AND YOU KNOW I AIN'T LYIN'. GO BEHIND THE SCENES OR YOU KNOW SOMEONE'S DYIN'."
MAN... NOT EXACTLY SHAKESPEARE. IS THIS REALLY THE KIND OF STUFF YOU GUYS HAVE TO PUT UP WITH?
"LABORS"... "LYIN"... OH, I GET IT. A PUN. WELL, "LABORS" AND "LION" MUST REFER TO HERCULES, RIGHT? SO THAT COULD ONLY APPLY TO ONE PLACE.

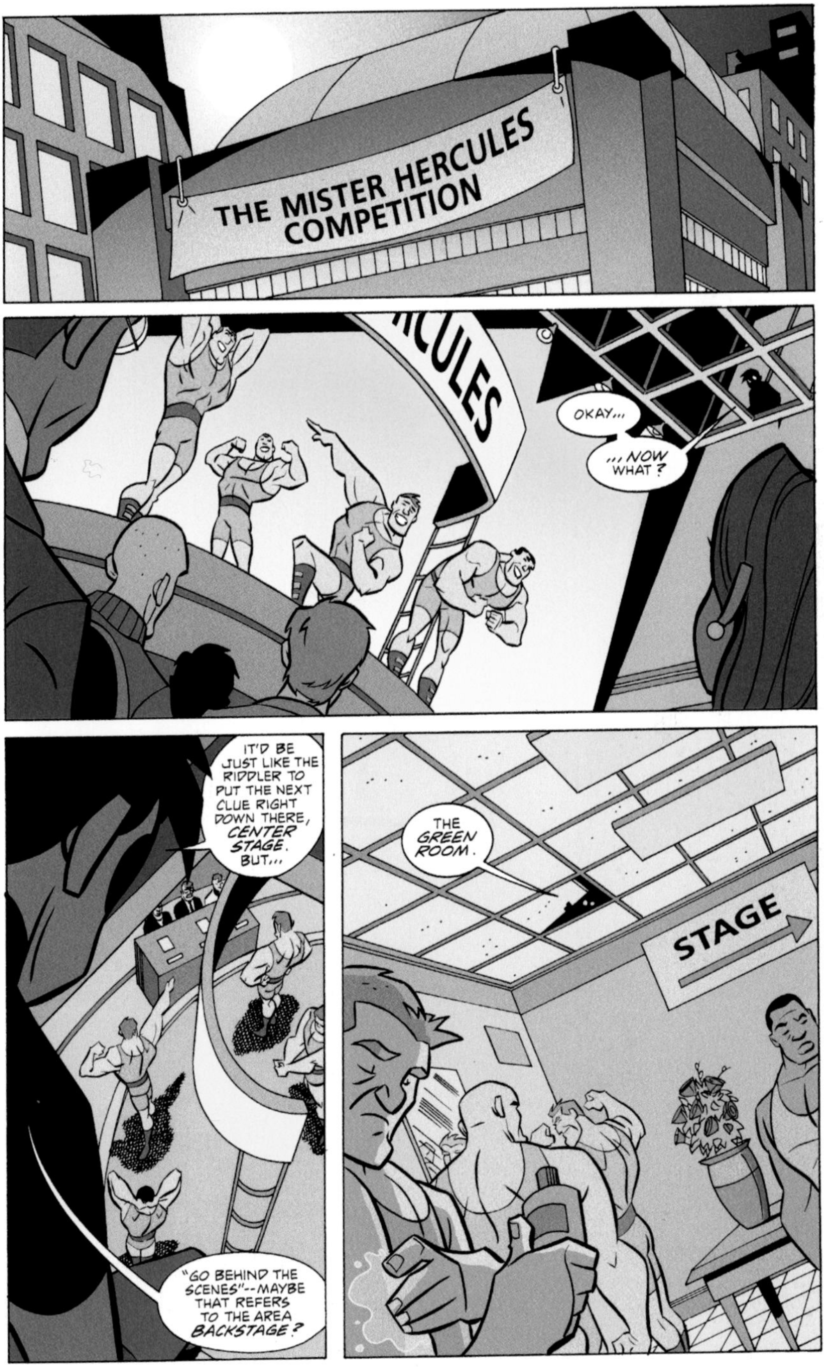
THE MISTER HERCULES COMPETITION
OKAY...
...NOW WHAT?
IT'D BE JUST LIKE THE RIDDLER TO PUT THE NEXT CLUE RIGHT DOWN THERE, *CENTER STAGE*. BUT...
"GO BEHIND THE SCENES"--MAYBE THAT REFERS TO THE AREA *BACKSTAGE*?
THE *GREEN ROOM*.
STAGE

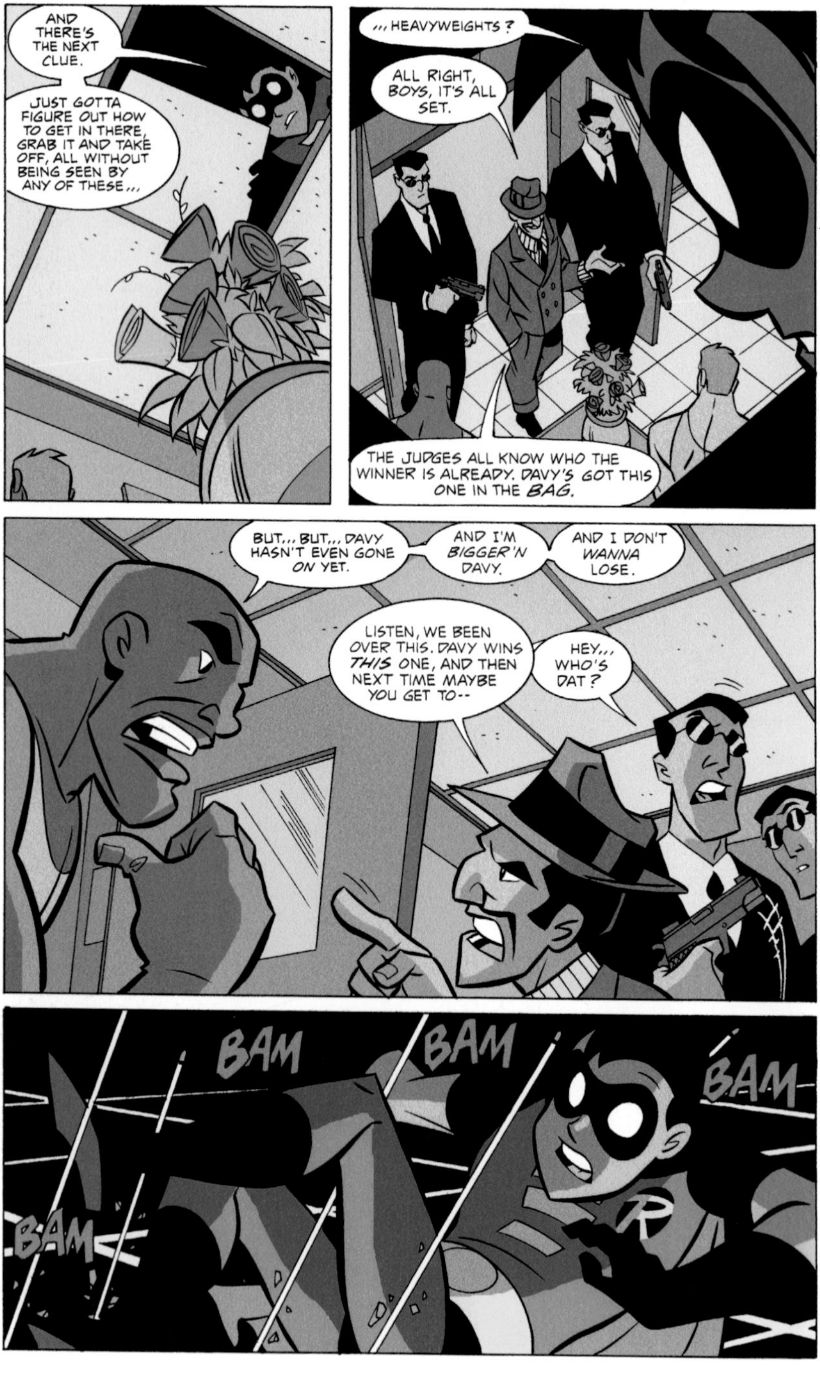
AND THERE'S THE NEXT CLUE.
JUST GOTTA FIGURE OUT HOW TO GET IN THERE, GRAB IT AND TAKE OFF, ALL WITHOUT BEING SEEN BY ANY OF THESE...
...HEAVYWEIGHTS?
ALL RIGHT, BOYS, IT'S ALL SET.
THE JUDGES ALL KNOW WHO THE WINNER IS ALREADY. DAVY'S GOT THIS ONE IN THE *BAG*.
BUT... BUT... DAVY HASN'T EVEN GONE ON YET.
AND I'M *BIGGER'N* DAVY.
AND I DON'T *WANNA* LOSE.
LISTEN, WE BEEN OVER THIS. DAVY WINS *THIS* ONE, AND THEN NEXT TIME MAYBE YOU GET TO--
HEY... WHO'S DAT?
BAM
BAM
BAM
BAM

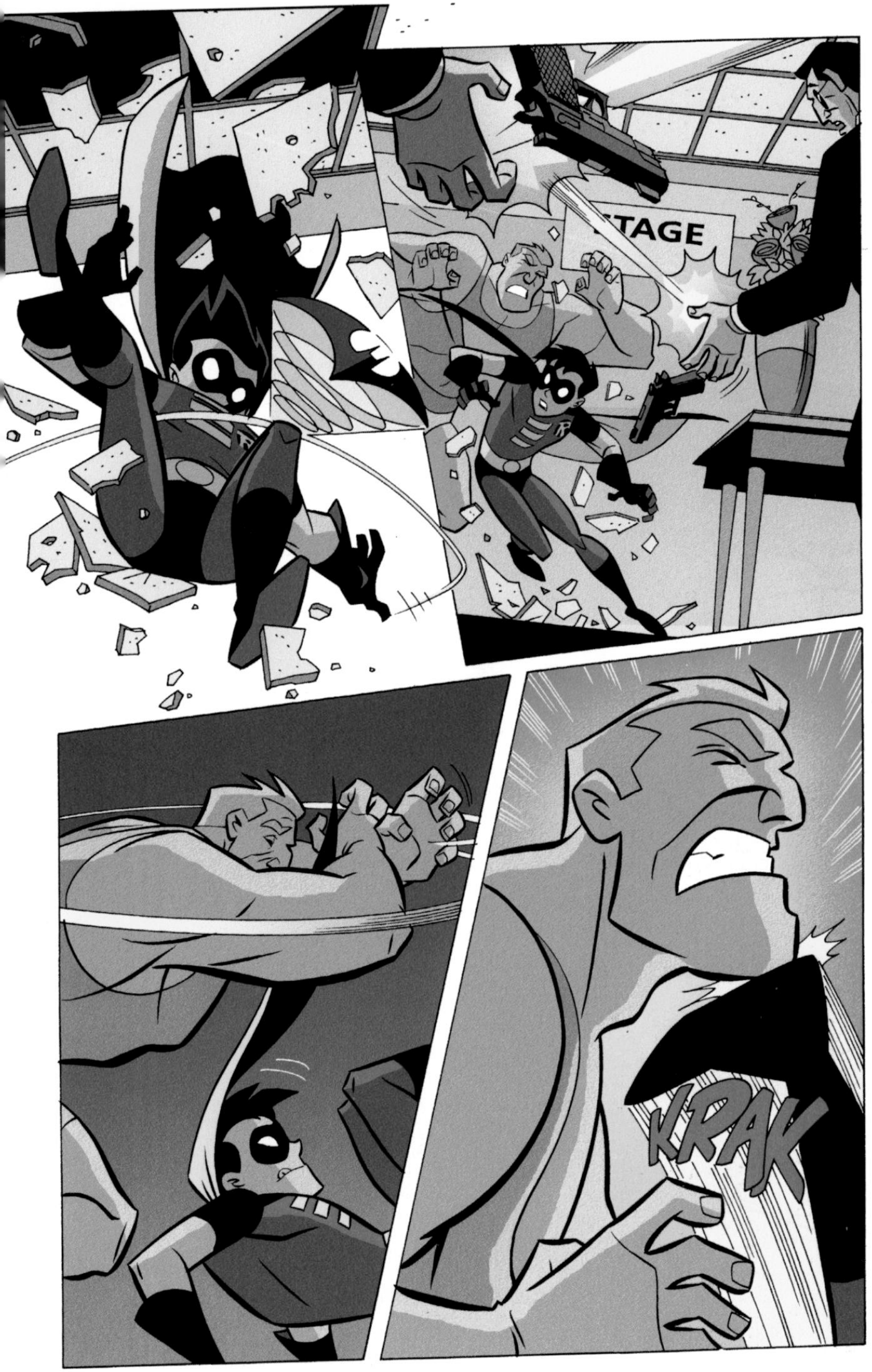
STAGE
KRAK

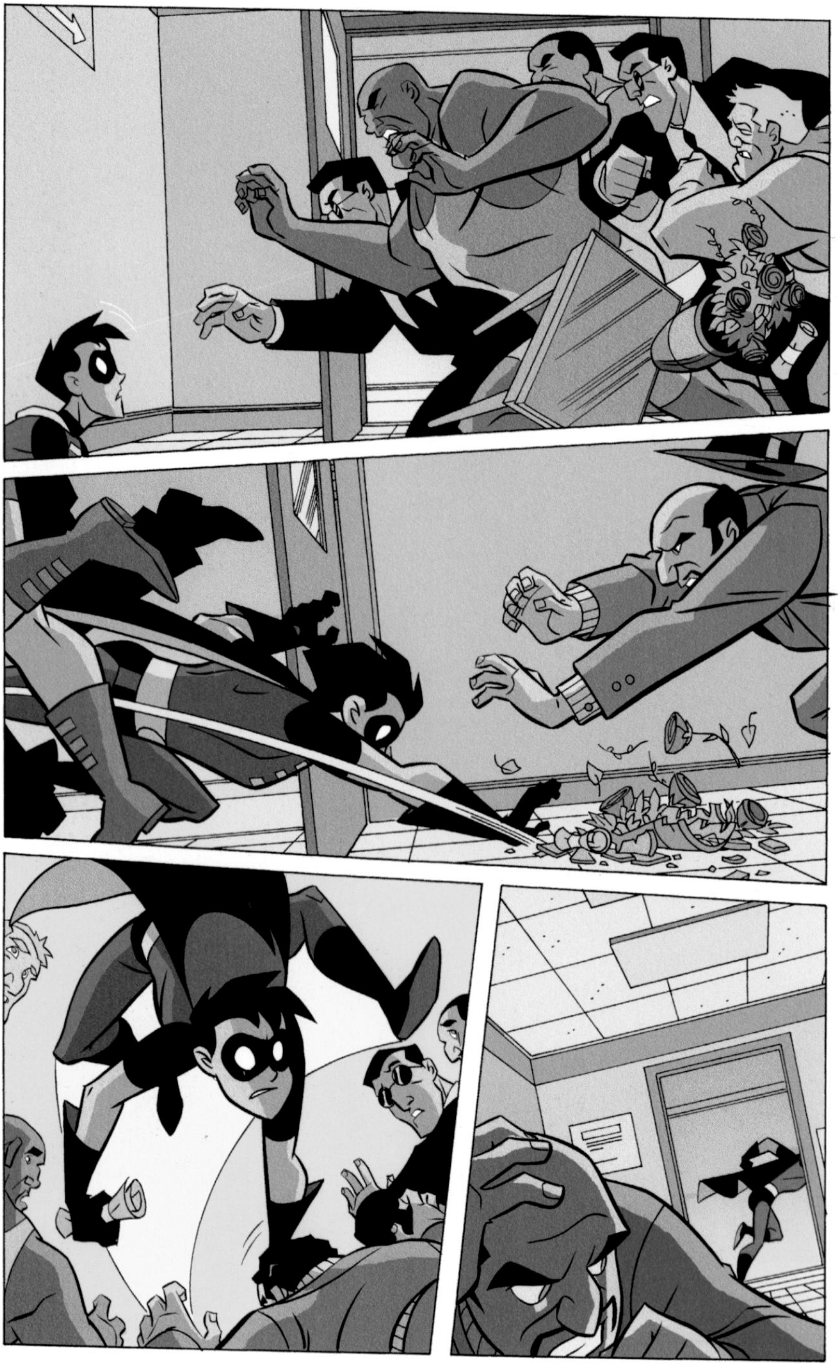

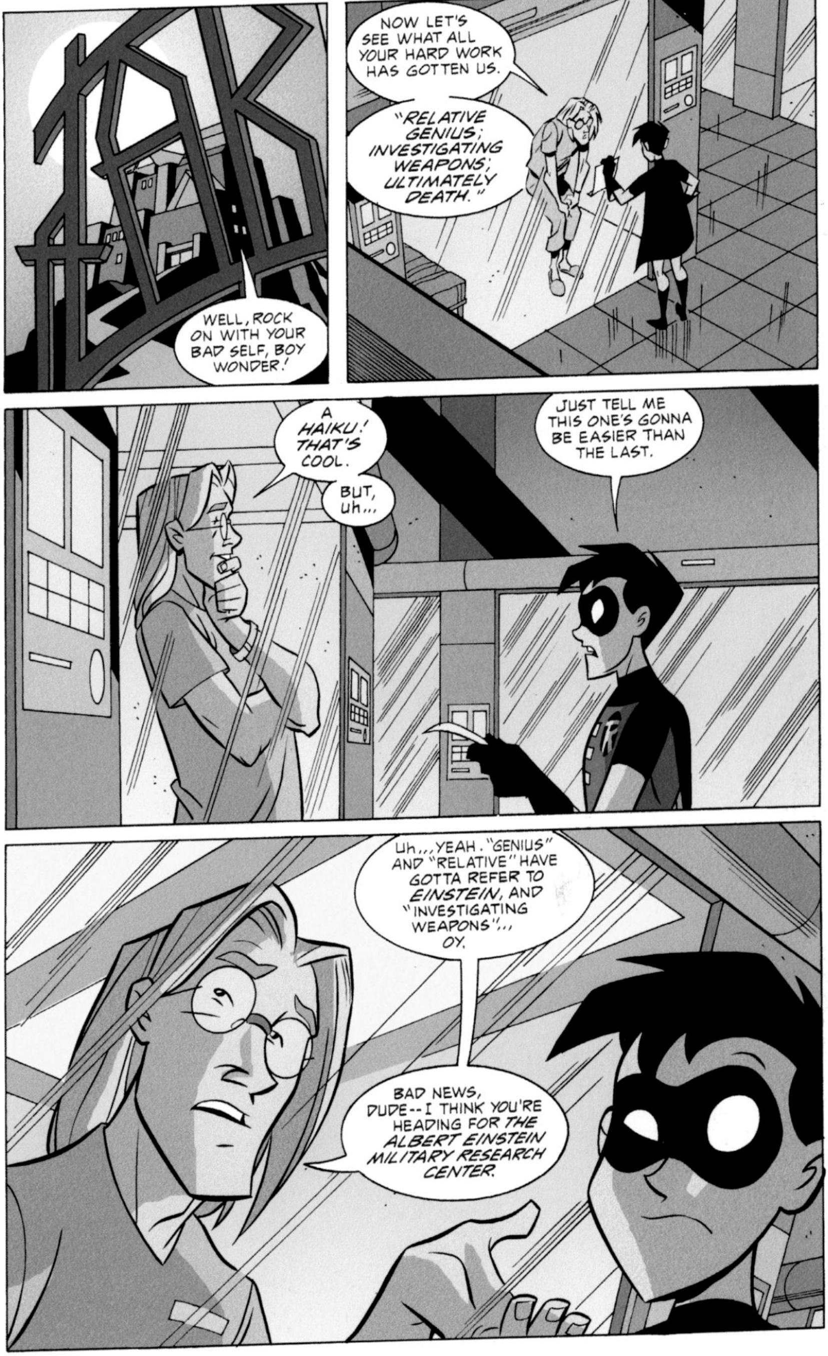
WELL, ROCK ON WITH YOUR BAD SELF, BOY WONDER!
NOW LET'S SEE WHAT ALL YOUR HARD WORK HAS GOTTEN US.
"RELATIVE GENIUS; INVESTIGATING WEAPONS; ULTIMATELY DEATH."
A HAIKU! THAT'S COOL.
BUT, uh...
JUST TELL ME THIS ONE'S GONNA BE EASIER THAN THE LAST.
Uh... YEAH. "GENIUS" AND "RELATIVE" HAVE GOTTA REFER TO EINSTEIN, AND "INVESTIGATING WEAPONS"... OY.
BAD NEWS, DUDE--I THINK YOU'RE HEADING FOR THE ALBERT EINSTEIN MILITARY RESEARCH CENTER.

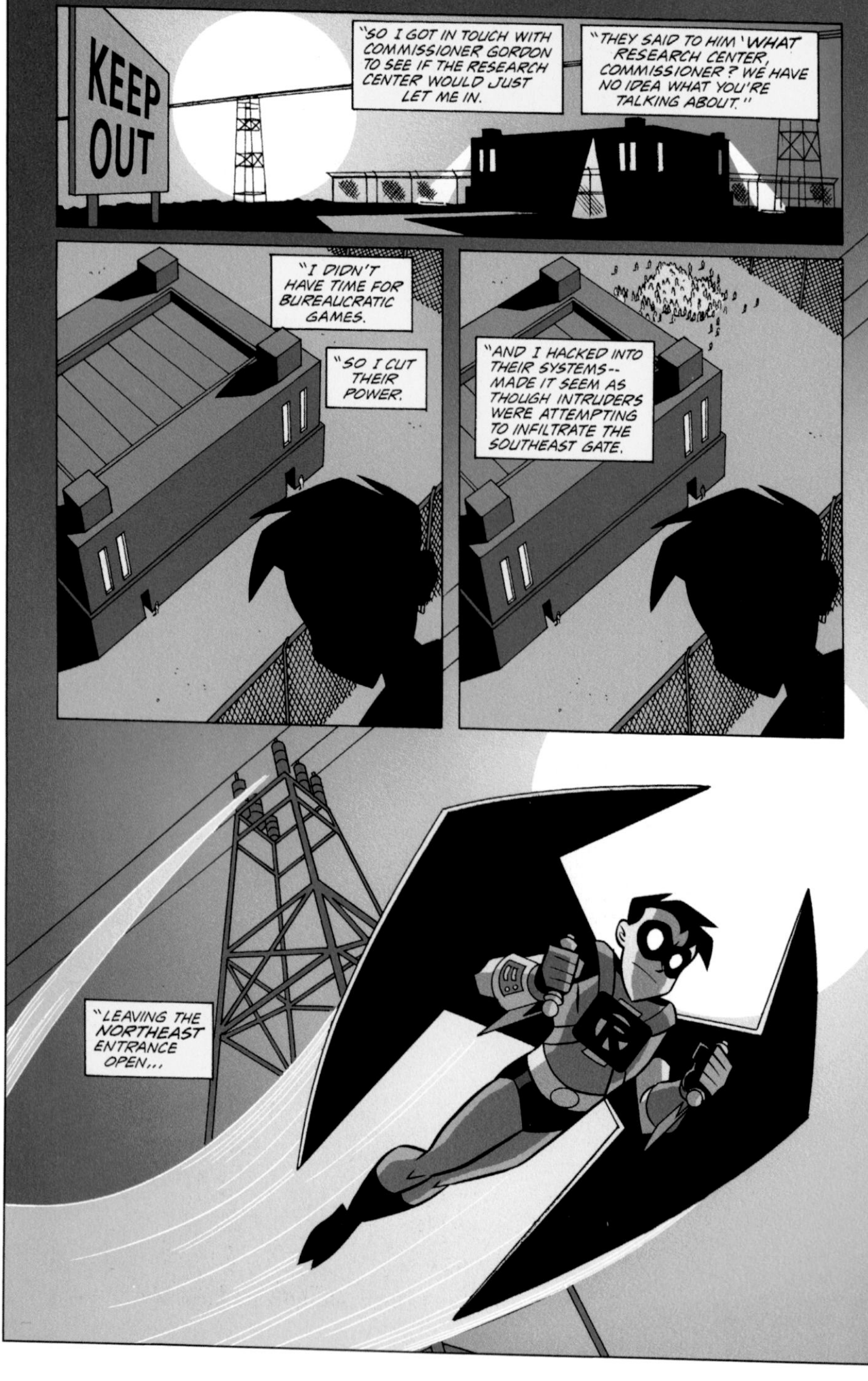
KEEP OUT
"SO I GOT IN TOUCH WITH COMMISSIONER GORDON TO SEE IF THE RESEARCH CENTER WOULD JUST LET ME IN.
"THEY SAID TO HIM 'WHAT RESEARCH CENTER, COMMISSIONER? WE HAVE NO IDEA WHAT YOU'RE TALKING ABOUT.'"
"I DIDN'T HAVE TIME FOR BUREAUCRATIC GAMES.
"SO I CUT THEIR POWER.
"AND I HACKED INTO THEIR SYSTEMS-- MADE IT SEEM AS THOUGH INTRUDERS WERE ATTEMPTING TO INFILTRATE THE SOUTHEAST GATE.
"LEAVING THE NORTHEAST ENTRANCE OPEN...

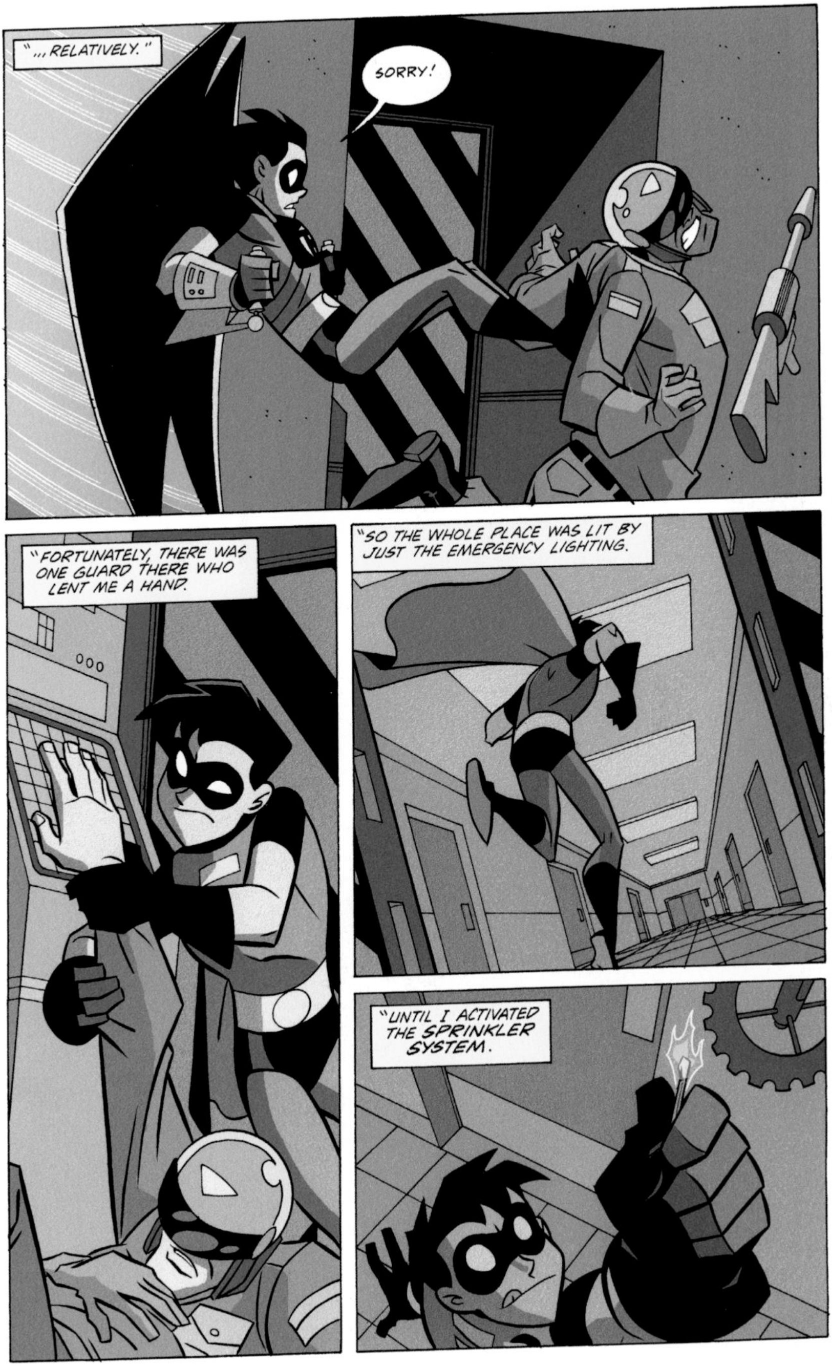
"...RELATIVELY."
SORRY!
"FORTUNATELY, THERE WAS ONE GUARD THERE WHO LENT ME A HAND.
"SO THE WHOLE PLACE WAS LIT BY JUST THE EMERGENCY LIGHTING.
"UNTIL I ACTIVATED THE SPRINKLER SYSTEM.

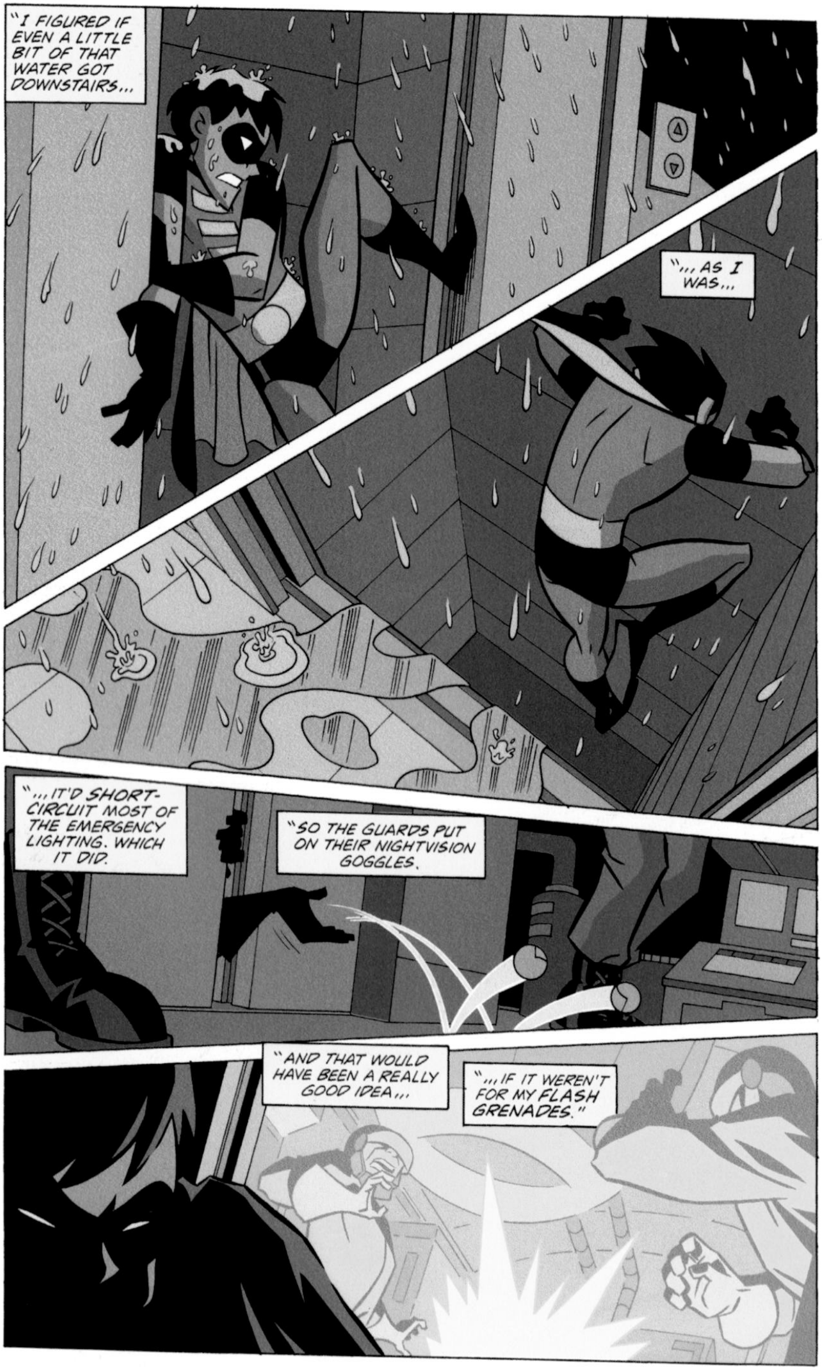
"I FIGURED IF EVEN A LITTLE BIT OF THAT WATER GOT DOWNSTAIRS...
"... AS I WAS...
"... IT'D SHORT-CIRCUIT MOST OF THE EMERGENCY LIGHTING. WHICH IT DID.
"SO THE GUARDS PUT ON THEIR NIGHTVISION GOGGLES.
"AND THAT WOULD HAVE BEEN A REALLY GOOD IDEA...
"... IF IT WEREN'T FOR MY FLASH GRENADES."

I JUST WALKED IN, FOUND THE NEXT CLUE AND SPLIT.

HEY, MAN, I'M STARTING TO SEE WHY THE BATMAN KEEPS YOU AROUND.

OKAY, LET'S TAKE A LOOK.

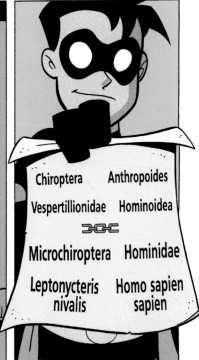

Chiroptera   Anthropoides

Vespertillionidae   Hominoidea

Microchiroptera   Hominidae

Leptonycteris nivalis   Homo sapien sapien

GOT ME, DUDE.

WHAT?

WHAT?

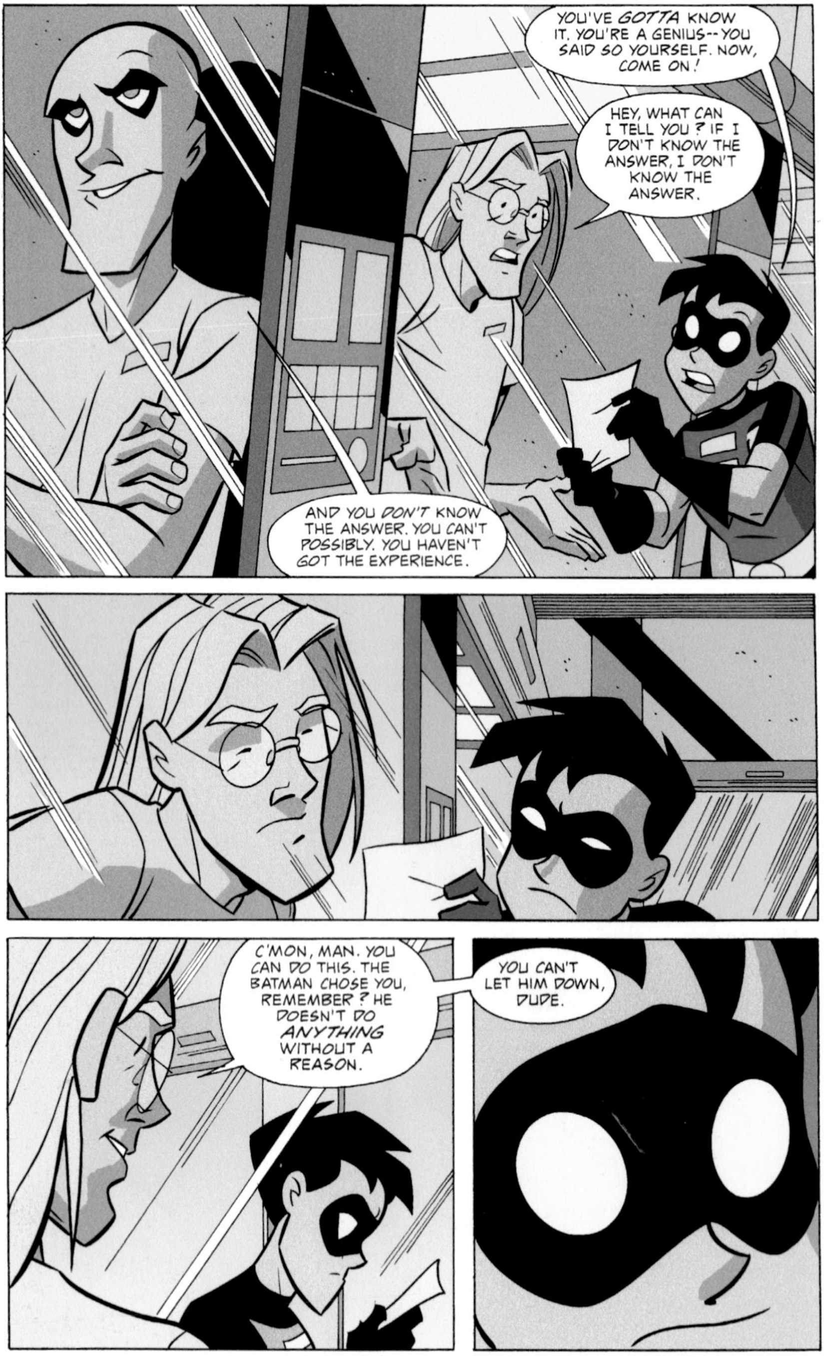
YOU'VE GOTTA KNOW IT. YOU'RE A GENIUS--YOU SAID SO YOURSELF. NOW, COME ON!
HEY, WHAT CAN I TELL YOU? IF I DON'T KNOW THE ANSWER, I DON'T KNOW THE ANSWER.
AND YOU DON'T KNOW THE ANSWER. YOU CAN'T POSSIBLY. YOU HAVEN'T GOT THE EXPERIENCE.
C'MON, MAN. YOU CAN DO THIS. THE BATMAN CHOSE YOU, REMEMBER? HE DOESN'T DO ANYTHING WITHOUT A REASON.
YOU CAN'T LET HIM DOWN, DUDE.

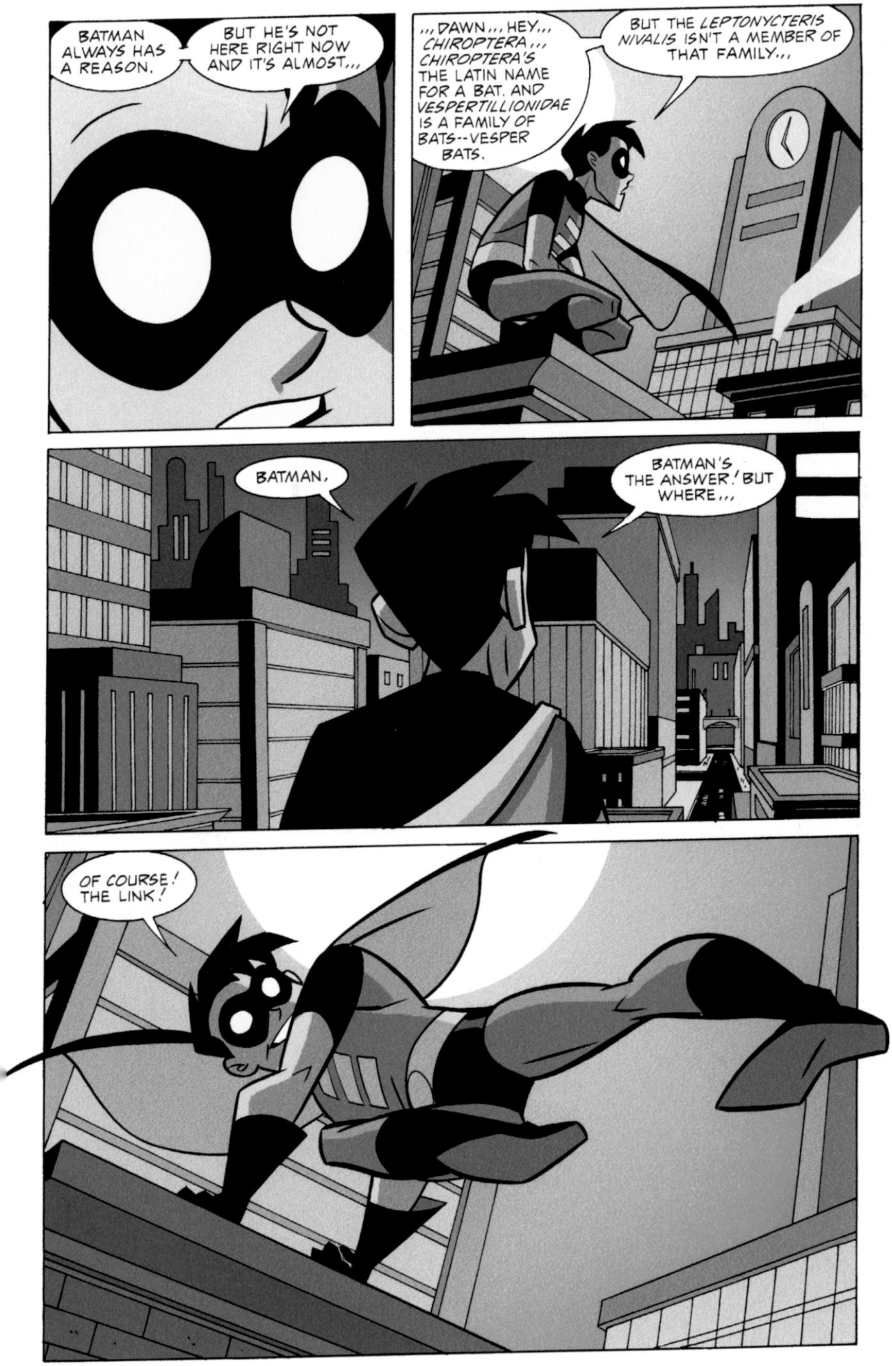
BATMAN ALWAYS HAS A REASON.
BUT HE'S NOT HERE RIGHT NOW AND IT'S ALMOST...
...DAWN... HEY... CHIROPTERA... CHIROPTERA'S THE LATIN NAME FOR A BAT. AND VESPERTILLIONIDAE IS A FAMILY OF BATS--VESPER BATS.
BUT THE LEPTONYCTERIS NIVALIS ISN'T A MEMBER OF THAT FAMILY...
BATMAN.
BATMAN'S THE ANSWER! BUT WHERE...
OF COURSE! THE LINK!

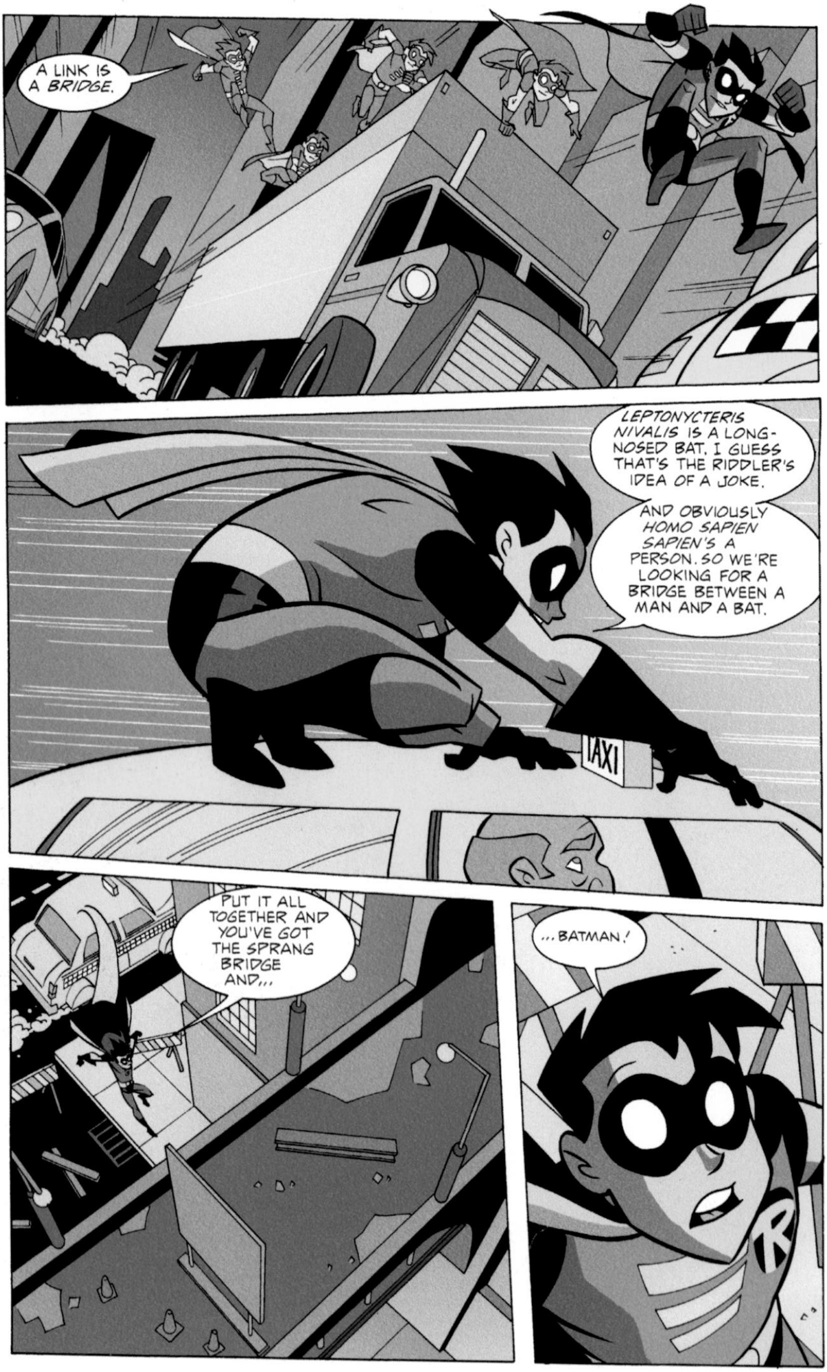
A LINK IS A *BRIDGE*.
LEPTONYCTERIS NIVALIS IS A LONG-NOSED BAT. I GUESS THAT'S THE RIDDLER'S IDEA OF A JOKE.
AND OBVIOUSLY *HOMO SAPIEN SAPIEN'S* A PERSON. SO WE'RE LOOKING FOR A BRIDGE BETWEEN A MAN AND A BAT.
TAXI
PUT IT ALL TOGETHER AND YOU'VE GOT THE SPRANG BRIDGE AND...
...BATMAN!

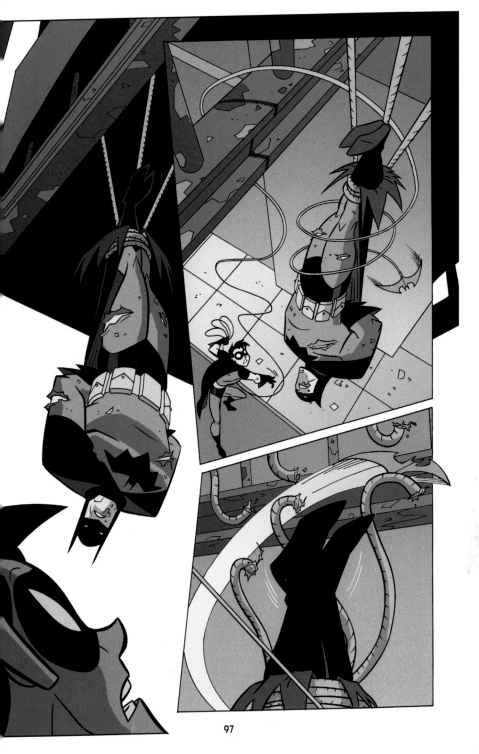

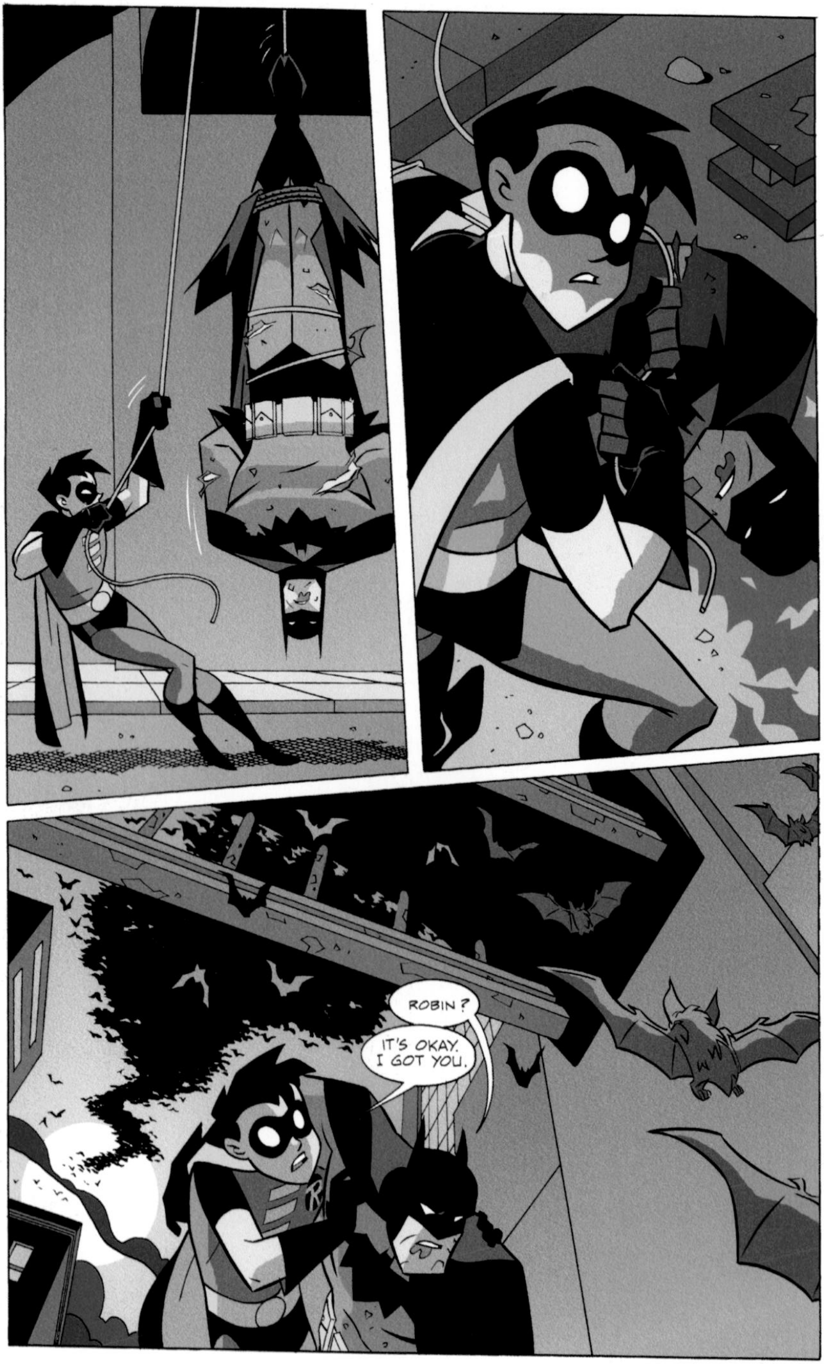
ROBIN?
IT'S OKAY. I GOT YOU.

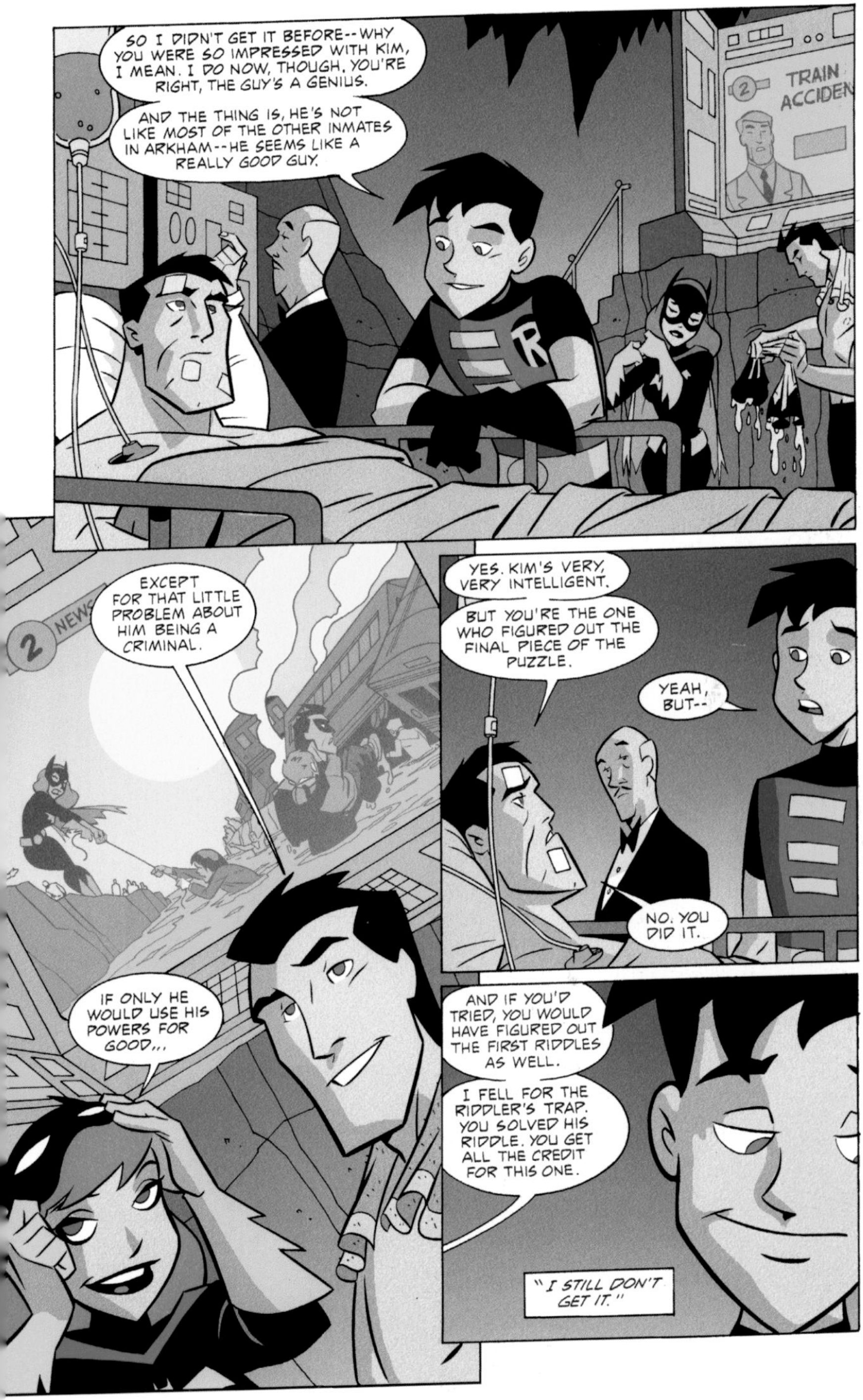
SO I DIDN'T GET IT BEFORE--WHY YOU WERE SO IMPRESSED WITH KIM, I MEAN. I DO NOW, THOUGH. YOU'RE RIGHT, THE GUY'S A GENIUS.
AND THE THING IS, HE'S NOT LIKE MOST OF THE OTHER INMATES IN ARKHAM--HE SEEMS LIKE A REALLY GOOD GUY.
2
TRAIN ACCIDEN
2 NEWS
EXCEPT FOR THAT LITTLE PROBLEM ABOUT HIM BEING A CRIMINAL.
IF ONLY HE WOULD USE HIS POWERS FOR GOOD...
YES. KIM'S VERY, VERY INTELLIGENT.
BUT YOU'RE THE ONE WHO FIGURED OUT THE FINAL PIECE OF THE PUZZLE.
YEAH, BUT--
NO. YOU DID IT.
AND IF YOU'D TRIED, YOU WOULD HAVE FIGURED OUT THE FIRST RIDDLES AS WELL.
I FELL FOR THE RIDDLER'S TRAP. YOU SOLVED HIS RIDDLE. YOU GET ALL THE CREDIT FOR THIS ONE.
"I STILL DON'T GET IT."

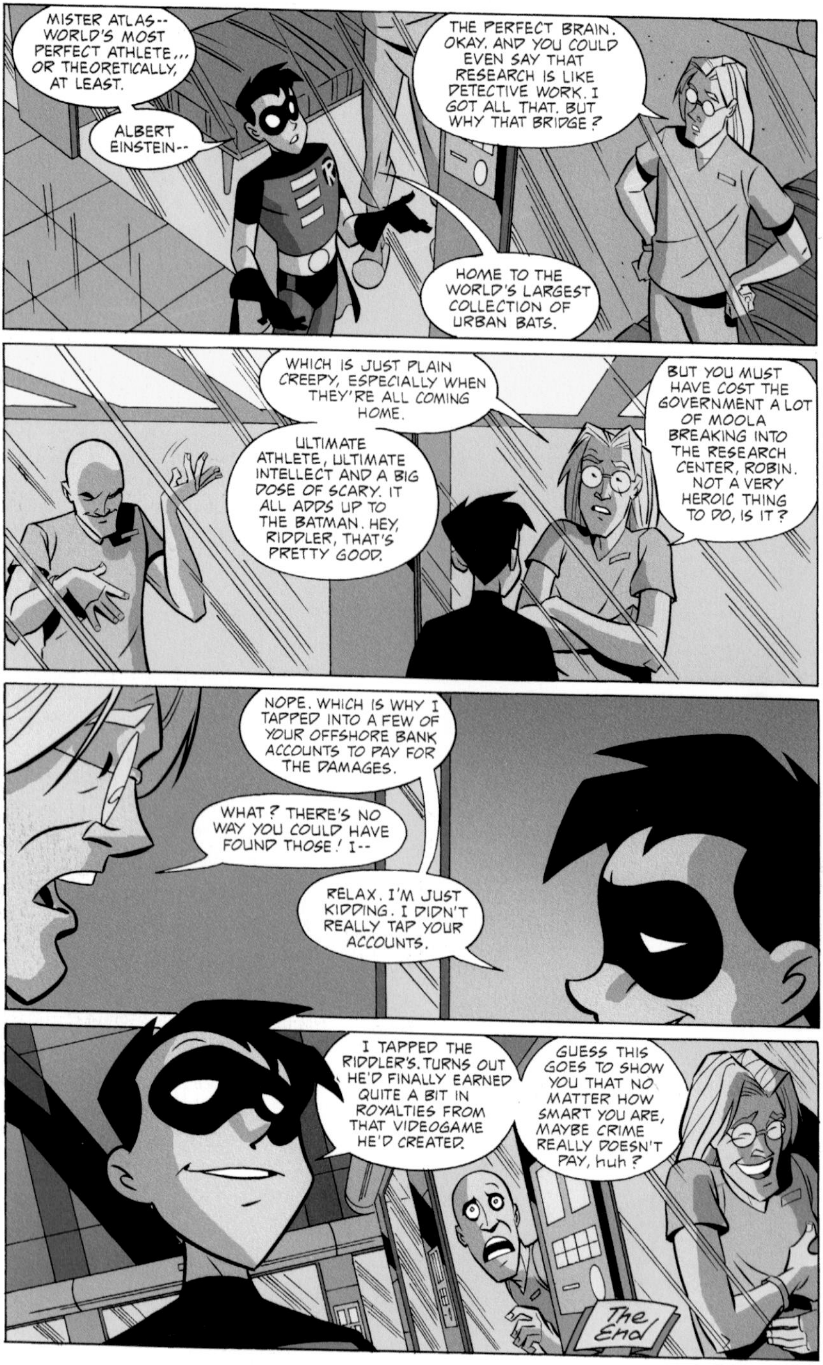
MISTER ATLAS-- WORLD'S MOST PERFECT ATHLETE... OR THEORETICALLY, AT LEAST.
ALBERT EINSTEIN--
THE PERFECT BRAIN. OKAY. AND YOU COULD EVEN SAY THAT RESEARCH IS LIKE DETECTIVE WORK. I GOT ALL THAT. BUT WHY THAT BRIDGE?
HOME TO THE WORLD'S LARGEST COLLECTION OF URBAN BATS.
WHICH IS JUST PLAIN CREEPY, ESPECIALLY WHEN THEY'RE ALL COMING HOME.
ULTIMATE ATHLETE, ULTIMATE INTELLECT AND A BIG DOSE OF SCARY. IT ALL ADDS UP TO THE BATMAN. HEY, RIDDLER, THAT'S PRETTY GOOD.
BUT YOU MUST HAVE COST THE GOVERNMENT A LOT OF MOOLA BREAKING INTO THE RESEARCH CENTER, ROBIN. NOT A VERY HEROIC THING TO DO, IS IT?
NOPE. WHICH IS WHY I TAPPED INTO A FEW OF YOUR OFFSHORE BANK ACCOUNTS TO PAY FOR THE DAMAGES.
WHAT? THERE'S NO WAY YOU COULD HAVE FOUND THOSE! I--
RELAX. I'M JUST KIDDING. I DIDN'T REALLY TAP YOUR ACCOUNTS.
I TAPPED THE RIDDLER'S. TURNS OUT HE'D FINALLY EARNED QUITE A BIT IN ROYALTIES FROM THAT VIDEOGAME HE'D CREATED.
GUESS THIS GOES TO SHOW YOU THAT NO MATTER HOW SMART YOU ARE, MAYBE CRIME REALLY DOESN'T PAY, huh?
The End

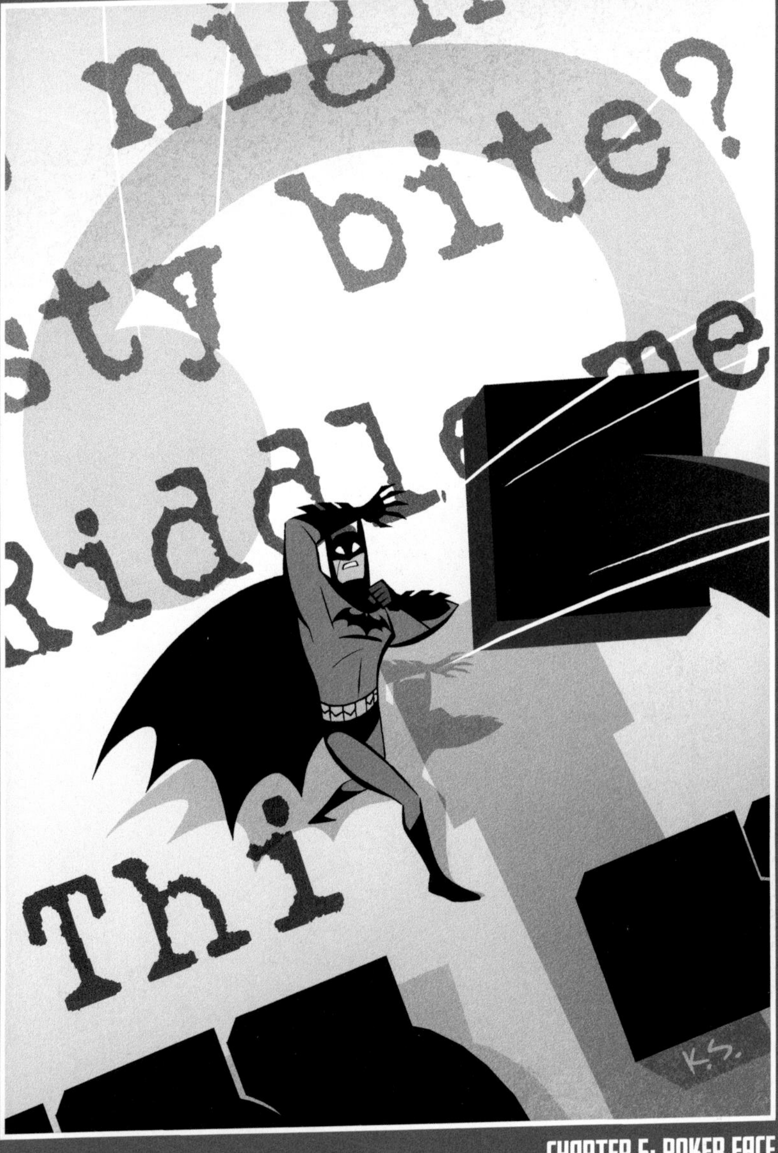

CHAPTER 5: POKER FACE

RIDDLE ME THIS

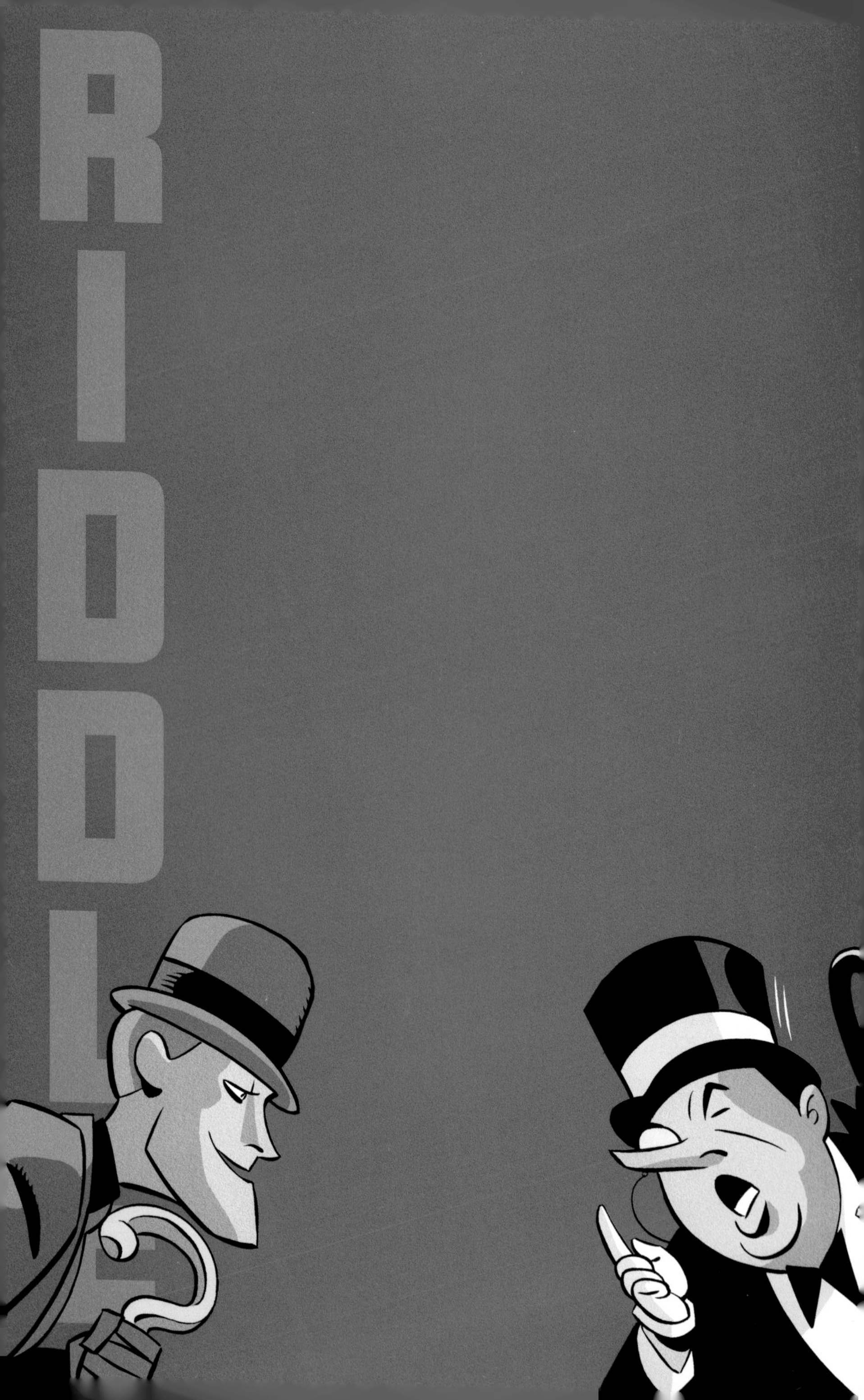

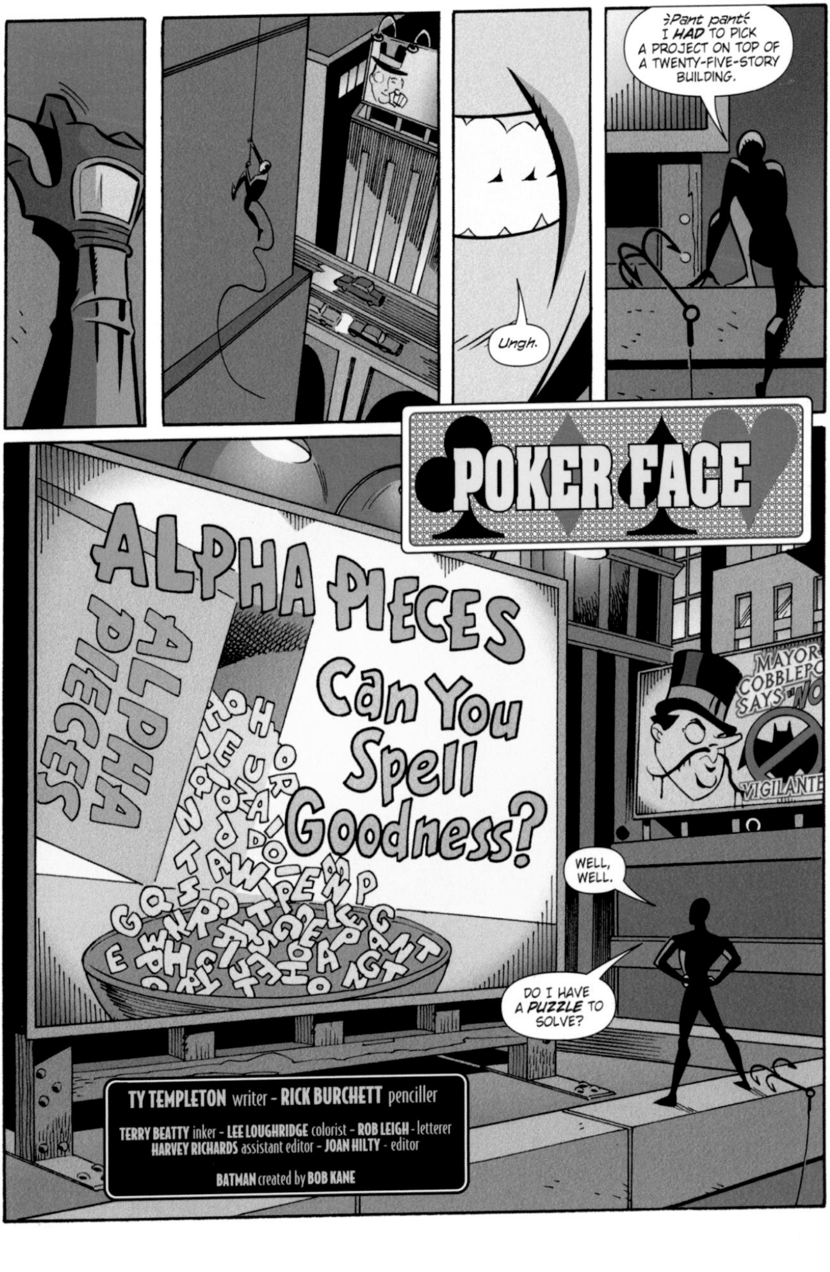
Ungh.
»Pant pant« I HAD TO PICK A PROJECT ON TOP OF A TWENTY-FIVE-STORY BUILDING.
POKER FACE
ALPHA PIECES
Can You Spell Goodness?
ALPHA PIECES
MAYOR COBBLEPO SAYS "NO" VIGILANTE
WELL, WELL.
DO I HAVE A PUZZLE TO SOLVE?
TY TEMPLETON writer - RICK BURCHETT penciller
TERRY BEATTY inker - LEE LOUGHRIDGE colorist - ROB LEIGH - letterer
HARVEY RICHARDS assistant editor - JOAN HILTY - editor
BATMAN created by BOB KANE

NEXT MORNING.

ALPHA PIECE

ALPHA P

Can You Spell Goodness

BATMAN Goodness

LARGEST ANT

PITTS HOME

FIVE A M

COME ALONE

I SAID THIS SORT OF THING WAS GOING TO **STOP!!**

GOTHAM GAZE

RIDDLER'S BACK!

HAS EDWARD NYGMA RETURNED TO A LIFE OF CRIME?

WHAT DO **YOU** CARE IF THE RIDDLER HAS A LITTLE FUN, MR. MAYOR? IT AIN'T ONE A' **YOUR** BILLBOARDS HE WAS DEFACING.

THE CITIZENS BEEN DOIN' ENOUGH OF **THAT** ON THEIR OWN.

I GAVE MY **WORD** TO THE PEOPLE OF THIS CITY I WOULD PUT AN **END** TO THE LUNATICS IN MASKS AND THEIR DANGEROUS GAMES.

MY INCOMPETENT POLICE FORCE MAY NOT BE ABLE TO BRING IN BATMAN, TO STAND TRIAL...

BUT WE **KNOW** WHERE NYGMA LIVES.

I GOT **BETTER** THAN KNOWING WHERE HE LIVES, BOSS.

I KNOW WHERE HE IS RIGHT **NOW...**

ON THE TV.

MR. NYGMA! MR. NYGMA! A **COMMENT,** PLEASE?

NYGMATECH

LIVE

104

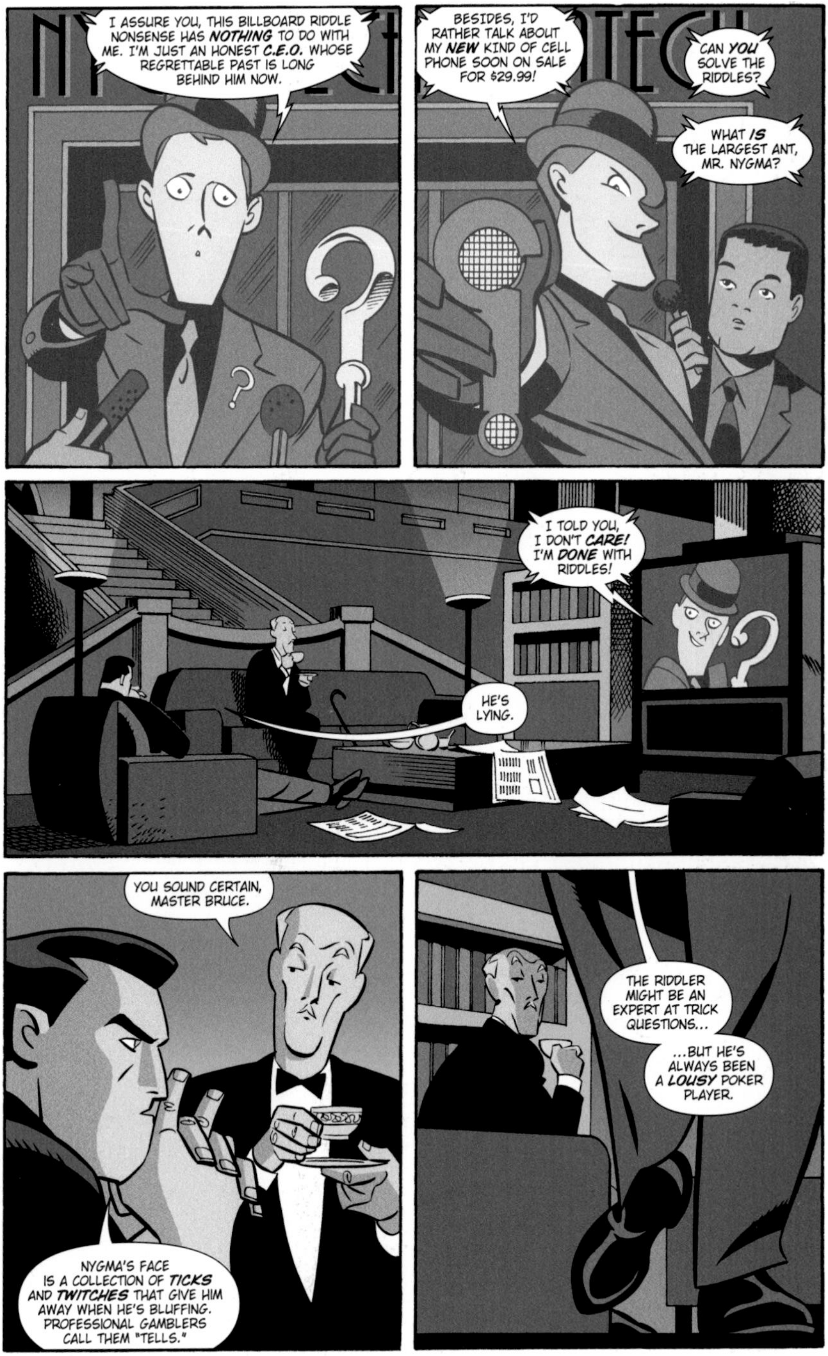
I ASSURE YOU, THIS BILLBOARD RIDDLE NONSENSE HAS **NOTHING** TO DO WITH ME. I'M JUST AN HONEST **C.E.O.** WHOSE REGRETTABLE PAST IS LONG BEHIND HIM NOW.
BESIDES, I'D RATHER TALK ABOUT MY **NEW** KIND OF CELL PHONE SOON ON SALE FOR $29.99!
CAN **YOU** SOLVE THE RIDDLES?
WHAT **IS** THE LARGEST ANT, MR. NYGMA?
I TOLD YOU, I DON'T **CARE!** I'M **DONE** WITH RIDDLES!
HE'S LYING.
YOU SOUND CERTAIN, MASTER BRUCE.
NYGMA'S FACE IS A COLLECTION OF **TICKS** AND **TWITCHES** THAT GIVE HIM AWAY WHEN HE'S BLUFFING. PROFESSIONAL GAMBLERS CALL THEM "TELLS."
THE RIDDLER MIGHT BE AN EXPERT AT TRICK QUESTIONS...
...BUT HE'S ALWAYS BEEN A **LOUSY** POKER PLAYER.

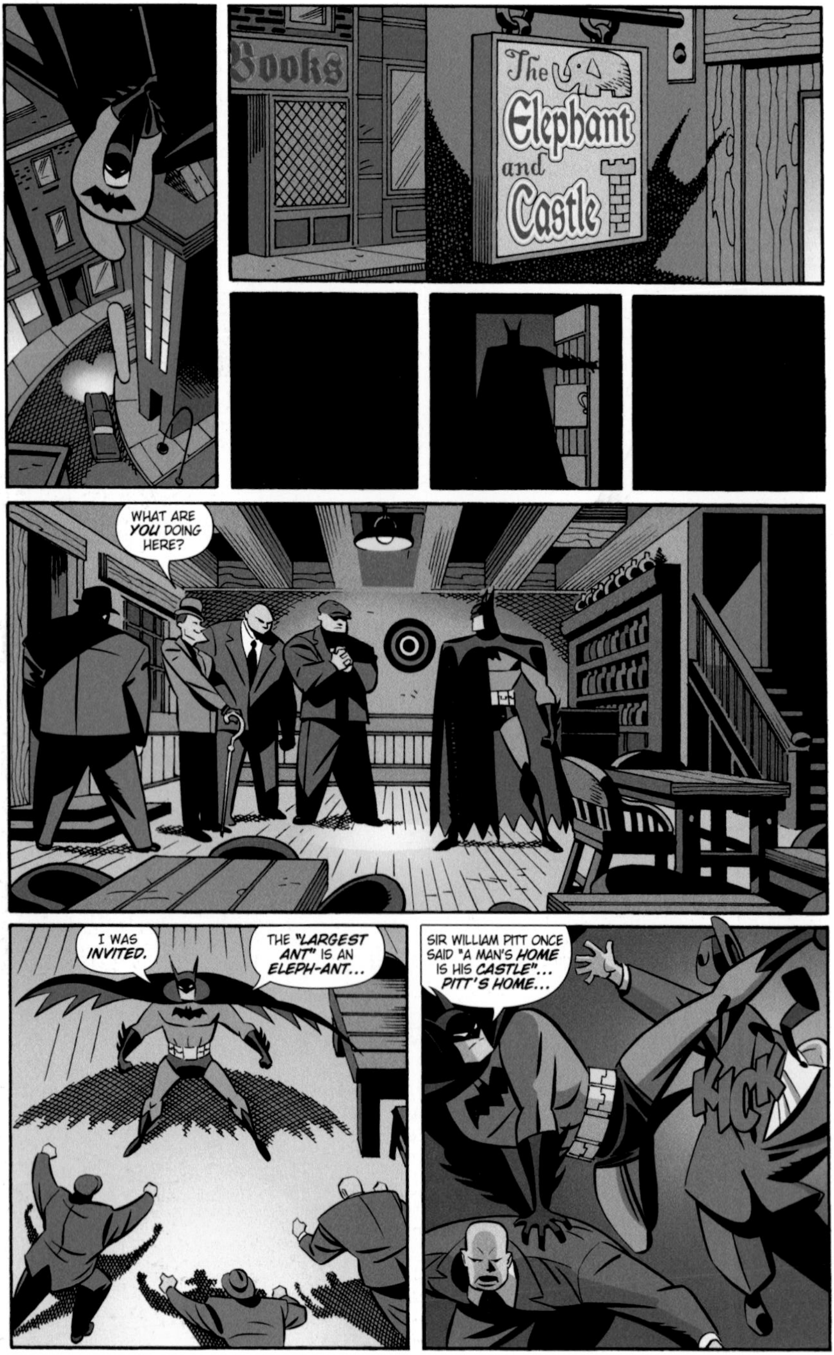
Books
The Elephant and Castle
WHAT ARE YOU DOING HERE?
I WAS INVITED.
THE "LARGEST ANT" IS AN ELEPH-ANT...
SIR WILLIAM PITT ONCE SAID "A MAN'S HOME IS HIS CASTLE"... PITT'S HOME...
KICK

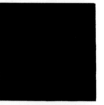

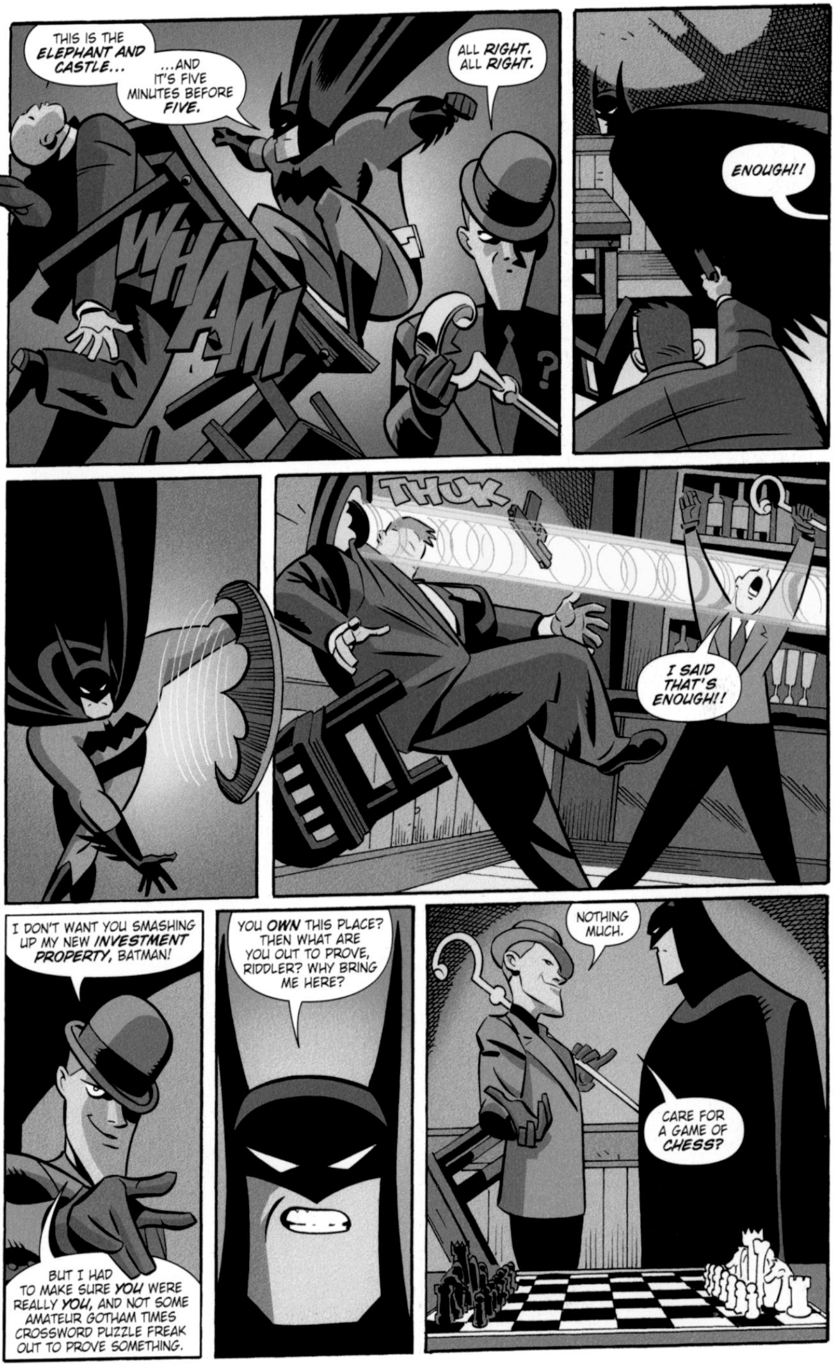
THIS IS THE ELEPHANT AND CASTLE...
...AND IT'S FIVE MINUTES BEFORE FIVE.
WHAM
ALL RIGHT. ALL RIGHT.
ENOUGH!!
THUK
I SAID THAT'S ENOUGH!!
I DON'T WANT YOU SMASHING UP MY NEW INVESTMENT PROPERTY, BATMAN!
BUT I HAD TO MAKE SURE YOU WERE REALLY YOU, AND NOT SOME AMATEUR GOTHAM TIMES CROSSWORD PUZZLE FREAK OUT TO PROVE SOMETHING.
YOU OWN THIS PLACE? THEN WHAT ARE YOU OUT TO PROVE, RIDDLER? WHY BRING ME HERE?
NOTHING MUCH.
CARE FOR A GAME OF CHESS?

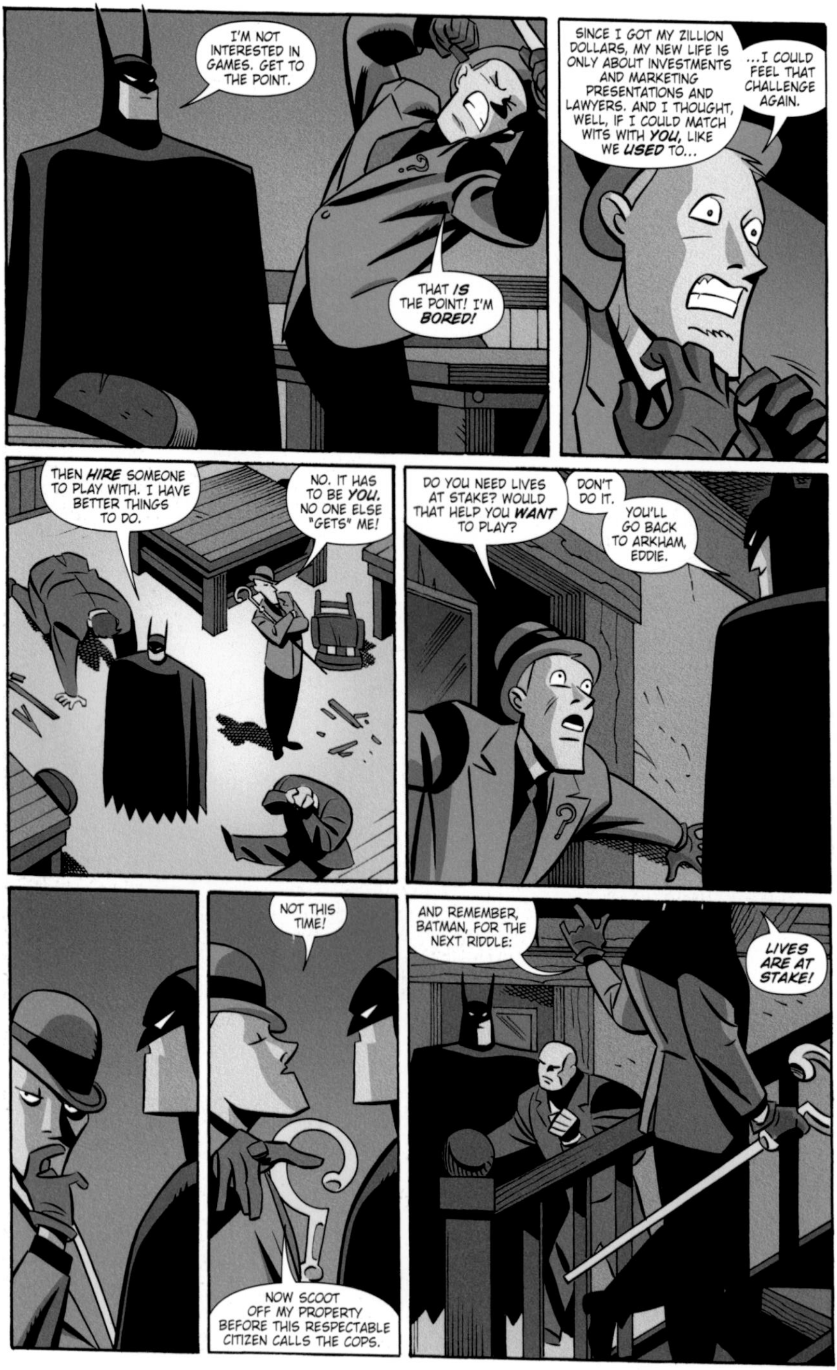
I'M NOT INTERESTED IN GAMES. GET TO THE POINT.
THAT IS THE POINT! I'M BORED!
SINCE I GOT MY ZILLION DOLLARS, MY NEW LIFE IS ONLY ABOUT INVESTMENTS AND MARKETING PRESENTATIONS AND LAWYERS. AND I THOUGHT, WELL, IF I COULD MATCH WITS WITH YOU, LIKE WE USED TO...
...I COULD FEEL THAT CHALLENGE AGAIN.
THEN HIRE SOMEONE TO PLAY WITH. I HAVE BETTER THINGS TO DO.
NO. IT HAS TO BE YOU. NO ONE ELSE "GETS" ME!
DO YOU NEED LIVES AT STAKE? WOULD THAT HELP YOU WANT TO PLAY?
DON'T DO IT.
YOU'LL GO BACK TO ARKHAM, EDDIE.
NOT THIS TIME!
NOW SCOOT OFF MY PROPERTY BEFORE THIS RESPECTABLE CITIZEN CALLS THE COPS.
AND REMEMBER, BATMAN, FOR THE NEXT RIDDLE:
LIVES ARE AT STAKE!

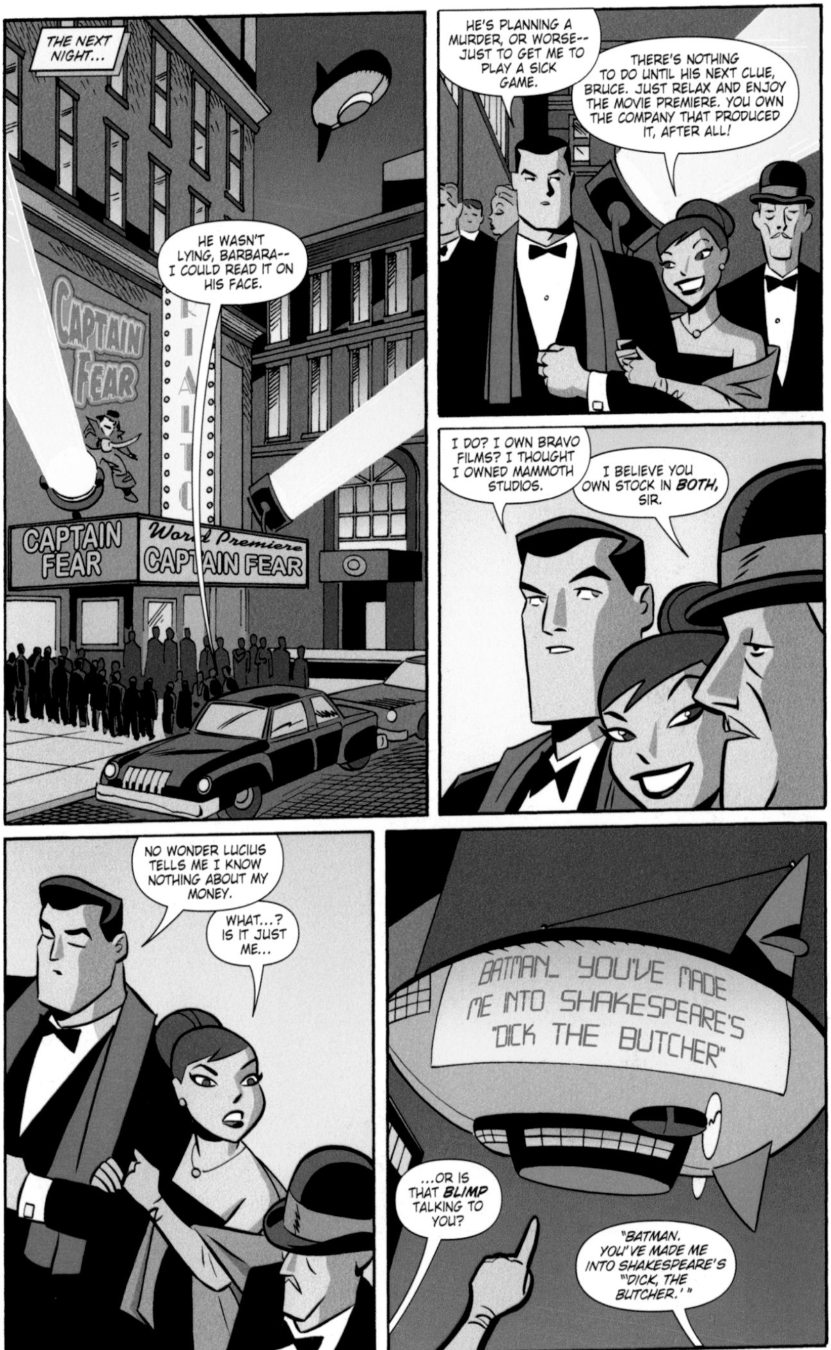
THE NEXT NIGHT...
HE WASN'T LYING, BARBARA-- I COULD READ IT ON HIS FACE.
CAPTAIN FEAR
RIALTO
CAPTAIN FEAR
World Premiere
CAPTAIN FEAR
HE'S PLANNING A MURDER, OR WORSE-- JUST TO GET ME TO PLAY A SICK GAME.
THERE'S NOTHING TO DO UNTIL HIS NEXT CLUE, BRUCE. JUST RELAX AND ENJOY THE MOVIE PREMIERE. YOU OWN THE COMPANY THAT PRODUCED IT, AFTER ALL!
I DO? I OWN BRAVO FILMS? I THOUGHT I OWNED MAMMOTH STUDIOS.
I BELIEVE YOU OWN STOCK IN BOTH, SIR.
NO WONDER LUCIUS TELLS ME I KNOW NOTHING ABOUT MY MONEY.
WHAT...? IS IT JUST ME...
BATMAN_ YOU'VE MADE ME INTO SHAKESPEARE'S "DICK THE BUTCHER"
...OR IS THAT BLIMP TALKING TO YOU?
"BATMAN. YOU'VE MADE ME INTO SHAKESPEARE'S "DICK, THE BUTCHER.' "

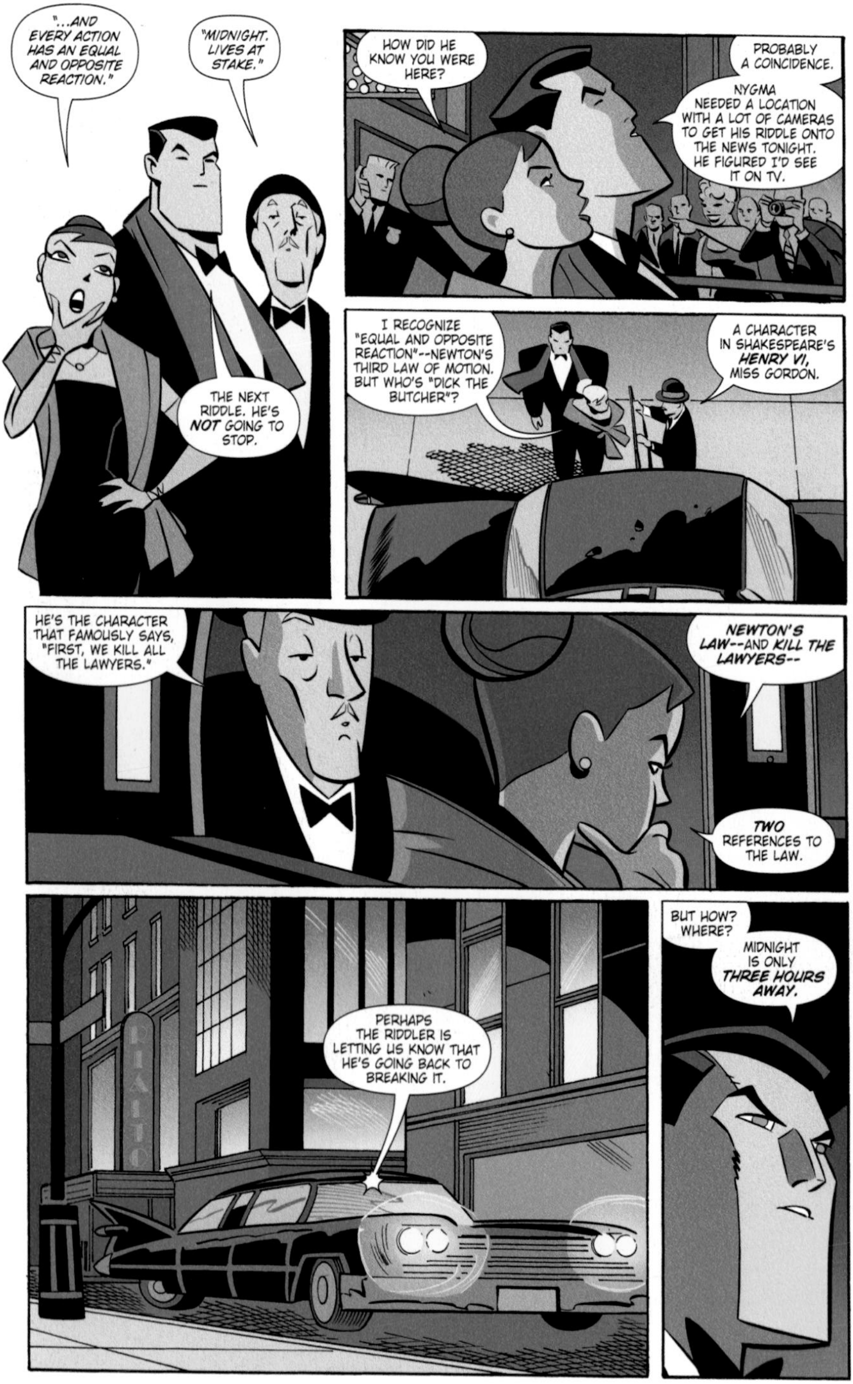
"...AND EVERY ACTION HAS AN EQUAL AND OPPOSITE REACTION."
"MIDNIGHT. LIVES AT STAKE."
THE NEXT RIDDLE. HE'S NOT GOING TO STOP.
HOW DID HE KNOW YOU WERE HERE?
PROBABLY A COINCIDENCE.
NYGMA NEEDED A LOCATION WITH A LOT OF CAMERAS TO GET HIS RIDDLE ONTO THE NEWS TONIGHT. HE FIGURED I'D SEE IT ON TV.
I RECOGNIZE "EQUAL AND OPPOSITE REACTION"--NEWTON'S THIRD LAW OF MOTION. BUT WHO'S "DICK THE BUTCHER"?
A CHARACTER IN SHAKESPEARE'S HENRY VI, MISS GORDON.
HE'S THE CHARACTER THAT FAMOUSLY SAYS, "FIRST, WE KILL ALL THE LAWYERS."
NEWTON'S LAW--AND KILL THE LAWYERS--
TWO REFERENCES TO THE LAW.
PERHAPS THE RIDDLER IS LETTING US KNOW THAT HE'S GOING BACK TO BREAKING IT.
BUT HOW? WHERE?
MIDNIGHT IS ONLY THREE HOURS AWAY.

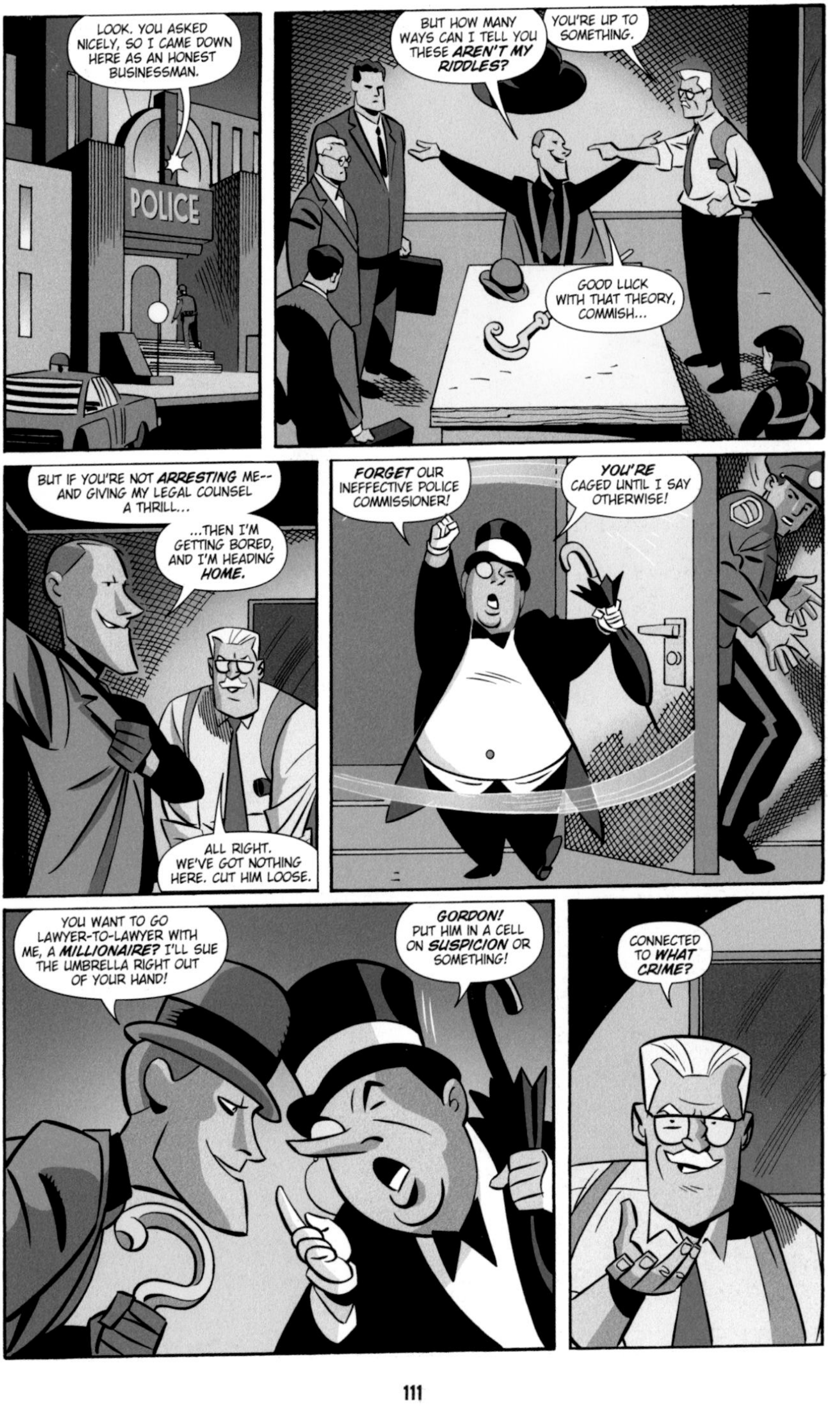
LOOK. YOU ASKED NICELY, SO I CAME DOWN HERE AS AN HONEST BUSINESSMAN.
POLICE
BUT HOW MANY WAYS CAN I TELL YOU THESE AREN'T MY RIDDLES?
YOU'RE UP TO SOMETHING.
GOOD LUCK WITH THAT THEORY, COMMISH...
BUT IF YOU'RE NOT ARRESTING ME-- AND GIVING MY LEGAL COUNSEL A THRILL...
...THEN I'M GETTING BORED, AND I'M HEADING HOME.
ALL RIGHT. WE'VE GOT NOTHING HERE. CUT HIM LOOSE.
FORGET OUR INEFFECTIVE POLICE COMMISSIONER!
YOU'RE CAGED UNTIL I SAY OTHERWISE!
YOU WANT TO GO LAWYER-TO-LAWYER WITH ME, A MILLIONAIRE? I'LL SUE THE UMBRELLA RIGHT OUT OF YOUR HAND!
GORDON! PUT HIM IN A CELL ON SUSPICION OR SOMETHING!
CONNECTED TO WHAT CRIME?

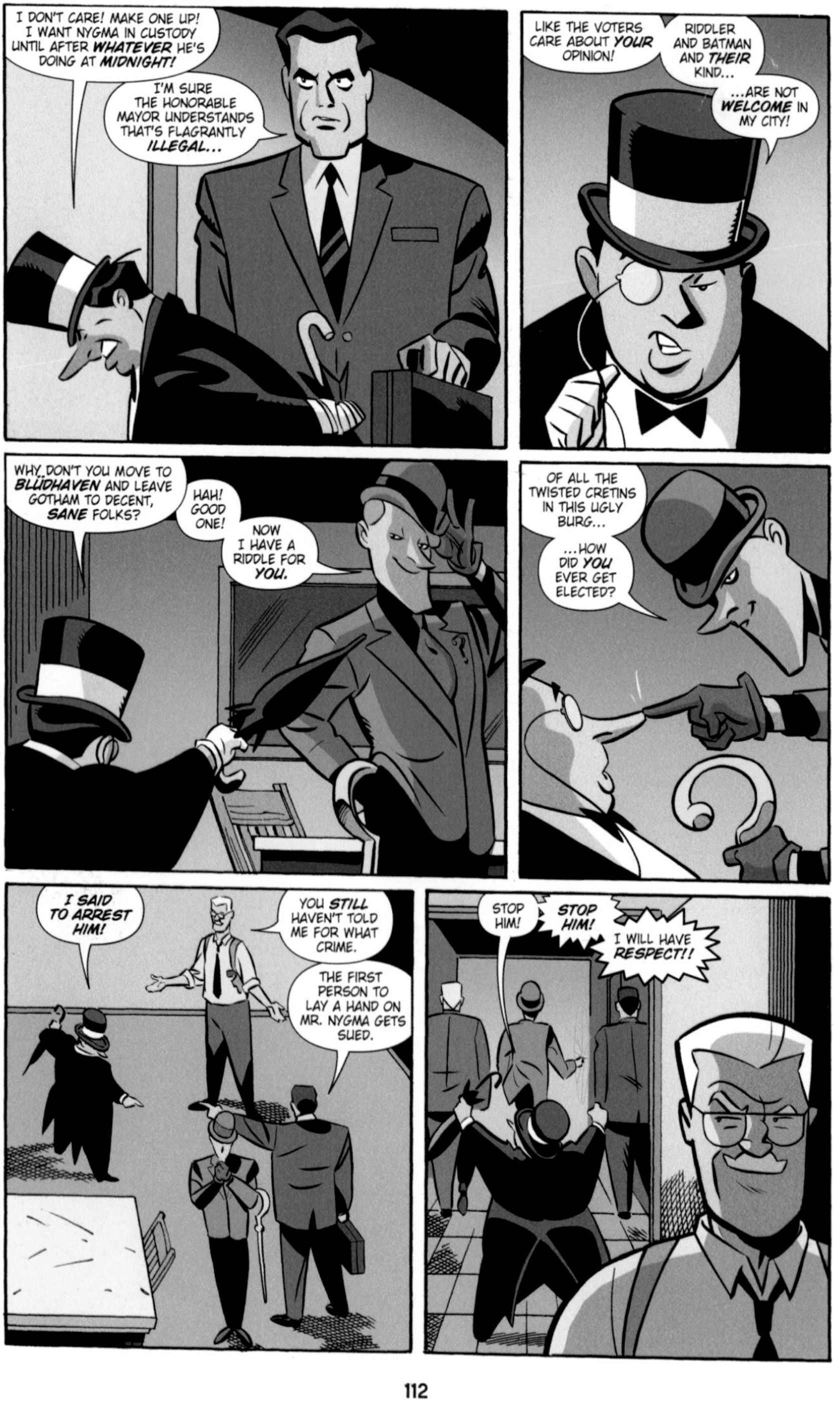
I DON'T CARE! MAKE ONE UP! I WANT NYGMA IN CUSTODY UNTIL AFTER WHATEVER HE'S DOING AT MIDNIGHT!
I'M SURE THE HONORABLE MAYOR UNDERSTANDS THAT'S FLAGRANTLY ILLEGAL...
LIKE THE VOTERS CARE ABOUT YOUR OPINION!
RIDDLER AND BATMAN AND THEIR KIND...
...ARE NOT WELCOME IN MY CITY!
WHY DON'T YOU MOVE TO BLÜDHAVEN AND LEAVE GOTHAM TO DECENT, SANE FOLKS?
HAH! GOOD ONE!
NOW I HAVE A RIDDLE FOR YOU.
OF ALL THE TWISTED CRETINS IN THIS UGLY BURG...
...HOW DID YOU EVER GET ELECTED?
I SAID TO ARREST HIM!
YOU STILL HAVEN'T TOLD ME FOR WHAT CRIME.
THE FIRST PERSON TO LAY A HAND ON MR. NYGMA GETS SUED.
STOP HIM!
STOP HIM!
I WILL HAVE RESPECT!!

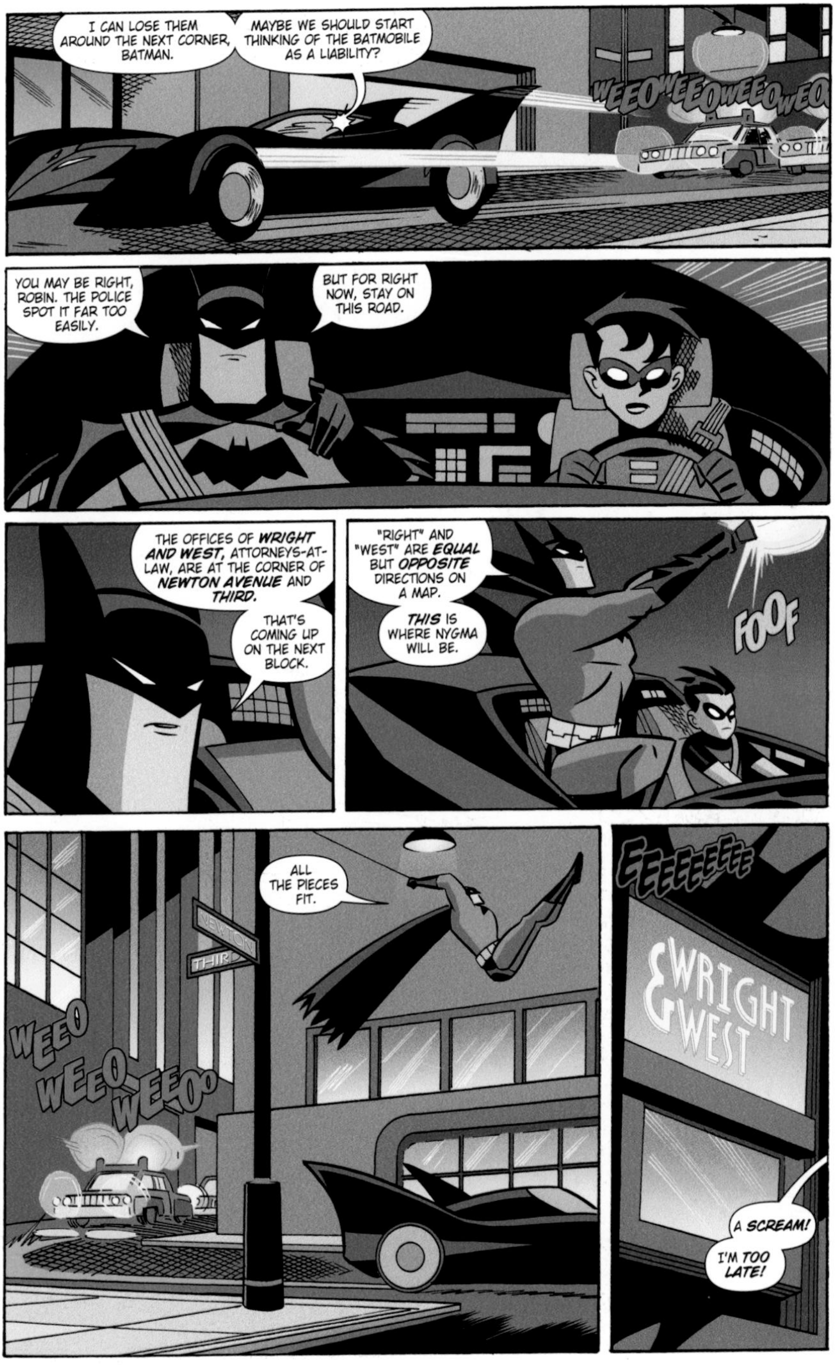
I CAN LOSE THEM AROUND THE NEXT CORNER, BATMAN.
MAYBE WE SHOULD START THINKING OF THE BATMOBILE AS A LIABILITY?
WEEOWEEOWEEOWEO
YOU MAY BE RIGHT, ROBIN. THE POLICE SPOT IT FAR TOO EASILY.
BUT FOR RIGHT NOW, STAY ON THIS ROAD.
THE OFFICES OF WRIGHT AND WEST, ATTORNEYS-AT-LAW, ARE AT THE CORNER OF NEWTON AVENUE AND THIRD.
THAT'S COMING UP ON THE NEXT BLOCK.
"RIGHT" AND "WEST" ARE EQUAL BUT OPPOSITE DIRECTIONS ON A MAP.
THIS IS WHERE NYGMA WILL BE.
FOOF
ALL THE PIECES FIT.
NEWTON
THIRD
WEEO WEEO WEEOo
EEEEEEEEE
WRIGHT & WEST
A SCREAM!
I'M TOO LATE!

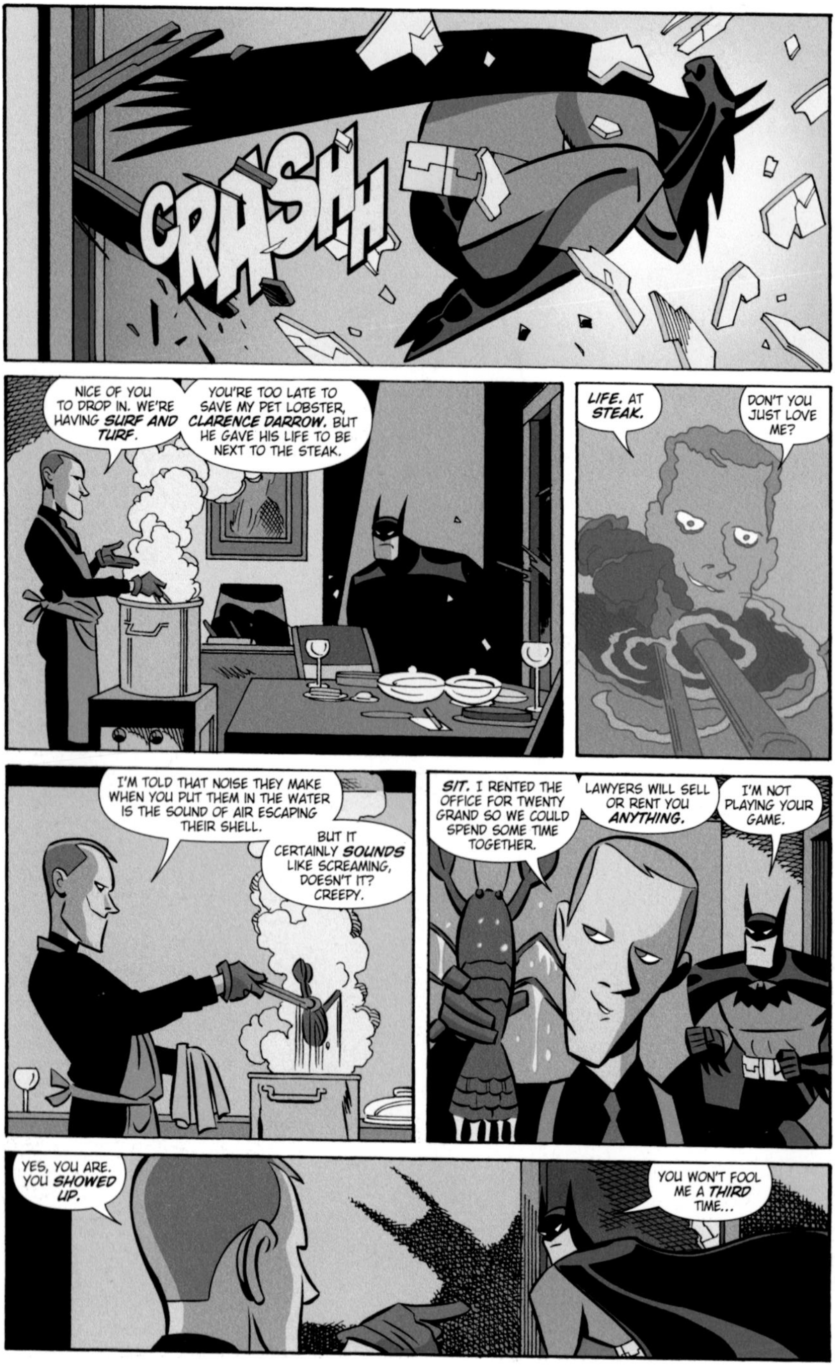
CRASHH
NICE OF YOU TO DROP IN. WE'RE HAVING SURF AND TURF.
YOU'RE TOO LATE TO SAVE MY PET LOBSTER, CLARENCE DARROW. BUT HE GAVE HIS LIFE TO BE NEXT TO THE STEAK.
LIFE. AT STEAK.
DON'T YOU JUST LOVE ME?
I'M TOLD THAT NOISE THEY MAKE WHEN YOU PUT THEM IN THE WATER IS THE SOUND OF AIR ESCAPING THEIR SHELL.
BUT IT CERTAINLY SOUNDS LIKE SCREAMING, DOESN'T IT? CREEPY.
SIT. I RENTED THE OFFICE FOR TWENTY GRAND SO WE COULD SPEND SOME TIME TOGETHER.
LAWYERS WILL SELL OR RENT YOU ANYTHING.
I'M NOT PLAYING YOUR GAME.
YES, YOU ARE. YOU SHOWED UP.
YOU WON'T FOOL ME A THIRD TIME...

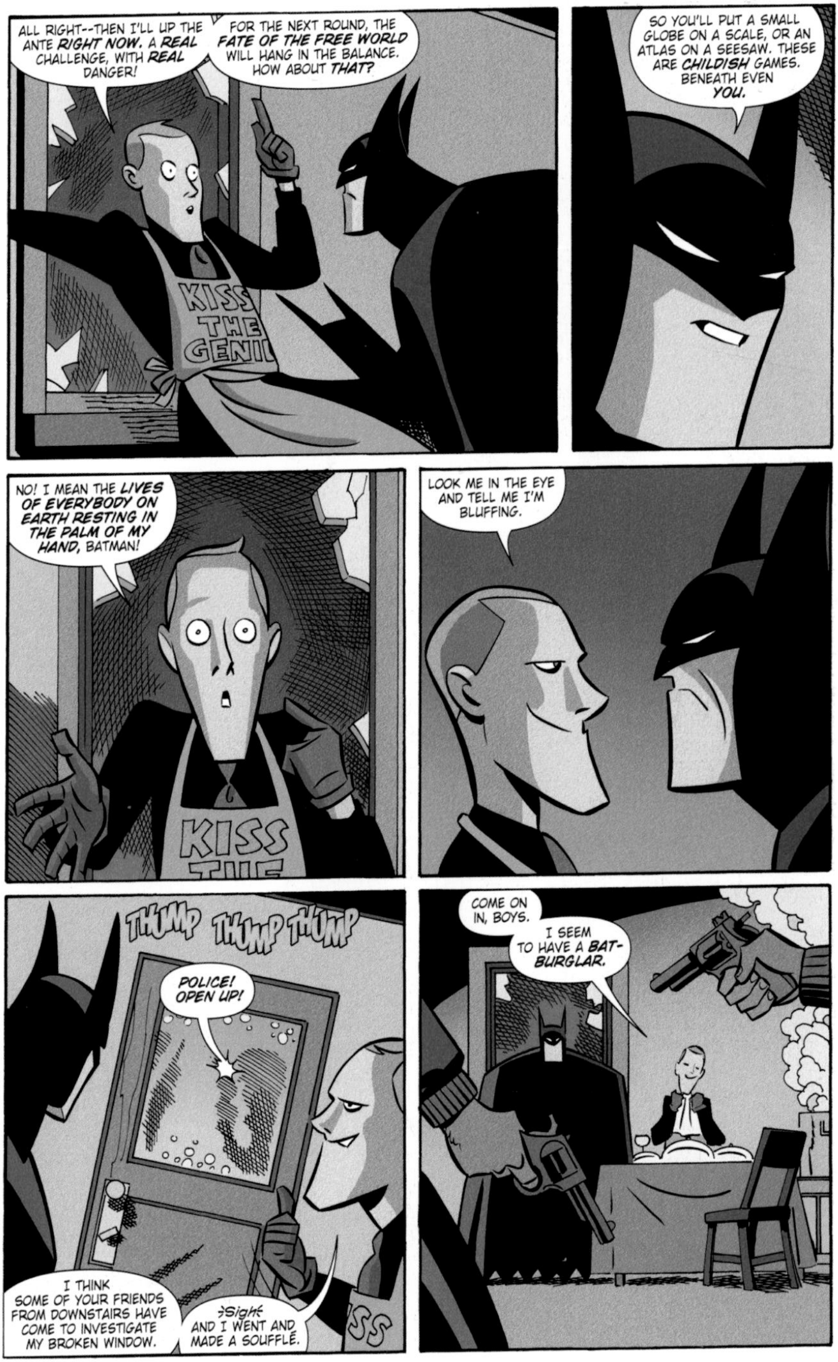
ALL RIGHT--THEN I'LL UP THE ANTE RIGHT NOW. A REAL CHALLENGE, WITH REAL DANGER!
FOR THE NEXT ROUND, THE FATE OF THE FREE WORLD WILL HANG IN THE BALANCE. HOW ABOUT THAT?
KISS THE GENI
SO YOU'LL PUT A SMALL GLOBE ON A SCALE, OR AN ATLAS ON A SEESAW. THESE ARE CHILDISH GAMES. BENEATH EVEN YOU.
NO! I MEAN THE LIVES OF EVERYBODY ON EARTH RESTING IN THE PALM OF MY HAND, BATMAN!
KISS
LOOK ME IN THE EYE AND TELL ME I'M BLUFFING.
THUMP THUMP THUMP
POLICE! OPEN UP!
I THINK SOME OF YOUR FRIENDS FROM DOWNSTAIRS HAVE COME TO INVESTIGATE MY BROKEN WINDOW.
Sigh
AND I WENT AND MADE A SOUFFLÉ.
COME ON IN, BOYS.
I SEEM TO HAVE A BAT-BURGLAR.

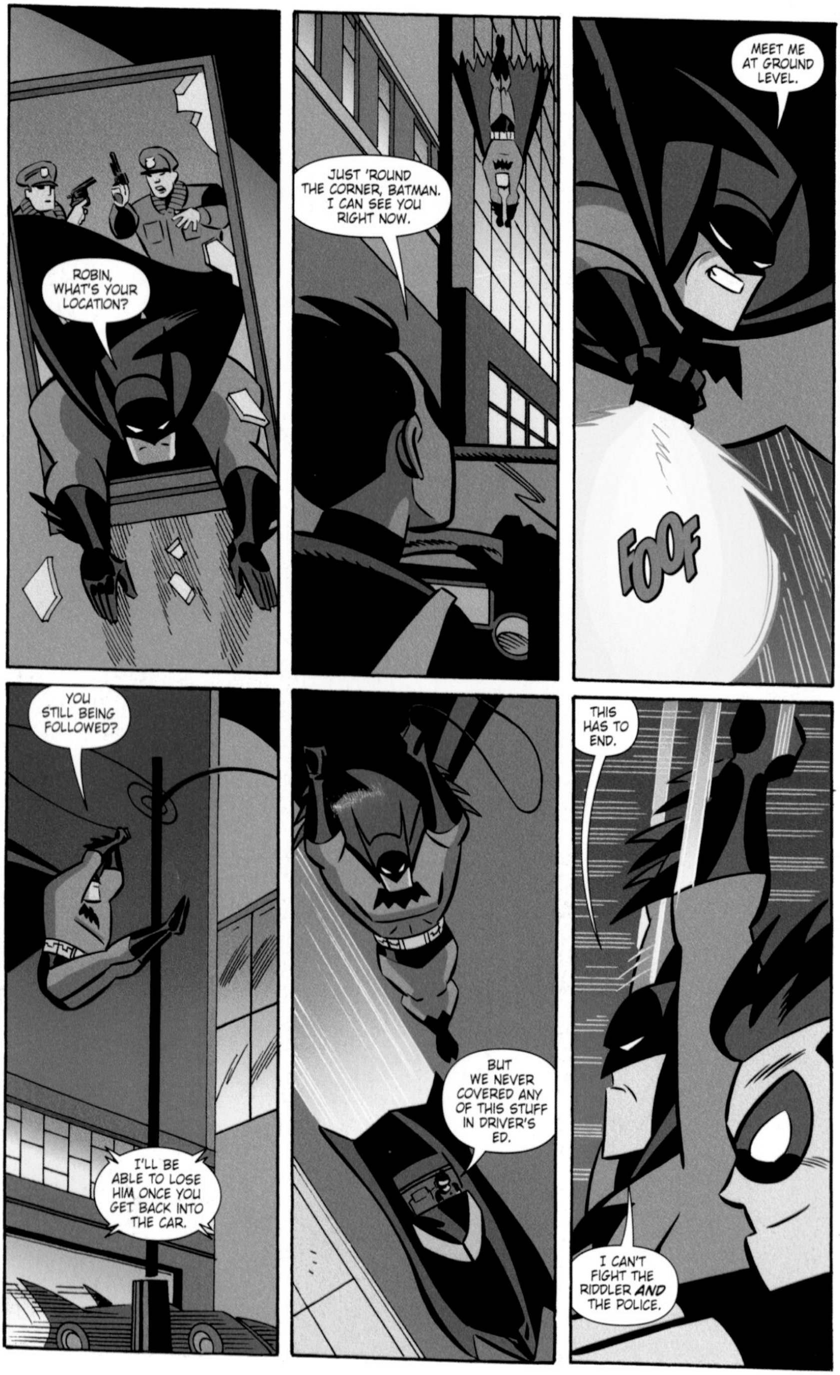
ROBIN, WHAT'S YOUR LOCATION?
JUST 'ROUND THE CORNER, BATMAN. I CAN SEE YOU RIGHT NOW.
MEET ME AT GROUND LEVEL.
FOOF
YOU STILL BEING FOLLOWED?
I'LL BE ABLE TO LOSE HIM ONCE YOU GET BACK INTO THE CAR.
BUT WE NEVER COVERED ANY OF THIS STUFF IN DRIVER'S ED.
THIS HAS TO END.
I CAN'T FIGHT THE RIDDLER AND THE POLICE.

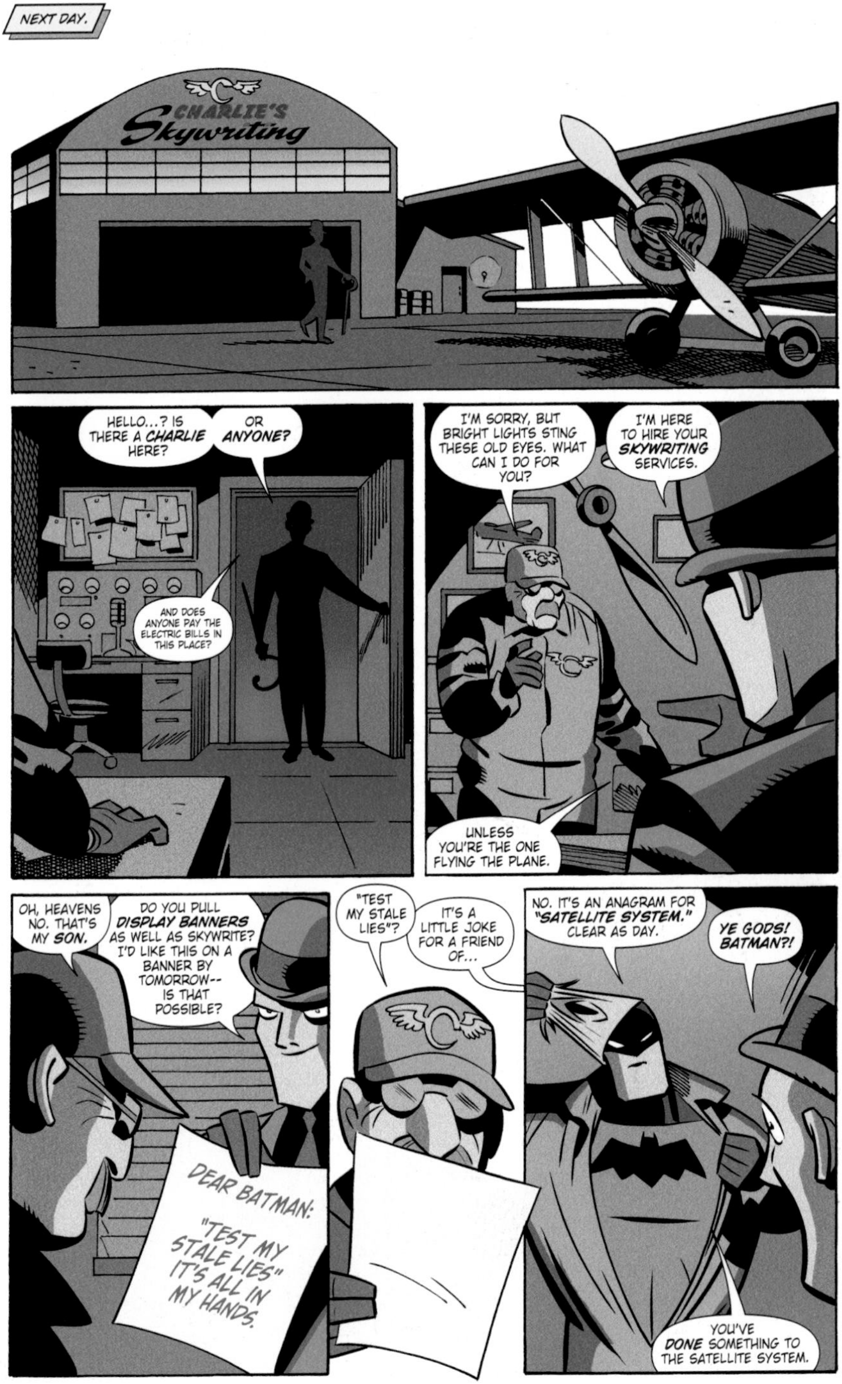
NEXT DAY.
CHARLIE'S Skywriting
HELLO...? IS THERE A CHARLIE HERE?
OR ANYONE?
AND DOES ANYONE PAY THE ELECTRIC BILLS IN THIS PLACE?
I'M SORRY, BUT BRIGHT LIGHTS STING THESE OLD EYES. WHAT CAN I DO FOR YOU?
I'M HERE TO HIRE YOUR SKYWRITING SERVICES.
UNLESS YOU'RE THE ONE FLYING THE PLANE.
OH, HEAVENS NO. THAT'S MY SON.
DO YOU PULL DISPLAY BANNERS AS WELL AS SKYWRITE? I'D LIKE THIS ON A BANNER BY TOMORROW-- IS THAT POSSIBLE?
DEAR BATMAN: "TEST MY STALE LIES" IT'S ALL IN MY HANDS.
"TEST MY STALE LIES"?
IT'S A LITTLE JOKE FOR A FRIEND OF...
NO. IT'S AN ANAGRAM FOR "SATELLITE SYSTEM." CLEAR AS DAY.
YE GODS! BATMAN?!
YOU'VE DONE SOMETHING TO THE SATELLITE SYSTEM.

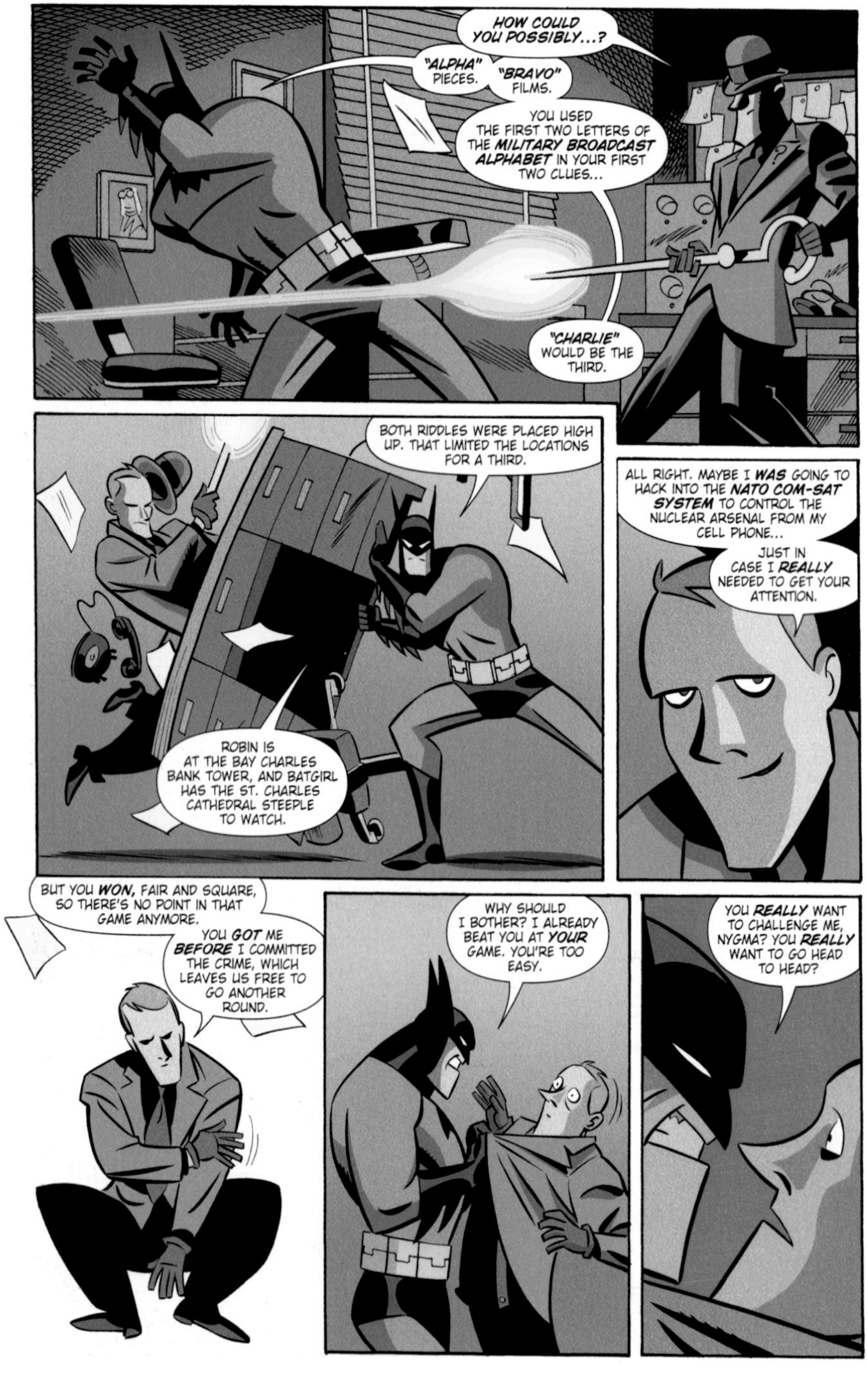

HOW COULD YOU POSSIBLY...?
"ALPHA" PIECES.
"BRAVO" FILMS.
YOU USED THE FIRST TWO LETTERS OF THE MILITARY BROADCAST ALPHABET IN YOUR FIRST TWO CLUES...
"CHARLIE" WOULD BE THE THIRD.
BOTH RIDDLES WERE PLACED HIGH UP. THAT LIMITED THE LOCATIONS FOR A THIRD.
ROBIN IS AT THE BAY CHARLES BANK TOWER, AND BATGIRL HAS THE ST. CHARLES CATHEDRAL STEEPLE TO WATCH.
ALL RIGHT. MAYBE I WAS GOING TO HACK INTO THE NATO COM-SAT SYSTEM TO CONTROL THE NUCLEAR ARSENAL FROM MY CELL PHONE...
JUST IN CASE I REALLY NEEDED TO GET YOUR ATTENTION.
BUT YOU WON, FAIR AND SQUARE, SO THERE'S NO POINT IN THAT GAME ANYMORE.
YOU GOT ME BEFORE I COMMITTED THE CRIME, WHICH LEAVES US FREE TO GO ANOTHER ROUND.
WHY SHOULD I BOTHER? I ALREADY BEAT YOU AT YOUR GAME. YOU'RE TOO EASY.
YOU REALLY WANT TO CHALLENGE ME, NYGMA? YOU REALLY WANT TO GO HEAD TO HEAD?

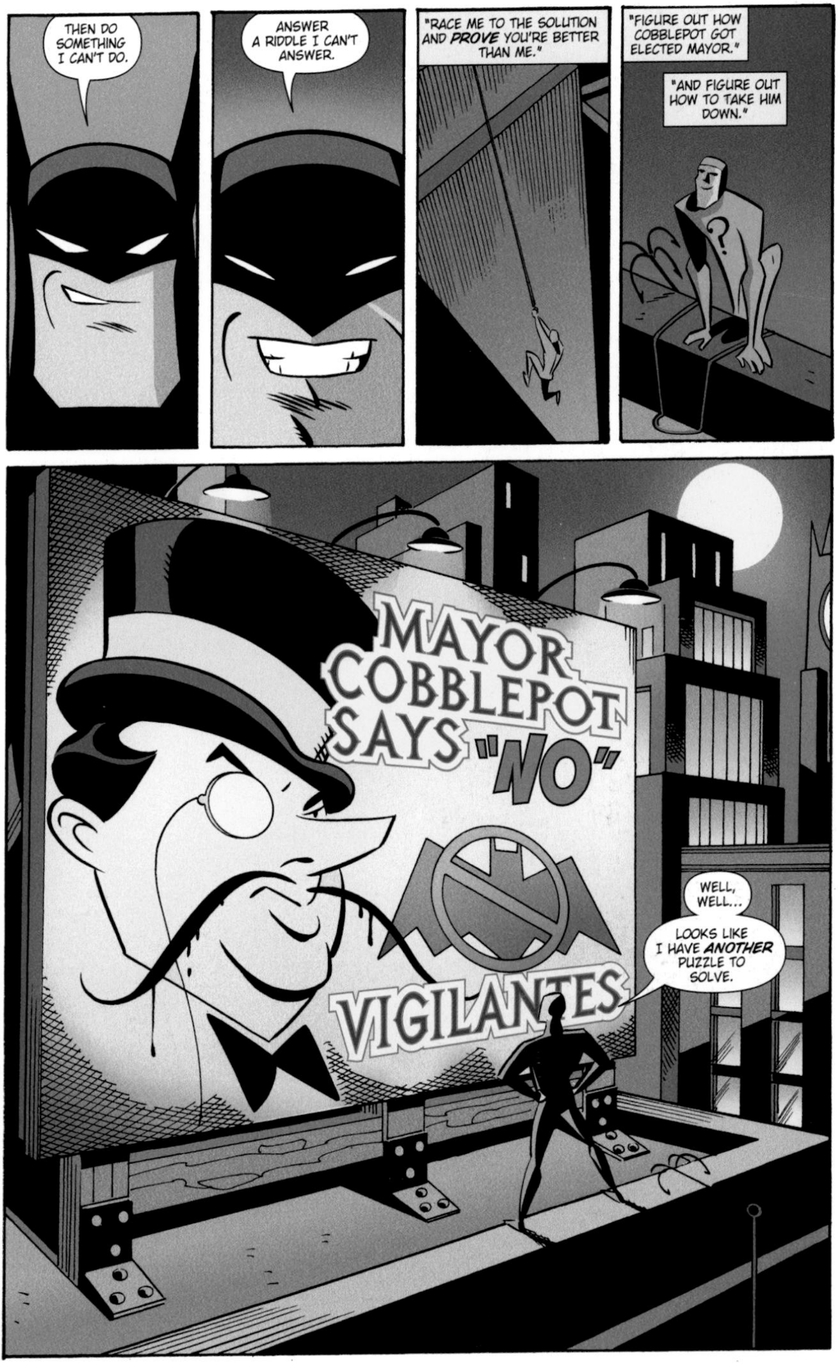
THEN DO SOMETHING I CAN'T DO.
ANSWER A RIDDLE I CAN'T ANSWER.
"RACE ME TO THE SOLUTION AND PROVE YOU'RE BETTER THAN ME."
"FIGURE OUT HOW COBBLEPOT GOT ELECTED MAYOR."
"AND FIGURE OUT HOW TO TAKE HIM DOWN."
MAYOR COBBLEPOT SAYS "NO" VIGILANTES
WELL, WELL...
LOOKS LIKE I HAVE ANOTHER PUZZLE TO SOLVE.

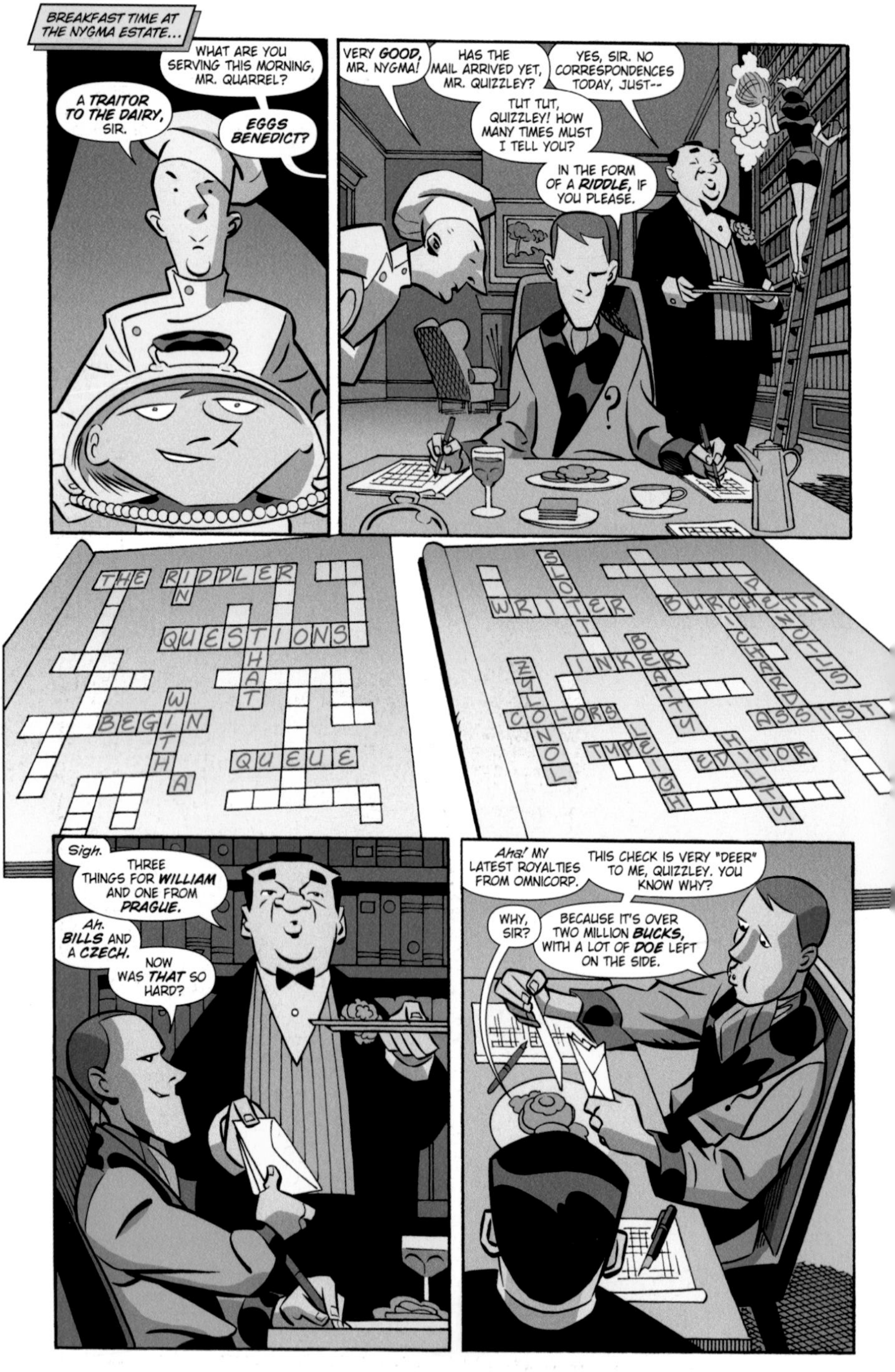
BREAKFAST TIME AT THE NYGMA ESTATE...
WHAT ARE YOU SERVING THIS MORNING, MR. QUARREL?
A TRAITOR TO THE DAIRY, SIR.
EGGS BENEDICT?
VERY GOOD, MR. NYGMA!
HAS THE MAIL ARRIVED YET, MR. QUIZZLEY?
YES, SIR. NO CORRESPONDENCES TODAY, JUST--
TUT TUT, QUIZZLEY! HOW MANY TIMES MUST I TELL YOU?
IN THE FORM OF A RIDDLE, IF YOU PLEASE.
THE RIDDLER
IN
QUESTIONS
THAT
BEGIN
WITH A
QUEUE
SLOTT
WRITER
BURCHETT
PENCILS
RICHARD
INKER
BEATTY
ZYLONOL
COLORS
TYPE
LEIGH
ASSIST
EDITOR
HILTY
Sigh.
THREE THINGS FOR WILLIAM AND ONE FROM PRAGUE.
Ah. BILLS AND A CZECH.
NOW WAS THAT SO HARD?
Aha! MY LATEST ROYALTIES FROM OMNICORP.
THIS CHECK IS VERY "DEER" TO ME, QUIZZLEY. YOU KNOW WHY?
WHY, SIR?
BECAUSE IT'S OVER TWO MILLION BUCKS, WITH A LOT OF DOE LEFT ON THE SIDE.

"IT'S SUCH A LOVELY DAY, WHY DON'T I DROP BY THE BANK AND DEPOSIT THIS MYSELF?"

GUESS THE NUMBER OF JELLYBEANS AND WIN A HAM

HEY!

SIX-OH-TWO-TWO.

GUESS THE NUMBER OF JELLYBEANS AND WIN A HAM

MATE IN SIXTEEN.

Huh?

MATE IN TWELVE.

WHAT?

STALEMATE IN TWENTY.

YOU SURE?

AM I SURE?

Gnnn!

NOW I ASK YOU...

YAY!

GOTHAM 1ST NATIONAL BANK

...WHAT KIND OF QUESTION IS THAT?

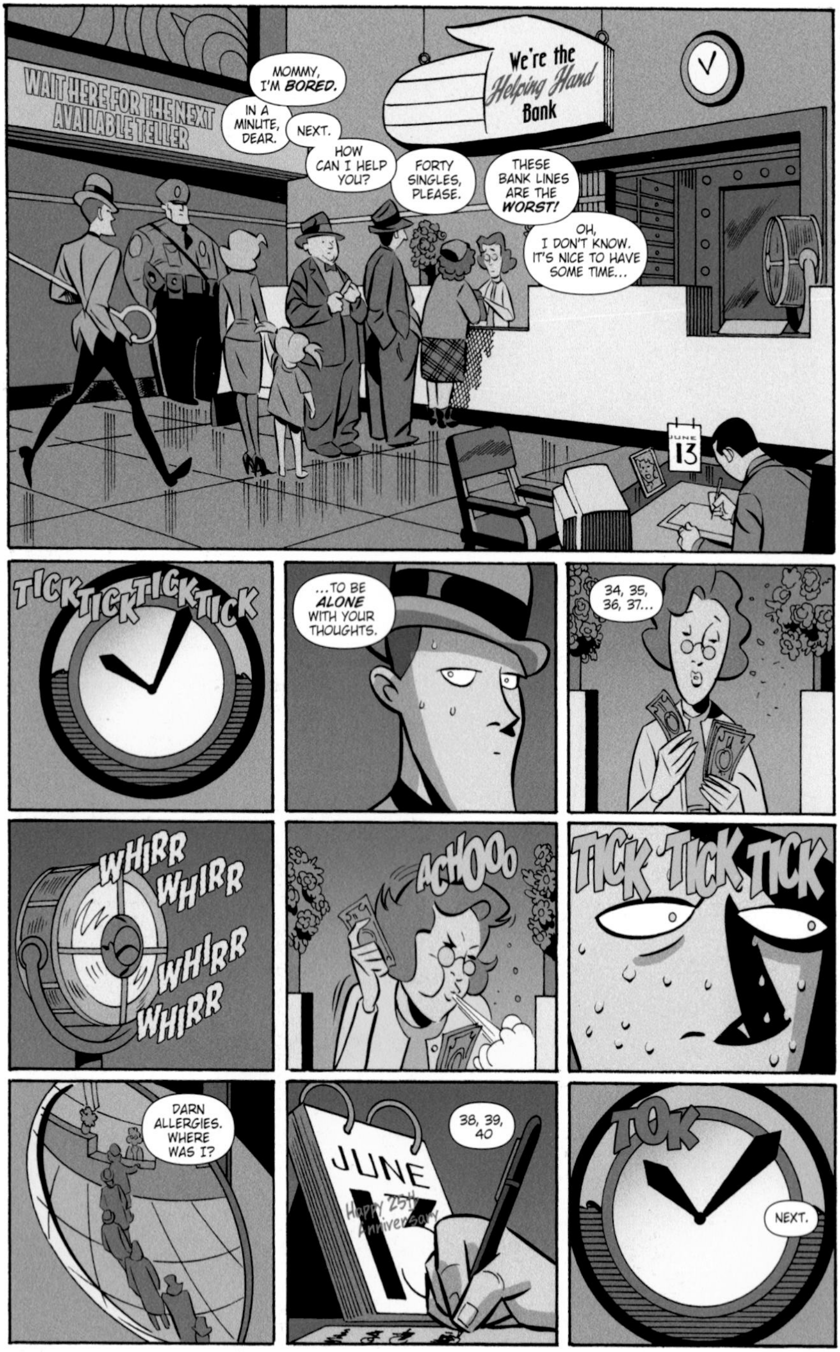
WAIT HERE FOR THE NEXT AVAILABLE TELLER
We're the Helping Hand Bank
MOMMY, I'M BORED.
IN A MINUTE, DEAR.
NEXT.
HOW CAN I HELP YOU?
FORTY SINGLES, PLEASE.
THESE BANK LINES ARE THE WORST!
OH, I DON'T KNOW. IT'S NICE TO HAVE SOME TIME...
JUNE 13
TICK TICK TICK TICK
...TO BE ALONE WITH YOUR THOUGHTS.
34, 35, 36, 37...
WHIRR WHIRR WHIRR WHIRR
ACHOOO
TICK TICK TICK
DARN ALLERGIES. WHERE WAS I?
JUNE
Happy 25th Anniversary
38, 39, 40
TOK
NEXT.

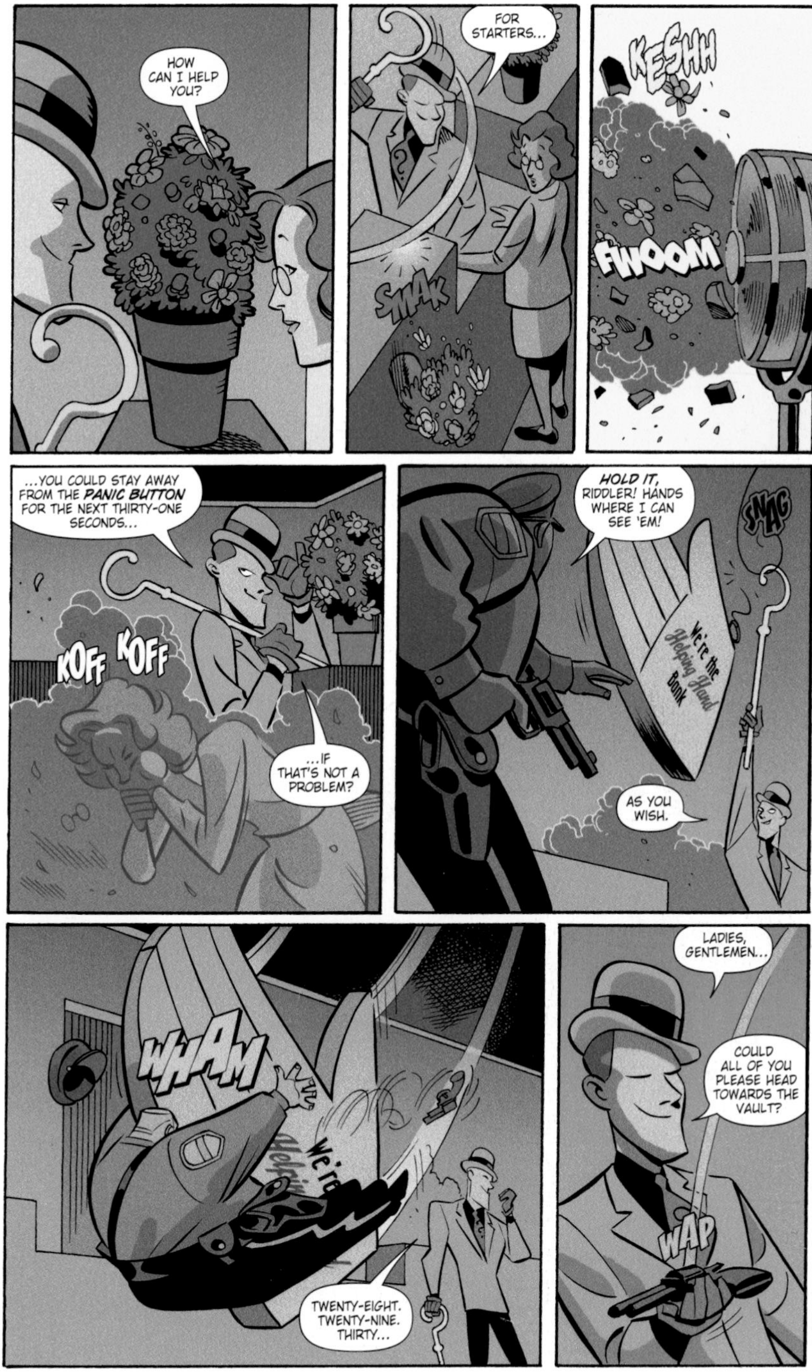
HOW CAN I HELP YOU?
FOR STARTERS...
SMAK
KESHH
FWOOM
...YOU COULD STAY AWAY FROM THE PANIC BUTTON FOR THE NEXT THIRTY-ONE SECONDS...
KOFF KOFF
...IF THAT'S NOT A PROBLEM?
HOLD IT, RIDDLER! HANDS WHERE I CAN SEE 'EM!
SNAG
We're the Helping Hand Bank
AS YOU WISH.
WHAM
TWENTY-EIGHT. TWENTY-NINE. THIRTY...
LADIES, GENTLEMEN...
COULD ALL OF YOU PLEASE HEAD TOWARDS THE VAULT?
WAP

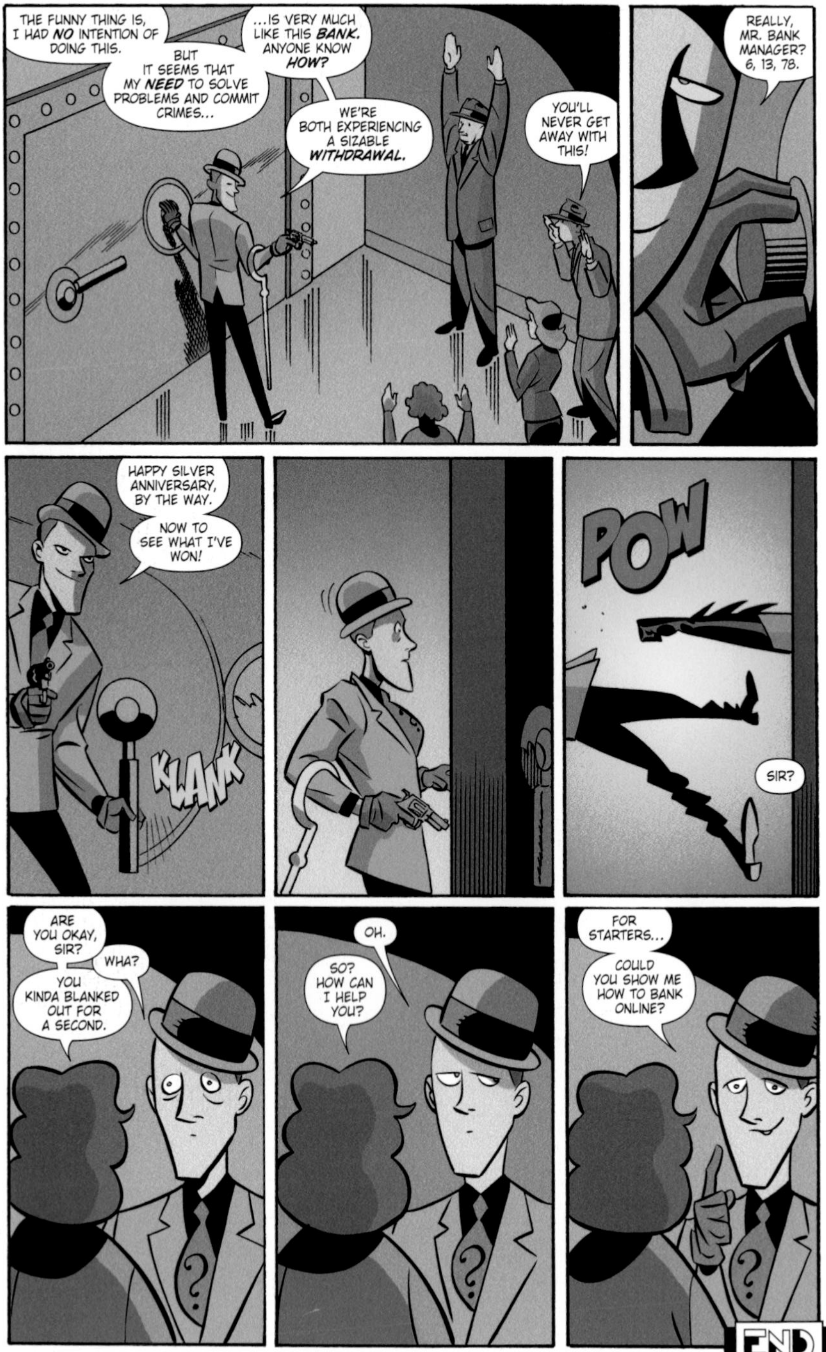
THE FUNNY THING IS, I HAD NO INTENTION OF DOING THIS.
BUT IT SEEMS THAT MY NEED TO SOLVE PROBLEMS AND COMMIT CRIMES...
...IS VERY MUCH LIKE THIS BANK. ANYONE KNOW HOW?
WE'RE BOTH EXPERIENCING A SIZABLE WITHDRAWAL.
YOU'LL NEVER GET AWAY WITH THIS!
REALLY, MR. BANK MANAGER? 6, 13, 78.
HAPPY SILVER ANNIVERSARY, BY THE WAY.
NOW TO SEE WHAT I'VE WON!
KLANK
POW
SIR?
ARE YOU OKAY, SIR?
WHA?
YOU KINDA BLANKED OUT FOR A SECOND.
OH.
SO? HOW CAN I HELP YOU?
FOR STARTERS...
COULD YOU SHOW ME HOW TO BANK ONLINE?
END

You thought only heroes got fan mail?
Think again!

NEW YORK TIMES BESTSELLING AUTHOR MICHAEL NORTHROP
DC
DEAR SUPER-VILLAINS
LL 1979
ILLUSTRATED BY GUSTAVO DUARTE

Keep reading for an evil sneak peek at

DEAR DC SUPER-VILLAINS

the next book from Michael Northrop and Gustavo Duarte!
Coming Spring 2021.

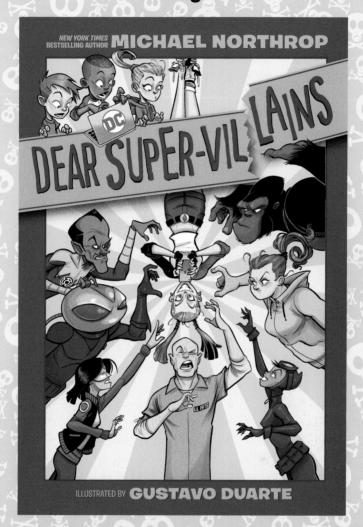

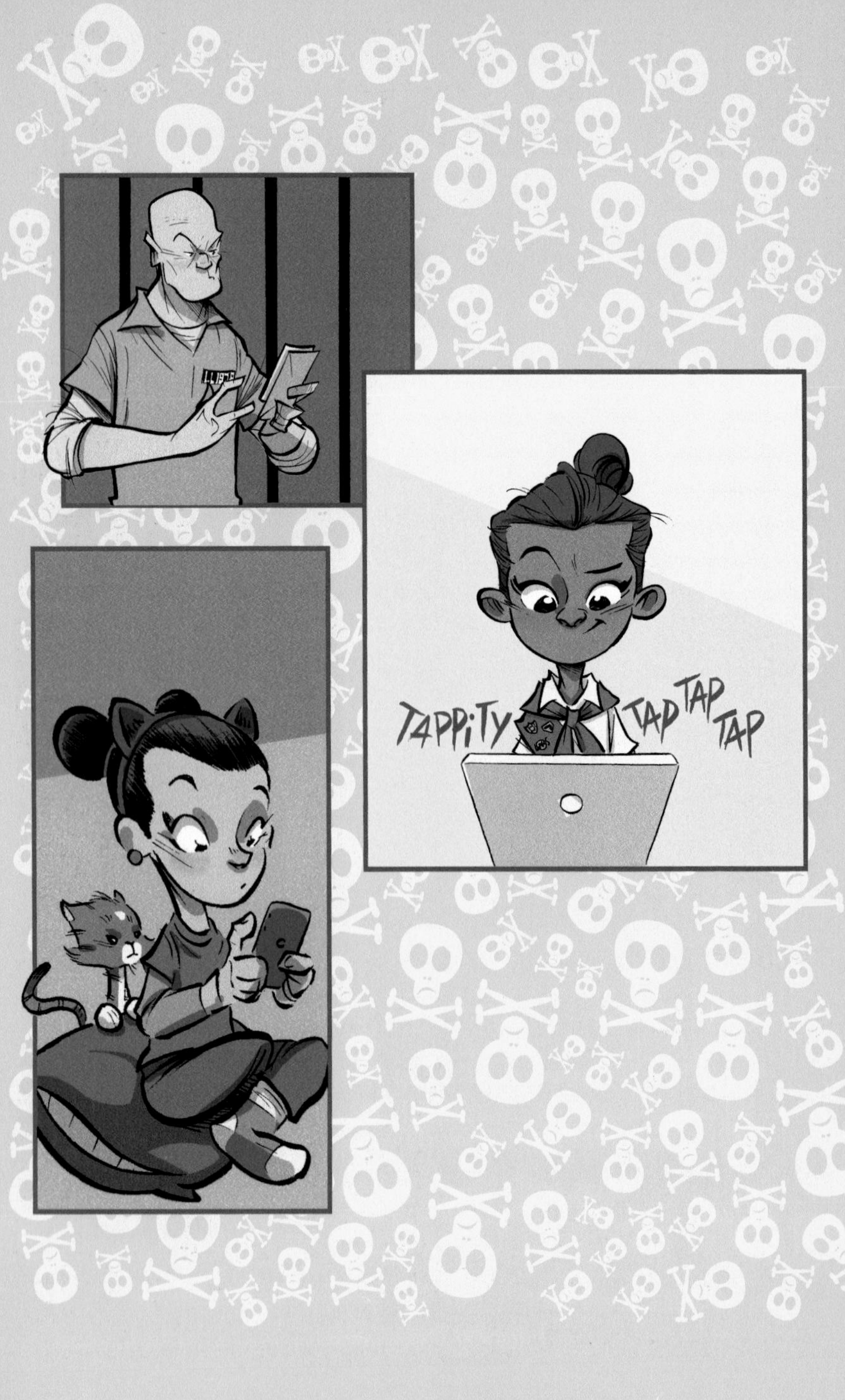
TAPPiTY
TAP TAP TAP

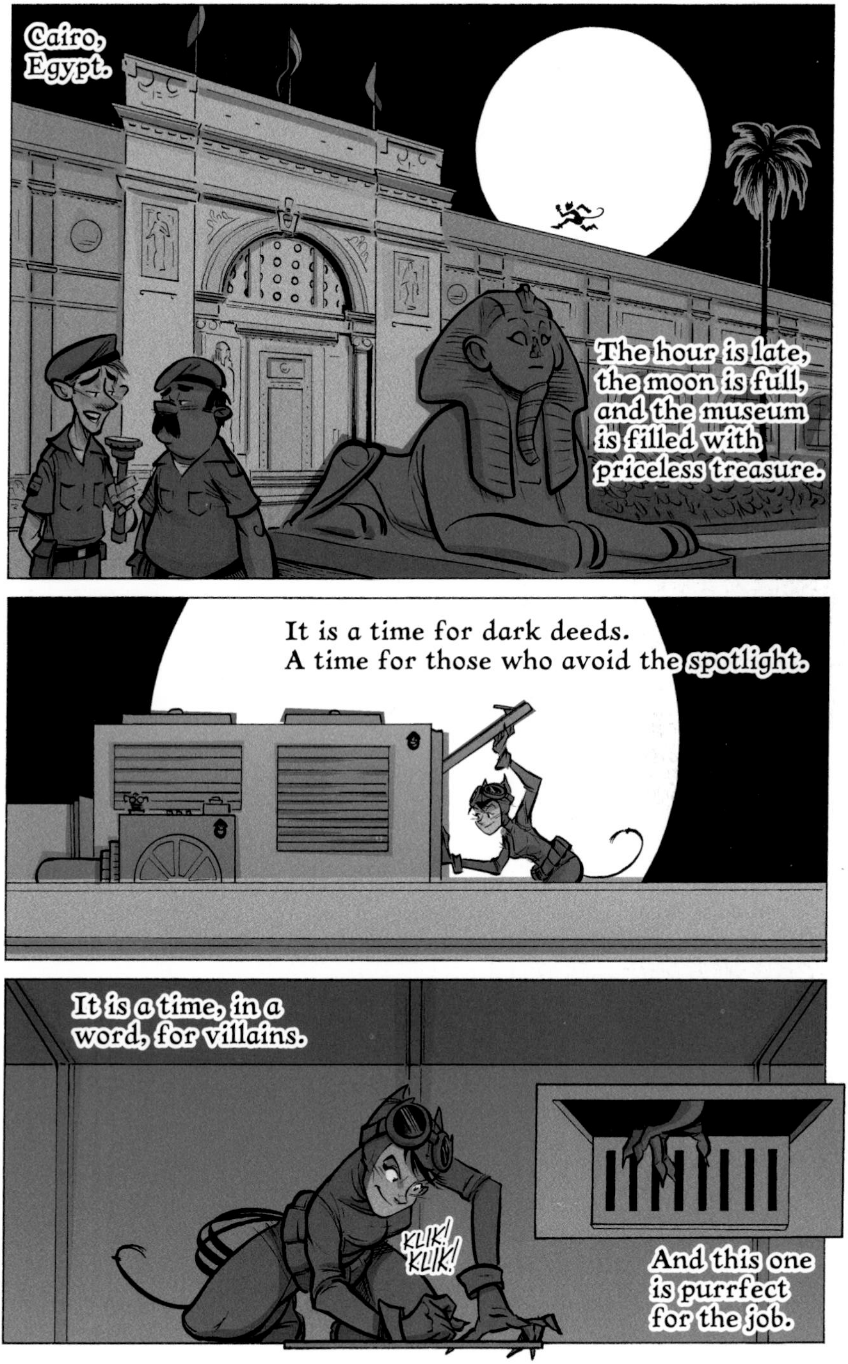
Cairo, Egypt.
The hour is late, the moon is full, and the museum is filled with priceless treasure.
It is a time for dark deeds.
A time for those who avoid the spotlight.
It is a time, in a word, for villains.
KLIK! KLIK!
And this one is purrfect for the job.

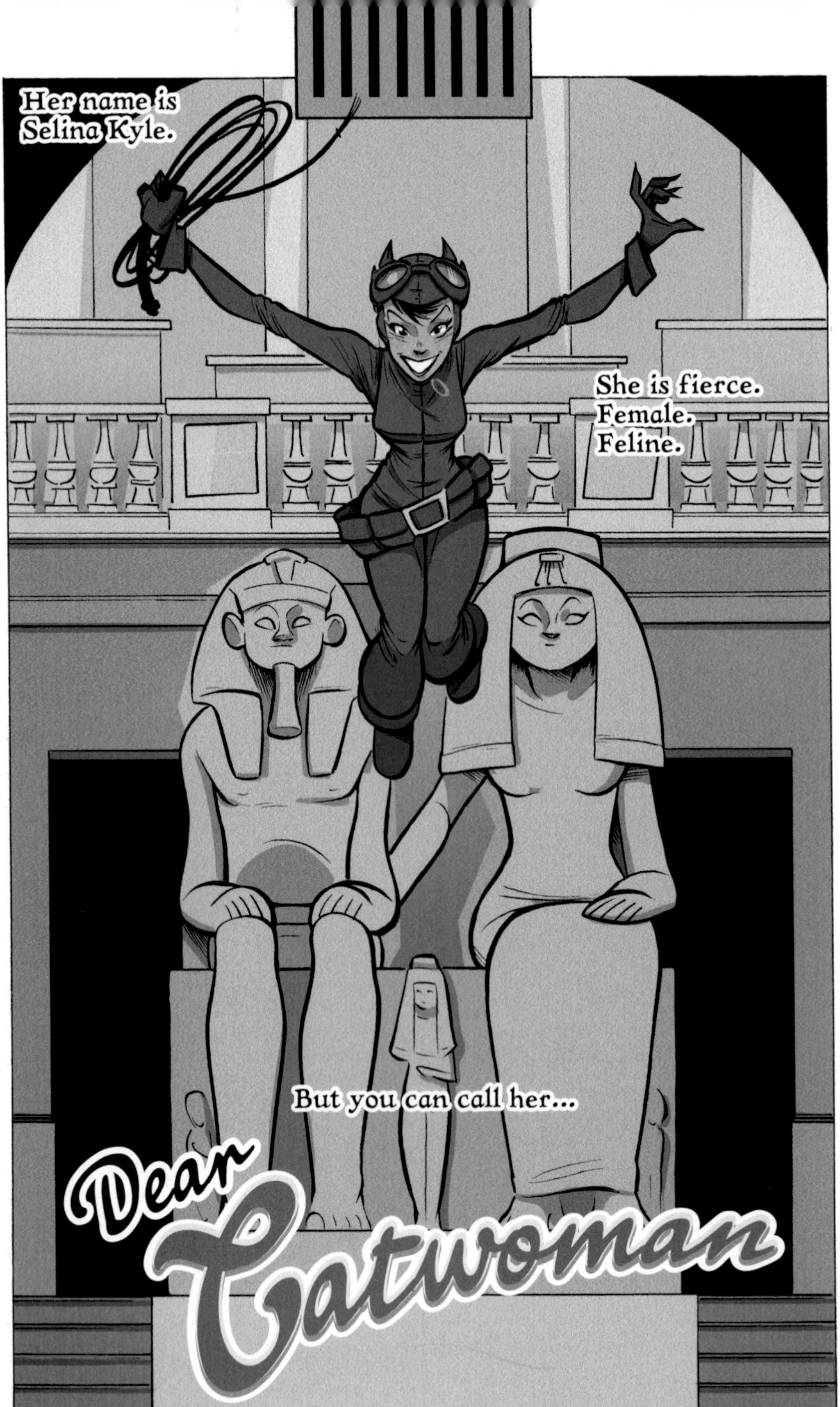
Her name is Selina Kyle.
She is fierce. Female. Feline.
But you can call her...
Dear Catwoman

And like a cat,
she always lands
on her feet.

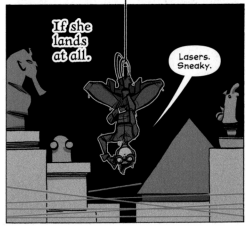

If she
lands
at all.

Lasers.
Sneaky.

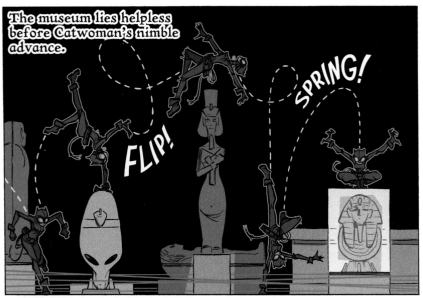

The museum lies helpless before Catwoman's nimble advance.

FLIP!

SPRING!

And she doesn't plan on leaving empty-handed.

FLOP!

LOOT SACK!

No item is safe.

Especially if it's shiny.

GLEAM!

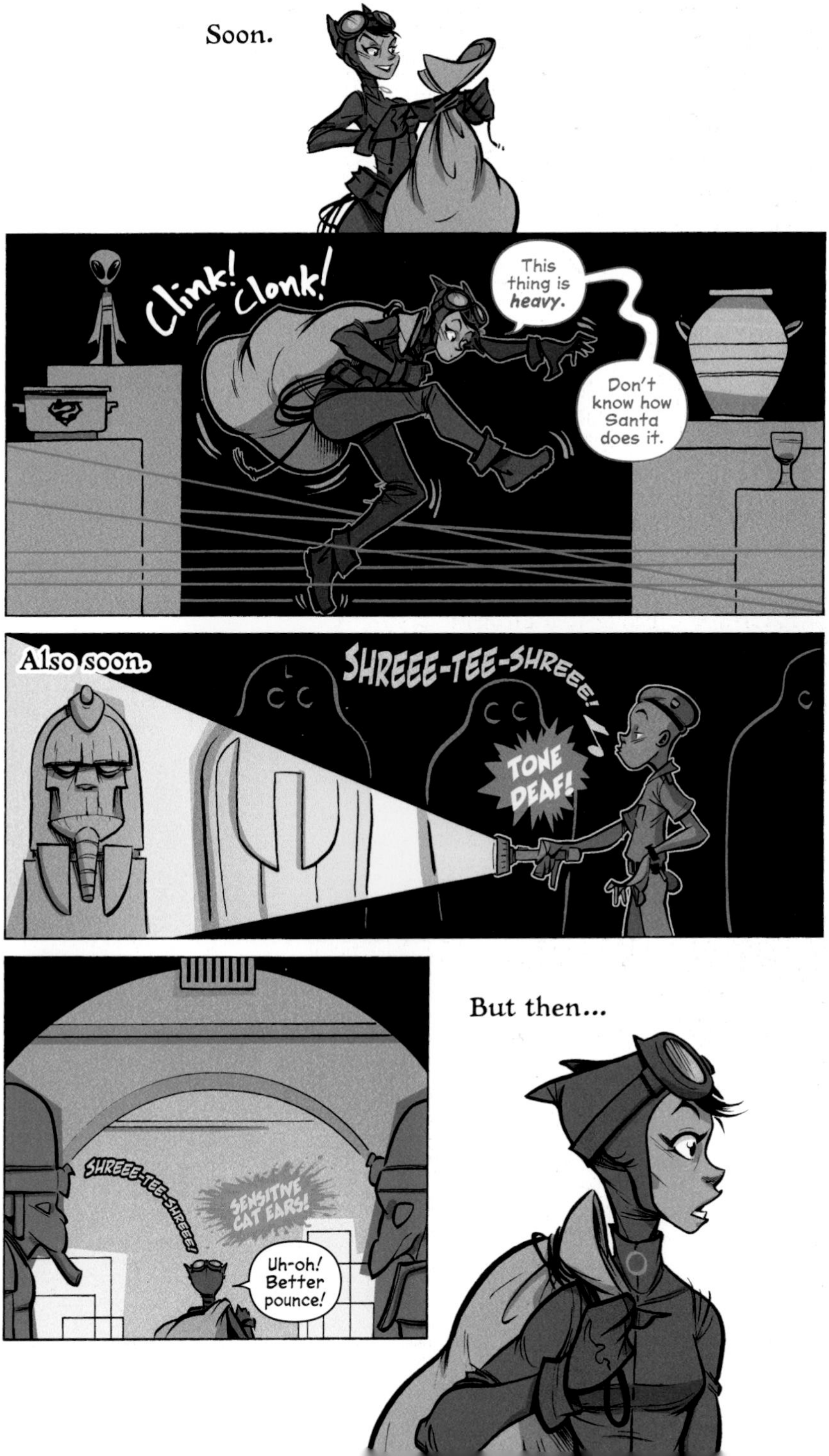
Soon.
Clink! Clonk!
This thing is heavy.
Don't know how Santa does it.
Also soon.
SHREEE-TEE-SHREEE!
TONE DEAF!
But then...
SHREEE-TEE-SHREEE!
SENSITIVE CAT EARS!
Uh-oh! Better pounce!

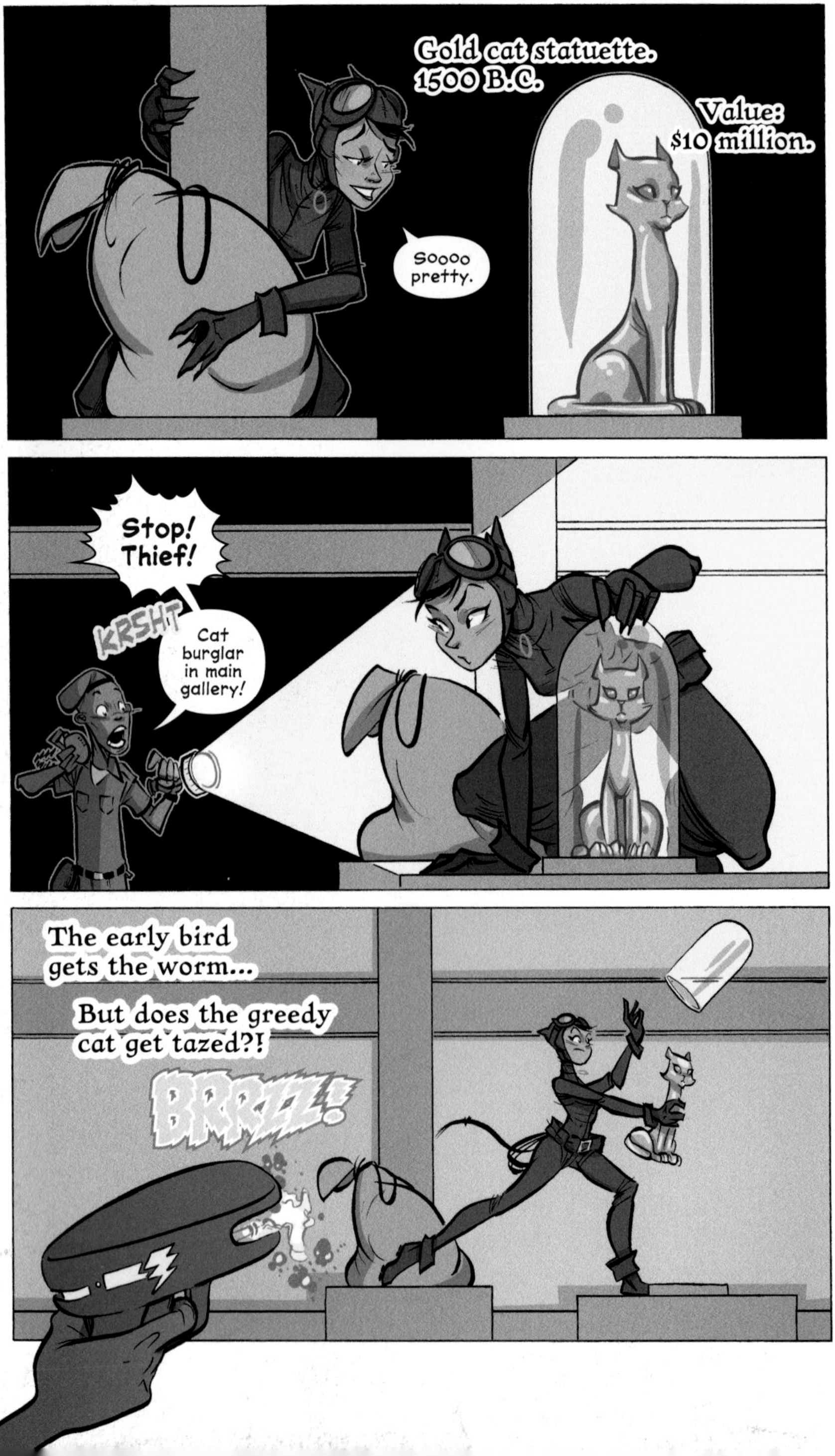
Gold cat statuette.
1500 B.C.
Value:
$10 million.
Soooo pretty.
Stop! Thief!
KRSHT
Cat burglar in main gallery!
The early bird gets the worm...
But does the greedy cat get tazed?!
BRRZZZ!

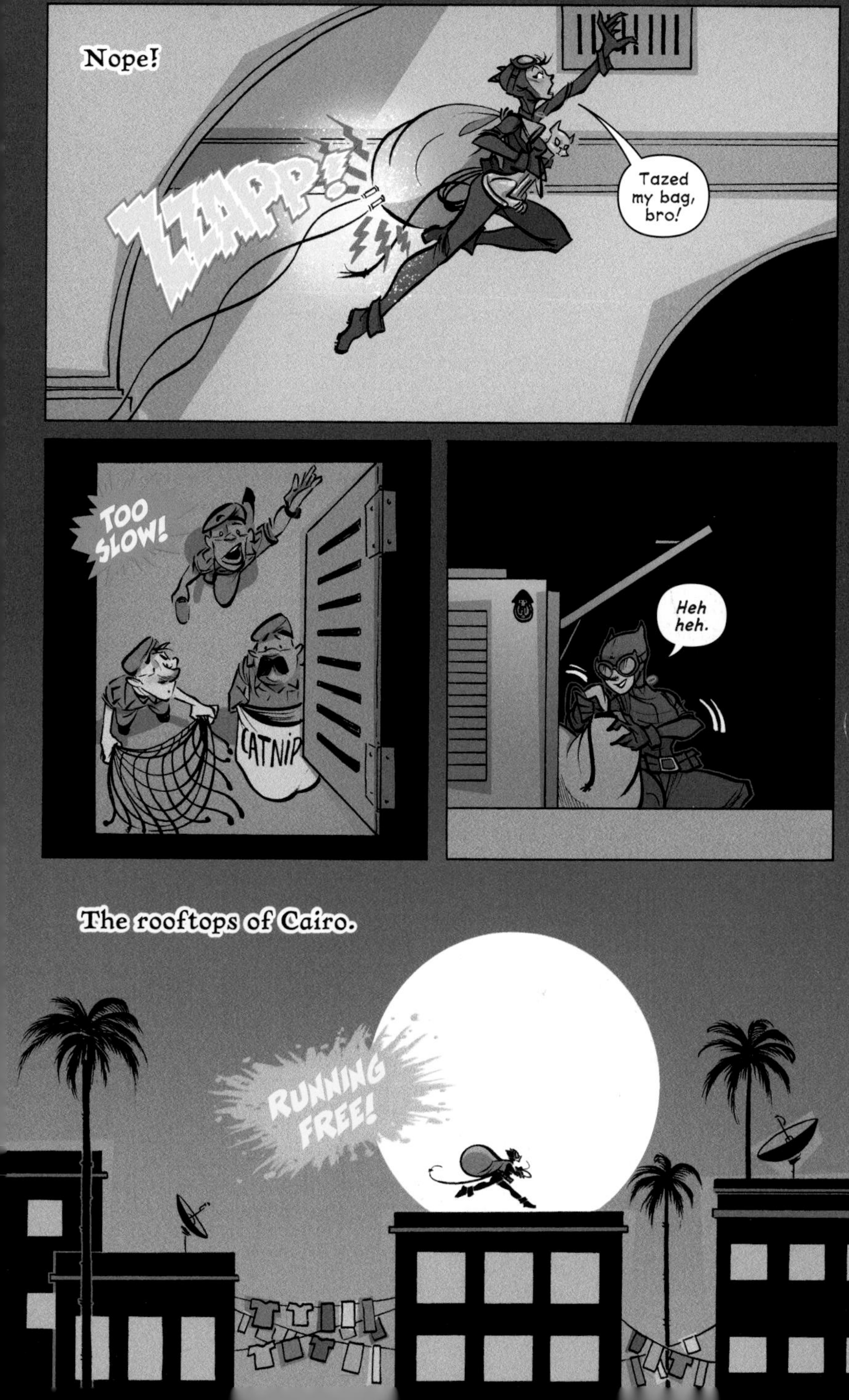
Nope!
ZZAPP!
Tazed my bag, bro!
TOO SLOW!
CATNIP
Heh heh.
The rooftops of Cairo.
RUNNING FREE!

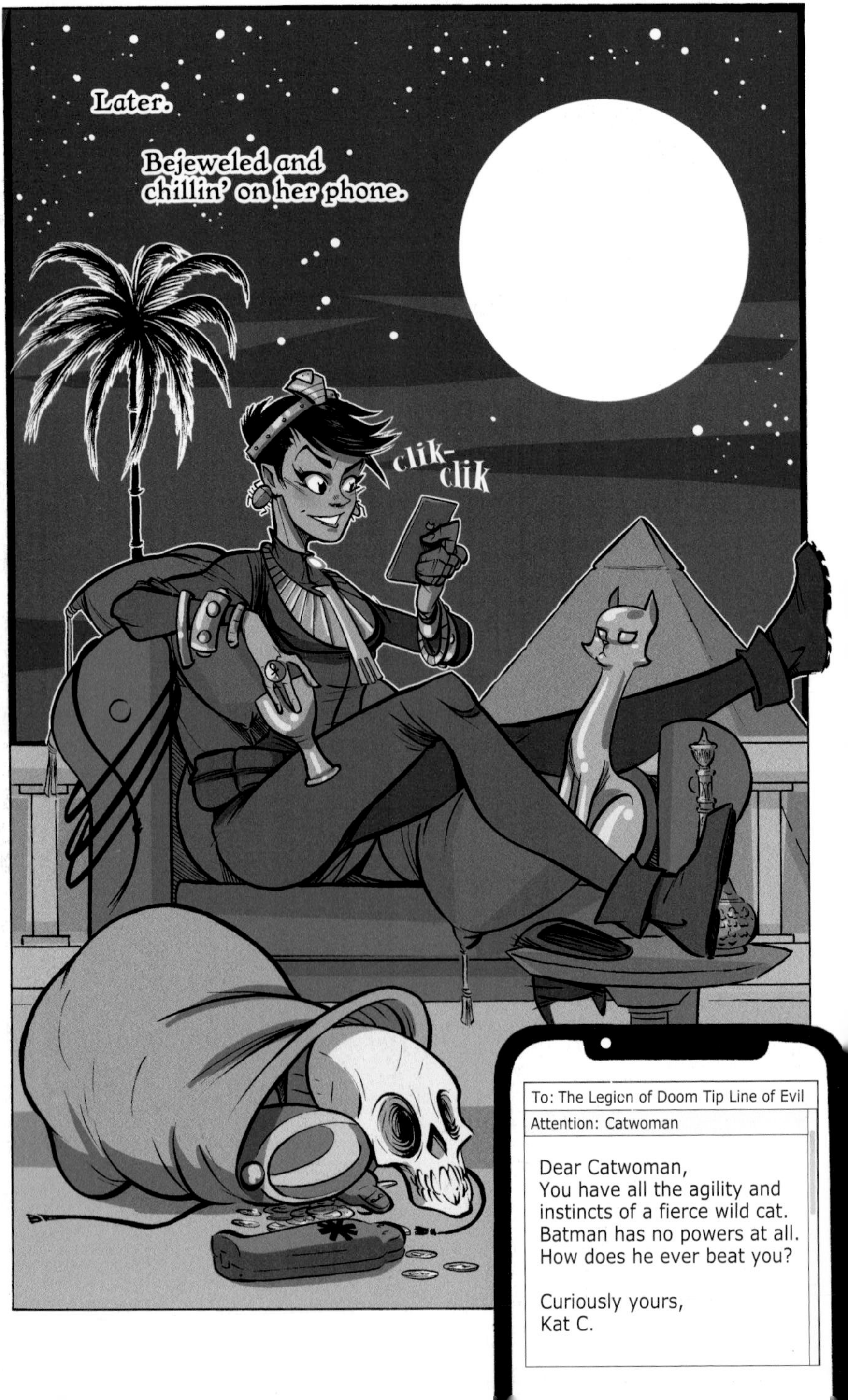
Later.
Bejeweled and chillin' on her phone.
clik-clik
To: The Legion of Doom Tip Line of Evil
Attention: Catwoman
Dear Catwoman,
You have all the agility and instincts of a fierce wild cat. Batman has no powers at all. How does he ever beat you?
Curiously yours,
Kat C.

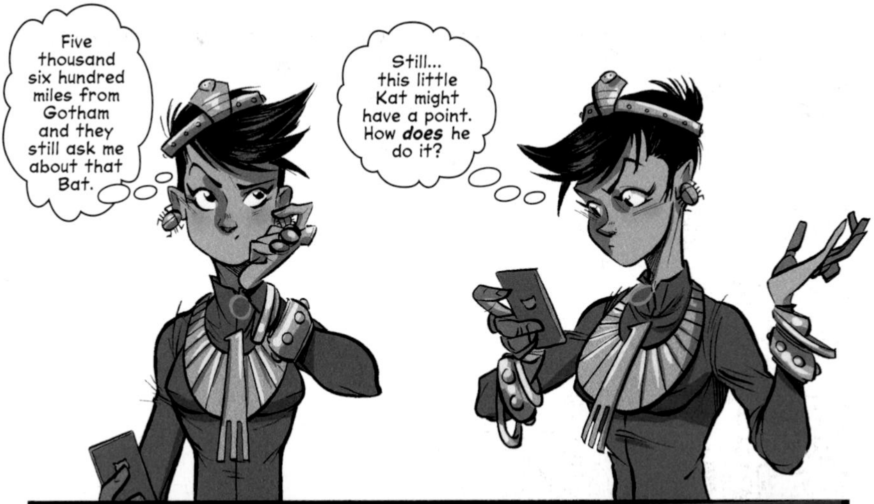
Five thousand six hundred miles from Gotham and they still ask me about that Bat.
Still... this little Kat might have a point. How *does* he do it?

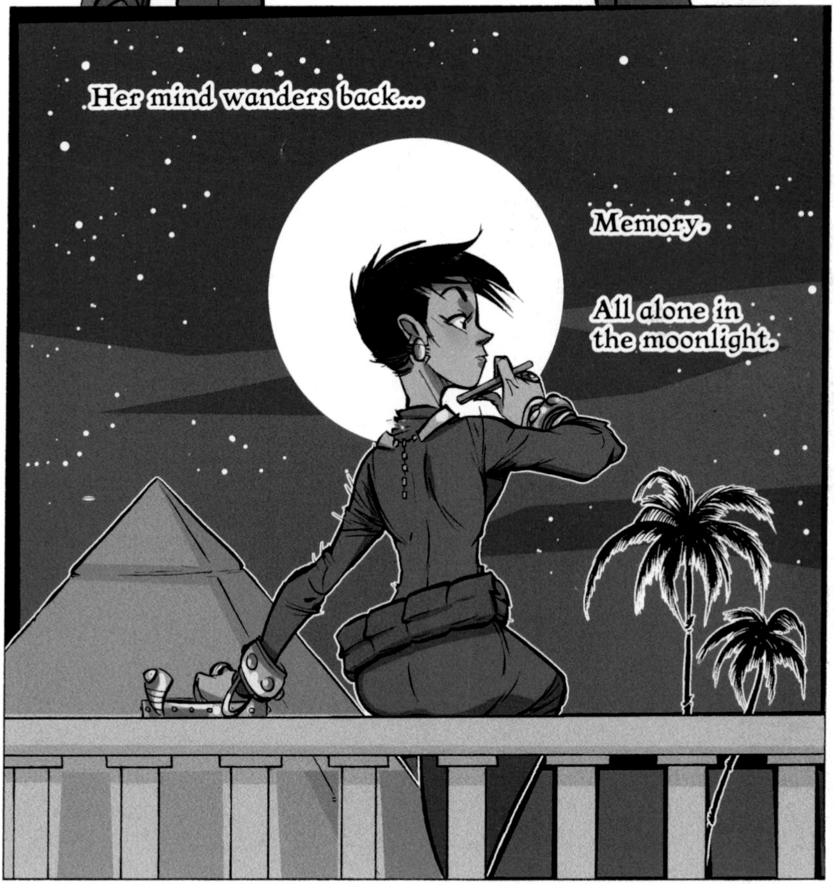
Her mind wanders back...
Memory.
All alone in the moonlight.

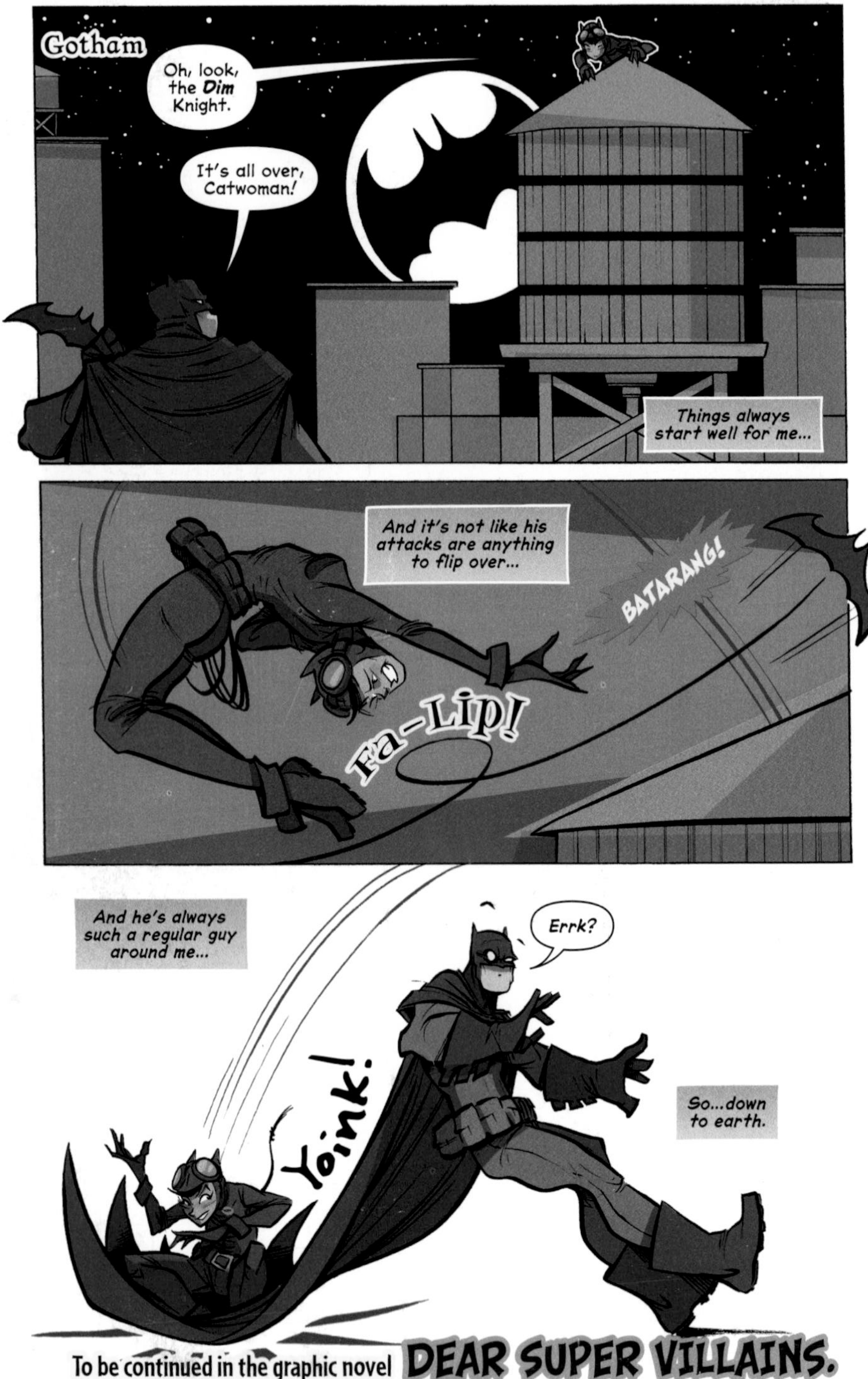
Gotham
Oh, look, the *Dim* Knight.
It's all over, Catwoman!
Things always start well for me...
And it's not like his attacks are anything to flip over...
BATARANG!
Fa-Lip!
And he's always such a regular guy around me...
Errk?
Yoink!
So...down to earth.

To be continued in the graphic novel **DEAR SUPER VILLAINS.**